Author's Note:

From a dream to a reality.

Etherea; The Lost daughter was inspired by a childhood filled with Irish myths and legends. It brings to life the creatures I grew up hearing of and the beautiful landscape I had the honour of being born to.

Thank you from the bottom of my heart for joining me in this adventure across the land of Etherea.

To my family, to my friends, to those who listened to me harp on for months about my book; you are the real ones, I could not have done this without you.

And of course, to my partner John who was forced to hear me clicking away for months; I issue an apology in advance, for there is much more to come!

Etherea: The Lost Daughter

Prologue

What would you do if you had an entire world within your grasp? What if the only thing stopping you was one girl; one clueless, little girl? Ciar would do anything, he would drag her to his castle; if it were only that easy. He had found her, at last. Over two centuries spent searching- and failing- at last, his faithful lieutenant had returned with news which filled his blackened heart with delight.

It would be a simple task, no? For Duane to woo the foolish girl, so that she may come to him; oh, what a delight that would be. The girl who Etherea had tried so desperately to protect, left defenceless by their aid. So, Duane had set out; with an arsenal of charm and enchantments. He knew he could not fail for he had failed once before, with her mother, and he would not do so again. Duane had found her so easily, hunting in that meadow; of course he did, for she was mortal and alone in this world; she did not stand a chance. The girl had startled at first, wide-eyed and shaking she had aimed her bow so quickly at him that for a moment he forgot she was merely human; for now. It took him days before she would allow him to come close. The moment she lowered her defences, he began to fill her head with fairy tales of mystery and magic. Duane told her of things that did not exist in her world, things she could scarcely believe; her will was stronger than he had anticipated, yet he continued with his plan. For that he would curse himself eternally.

"Etherea is a glistening land of beautiful jewels, if you'd join me there, you could have everything. You could have the world." He had whispered in her ear. Sweet words from a sweeter Prince, and while her curiosity had peaked, she could not justify following him; not when she barely believed a word he said, who would? It took weeks for Nia to take the young prince's hand and allow him to lead her to the magical far-off land he had spoken of. The weeks flew by with whispers of sweet nothings and promises, she was wrapped in a dream. Duane knew he would need more to convince her to join him, he should have known she would not follow him so easily; she was just like her mother. As he revealed a fraction of his magic, she finally began to believe him. Too curious for her own good, she could not help herself when she decided she would follow him to his 'Etherea' as he called it. Duane took her hand with a smirk she could not see and led the girl into his trap. It would take weeks, months even, to weave the web of lies that would convince her to destroy Etherea once and for all.

The last defence of Etherea, poisoned by dark magic, who would have thought?

Chapter One:

The air was crisp and cold on the morning which would change Nia's life forever. The woods were silent as the morning dew dripped from the flowers beneath her feet, the sun had just begun to rise. It coated her frost pinched cheeks with golden light, offering the young girl a small reprieve from the frosted morning. She had set out before the birds, with her hand-crafted bow in her palm. Nia, like many in her village, hunted for necessity. Far from any town or market, what they had they made or scavenged.

She often wondered why they had stayed in this abandoned quarter of the earth for so long when there were such wonders just past their borders. Travelling merchants seldom passed by, but when they did- oh the tales they would tell. Nia found solace in the confirmation that there was much more to this world than her dreary village and the sour folk that inhabited it. They were not all bad, of course, but Nia had been dealt enough suffering at the hands of her peers to hold little loyalty in her heart. She would never abandon them in times of need, would always protect them from the harms of the forest; but she longed for more.

 Nia recollected a morning, much warmer than this, many weeks before; when the sun rose early, and the world was alive with birdsong and wildlife. She had stood in this clearing just the same when he had emerged from the treeline north of her. Nia took one look at the vibrant gold eyes staring back at her and prepared to fire an arrow. He was not human, not natural. It unnerved her, she had bolted as he raised a foot to step towards her. He returned day after day, sometimes with gifts, sometimes with conversation; Nia had tried so ridiculously hard to ignore him, but her curious nature would always get the better of her. Duane had whisked her off her feet to a faraway land with glistening seas. She had never seen such green before.

He called it Etherea.

It was there she learned of the Fae, magical creatures with immense power and terrifying beauty. It had taken her a long time to follow the black-haired boy with glowing gold eyes far north into this magical land; seeing its beauty had filled her with regret for her caution. It had been breathtaking, as had he. Since then, Nia had found herself in the woods searching for her Fae Prince while she hunted; most days he joined her as the sun rose, it seemed this would not be one of those days. Her heart ached, it unnerved her; she had never been inclined to focus on boys and relationships, always too devoted to keeping herself and her village alive. She snorted to herself, for the men she had known paled in comparison to Duane; she wished he would meet Tristan, the vicious little boy would never dare touch her again.

Nia watched with cautious eyes as the silent forest began to stir, her footsteps barely a whisper as she wove through the wood. As she scoured the mud for tracks, Nias eyes widened at the sheer length of the deep impression in the mud at her foot. *Too large for a wolf, a bear maybe?* But no bears roamed these woods, her mother had told her of the large creatures that roamed North of this land, but they would never venture this far south. Her mind flashed to what few Fae creatures her Prince had warned her of.

Her blood ran cold.

Nia felt for the silver-handled steel dagger at her side for reassurance. It was a beautifully crafted weapon, gifted to her by her mother, with intricate twisting designs and a deep red jewel adorning the hilt. Even her Prince had commented on its beauty. Reassured by its presence she let out a shaky breath. With both hands now firmly on her matching bow and a silver tipped arrow nocked against the sturdy sting, Nia set out quietly after the beast, with only the slightest nagging feeling that this was *not* a good idea. Nia knew a beast this size could feed many people in her village and its fur would see plenty through the winter, so she ignored the sinking feeling in her gut and pressed on quietly; swearing to herself that she would turn around and run should she find something she could not face. If only she had been honest with herself. Spurred on by hunger, Nia could not have known what danger she approached.

The tracks led further north, where her mother had warned her not to go; but it was a path she had walked so many times now, with him. Nia was about to abandon her search when there, through the hedge, stood a menacing mesh of dark fur and huge limbs. A dangerous curiosity filled her, she had always been more inquisitive than had been good for her, and Nia found herself stepping towards the beast; already breaking her oath to herself. Her trance cracked as a young boy stumbled through the hedge, across the clearing, right at the feet of the beast. It still had its back to her, she could have run, but Nia saw the sheer terror in the young child's face and all doubt left her mind.

Before the beast could raise a claw, her silver arrow whistled through the air, lodging itself in its shoulder. Nia silently cursed, she had been aiming for its neck, but the arrow had sunk deep enough to cause the creature discomfort. As it turned from the child, a brief sigh of relief escaped her. The boy looked at her, shock across his face. Nia could have sworn recognition flashed in his eyes. Nia knew she had seconds before it regained sense. She let loose another five arrows blindly. Her feet tore through the mud beneath them towards the little boy. His pale skin was covered in the wet mud and bright red scrapes, his light russet hair stuck up in all directions, his blue eyes welled with tears as Nia scrambled to grab him. She had seen what the child did not, an assembly of razor-sharp claws had come swinging towards him.

Nia did the only thing she could.

She wrapped her body around the child and waited for the agonising slice of her soft flesh.

Nia barely recognised her own mangled scream as she felt the red-hot pain tear through her back, white spots flashed in her vision. A sob beneath her brought Nia scrambling back to reality, her hand flew to the dagger at her belt. A last resort. She said a silent prayer to whatever God's her mother secretly prayed to at night as she wrapped her fingers around the cold metal, and with every ounce of strength she had left - which was not much all things considered- she swung.

Nia plunged the dagger between the beasts' eyes as it lunged towards her. She knew its skin would be too thick to pierce its heart. Shooting an animal between the eyes had never failed her, and yet; *It blinked*. Nia gasped and, in a panic, she twisted the dagger until her ears heard that disgusting squelch of opening flesh and the cracking of bones.

The beast went limp.

It hit the ground with a rumbling thud and only then did Nia let out the breath she held. She turned to check on the boy, only to find him gone. Knowing she would not have the strength to carry the beast, Nia pulled her dagger from its skull. None would believe her word alone; Nia could almost hear Tristans taunts if she tried to warn them without evidence. So, she took the fangs from its mouth and the claws from its paws, these alone would prove the monstrosity of what she had faced; if the gushing wound on her back was not enough. They needed to know; their village was no longer safe.

Nia could keep silent about the Fae and their glistening palaces; but this? These beasts would tear through her people in seconds.

Nia stumbled through the darkness, through twists and turns she could not remember, a sickening feeling rested in her gut as she stopped in her tracks, goosebumps raised across her flesh. *I am being watched,* she realised. Nia raised her final arrow and turned cautiously; silence fell over the darkened forest. Not even birds dared sing their song. Nia was not fooled; she had won against the beast with little to spare, there could be more. Minutes passed without movement. When she could trust that she had only imagined the eyes at her back, Nia ground her teeth and took off as fast as she could in hopes that she would reach her home before darkness overtook her.

Nia stumbled through the darkening forest frantically until she fell through the wooden door of her cottage "Elvinia!" Her mother screamed, her chestnut hair in a tidy bun, her green eyes wide with alarm. Riona was a tall and fierce woman, unlike many in this land, and raised her daughter to be the same. Nia was too weak to notice the fear in her mother's eyes as she scanned the forest from where Nia had just emerged. "What was it?" Riona demanded of her daughter as she hurried to tend to her wounds. "It was a huge beast; I have never seen anything like it. I tried to run but a boy ran from the other side of the hedge. I could not leave him, mother. He was barely ten, but I killed it." Nia pulled her proof from her satchel, Riona knew she should be proud of her daughter for defending the child, but fear had stricken her heart cold.

As quick as she could Riona applied an herbal remedy to the girls back while cursing everything under the sun. "There is something I must tell you Elvinia." Nia could tell it was serious, even without the foreboding in her mother's tone. The paste had soothed some of the sting, but Nia still squirmed with pain as she was bandaged. It became increasingly difficult to hear the words her mother spoke. "The creature you have seen, it is not of this world. Neither are we; I know it makes no sense, but the legends of the Fae are true, the fairytales of beasts and sorcery, all of it is true, every tale I have ever told you has been a sort of lesson. Oh, I wish I had more time to explain. You will remember my child. I have not been so foolish as to leave you wholly unprepared; but it will take time for you to regain your strength." Riona had begun frantically packing essentials into two rucksacks.

Nia stared at her mother, half feverish from the gash on her back, dazed and confused. Her words made some sense, Nia had already stepped into the Fae world, but to learn that it had been *her* world once was a revelation she had not expected. If only she had told her mother about her prince. "Oh, I have been so stupid, it has been so many years I thought someone would have stopped him, Elvinia listen to me very carefully. You come from a line of extremely powerful High Elves, I have done all I can to keep you safe and hidden in the hopes that we could live in peace as mortals. What a stupid hope that was, more will come, those beasts travel in packs. We are blessed that they have not come already." As Riona spoke, Nia noticed the pain disappear from her wounds. She felt *stronger* somehow.

"You will begin to change; I cannot explain it all now and I was a fool not to restore your memories sooner. Please forgive me Elvinia, all I did was for you." Nia was speechless as her mother pulled a sword and shield from seemingly nowhere, it was a matching set to her dagger and bow. "We need to leave, now." Her tone was stern despite her panic; and just as the words left her lips, their homely cottage door came flying from its stead.

Nia grabbed her spare set of arrows and stumbled in front of her mother in panic. With her arrow pointed squarely at the monster's eye, she had no idea where the sudden rush of courage had sprouted from. The same swell of protectiveness had overwhelmed her when she had spotted the young boy facing the beast by the hedge, in that moment her life paled in comparison. The beast roared; its unholy sound rattled the stone walls of their home. Books and trinkets fell from their shelves, before another guttural growl started from behind them. Nia said a silent prayer to her Fae Prince for help.

It was no use, she knew this; Nia would not be foolish enough to wait for aid from anyone. Nia understood that not even her village would come to their rescue. They would close their doors and shutter their windows, waiting for the creatures to leave; hoping that Nia and her mother were enough to sate the monster's hunger.

Despite this, the young girl had a spirit filled with determination to survive; she had lived through mortal horrors; she would not die this day at the hands of a Fae creature. The sound of shattering glass was too late a warning before her mother screamed behind her. Nia's neck almost snapped as she turned, before lunging at the beast with all her might. Though her small frame barely made a dent against the monstrosity before her. Nia sunk her dagger into its torso and fought the urge to cover her ears as it let out an ungodly shriek, the red jewel atop the dagger glowed furiously. If it had not been for the snarl behind her, Nia might have dropped the dagger in shock. Instead, she yanked it from its fleshy resting place and threw herself at what she hoped would be her final foe for the night.

The last creature bared its giant fangs at the lunging girl and swiped its monstrous paw at her. It sent her barrelling backwards. The force knocked every ounce of breath from Nia's lungs as she bounced against the stone wall, clattering unceremoniously into the debris of a broken vase of flowers. Nia felt the wounds on her back split and her head spun as warm wet liquid spilled down her face. The creature stalked towards her and picked her aching body off the floor before flinging her mercilessly against the adjacent wall.

This time, she heard her own bones *break*.

Nia watched, helpless and terrified, as the beast turned towards her unconscious mother; it was as if it laughed as it picked her up. Nia tried to scream, but her voice was strangled by the blood which had begun to gurgle up her throat. The world began to fade as she watched that horrendous thing carry her mother's limp body from the cottage. *I must get up*. She told herself, but her body and her mind had become two separate entities. Nia willed herself to move, to scream, to do anything to help her mother. Instead, she lay flat, lifeless on the cold wood floor. She watched as her vision blurred, the beast stalk towards the forest; to Etherea. As her spirit slipped away, Nia said a silent prayer that her mother would escape; even if she would not live to see her again.

"Hurry, she is here!" A small, shrill voice screamed. The sound felt so far away, her ears burned as her blood gushed from her body; watering the earth beneath her frail form. If Nia had the strength, she might have told them to be quiet; she had finally begun to drift away in peace. Her mind was as broken as her body; Nia barely noticed the blood clearing from her lungs. Footsteps shuffled around her. "By the Fates, there were two of them, how is she still alive?" A man's voice questioned; the air had begun to clear. Nia found herself able to open her eyes, to breathe, there was still pain; but Nia knew she should not be alive.

When she did open her eyes, Nia could not have prepared herself for what stood before her. The young boy from the woods stood flanked by two men, *no*, men was a poor way to describe the two ethereal beings in front of her. Although they looked like men, both had a glow surrounding them like glittering jewels. As her vision cleared even more, Nia almost gasped. They were gorgeous; like nothing she had ever seen this side of the veil. The shorter of them had a lush green aura surrounding him, his blonde hair elegantly styled, green eyes sparkling with a cheerful disposition; despite the worry on his face. The tallest of the two glowed sky blue and seemed a stark contrast to his counterpart. He looked like an older, angrier version of the child, with dark stormy blue eyes, copper hair askew, a pointed nose and strong jawline. Nia dared not look any further than his lips, cursing herself for her girlish stupidity. They were Fae, she had spent enough time with her Prince to know this much.

"What is happening?" Nia spluttered; the blonde man spoke first. "You are safe now. We are Fae, we come from a land far away. I am Uaine Ó Loinsigh. This is Torrin Ó Cinnéide and his young brother Rian; the last High Lords of the Sapphire Court, the beast you saved him from was a Faelcu. Bastardised versions of the Faoladh." Nias head spun. "She does not know what they are you fool." The one called Torrin spoke, and she realised he was who had commented on her battered form when they first walked in. "I do not care what it is called, it has my mother!" Nia exclaimed when she found she had regained strength. Everything had become too much of a blur to question how or why she no longer felt like her bones were broken. Only one thing remained, to retrieve her mother.

She grabbed the bloody, abandoned shield and sword from the floor and pulled herself to her feet. Nia limped past the trio of Fae around her, she ignored their shocked looks. She *should* have been terrified of them, yet she shoved through them as if they were regular folk. The mortal world had no knowledge of Etherea; and yet, she did not bat an eyelid at their revelation, "and where, pray tell, are you going?" Torrin scoffed, although he was impressed. Many Fae would have lay lifeless on that floor, would have begged for death even after he had healed them; but not her. The strawberry haired girl limped further into the darkness, muttering bitterly with each step.

"I'm going to kill every last one of those bastards and bring my mother home."

Unbeknownst to Nia, the further she limped from Torrin, the weaker his healing spell became. A few steps further and the young girl dropped like a dead weight on the path. "Well, I must say I admire the effort." Uaine commented to his friend as she slumped to the ground. "We have to help her." Rian pleaded with his brother, knowing Torrin would easily let the girl freeze to death if it meant the Faelcu would leave them be. To give Torrin some credit though, the girl had saved his brother's life, she had stood her ground against three Faelcu in total and although it had been barely, she also lived to tell the tale.

So, it was decided, as Torrin gently took the girl in his arms; that they would take her from her mortal lands and shelter her from whatever misfortune had brought the Faelcu here. In truth, Torrin owed her a great deal; he knew this as he looked at her soft and battered face. His young brother would have been ripped to shreds by the Faelcu.

Instead, this girl and her mother paid the price for Rian's recklessness.

It would be three days before Nia awoke to a heavenly dose of sunlight and silk. *Maybe I did die,* she thought. Nia remembered though, as she shot so fast from soft bed that her head spun. *Those claws, those dead eyes.* Vomit rose in her throat as she ran to the adjoining bathroom. With no time to admire the white marble room, she swiftly fell to the floor as the contents of her stomach emptied into the toilet bowl. Her hands shook as she gripped the crisp white ceramic beneath her cold fingers. Everything around her was sickeningly clean; despite her mother's best efforts, there had always been dust and grime covering their home. This place was positively sterile in comparison.

Nia had felt her ribs crack in her chest, her shoulders had popped from their sockets, blood had swelled within her; like a crashing wave it had choked her until she could not breathe. *How is this possible?* She questioned, she supposed she should not be surprised. Nia still could not believe this world existed after weeks of visits; mere hours could not allow the trauma of what had just transpired to dissolve. She felt those sharp claws at her back once more and shuddered.

Her bare feet met warm wooden panels as she stepped from the bathroom; her silk nightgown hung down to her ankles, clung to her back now drenched in sweat. Nia felt disturbed, with no idea where she was, who had dressed her, or whether her mother had survived; she pressed on, searching the cupboards around her for more suitable clothing. Nia knew she did not want to be caught wandering in a nightgown of all things. Her skin crawled as she thought again of who had changed her from her blood-soaked clothes.

If I am in Etherea, I should find my prince; for he would not leave me in this strange home if he knew what had happened.

With no hope of finding her weapons, and the slightest hope that she could find safety with Duane, Nia donned a beautiful light blue dress and some flat shoes and set out to the corridor. The house, if one could even call it such, was enormous. Long, winding echoey corridors filled with paintings and armour. Nia had almost given up trying each door she passed when she finally heard a voice. It was Uaine, and Nia let out a breath of relief. Torrin's face, his sharp cheekbones, those storm-blue eyes; Nia did not think she could face him yet. Guilt racked her as she thought then of Duane, *he will be so worried about me, I must write to him*. "Ah, our sleeping beauty has awoken." Uaine smiled softly as she approached, he knew the trepidation in her eyes all too well. Like a cornered animal, confused in unfamiliar territory. "Do not be frightened, you are safe here. The boy you saved in the woods was Rian, brother to the High Fae of the Sapphire Lands, Lord Torrin." Uaine's green eyes twinkled as he watched the girls face twist with thought; his gentle voice comforted her.

Nias mind raced, if Torrin was some Fae Lord then surely, *he* could get her mother back. Then, she reconsidered, he had been as fearful of the Faelcu as she; so maybe he could not help after all; at least he might know how to contact Duane. Then, her mother's words rang in her ears, she had told Nia they were descendants of High Elves. Duane had not told her of Elves in Etherea, only Fae. Nia wondered if she were related to some powerful Elven Lord who could help her. But then if her mother had allies in this world why would she flee? Perhaps if she asked Duane, he could find a way to help her.

"What is your name?" Uaine asked, breaking her from thought. Nia contemplated it, still not entirely trusting of this stranger, she decided it best not to give her full name. With a twisting in her gut and a headache swiftly forming in her mind; she lifted her chin to meet his curious green eyes. "Nia, my name is Nia." She told him firmly. Uaine could not decipher whether she was lying, and this fact unnerved him completely. He looked at the mortal girl, small and weak; yet strong all the same. She was a survivor if nothing else, and Uaine could relate to this above all.

Uaine had the gift of Half-Sight, unable to foresee like an oracle or seer but still extremely useful; he could see far more than those around him. It was this gift which allowed him to see a light Golden mist swirling around the young girl's head, like a spell; Uaine said nothing about it as he smiled at her. *She has been through enough*, he decided, *it will do no good to terrify her further.* "Come then Nia, Torrin will want to talk to you." Uaine gestured to the corridor before them, and Nia fell in step beside him with her gut still twisting. *They would not harm me*, she hoped, *not after saving me*. She recalled her mother's bedtime stories of powerful Faeries of all kinds, some could shape-shift, some had ungodly strength, yet Nia could barely remember those stories now. If only she had paid more attention, but why should she? For they were only stories; until they were not.

Her time with the prince had been summer walks and beautiful banquets, not discussions of horrible creatures and Nia cursed herself for not asking more questions. After a few twists and turns in silence. Both consumed by their own thoughts of the situation. It troubled Uaine, that the Faelcu had ventured so far into the mortal lands; for it should not have been possible. They came upon two giant cherry wood doors with intricate carved Sapphire adorning its entirety. Nia let out a breath in awe at their sheer beauty and Uaine watched with curiosity as her hands trailed the many crystal carvings across the panel. "It is but a door." Uaine laughed, Nia could not help the scowl she threw the Fae at her side. His eyes twinkled in response to her sour face, she was a strange mortal; even if Uaine did not have much to reference, he knew she should not be so calm as to glare at him.

"You see a door, I see the hours sat painstakingly chiselling each line, the sweat soaked into the gold dripped along its edges, I see the pride as its crafter stood back to witness their masterpiece take life. Proud that their work would adorn a High Lords home, in hope it would inspire awe and bring beauty into this world."

Nia knew how difficult it would be to craft something this magnificent. Uaine looked at the girl even more curious than before. Hundreds of years he had passed these doors, not once had he considered the hands which made them. "I had never thought of it like that." He admitted. "Have you ever tried to make a door like this?" Nia could not let it go; snobbery was a trait she could not stand, no matter how surreal this entire situation had become.

"I admit I have not."

"I would challenge you to try before you pass judgement."

A loud laugh bellowed from behind the doors before they swung open; revealing the one whom Nia wanted to face the least.

Torrin sat at the head of a small square table, much smaller than Nia had anticipated. The Manor was huge, it would only seem fitting that it held many people. He appeared much less tense than she had seen him last, Nia felt the breath leave her lungs once again. He was *magnificent*. His legs lazily draped across the arms of his golden chair, Torrin looked at his friend and their guest in the doorway with a lazy grin. He had heard her scalding words to Uaine and admired her spark; but Torrin questioned her sanity all the same.

Most mortals would have ran screaming from his Manor the moment they awoke, but then again, most mortals would not have survived an attack from the Faelcu.

"I see you have made yourself comfortable enough to torment one of your saviours." Torrin commented, Nia glared in return; in a flash her attraction ebbed. *Saviors*, she almost laughed aloud. "If your brother had not run into that clearing, I would not have needed to be saved, and you saw yourself comfortable enough to have me undressed." Nia snapped back at the Lord before her, while she knew it was probably not the best idea; she could not help herself.

The fog from her head had cleared and she finally had time to comprehend what had happened. Her mothers broken body, carried away in the arms of that beast; it burned in her mind. Uaine watched with surprise as the fiery young girl stalked up to one of the most powerful Fae in the land and stuck her finger in his chest without hesitation. "I want my weapons back." She said firmly. The shock in their eyes gave her a shiver of delight; for they did not know she knew of their world. *I will tear this land apart for my mother*, she thought. They owed her. Rian would be a slab of blood and bone had she ran from that clearing; her mother would not be half-way across this strange realm.

Torrin stared at the finger stabbing his chest before meeting Nias gaze, she almost faltered when those blue eyes bore into her own so furiously. Almost. For Nia was as stubborn as any Fae; a fact they would soon understand. Torrin rose from his chair, Nia stumbled back a few paces as he towered above her. She began to question her own sanity, *why couldn't I have kept my mouth shut?* She thought. Uaine waited for the outburst, for Torrin's temper to make an appearance, he was pleasantly surprised that his friend simply walked past the girl. The relief was short lived as the Lord turned and glared at the girl. "Well, are you coming?" Nia grinned and chased after him, Uaine shook his head; praying that Torrin would keep his temper in check, that he would not send the girl out into the dark jaws of Etherea.

Nia followed Torrin as he stalked through the Manor. If her hands did not shake so violently at her sides, she might have found the courage to scold him further. He cast a weary glance at the girl trailing behind him, her eyes darted this way and that; observing every inch of the corridors they roamed. He supposed he owed her some reprieve; *she is only human after all.*

"Rian will want to see you later, he has been worried about you." Torrin sighed as they turned towards the courtyard, slowing his pace until they fell in step beside each other. Nia let out a breath of relief, so she had not given him cause to kill her. *Yet.* "What about my mother? I must help her." her voice was quiet for the first time, Torrin heard the tremble of her lip and felt something in his heart he thought had left him long ago. "We will do what we can, but the Faelcu are only a fraction of the forces that hold your mother. They are the attack dogs of Duane, and I am sorry to say not many have survived them." Nias blood ran cold as her feet stilled. Torrin stopped to look at the girl as her already pale face blanched paper white.

"You cannot mean... He would not have meant to..."

Her thoughts seemed scrambled for a moment, Torrin raised his hand to shake her from her thoughts, but Nia's eyes snapped to meet his own. The worry that flashed through his core surprised even him, he pitied her; mortal, alone, unprotected, and in the path of danger. She was more beautiful than any mortal he had ever seen, Torrin selfishly played with the idea of keeping her there; he knew he could not, for a mortal in the lands of Fae would be in danger at every turn.

"Tell me you do not mean Prince Duane." Panic shook her voice.

Torrin's brows drew close. *She knows him.*

He could not believe it. What would Duane want with this mortal girl? Why would he send his dogs to rip her to shreds? This only strengthened Torrin's decision, he would bring her back to her lands; send her safely on her way with gold and jewels, to never return to this wicked realm. "*Prince Duane.*" It felt like acid on Torrins tongue. "Is what he has been named, in truth he is one false Prince to the false King, who has killed almost every beautiful thing in this damned land." He seethed; anger radiated from him. Nia could not believe it, the gentle boy she had spent so many weeks with; her mind filled with images of his fabulous castle by the sea, with lush green lands as far as the eye could see. "You must be wrong; Duane would not do such a thing." Nia argued.

Torrin glared at her, fury in his eyes at her defiance. Nia held firm; her gaze unwavering. She would not have followed Duane unless she trusted him completely; and she would not allow this stranger to bring doubt to her mind. Nia did not care how attractive Torrin was, she would not be lied to. He resisted the urge to roar at her, to shake her for her stupidity as her eyes narrowed. "Come with me." Torrin guided the distraught girl to the High Tower on the North side of his property, one that would allow her to see the true nature of her *Prince*. Torrin could not call him so with sincerity, Duane had been a High Lord, and he would remain nothing more in Torrin's eyes.

Nia followed up the steps of the tower with trepidation, her mind whirled. Would Duane lie to her? *No*, she thought, *Torrin must be wrong*. Once they reached the top, she could hardly believe the sight before her. Torrin had managed to keep some greenery on his own property; sickly hedges and bushels of half-dead flowers, outside his gates lay a barren wasteland, a clear border had been marked by a blackened forest on the horizon; scorched earth and smoke filled what should have been a beautiful landscape. Nia gasped with horror; it looked as though life itself had been sucked from his lands. "What happened here?" Her voice was barely a whisper, Torrin glared solemnly at the dusty earth surrounding his Manor.

"Many years ago, this realm was divided by five. Defined by the jewels littering each land, this is the remnants of the Sapphire Court." Pain filled his eyes, Nia felt sympathy for the High Lord. It would be a terrible thing to be a Lord with no people. The Silver Court is past our border, then there is the Emerald Court and the Golden Court by the coast which your *prince* hails from." Nia felt the sarcasm rippling from him and flinched, but he had named only four; so, she continued to listen intently. "Above us all lies the Ruby Court, once filled with the highest forms of Fae- The Elves. Unmatched in beauty and power they once brought peace and prosperity to the land. It was said their spirit poured energy back to the earth and that is where they drew their power, in a sort of symbiotic relationship. The Ruby Court held the High King Ainmuire and High Queen Katell, the Queen tragically died giving birth to their only child. Princess Riona." Nias ears pricked at her mother's name, *surely it could not be*. Her mother had said they were descendants of powerful Elves, *but royalty? No, I could not be a princess.*

"Riona was a fiercely kind woman, all who knew her would fall on their swords in a heartbeat to save her... some eventually did. You see, Riona fell for an evil Prince from a far and forgotten band of Dark Elves. They had been banished eons ago for the dark magic they practiced, where the Ruby Court Elves replenished the earth, Dark Elves only took from it. By the time Riona realised his ruse, it was too late. They had been married and Riona was expecting a child. Ciar had summoned the remaining Dark Elves to the Palace and those who did not bow had their lands plundered. Some of us, High Lords like myself still have enough power left in us to resist but only barely, as you can see. Ciar's power has waned over the years, but his influence has not. Duane is one of Ciars fiercest soldiers, along with the six High Lords of the Silver Court, they have taken the titles of Princes of Etherea." Torrin spat as he spoke the words.

"A bloody war ensued; Duane set his damn dogs on anyone that crossed his path. Women, children, it did not matter. Hope was almost lost, until Riona did the unthinkable. None knew exactly what happened on that fateful night, but when morning dawned after a bloody battle, Riona had disappeared from this land, leaving behind one final defence of her people. Riona had set a curse upon Ciar. Over time he has grown weaker and weaker; he has not left the castle in a hundred years, but his original curses remain, and his 'Princes' ensure that any rebellion is swiftly quashed. As you can see."

Bile rose in her throat as Nia contemplated Torrin's words. He saw no harm in telling her Etherea's story, if nothing else, he hoped it would deter her from searching for her mother.

For if she had any sense, she would run from him now. Nia remained; her brows creased with thought. She could not tell him what she knew. *If this Dark Elf is my father, they will never help me.* A chill ran through her bones as a terrible thought filled her mind; *what if I am like him?* Torrin blinked and shook his head, as if he had been reliving the past.

Nia knew from Duane that Fae aged differently to mortals, so it was very possible that he *had* lived through those dark times. "And what of her child?" Nia could not help herself; curiosity had taken over. Torrin shook his head as he looked over the bleak horizon. Nia cursed herself for her nosiness and rose an unsteady hand to clasp his own. Torrin blinked twice at their interlocking fingers, a warmth spread through him like no other. It gave him the strength to answer. "None know for sure; some say she bargained her first born son for safe passage; some say she sacrificed the boy for the curse she set upon Ciar. There are those who believe the child *is* the curse she set forth. Others believe the child is the key to returning Ciars power, or another Ciar in the making. I hope she is out there somewhere, at peace, for all that is still wrong in this land we owe our lives to Riona." Nia felt bile rise at that, if her mother was their lost Queen then she was most surely not at peace.

Torrin knew the child would be a blight on Etherea; just like its father. "I need to find my mother." Nia said once again, Torrin sighed and shook his head at her. He could not believe she would still want to, after all that he had told her. "Have you not been listening to me? Duane is a demon, a vicious mongrel, I am sorry to tell you Nia, but your mother is most likely dead if he has her. You do not know the history they share." Her head snapped upwards at that. Anger swirled in the young girls' eyes. "If my mother is dead then Duane will answer to *me*, but the man you are describing does not sound like *my* Duane. I will find him and ask him myself if you are so unwilling to help."

Nia glared up at the Fae in front of her. His intense stare sent her knees knocking; Nia refused to waver. "You are a fool, girl. But I will not send you out into those woods chasing that bastard unprepared. Your weapons are on your bed, meet me in the courtyard at dawn and I will teach you how to not get yourself killed." With that Torrin stormed away, the hand which held hers now cold and empty. Nia watched his form disappear down the stairs and waited before doing so herself with a huff. Her fingers tingled where his had just been, like sparks dancing across her skin. She noticed then, in the silence of the tower; her entire body felt electric.

Nia had never felt like this before.

She did not get to speak with Rian that night, too overwhelmed by the day's events to speak to yet another Fae. She found the doorway to what she supposed was her new room and clutched her mother's silver hilted sword as she lay in the regal bed. Her mind reeled as she wondered, *if I was born of powerful magic; what can I do?*

Chapter Two:

"What do you mean you left her to die?" Duane roared at his Faelcu, he had sent out three; yet only one remained. The beast bowed its head to its master. "You were meant to bring her here, so that she may unlock her powers, so that we may turn her, not *kill her.*" Duane paced feverishly, anger boiled his blood; his arm flew in the direction of the Faelcu in a blind rage, sending waves of golden light from his fingertips.

The beast flew backwards against the wall like a leaf in the wind, struggling as Duane sizzled the blood in its veins. "How *did* she survive against *three* of you?" He snarled. His magic swirled within the creature, white hot against its insides. "We were hunting, enclosing on her, when a boy distracted one of us; she jumped in to save the boy and killed it with an elven blade. When one tried to kill her mother, she pierced its chest with that same blade. I took the mother and fled." Duane glared at the beast for its idiocy.

"You took the mother, not the girl; the one who we have worked tirelessly to turn? You should have killed Riona when you had the chance." With each word Duane said through grit teeth, the magic coursing from his fingers grew more intense; the Faelcu's blood boiled hotter and hotter, its screams could be heard throughout the castle until finally, the beast became a molten puddle of goo and bone.

Duane glared out across his court; he held no remorse for the creature he had killed. "Prepare a carriage, I think it is high time I pay Torrin a visit." He sneered at his servants. Duane knew that he must find her and convince her to come with him; now that he had her mother in his dungeons, he was sure he would not have much trouble. Duane laughed coldly at that, the great Riona locked in his castle and her daughter clueless to his plans. Even if Torrin told her of his cruelty, Duane had spent weeks filling Elvinia's head with wonder. He could not wait to turn that same wonder into a vicious weapon. He had been the one to fail his master all those years ago, he would be the one to return Ciars power. *He would not fail again*.

Uaine watched his friend with wariness as the High Lord glared at his breakfast. "What is it?" He asked, Torrin had not been the same since the attack which saw his Court decimated. He had always been quiet, withdrawn without his people around him, afraid that Ciar would return for what was left of his family; in recent years he had spent his days patrolling the border, awaiting the armies return.

Torrin cursed himself for not noticing Duane slipping through. The Faelcu, he had sensed *them* the moment they stepped foot on his lands; Torrin cursed his brother once more. He had dashed to the border, could not lie to himself that he relished the thought of cutting down Duane's dogs. He could not understand how they got by him or how they crossed into the mortal lands, only that Rian had found him. The boy was covered in sweat, mud, and blood; Torrin had been terrified as he looked his brother over, only it was not Rian's blood which covered the child. It was Nia's. His thoughts flickered to the girl once more, there was something so familiar about her; he could not place it.

"Something is wrong with her." Torrin said with a shake of his head. No mortal could have lost so much blood and survived; nor would Duane waste his time with her. "After what she has been through, Torrin, it is natural that she be... disturbed. You know how mortals are." Uaine dismissed his friend, but Torrin only stared into the distance with more intent. "That is just it Uaine, she is not disturbed; she is unnaturally calm about this entire situation. I am not sure she is entirely mortal." He had sensed it the moment Nia arose outside her worn-down cottage, battered, bruised and ready to chase after her mother.

She possessed a strength most Fae could not create no matter what magic they may have. There was something inhuman about her. "I know what you mean. When I asked for her name, she looked as if she did not wish to tell me." Uaine paused for a moment in thought. "It is not unheard of;

that Fae men would sneak into the mortal Realm through tears in the veil, to leave a trail of half fae children in their wake. Perhaps she knows more of this world than we assume." It was the only explanation Uaine could give. Torrin supposed it could be true, but he could not ignore the feeling in his gut; something was amiss.

Nia rose from a fitful sleep, visions of a bloody war she could not have witnessed had seeped into her consciousness. A dark man cloaked in shadow, glowing scarlet eyes. Clashing swords and screaming Fae plagued her thoughts, Nia decided this was due to her conversation with Torrin and nothing more. Although she had managed to stay calm thus far, Nia was unsure just how long she could remain so. It had all happened so fast. Images of her mother, limp, and bleeding, being dragged away from their home brought tears to her eyes.

Nia rummaged through the wardrobe, blinking those tears away, she managed to find a pair of silk brown trousers and a comfortable white tunic and reminded herself to ask Uaine where she might find more. Nia adored the dresses adorning her wardrobe, she could never have imagined such exceptional fabrics would be beneath her fingertips; but something in Nia's gut told her she would need to be ready to always run in this realm. Fastening her belt and holstering her dagger, she would take no chances, Nia began her journey through the quiet Manor.

She wondered where his servants must be, even human Lords had servants; although she detested the practice, she was not naive. A flash of that barren land came to her mind and Nia had a thought that churned her insides. *There was none left to serve.* Nia shook the macabre thought from her head and continued towards the dining room, retracing her steps from the day before. As she turned a corner, still far from her destination, Nia's ears picked up a sound. It was Torrin and Uaine speaking about her. Nia turned, expecting to find the pair next to her, but found only the empty hallway. *Curious,* she thought and continued.

Their voices grew louder as she walked and Nia noticed even more curious sounds, it was as if she could hear birds chirping in the courtyard and trees rustling in the wind. Nia questioned her sanity, for she was far too deep within the Manor to hear what she could. *I must have hit my head much harder than I realised,* she thought, *maybe I will wake up and this will all have been some terrible nightmare. Perhaps there is a window open somewhere*, Nia tried to reason with herself. Her mother's words rang in her mind and stopped her cold.

"You will change."

In the whirlwind of the attack, Nia had not had time to contemplate what this could all mean. What she had gathered thus far was that she was not just Fae, but an Elf; the daughter of two powerful magical, royal beings and surely that meant she would have magic of her own. Nia decided instantly that if she were a descendant of great and terrible magic then surely, she would find the strength to rescue her mother; with or without help. Determination filled her as Nia arrived at the dining room and pushed those grand doors open to finally find the owners of the voices that had chased her through the halls.

Nia knew that neither believed her to be truly mortal, but *she* did not yet believe *them* to be trusted.

Both Fae men stared at the young girl as she stepped into the room. Nia was highly aware of their eyes watching her every move. She looked taller somehow, brighter, Torrin could not tear his eyes from her as she took a seat before them. His suspicion almost forgotten. Uaine looked on in disbelief at the sheer rapture on Torrins face, in the eons that they had known each other Uaine had never seen his friend so enthralled.

By a mortal woman no less, Uaine almost snorted until Torrins foot came smashing down on his own. He had forgotten for a moment, that Torrin could hear every whisper in his mind with little effort. It was a trait all Fae shared, but it had its limitations; one must be open to communication. It was a blessing that none had the ability to truly invade another's mind, Etherea would be a much darker place than it had already become.

Okay, you grumpy old fool, a somewhat mortal woman, Uaine reasoned with a smirk. Nia watched with curiosity as the two seemed to have a silent conversation. Before she had a chance to ask, Nia heard the bounding footsteps of a child coming through the corridor. Forgetting for a moment, that she should not have been able to hear him, Nia turned with a smile. "Here comes the more civilised member of your clan." She quipped, Torrin noticed it instantly; he had been waiting for any indication that she was not human. His brother was at least two corridors away and even a clumsy Fae child is much stealthier than even the most skilled mortal hunter. He eyed the young girl with renewed curiosity, *half Fae at least. That much is clear, but how much does she know?* He questioned.

A barrier had been created between their two worlds eons ago, after the first war ensured neither race could coexist. Though, like most things over time, cracks had formed. The human world had forgotten all about this other realm. It was for the better, as they would surely wage war once more should they discover their powerful neighbours. Torrin remembered the flash in her eyes in the tower. When he said Riona's name. "What is your mother's name Nia?" Torrin asked suddenly, he had watched her face whilst he spoke of Etherea's tragic tale. She had recognised it, maybe not entirely, but there had been something in her eyes that told him she knew more than she would say. Paired with Duane's interest in her, Torrin's nerves were shot. His family had suffered more loss than most in the fight at Riona's side, he knew first hand Ciars power of deceit. If she was who he suspected and she had already allied with Duane, all hope was lost.

Uaine looked on curiously between the pair, as the girl froze before turning slowly to look at Torrin. Once again, she bore that look of an animal trapped. Uaine had his own suspicions of what the girl could be, as her eyes watched every movement around; there was an instinct in her, to never let her guard down. Nia stared at the High Lord.

Does he know?

"Why?" Nia evaded, willing Rian to burst through the door and save her from this line of questioning. "If I am to send a search party out for someone, I would much prefer to know whom it is they are searching for. Uaine and I had just been discussing such before you joined us." Torrin had a glint in his eye as he stared at her, like a cat that caught his prey.

It sent goosebumps across her skin. Nia knew he was telling a lie, but how could she say so without exposing herself? She also knew she was enjoying his stare far too much to be comfortable with. Nia had never cared much for men, until Duane. Her heart fluttered once more in her chest at the thought of him. *He must be so worried.*

Nia stood. Hands shaking. Undecided, she took a breath. Rian's footsteps grew closer. Torrin's eyes bore into hers. The young boy barrelled into Nias arms as she silently thanked the Gods. "I'm so glad you're okay!" The child gushed; his cheeks red from running. "Thank you, for saving my life." Rian had suddenly straightened up before bowing low to the ground. Nia could not stand it and raised the child to be level again, sticking a finger under his chin so that he met her eyes; Nia smiled softly.

"You never need bow to me, I saved your life as you saved mine, we are equals Rian. You faced that beast and survived, just like I. That is something that none can challenge." Torrins heart swelled once again as he watched his brother's face light with happiness before he once again threw his little arms around her. Nia laughed, the sound like bells dancing in the air, and Torrin found himself standing with a lightness in his soul that he had not felt in ages. "Come, if you are to rescue your mother you must be prepared." Uaine glanced in shock at Torrin.

Rescue her mother? If Duane has her, she is dead. He could not understand the look Torrin threw him as Nia said farewell to Rian and followed him to the courtyard.

"I only brought my dagger." Nia admitted as they reached a plethora of targets and straw figures, a suit of armour stood sword and all in the far-right corner. Torrin chuckled softly and waved his hand across the table. Nias eyes widened as her weapons lay neatly across the light wood surface. "You seem to be very familiar with that dagger, show me your skills with something else." Torrin leaned against the stone wall, arms crossed as he watched her examine the table. In truth Nia was simply trying to ignore staring at his defined arms, flexing as he crossed them. Her nimble fingers traced the wooden bow, made from a glorious Yew tree; Nia had never held a bow so easily than this one.

True to the rest of her mother's gifted weapons it was no simple Yew bow, tipped with silver and delicately embedded with red jewels it was a magnificent weapon. Nia picked it up swiftly along with a dozen arrows in her quiver and turned towards the targets. She faltered for a second as the targets began to move, this way and that until she felt dizzy. Nia shook her head and drew a breath along with her first arrow. In truth, Nia had picked her most favored weapon, even the dagger could not compare to the rush of loosing an arrow.

She felt as if she was flying, each silver bolt sank further into every target until she found no arrows left. "You cheated." Torrin could not help but smile, she clearly knew her way around a bow. "You did not require I have no experience with my choice of weapon, only that I did not choose the dagger." Nia smirked at the shocked Lord, glad that she had begun to gain the upper hand. Torrin shook his head with a light laugh. "Remind me not to make a deal with you." He joked, as he pushed the sword into her hand. "Now, are you as familiar with this?" Truthfully, a sword and shield were not weaponry her mother had trained her with.

The sword felt heavier than it had the night her mother was taken, although she found it growing lighter in her grip with each passing second. Nia raised the sword clumsily above her head and ran towards the straw figure before her. To her astonishment, the figure moved. A flimsy wooden stick swatted against her rib cage before her blade could reach the mannequin's neck. "You're dead." Torrin mused as Nia huffed. So, they continued, for hours; Torrin mostly helped her, but he could not resist taunting her inexperience.

Nias bones screamed at her as she finally dodged the figurines false blade and sliced her steel through its belly. A slow, sarcastic clap came from Torrin. "Well done little one, you only died about a dozen times." Nia glared at the condescending Fae before her and bit her lip. *I will show him.* Nia simply swallowed the insults dancing on her tongue and smiled up at the confident Lord. Torrin felt the wind knock from his lungs as she smiled kindly up at him, her soft hands wrapped around his own. "A student owes what she learns only to those who teach her." Nia gently said and watched as the Lords guard lowered.

His eyes travelled her face and Nia almost forgot her intention. *Almost.* With one hand caressing his chiselled face, Nia drew her dagger from its hold. She moved with a swiftness she did not know she possessed and before Torrin could blink the girl was on his back with her blade at his throat. "Now you are dead, *my lord.*" She said it with a sneer, but it sent ripples of delight through his veins. It was such a pleasant surprise, and Nia could not hide her shock as Torrin burst into a fit of laughter.

He shook the would-be assassin from his back and looked to Nia with a renewed respect, even if she *had* fallen on her ass.

"You are a very curious mortal; you do know this?" Torrin asked with an extended palm, Nia took it as a truce and regained her balance with his help. "You adapt or you die in my world." Nias mind flashed back to frigid winter nights in the wood, starving children in her village, how she would stay until her boots had soaked through and frozen; she would not leave empty handed. Nia thought of her village with sadness, there was few hunting folks left, most were children. "What is troubling you, Nia?" Torrin asked as the spirited girl fell quietly in step at his side.

"My village, most have become elderly, there was only a handful of us who could still hunt. Most scavenge or farm fruit and vegetables, but that does not see them through the winter. I fear what will happen to them should I not return with my mother soon." It pained her heart, although this fascinating world beckoned her, Nia knew she must return and help those she knew could not help themselves.

"I will send supplies for them; no harm will come of your village." Torrin commanded, Nia quirked a brow and looked around the empty corridor. "With your mighty army?" Regret filled her instantly at the shame on Torrins face. "Most Fae live underground now, a curse set upon them by Ciar while he still had his strength, *if I shall be king of nothing then let them be Lords to no-one*, he had roared. I became cursed to walk a barren Court while my people suffer the loss of light. We have found our ways to communicate, but as they cannot leave, we too cannot enter. Your realm, however, is a sort of grey area. Not touched by Fae magic, our curses disappear once we cross the veil between. It is a rumour, that there are tunnels within the earth which lead to the mortal realm. I have not heard anything which confirms it. I do not think Ciar expected them to survive, yet they have created their own society." Nias heart clenched, an entire people trapped beneath the earth, *how awful.*

The barbarity of it all made her gag. "How could she ever have loved someone so horrid?" Nia wondered aloud. "As brutish as Ciar is, he *was* also just as charming, he lured many Lords, Elves, High Fae and other creatures to his side with his corruption. Tempted them with their most wicked desires and perverted their power into a sadistic force with none the wiser to his plans. I assume he tried to turn Riona, but our Queen resisted, and it is only through her strength that we even live to tell the tale. No matter the cost." The awe in his tone made Nia wish that she could have seen her mother in this world, in all her glory.

Nia felt something tugging at her essence and shook her head. *Something,* though she did not know what, called to her. She had the overwhelming urge to run into the courtyard. They arrived once again at the dining room, only Nia could not ignore the pull in her soul any longer. "I shall join you in a moment." She told him curtly and darted in the direction that sang to her. Torrin watched in confusion as she ran abruptly, feet barely hitting the floor, towards the gardens.

Uaine glanced at his friend, standing abandoned in the doorway, with trepidation before both Fae took chase after that strange girl. Nia could not describe the wonder that filled her heart, her feet were burning, she did not know where she was going but she knew that she could not rest until she reached it. Nias body was not her own, she felt weightless as the cool night air whipped her cheeks. Delirious, she laughed into the darkness, it was if she was drunk. Torrin heard her laughter, like soft silver bells carried by the wind and felt his heart beat faster. She felt like a child once again.

Bursting blue lights had begun to light Nias pathway and she knew she must follow them. Torrin, however, cursed when he saw the imitation will o' wisps. He knew what she was running gleefully towards, a Pùca. Once harmless pranksters, they had become another of the shape-shifting Fae bound and controlled by Ciars force. Now, these creatures spent their nights luring the children of High Fae to their deaths as their magic presented itself. What it wanted with Nia, Torrin could not decipher.

Blissfully unaware, Nia followed her shining guides with determination until she came to a beautiful field untouched by the curse around the wood. In that clearing stood a great dark stag, regal and grand, Nia felt the urge to bow to its sheer power. The stag, however, bowed its head to her. Nia placed her hand between its eyes, its soft fur slipping between her fingers and smiled as she closed her eyes. It was a majestic creature, warmth filled her as her lids grew heavy. Torrin watched with horror as red embers began to float from Nias body towards the Pùca. "That should not be happening." Uaine gasped as red sparks flew. Torrin blinked away his shock and lunged towards the Pùca. The blood in Nias veins froze like ice the moment the spell had been broken. Her limbs shook and her mind blanched before she fell limp against the scorched field. The luscious grass had been a glamor. *She had been a fool.*

Chapter Three:

Nia woke once again foggy and unclear. Vague memories of a horned beast invaded her consciousness. She could not help the groan that passed her lips. *How many times must I face these creatures?* Nia decided if she were to stay in this Realm long enough to rescue her mother then she must arm herself with not just weapons but knowledge, as it was her mother who taught her that knowledge could be the most powerful weapon of all. Nia left her room in search of someone, anyone really, whoever would give her the most answers would suffice.

Their voices carried through the hallways once again, Uaines usual humorous lilt had vanished, Torrins grave seriousness was in full effect. Nia ignored the urge to roll her eyes as they whispered about her. Questions of her mortality, of her loyalty, of her heritage. Nia's heart felt heavy although she did not blame them, not entirely, she had questioned herself a million times already. Nia knew in her core that she could not be like her father, she only hoped she was not wrong. "We need to find out what she is, no mortal woman could bear the child of an Elf. I know Fae men are weak to mortal women, but have you ever seen a Red Faerie?" Torrin questioned. It was fair enough, she supposed; if most of the Red Elves were trapped beneath the earth, it made sense that they would be curious to find they had taken one into their care. Nia decided she should find out more about her lineage and then she would tell them who she was. Taking the opposite turn she found what she had been searching for. The library. Its doors were laden with delicate scenes of battles and magical creatures. Nia gasped as the figures began to move, in an epic fight scene. When she could finally tear her eyes from the door, she ventured inside. It was vast and dusty, yet cosy and clean at the same time. Nia scoured the shelves for each book on Fae Lore and immersed herself into learning all she could.

When her head was filled with information on so many creatures she could scarcely believe, Nia took a moment to reflect on what she had learned. Winged creatures hid deep within the mountains, clans of Giants lived above them, music once filled Etherea through traveling bands of pixies, the wailing banshee would come to warn the souls of those about to die. The Faoladh were once sacred protectors of the Elves before they were contorted by dark magic into the monsters she had faced. There were many types of shapeshifters in the Fae world. Mermaids and sirens, seers and sorcerers could pass freely between this world and the next. Guilds of healers and scholars once stood in glittering cities. It was all lost to dark magic. Dark Elven magic.

The more Nia read, the more she understood Uaine and Torrins worry. It was after all, the same magic running through her veins. Her hands shook as she turned each page, illustrations of her ancestors filled the parchment. Nia noticed there was far more information on her mother. Ciar's ancestry could be tracked only to his father and grandfather, two powerful High Elves who had been banished during the first war. They had committed unspeakable war crimes, tears pricked Nia's eyes as she read. Her hands shook as she turned the page; hope filled her as her mother's ancestry appeared much less terrible. Nia noticed with a frown as she read each woman's cause of death, every first-born daughter died in childbirth. Daughters born once the Kings had remarried seemed to fare much better. *Strange,* Nia thought as she looked back to her mother's description. Riona had been the first born, her mother had died in childbirth; yet Riona had survived the birth of her own daughter.

Nia shook her aching head and slipped the book beneath her pillow. She wished to learn of their powers, so she may find her own. Deciding to take a reprieve, Nia picked up a novel she had found about the High Fae of Etherea. It was a gossip reel, she snickered at the pages describing Torrin as the ultimate playboy; she could not find anything of Uaine. Her pulse quickened as footsteps approached, Nia dropped the book to her side. "Can you hear me, Nia?" She knew he was whispering from the hallway, yet it was as if his lips had been right at her ear. Nia ignored him and his frustrated sigh, her heart beat furiously in her ears. What would they do to her once they knew what she was? They had every reason to despise her. Fear thwarted her decision to tell them anything.

Torrin knocked firmly. "Come in." Her voice shook, and worry filled him. Torrin carried a tray of food and wine, suddenly Nia realised how hungry she had become. Her stomach chose that moment to announce itself. The pair laughed at her grumbling middle and Torrin extended the tray to the girl. "I was worried when you did not arrive for lunch or dinner." Torrin admitted truthfully. "I decided I could not stay ignorant to the workings of your world if I intended to spend time here." Nia answered as she ate, his eyes darted to the book at her side and Torrin could not help the embarrassed groan that surpassed his lips.

Nia smiled at that; it read like a gossip reel on Ethereas nobility. "Perhaps it was for the best that you have been separated from the ladies, you seemed intent to leave a trail of little Lords in your wake." Nia could not help herself, as she drank the wine, she felt a weight lifted from her shoulders. Torrin scratched the nape of his neck with a laugh, Nia understood the temptation those women must have felt as she watched him. "You wound me Nia, but I can assure you those ladies never left unsatisfied." Torrin winked and felt his bones tingle as her face turned beet red. Nia swallowed the food in her mouth with a gulp. "Are there still mermaids?" She averted, changing from that heady subject, for fear her more girlish impulses may take over. Torrin glanced at the illustrations adorning the page of each book before her, she had intensely delved into their histories. "Magical creatures are still free to roam the lands, although I wouldn't go searching for friendship with the merfolk. They are as sinister as they are beautiful."

Nia felt her shoulder slump with despair and could not help the words that fell bitterly from her lips. "Are there any

creatures in this damned land that won't try to kill me?"
Torrin supposed he owed her some sympathy, she must have
had friends in her village, he had become accustomed to
these empty halls. The Lords and their families had become
bored of holding up traditions like dinners and balls. What
was the point, with so few left to enjoy them? He supposed
there was a point now. "I shall hold a dinner for you, so that
you may meet some of Ethereas more civilised folk." Nia did
not miss that it was her own words being thrown back at her
but accepted the offer of comfort, nonetheless. "Thank you."
She breathed with relief. As civilised as they *had* been, the
idea of continuing her days with only Uaine, Torrin and Rian
as company was unnerving. Nia knew she would need allies
in this world.

Torrin shuffled quietly, deep in thought. "I need to tell you
something." He started, cutting Nias own revelation dead in
its tracks. The Lord found himself restless and
uncomfortable, her reaction would tell him all he needed to
know. Yet he found himself unwilling to end the playful
banter that had begun between them. Nia was about to ask
what he was trying to say when Torrin went rigid. His eyes
glared out of the window. Nia could not see a thing when she
followed his gaze. "Do not move, do not speak, stay here
until I come for you." He said suddenly. Nia felt like a warm
sheet had been wrapped around her body and if Torrin had
not been so tense, she might have considered sleeping right
there. He darted from the room like hot coals had been
pressed against his heels and Nia found she could not move.

Nia heard it then, the low growl of the beast that carried her mother away. Her blood boiled, but still, she could not move. Nia cursed whatever force had bound her and fought with every ounce of her strength. She managed to make it to the window with great difficulty. Sweat dripped from her brow. As she watched the beast stalk towards him, she remembered Torrins words and decided it best to heed them. The Faelcu came followed by a shining gold carriage; she knew that carriage. *Duane*. Nias heart leapt as she tugged against her bindings. If what Torrin had said was true, Duane would show his true colours. Her skin crawled as the magic tightened around her, Nia felt as though she might explode.

"Torrin, please, let me go." She whimpered. Torrin's shoulders tensed.

Duane stepped from the carriage, a grin on his face.

As he stepped out, a fitted black suit slick against his skin, he was truly glorious. Nia felt her skin flush with heat, her heart called out to him, begging him to save her. Torrin suddenly paled in comparison next to her Prince. Nia prayed that Torrin was wrong. A smile spread out across Duanes lips, but there was something sinister behind it. He seemed colder than before. Nia blinked as she watched; still scratching against the invisible force which held her. "Torrin my old friend! How long has it been?" Nia could have sworn she heard Torrin say '*Not long enough*' but his lips had not moved. "What do you want Duane?" Torrin asked through grit teeth, Duane *tsk'd* at the fool before him. "You have something that is not yours Torrin." Duane taunted and took a step closer.

Nia watched his expression change. Duane glanced behind Torrin for a second, she could have sworn he met her eye. Duane saw nothing but an empty window, but he felt her there. Duane raised a brow as he realised Torrin had cloaked her. *Clever boy*, he mused to himself. "This foolish beast has taken a dear family member of someone who I must say, is very important to me. If you should see Elvinia, tell her that I miss her, that I wish to see her once more. Riona and her father would very much like to have her home, being royalty and all that." With a wink, he shrugged nonchalantly; as if he had not just revealed her secret.

Nia felt the blanket of magic restrict her tighter. She fought to run after him, as Torrin threw his hands towards Duane. Nia screamed as Sapphire Light burst from his palms. Duane disappeared. Her blood bubbled in her veins. Duane was not worried, for he had spent weeks sowing enchantments that would blind her to his true nature when in his presence. Seeing him would start an itch in her veins until she found him again. He was right, as Nia almost tore herself to pieces to escape Torrin's bindings; her mind was consumed with the need to follow him. Torrin turned, fury in his eyes as he glared up at the girl, no, *the Elf*.

What have I brought into my home?

Torrin stormed his way through the Manor. It made so much sense, why the Faelcu came and how she survived; why the púca drew her in. It was her power. It had called out to them.

Uaine heard the thunderous roar that coursed through the walls and jumped to chase after his friend. Nia had managed to break through her bindings just as Torrin skidded to a halt in the doorway. "Who are you?" He boomed; the sound scorched her sensitive ears. Nia choked on her answer, *I must find Duane*. She suddenly did not care how Torrin saw her, she would not let them stand in her way. "I have to go to him." She pleaded. Disgust filled Torrins blue eyes. "You will do no such thing, tell me who you are." He demanded; Nia felt that weight fall upon her body once again.

Fear and anger washed through her. "Let me go." Nia warned, Torrin almost faltered as her eyes pierced his, but he did not heed her words. Panic set in as Nia felt the binds tighten. "Nia just tell us who you are, and he will let you go." Uaine pleaded in the doorway. Nia felt herself drifting as the binds tightened, a harrowing calm stilled her as the sound of a faraway babbling brook soothed her senses. Torrin and Uaine exchanged a worried glance at her serene demeanour. They had little choice but to bear witness as the unthinkable happened.

A red mist burst from Nias body, her aura aflame. All serenity shattered from her face as her eyes flew wide, green orbs replaced by glowing red. She could see it now, the glowing white rope fastening around her limbs. Uaine blinked as he realised, she saw it too, the magic which most Fae believed to be an invisible spell twisting and turning towards her. Nia let out a shriek as the rope shattered in her grasp, it burst violently into a thousand shards of light. Red lightning cracked through the room, sending the trio barrelling to the floor. Nia gasped for air as she scrambled to her feet, with no idea how she had just done what she did, she clutched her dagger as Torrin and Uaine rose. While she had wished to discover her magic, this was not how she envisioned it.

"I don't know who I am exactly." Nia spluttered with panic as they steadied themselves. Uaine looked at her with pity, the dagger outstretched and darting between them as if she did not have access to great power. "It is true, my name is Elvinia and my mother is your lost Queen. I had not been sure that my Riona was also yours, until Duane spoke of her outside. Before the Faelcu attacked I was just a human girl who had somehow found a Faerie Prince and that my life was set to become a fairytale. I had no idea who my mother truly was, and I still do not know what I am. Since I have been here, things have changed, I can hear things and see things that I should not. My dreams are filled with battlefields that I could not have seen, and I feel... *I feel wrong.*" Yes, wrong was the best word to describe the feeling that had crept into Nias soul. Uaine did something that churned her stomach, he *bowed*. Lowering until his forehead touched the ground. Torrins blue eyes bore into her soul.

The girl looked disgusted. In truth she was. Nia had always held the belief that no one man should bow to another and reached for Uaines arm. "Please do not bow to me, I am no one to bow for." Nia reasoned as she tugged at the cloth of Uaines shirt. His green eyes met Torrins as he rose, *she has no idea what this means*, he communicated silently with his friend. Torrin could only glare at the girl, *we have brought death into our world*. Although they made no sound, Nia saw wisps of blue and green dancing in the air between them. Twice she blinked and yet the wisps remained. She suspected what it meant; they used magic to communicate.

The anger radiated from Torrin and Nia found herself feeling suddenly small. "Come, Elvinia, we shall take a walk in the gardens, and I will offer what explanation I can." Uaine said hurriedly, as shiny metallic claws began to sprout from Torrins knuckles, an ability he had kept secret for decades. *The girl has done nothing wrong, not yet anyway, you know there are two choices before her. Do not aid the darkness by pushing her towards that bastard.* Uaine left no time for Torrin's response as he whisked Nia towards the gardens. Her mind raged, that power still stung her veins. Nia felt as though she might shatter into a thousand pieces. Torrin could not let them leave alone, so quietly he stalked behind the pair and willed himself to relax. Uaine was right after all, he could not be sure what Nia would choose. The choice itself struck fear into the heart of Fae, as although they longed for Rionas return, they knew her child could bring about the end of days.

The wintry night air offered little reprieve as Nia struggled to breath, her eyes closed of their own accord as she felt the air around her as if for the very first time. The wind whispered in her ears, bat wings slapped together in the distance, the breath of wolves and the panicked heartbeat of their prey. She felt the goosebumps raise on Torrins arm at the entrance to the courtyard, the rustling of his cloth tunic, the smell of fresh apples and cinnamon invaded her senses as she found herself focusing on him. She shook him from her mind and let her senses wander into the ether. It was if the world was within her. Nia had never felt such serenity, and yet there was something amiss. A stench she could not place, a dead coldness to the nights chill. It caused a ripple of pain through her heart.

The girl doubled in agony as her senses ventured further into the darkness, the scraping of steel against stone, the cracking of bones, the wails of mothers for their children. Tears formed a river along Nias cheeks as she tore her eyes open and turned to her two spectators. "That pain... Their screams... Can't you hear them?" She asked them frantically as her hands tore at her temples. Uaines green eyes glowed furiously as he looked at the girl, truly looked, with his magic. What he saw almost brought him to his knees. Uaine turned with tears in his eyes, and whispered an apology as he allowed Torrin to see what he could see.

Both men stared in awe or horror, they could not decide, as the magic allowed them to pierce Nias mortal reflection. An iridescent red silhouette radiated from the girl, so bright it almost burned their eyes. Hair like blood and nails sharp as daggers, great furious wings lay rested against her back.

Elves had been known to take another form when accessing their powers, but Torrin had been a boy when the Elves went to the mountains and had never bore witness to such a sight before.

He felt as though his eyes might burn but could not look away as her magic washed over him. It was not to harm him he realised, but as if she were examining him. He could not look away, even though she had her back to him. Only when she turned, frantically attempting to scratch out her own mind did Torrin notice what had been around her aura the whole time. A million white threads had formed, like a spiderweb outstretched across the entire land. One section of the threads, thousands in all, lead straight towards the darkest parts of Etherea.

They had been taught, as all Lords were, of every magical being and power that existed but Torrin had not expected this. "*They're real.*" He breathed as Uaine arrived at the same realisation. "Fate Swayer." Uaine confirmed. Both men spurred into action as Nia shrieked again. "Why are you just standing there?" She cried at the pair. Nia fell to her knees, all sense lost as she clutched her hands together in a prayer. "Please, please Torrin." He realised she had never used his name before, and while a forgotten part of him longed to hear it again, her desperate tone sent ripples of pity through him.

"I cannot remember the Lore Uaine, how did they cope with their power?" Torrin asked frantically. Uaine had always been the more scholarly of the two and yet for all his knowledge, he could not remember a single thing. It was as if it was locked away from him. "I do not know; it is as if it has been hidden from me." Torrin knew what he meant. It had to be some rotten curse set forth by Ciar. "I can help." A quiet voice came from the shadows as Nia howled once more, Uaine had taken hold of her arms for fear that she may pierce her skull with her ferocity.

Rian stepped from the hedge he had been hiding in, the small boy had been following his older brother since Duane arrived. The men watched with caution as the young Fae stepped towards the thrashing girl in the courtyard. Nia felt as if she would explode, tendrils of black ink shot out towards Uaine and Torrin, it took all her strength to keep Rian from becoming a target to the suffering leaking from her body. "I'm sorry." She sobbed to Torrin and Uaine as their faces contorted with pain. Both Fae fell to their knees as they felt a fraction of the agony Nia could feel in the world. "There is just so much, it is everywhere." Rian stepped closer to Nia as her skin began to burn. "Rian please, run. Take my dagger and go as far and as fast as you can from that darkness." She begged as Rian placed his tiny hand in hers.

Blue waves of light wrapped around her arms.

His lips did not move but Nia heard his voice, loud and clear in her mind '*focus Elvinia, what else do you hear?*' She could barely hear a thing above the chilling screams, but Nia shut her eyes once more and focused. *There had been light before the darkness*, she reasoned with herself, *there will be light once more.* It took all her strength but finally Nia turned towards the south, away from that horrendous feeling. *Soothe her you idiots,* Rian barked at their witnesses in his mind. Torrins brows raised at his brother, the youngling had been keeping secrets. "What do you hear?" Torrin asked tentatively. His voice sent shockwaves through Nia; it was like warm honey sliding across her senses. Knowing she could not tell him this, Nia willed herself to focus once again.

The southern winds carried sounds of joy, of humans. "I hear taverns filled with merriment, dogs howling to the moon, mothers sending children to bed and children's hushed giggling in those beds." Light had filled her once again as she chuckled at childish whims. Nia drew further back, and peace washed across her features. "And what do you smell?" Uaine pushed, they had seemed to pull her from the precipice she had found herself upon. "The air is so sweet, I can smell the roses, the earth, fresh apples and cinnamon, like a fresh pie sitting on a windowsill." Rian released her hand only once Nias breath levelled and her eyes opened like blossoming violets. Torrin blinked at the bright shade of lilac that stared back at him, it was almost enough to soothe the ice that had settled in his veins. For a moment he had heard their screams too, and it shook him to the bone.

Nia opened her mouth to speak, only she found herself drained of energy and could only weakly say, "I am sorry." Torrin's heart surged at this and an instinct like no other came over the Fae Lord. He took his cloak from his back and wrapped the exhausted girl in its warmth. "Take Rian to the study, I have questions for you." Torrin ordered Uaine with a pointed look to Rian. The young Fae only rolled his eyes and followed his brothers' companion to the study. Torrin scooped Nia into his arms and began a quiet journey to her room. Nia had felt too many emotions to comprehend as silent tears rolled down her face, she buried her head in Torrins shoulder with shame and blanched as the strong smell of apples and cinnamon hit her nostrils. It had been him, that smell that had chased her and soothed her since she first arrived.

"I should be the one to apologise." Torrin broke the silence as he gently lay her on the silk bed. He sat a respectful distance, yet Nia longed for the comfort of arms around her once more. "I... I did not tell you the totality of the curse Riona set upon Ciar before her disappearance. For every year you live, Ciars power will flow from his body to yours, your life brings his death closer with every breath you draw. Yet all curses demand a counterbalance, and so in his travels to break Rionas curse Ciar found that he would have three hundred years to find you. If he did find you, he had three hundred days to turn you to his side. If you chose darkness, it would mean the end of Etherea forever. If he failed in this, all his wicked magic would be reversed, and he will fall... Elvinia your mother left with you two hundred and ninety-eight years ago. There are two years left of his curse and suddenly you are attacked by three Faelcu and forced into this land? I let fear cloud my judgement, yes, I am sure it was Ciars dark forces that brought you here, yet I see now that you are nothing like him. Forgive me, Nia." Her head spun at the revelation, two hundred and ninety-eight years ago, but how could it be?

It was all far too much for one person to come to terms with, although there was one thought burning through her mind. Torrin turned to leave, to give the girl space, but a soft hand gripped forearm before he could remove himself from the bed. "Could you... I cannot..." Nia could not find the words; she had never felt so vulnerable in her life as she willed herself to look at Torrins face. "You have been through a great ordeal Nia, whatever you need, I am here." She could have cried at the care in his eyes. "Could you stay with me?" Nia finally breathed, embarrassment prickling her cheeks. "I understand I shall be a far cry from the beautiful company you once kept, but I fear if what you say is true there will be more beasts searching for me." Torrin wondered how she would feel should she learn it was a beast who she invited into her bed that night, he had managed to conceal his ability since Ciar set out to turn every last Fae who could do the same.

He found himself dumbstruck at her statement and shook his head. "You are correct." Torrin said with finality before quickly adding, "you are a far cry *better* than any company I have ever kept, and you'll know my words true when the Lords of Etherea fight like schoolboys for your attention at dinner." Torrin almost growled at the thought, yet calmed himself. He had no claim on her, yet as she patted the space at her side Torrin felt an odd sense of possessiveness roll over him.

Nia laughed at his words; the male gaze had never drifted her way. She supposed that had been why Duane had whisked her up so easily. *Duane*. Nia nearly shot from the bed. In the chaos she had forgotten him, the dull ache in her chest roared. "I have to go." Torrins brows drew with confusion as she started to climb out of bed. "You have to rest." He replied, as her knees buckled when she stood. For a moment, the ache eased as Torrin wrapped his arms around her body and gently guided her back into bed. Nia supposed he was right; she would find Duane when she had rested. It would not do to arrive at a prince's door in her state. So, Nia shut her eyes and begged for sleep to soothe the torment of her mind.

Torrin pushed his questions from his tongue as he lay silent beside the drifting girl. It seemed each day that she stayed in Etherea a new drama would present itself. When her breath evened and her shoulders eased, Torrin took a moment to really look at her. Her pale face awash with peace, cheeks blushed with exhaustion, supple lips parted with each breath. Torrin dared not look further than her face, even in simple tunic and britches she oozed beauty, he did not trust his thoughts if his eyes would wander. When he was sure that she had drifted into a peaceful sleep, reluctantly, Torrin peeled himself from her side and found Uaine and Rian in the study.

Rian sat lazily across an armchair while Uaine paced by the window. "How in the Fates did you know what to do?" Torrin asked his brother "I cannot explain it." Rian said simply as Uaine let out a frustrated groan. The boy had given him the same answer a dozen times. "You will explain it as best you can." Torrin challenged as the mousy haired child shut his eyes. "You have to swear you will not be angry." Rian said finally. Torrin and Uaine shared a look, for although they had many differences from their human counterparts' children were the same no matter which side of the veil they hailed from. "We won't be mad Rian, we are simply curious." Uaine explained in an attempt to soothe the boy, he could see Torrins patience had worn thin. "I cannot explain." Torrin almost lunged to shake his brother until Rian hastily continued, "I have to show you, but we will have to hurry."

Rian took off running, Uaine and Torrin on his heels, into the courtyard. His feet skidded to a stop at the large fountain adorning the centre of the garden. "What is going on Rian?" Uaine asked as Rian pushed a fang from its place within the stone lion's mouth. The fountain split the eerie silence with a rumbling groan and a light burst from within, it cut through the darkness of the midnight air.

Long winding stone steps spiralled downwards; their path illuminated by blue lights against stone walls. "We must hurry, it can only be accessed when the moon is shining and once the sun comes up, we will be stuck inside." Rian explained quickly before he ran down the steps. Uaine and Torrin glanced at each other before they once again followed the young Fae. Uaine felt it first, since his powers allowed him a much greater clarity to sense magic, whispers of ancient magic deep beneath their feet. It tickled his nose, made his lungs stuffy and Uaine found himself leaned against the stone wall gasping for air. "Uaine? Uaine what is it?" Torrin asked as he caught his friends stumbling form, "magic runs deep in these walls, I will be alright, we must go further." He wiped the sweat from his brow and willed his feet to carry on, whatever they ventured towards he must find out.

The trio descended into the clammy air beneath them. *How long has this chamber existed?* Torrin thought, surely, he would have noticed something like this. Then again, he remembered, there had not been much time for curiosity. Ciars triumph against Riona had decimated hope across the land, Fae had scrambled to protect their families and their homes. Uaine struggled with each step, his nose burned, his face was slick with sweat. Rian glanced at the pair with worry, he had vomited three times the first time he came to this stone room. He watched the pair as their expressions contorted between astonishment, confusion and fear at the silhouette hunched against the northern wall of the room.

Her expression was a mix of boredom and annoyance, her cold lilac eyes drifted to the trio in the doorway. Her face- a deathly shade of pale, Uaine ignored the urge to run fast and far in the opposite direction. Torrin barely managed to swallow the bile that rose as she stepped into the glow of a nearby wisp. If it had not been for her jagged teeth and the subtle differences in the structure of her face, Torrin could have sworn it had been Nia who stepped from the shadows. "Ah, the little lord returns, I thought you were to leave me to rot until the end of days.... Has it come so soon?" Her voice scratched at their ears, like claws against wood. "Who is this?" Torrin questioned his brother as he dragged his eyes from the girl before them.

Rian cast a wary look between them before her voice cut through his silence. "I am the one who came from her." She spat then. "Your princess is my spirit twin." She cackled then, as if it were all one huge jest. "My, how Ciar has been successful, you do not know enough to help her. Stupid Fae." At this Rian stepped forward and extended his hand. He blinked as a white cloud surrounded it. Within his palm a glowing sapphire encased in rubies and emeralds, with a silver and gold metalwork casing, appeared. "By the order of the Seven Powers that bind you, you will answer our questions honestly. No games, Fate-Swayer." The words left his mouth by instinct. Torrin and Uaine balked at the child as the girl's face contorted with pain. Rian looked at the stone with unease, he had a vague and cloudy memory of the shining artefact. "Fine." She relented, and the stone ceased its furious glow. "Ask what you will." Torrin set forth to gain the answers they had come for. "What is a Fate-Swayer?" At this she laughed. "Well, we know who didn't get the brains in the family."

Rians eyes turned dark, and her face fell flat. "I answered honestly." She said with a roll of her eyes. "If the name was not telling enough, we are the beings destined by the Fates to sway the outcome of the world in times of war and turmoil; while some have the gift of peering into one's soul, we can reach into the very essence of a being and change it to our will. One is born, one is made, rarely do two come from the same mother. My unfortunate soul had entered this wretched world at the same moment Riona pushed that bitch out. Thus, cursing me to be the dark counterpart to her sickly-sweet predisposition. Enjoy her sweetness while you can, Lord Torrin, for she will not be around for long. She *could* be your weapon if you were clever. Unfortunately for you all, I am definitely Ciars. Well, I was to be, am destined to be, see it how you will." Nessa waved her hand with nonchalance, it filled Uaine with unease.

"But what can you *do*?" Uaine pushed, at this she smiled. "Ah, so she has returned and Rionas protection spell has vanished. Oh, what I would give to see the pain on her pretty face as she heard their screams for the first time. It must have nearly broken her." There was no sympathy in her voice. Uaine wondered how she knew of Riona's protection spell. His eyes flickered to the uneasy child at their side. "We are the needle with which the threads of the world are woven, we can do many things. Has your princess boiled the blood from within anyone yet? She will. While we are born pre-determined for good or evil, the fates still allow a choice. It is their twisted way of allowing free will to remain. You should pray that your princess is better than I." At this she howled with laughter.

Rian snapped, the stone burned bright once more. "How do we help her control it?" He snarled as she retreated. "Bring her to me." She tried, yet upon seeing the incredulous looks on their faces the woman relented. "There is a man, a withering old man within a tree in the forest of Galeria, his name is Abbán, tell him the bane of his blood sent you." With a sinister smile her eyes glanced towards the stairway. "I hope you boys run fast; I hear the sun breaking the horizon."

With those words the trio turned and dashed towards the doorway, the weight of each step tripled as they ascended. Uaine lost the contents of his stomach as they ran. Rian urged the two to hurry. None who spent a night in that chamber ever returned. When fresh air hit their lungs they fell to the earth, at the very moment the stone fountain closed behind them. "What in the Fates Rian?" Torrin gasped at his brother.

"I found our fathers journals; he wrote once of this place. I did not search for it; I was in the Courtyard when I read the passage and the fountain opened. He wrote of a vow they swore that they would be the Fateful, the protectors of Fae against dark Fate-Swayers. They knew finding Riona would be impossible, so they followed the magic released the night Nia was born to find her. They let her be for years, until she proved her dark nature and then they trapped her behind a plethora of wards and spells. They believed that if she would not help us, she would at least not be able to hurt us." It made sense and yet, Torrin could hardly believe it. "And you've just kept it a secret all this time?" He asked, at this Rians temper flew.

"They are dead Torrin! Almost every person he wrote of has been butchered by Ciar. Our parents included. I could not let anyone know about her, I could not risk losing anyone else to that monster." Tears pricked at his eyes and at that, Torrin's heart broke. Uaine watched the young Fae, the child was hiding something, or something was hidden from the child; Uaine could not tell.

"Come Rian, we will talk more about this later. We all need to rest before continuing." With that, the trio returned dirty and exhausted back to the manor. A million questions in each of their minds.

Chapter Four:

Nia rose, a clarity in her mind unlike any she had ever experienced. It was if her bones called out to the world, and the world... *answered*. Leaves rustled in the distance, she could hear the babbling of a faraway flowing river, the water sloshing against the rocks as it ran through the forest. It glugged and gurgled as if she had laid her head right next to it. Nia could hear the crackling of the forest which bordered Torrin's barren lands, trees creaking as the wind whooshed through them. chirping rang out in the background; songbirds awakened by the rising dawn. Nia did not dare attempt to listen any further. It took every ounce of strength she had to reel her senses back, away from the river and the trees; back to the deafening quiet of Torrin's Court.

A glance in the mirror as she crossed the room sent Nia reeling towards the glass, her eyes glowed violet, her once light strawberry hair burned a violent blood red, and her skin... The palest she had ever seen it yet glowing all the same. She felt strong, stronger than she thought she ought to, and stepped out into the breezy corridor. Her untrained ears twitched at every sound, Nia willed herself to focus and found her targets. She recoiled at the word as she thought it, *they are not targets*. Her brain had become muddled as memories flashed too fast through her mind, foreign memories of whispered words from Duane had surfaced, she did not know what exactly he had done to her, yet Nia felt the wrongness creeping into her connection with him and knew that he, like Torrin, had used his magic against her. She felt her faith in Torrin slipping.

Throughout the night, memories had assaulted her unconsciousness, like an ancient trove had been unlocked, fragments began to leak through the wards her mother had placed. She had indeed lived for those two hundred and ninety-eight years, learned and absorbed everything in a locked away section of her mind. It had only begun to piece itself together, shards ripped apart by magic. Not in the way Torrin and Duane had wielded it against her, no, Nia knew her mother's spell was cast with love and protection. Riona had managed to raise her, train her, prepare her, and allow her to enjoy a mortal life. A renewed respect for her mother filled Nia. Even if she could not remaster her abilities as quickly as her mother may have hoped, Nia was grateful that Riona had tried.

The Manor was eerily silent as she ventured through the hallway. Nia wondered where her companions had gone, she wished to apologise for throwing such horrendous pain at them; although she could not forget how quickly Torrin turned on her, she understood his fear. It had almost consumed her, and the energy it took to stop focusing on it almost knocked her over. If this were the beginning, she did not think she would survive the end. Nia gritted her teeth and pushed on; a memory of her mother came to comfort her.

"Breathe Elvinia, you are the earth, and it is you. Focus your mind on the light and laughter, let it ground you. Let it fill your heart until you are aflame with happiness. Hold on to the light, keep your heart warm as you reach towards the darkness. You must not ignore the darkness Elvinia, use it to guide you where you are needed most but never touch the darkness with a heavy heart. It can consume you if it is allowed. You must focus on the light Elvinia."

With her mother's words to ground her, Nia took a breath with each step and thought of every ounce of goodness in the world. She decided she should make a list, of each good thing in her life, to recite if she began to struggle. For the time being, the shadows had been pushed away. Her steps lightened as she reached the courtyard and Nias eyes sparkled at the sight before her. Uaine, Torrin and Rian were completing various tasks around the garden, from banners to picnic tables laden with decor and glassware. "What is going on?" Nia questioned with a smile as Torrin directed Rian with a huff. "I promised you I would introduce you to other Fae. I also have the feeling that a party may do us all some good." This could not have been further from the truth. Torrin thought holding a ball was a terrible idea so soon after what had happened, if Duane made an appearance, it could end in a bloody mess and gods forbid the words of that hateful woman beneath their feet held any truth. Nia could rip a Lord to pieces if she chose. He had no choice, for he had sent the invitations before they faced Nessa; but he would not say so to Nia.

Torrin reasoned with himself as he looked at the girl aiding Rian with the silverware, no claws in sight, violet eyes replaced those glaring red orbs, if he had not witnessed it, he would not have believed the smiling Elf felt a fraction of the pain she had shot into his soul. It had only been moments and it had almost ripped him to shreds. Yet, looking at her, she showed no signs of that torment. He had hidden her for too long, things had already begun to shift in Etherea; he knew he needed to prepare her. Torrin may have isolated himself from the other Courts, but even he heard of tensions rising within his neighbours' lands; witch-hunts in the Emerald Court, slaves escaping from the Silver Court, garrisons training in the Golden Court, whispers of Ciar stirring once more in his castle, the Ruby lands once dormant now filled with terrible creatures. Nia stood oblivious to it all, he could not bring himself to tell her.

Nia felt Torrin studying her as she turned towards Uaine. "So, what should I expect tonight?" Nia asked with genuine curiosity. Uaine sighed, it was easy to forget she had not lived in their world for long. "You should expect a room filled with very curious Lords and Ladies; I suspect the High Lords will not make an appearance, nobody has seen the Emerald High Lord in centuries and the Silver Princes... Well, they know better. It will be mostly Noble Emissaries sent in their stead. Torrin's relationship with the Courts is not ideal, they will not believe it is you until their servants' scurry back with proof. Due to this, they will ask you more questions than you have answers for. The questions will stop once they are drunk enough, and then I expect there shall be dancing until the dawn breaks." Nia enjoyed the sound of the latter, not so much the thought of a million questions fired her way.

Torrin watched her brow furrow with thought for a moment. "Then I shall hope you have wine strong enough that I may only answer few questions." Uaine laughed at that and raised a wine goblet in toast to her words. "If the wine does not work, we could pull the whiskey casks from the cellar." Uaine joked, with a twinkle in his eye. At this Torrin groaned. "Those casks will stay where they are, with an armed guard if Ceallach is coming." He laughed as he said it, but Nia saw the seriousness in his eyes. "Ceallach is a cousin of ours, and an absolute disaster when drunk. He has not been invited to an event since before the war. I heard he left only the doors standing at Lord Brádachs home." Rian answered her curious eyes. They were good at that, she noted, answering questions she had not asked. Nia made a mental note to practice masking her expressions.

For hours they bustled around the manor, Nia felt her heart swell with appreciation as they stepped back to admire their work. A ballroom, which Nia had not even known existed, adorned with the brightest crystal hanging lights she had ever seen. Silk ribbons of all shades of blue framed the grand room, wrapped around glittering pillars. Flecks of blue, white, and gold twisted beneath the stone. The floor, it took her breath away. That same white marble, with veins of sapphire blue tracing a path towards its centre. There beneath the surface lay an enormous sapphire geode, the heart of the room. It was magnificent, like nothing she had ever seen before. Torrin drank in the wonder on her face as she surveyed the room, he could not understand it; for he had looked at these floors a thousand times and never once appreciated their beauty. "It is time to get ready Nia, wouldn't want to appear uncivilised." Uaine winked, it broke her from her admiration with a groan. "Is nothing I say private?" She huffed as she retreated to her room. The soft smile she shot at the trio as she left told them that maybe, she did not mind too much.

Nia glared at the wardrobe with frustration. It held nothing that could compare to the illustrations of High Fae she had seen, although it was all magnificent. She had fashioned her hair in a style her mother taught her years ago, braids framing a high chignon, two loose curls framed the sides of her face, but still, she could not face the Noble Fae of Etherea in her tunic and britches. A soft knock on the door only increased her panic. "I have something that might help." Torrin chuckled softly behind the door. Nia let him in and found him holding three magnificent gowns in his hands. "They were my sisters; she has hundreds more if you do not like them." Nia took the heavy fabrics gratefully and began laying them on the bed to decide. "There was a tailor here once, he made all of Taras gowns and my suits, I only wish he were still around to fashion one for you." Torrin remembered him fondly, Nia took in the beauty of the three dresses and nodded her head. "I would have been honoured to receive a gown from someone so talented. I made my own clothes back home, but never would we have such luxurious fabrics."

Torrin did not miss a beat.

"Rip them apart and make your own."

She gasped; a hand clutched to heart in horror. It was such a girlish action she surprised herself. He chuckled as she stared at him, mouth agape. "I could not." She replied, he laughed again and shook his head as he closed the gap between them. Shivers coursed through her as he stepped beside her, brushing a stray hair from her face. He opened his mouth, then closed it again; as if he could not find the words. Torrin cleared his throat and stepped back. Nia could not hide her disappointment. "I watched that man cut yards of fabric from a dress seconds before Tara entered a room, I believe he'd be honoured to have his old creations refreshed. Word still reaches the underground; it would give him pride to hear the lost princess has debuted herself in his fabrics." With that reasoning, Nia could hardly argue.

As Torrin stepped through the doorway, he turned to offer one final piece of reassurance. "You will be spectacular, no matter what you wear." Nia blushed bright red as the door closed behind him.

Nia sat in a clutter of sapphire, silver, and red. Her hands worked feverishly at a pace only an Elf could achieve. She decided her gown would be Sapphire. Nia felt it only appropriate that she should represent the lands which had saved her. Carefully she attached the silver lace to the hem of the deep sapphire skirt. Using the silver, she wove intricate designs across the hips of the sapphire lace bodice. Treading silver one last time Nia lined the sweetheart neckline with more designs. It sparkled in the light and Nia beamed with pride at her creation. It fit like a glove as she slipped it on.

A smile tugged at her lips as she found Torrin had left behind another thing she had forgotten. *Shoes*. The silver heels complimented her dress nicely, but Nia felt her feet hurt terribly. These types of shoes were not commonly worn in her village, no nobles lived there. She decided to push through it, *my mother fought in wars*, she thought bitterly, *I can brave these death-traps for a few hours*. With that thought to push her forward, Nia left her room. Surprised to hear voices already traveling through the hallway, a wave of panic washed through her. Rian laughed at the High Elf's worried face. "You looked less concerned facing the Faelcu." He jested as Nias hand reached back to retreat into her room.

Relief filled her, she would not have to face them alone. "Uaine and Torrin have taken a wager on which Lord you might insult first tonight." Rian told her as he took her arm and began the walk towards the ballroom. Nia threw her head back with a laugh. "Have either of them considered that I might offend them first?" She joked, Rian turned with a twinkle in his eye. "No, but I assume their egos will be dust before the nights end." "You know me well." Her laughter died as they neared the bustling ballroom.

Nia could hear all manner of voices, of footsteps and laughter. It was more than she had heard in her lifetime. It almost drowned her. "Think of them as overgrown children, vying for your attention, sneaky, crafty children." Rian said in attempt to soothe her, it worked for the most part as she laughed and took a step to the door. "Like yourself so." She chuckled as he feigned offense. "You know I am much older than I look." Rian argued, he resented his appearance with every fibre of his being. He should have grown at this point; he could not understand why he had not. Rian shook the selfish thought from his mind and pushed those great big doors open. Nia had no time to consider the darkness that flashed in Rian's eyes.

Silence washed across the room.

Only the lull of a cello remained.

"May I present." Nia stifled a laugh at the sheer drama in Rians tone. "Princess Elvinia, the lost daughter to our rightful King Ciar." A nervous applause scattered across the room. Nia had expected this, Ciar ruled these lands still. A slight against him could cause devastating consequences for those involved. Nia raised her chin and scanned the crowd. Her breathing steadied as she noticed Torrin and Uaine weaving towards her, she could see the panic in Torrin's eyes despite his calm demeanour as he casually pushed through the Fae in his path. "Good evening." Nia started, cursing herself for not preparing words to say.

"Thank you, for joining us tonight. I understand that most of you have come to confirm the rumours running through your courts. I would like to remove any confusion of my intentions. I have spent the last two hundred and ninety odd years in a glamor, unaware of your lands or my heritage. I am here only to get to know the world in which I had been born, so please, drink and be merry. Should we be merry enough, the whiskey might make an appearance and then... I will be keeping an eye on Ceallach." With that they roared with laughter, the tension dissolved in the room as people began to dance once more. The Fae were easily distracted, for they lived in a world of magic and unpredictability, and this was yet another drama in a saga of tragedies in Etherea.

"You were supposed to come for me once she was ready." Torrin scolded his brother in a hushed tone before turning to Nia. She blushed scarlet as Torrins blue eyes drank in every inch of her figure. He selfishly enjoyed that they would all see her adorned in his court colours. It would be an insult to Ciar, that he had found her and took her in; that Nia had made herself comfortable in the Court which worked so hard to destroy him. It was sort of poetic, he supposed, that for all Ciar's efforts to tear Torrin's family apart; he now had in his home the daughter that could ruin the false King. She took the arm he offered and felt her skin raise at the touch of his lips at her ear. "I can guarantee every lady in this room is envious of your gown, and every Lord is wishing to be me right now." With a grin at the sight of her glowing cheeks, Torrin withdrew quickly and led Nia through the room.

"Lord Torrin! What a pleasure it is to return to your home, what has it been? A hundred years?" An older man with salt and pepper hair, chestnut brown eyes and a five o'clock shadow stepped before them with a tight smile. "Aye, at least." Torrin began, his own smile rigid as he turned to Nia. "Elvinia, may I introduce Sir Sean, an emissary of the Silver Court." The emissary bowed to the young girl before him. "Princess Elvinia, please accept our sincerest welcome and allow me to present these gifts from our Princes." Nia's eyes widened as a cart of glittering jewels and luxurious dresses was pulled into the room by four Fae men, her gaze flickered to the white light shackling their feet. Torrin resisted the urge to roll his eyes, *of course they would make a grand gesture.* Elvinia gasped as she ran a hand over the smooth silks and soft furs. "Your gift is much appreciated Sir, I only regret I cannot thank your Princes in person." The men carrying the bounty turned to leave. "Wait." She called out to them, Nia had noticed their weary eyes and worn hands. Immortality had not ensured basic respect for the life of another.

It sickened her.

The room hushed as Nia took handfuls of jewels from the glittering silver cart and placed them into the hands of the Fae men. Their hazel eyes widened. Nia noticed that all High-born Fae had eyes which reflected the court they hailed from and all low-born had varying shades of brown. She wondered if Uaine too was High Fae, for his eyes glowed green. Nia's gaze flickered to look at him and realised he had changed his eyes to a shade of chestnut brown. With no time to question him Nia looked back to the shaking Fae before her; it pained her to see their fear.

"Thank you, kind sirs, for carrying such a heavy gift all this way. I do hope this is enough." Nia bowed her head with respect, the emissary blinked in surprise and looked nervously around the room. To dissolve the tension, he grinned and outstretched his arms. "Your kindness is matched only by your beauty, what a blessing you are!" The room cheered, yet Nia could see their eyes darting to one another. Torrin took her hand once more as a plethora of Fae Nobles bombarded the strange Princess. Most had arrived expecting a carbon copy of Ciar, none had expected the image of their lost Queen to enter the room.

Their names and faces became a blur, their questions the same. "When will you go to your father?" "What are you going to do?" "What can we do?" Nia had no clear answers for them as she politely replied to each as best that she could. "As soon as I can." "Whatever I can." "Take care of each other." Fae of all courts questioned and complimented her, she was grateful for the steady arm Torrin lent her, whispering the names of approaching lords and ladies. Some were pleasant, like the young woman named Erin from the Silver Court who gushed over her gown. Her questions of Nias designs a welcome reprieve from the seriousness of the older Fae. Others, however, gave her a sense of unease, like the smirking emissary of the Golden Court; he did not share Sir Sean's mastery of charm. For a moment, her mind flashed to Duane and Nia forced her mind to clear. It was a struggle, she could almost feel him at her side; for a second, she wished he were.

The Golden Fae grinned at her; Nia blinked; she had not been paying attention. "I am sure our princess would be delighted to receive whatever Duane has sent, Sir Tyrone." Torrin replied to the emissary, knowing Nia had not heard a word the man said. Nia suppressed a groan, she did not want his gifts or pleasantries, she wanted *him*. Meeting Etherea's Fae had not been the grand affair she had hoped for. The girls in her village told tales of high society events with food and champagne and dashing men daring to sweep a maiden off her feet; it was at these events most marriages were secured. The doors burst open once more, Nia's heart fluttered as three carts rolled into the room of their own accord; no enslaved Fae in sight. Torrin could have strangled him *'clever bastard'* Uaine mused in Torrin's mind, only to recoil at the glare he received in return.

Nia stepped forward as a plethora of gifts came towards her. There were jewels, yes; but Duane had spent enough time with her to know she did not care for them. Nia could have cried at the sight of her mother's gold sewing machine; Riona had kept very few items from her past, this was one Nia adored. She had seen it one night, when she had followed the sound of her mother's muffled sobs. Riona had been sat at their tiny table, staring at the device; Nia had never seen anything like it. Atop the machine sat a golden note, the words *'I am sorry, my love'* burned bright in her eyes. Torrin could not believe what he was seeing, it was almost like she had forgotten all about the attack as she ran her fingertips across the golden bounty. Nia turned to Tyrone, a mist in her eyes. "Tell Duane, I thank him greatly for his gift; all is forgiven." Uaine and Torrin shared an uneasy look as Tyrone grinned and bowed.

True to Uaines word, the Fae soon became distracted by their own revelry. Nia felt relieved as the questions faded and the gifts were stored, the High Fae became much too concerned with each other to bother her anymore. It was refreshing, she had expected a much more dramatic affair. Torrin felt her lighten in his embrace as they walked the room and turned to her with a smile. Nia eyed his extended hand and rolled her teeth against her lips sheepishly. The action drew Torrins gaze in a heartbeat, goosebumps raised across his flesh. "I am afraid, I do not know how to dance." Nia admitted. Torrin cursed himself for his haste, he had not considered she may not be prepared for such an affair. "Take my hand, I promise I will not let you fall." Torrin assured her. Her eyes had cleared at least, he would not question her about it here.

Tentatively, Nia took his hand in hers, a soft gasp escaped her lips as his arm wrapped around her waist. The sheer fabric did nothing to stop the warmth of his hand from sending shivers up her back. Torrin led her to the floor, Nia did not miss how the Fae parted as they glided through. Torrin saw her lilac eyes dart around the room and lay his hand gently against her jaw. Nia sucked in a breath; her eyelids fluttered closed at his touch. "Keep your eyes only on me." A gasp caught in her throat. His breath blew hot against her ear as he spoke, and in an instant he had withdrew.

Nia shook the mist from her mind and met his gaze. Uaine watched the pair glide across the floor, almost flying. He did not miss the murmurs within the crowd as a halo of light surrounded Nia. Torrin could not take his eyes from the beautiful being in his arms. Nia felt weightless as he spun her, an orchestra of Fae instruments matched the pace of their steps. She did not know for how long they stayed like that, locked in one another's gaze, but soon; the merriment had moved outside.

The courtyard was aflame with light, Nias violet eyes sparkled as she absorbed her surroundings. Sweet music filled her ears, in a foreign yet familiar language. "The language of the Elves." Torrin answered her silent question as she stared at the ceílí forming in the courtyard. Her feet were not her own as the beating of a drum began, her body drawn towards the dancing Fae. Torrin decided against interrupting her, had she been human he would have ripped her from his courtyard the moment that fiddle began. She deserved to dance, to enjoy the revelry, Gods knew she had seen enough horrors thus far. Torrin watched her as he leaned against an oak tree, despite her earlier claims that she could not dance; he found himself captivated by the sway of her hips.

Three beautiful women danced in the middle of the circle that had formed, like three sisters fighting, Nia found she *understood* the words they sang. It was not just a song but a story, of two sisters battling the wild nature of the third, who wished no more than to run wild with sailors. Many stories were sung before the moon rose, yet Nia felt lighter than ever as she continued to dance. Torrin watched as serenity washed across Nia's face, a rainbow of light poured from her. The Fae were singing an old lullaby, one her mother had sung to her long ago. Her heart pained as she realised there would be many memories of her mother that should have been treasured and yet; were a necessary loss.

A chorus of male fae started the song, their voices a match to the aggression of the drums, then silence. Nia only realised once the drums had begun once more what had halted their revelry, *she* had spun into the middle of the circle and her voice led the chorus. Torrin watched in wonder as she flitted across the field, it was an old song of two lovers of separate classes, a highborn elf, and a lowdown fae, his pleas to her father. A soft masculine voice joined in her verse and Nia almost stumbled as a man stepped in to dance with her. Torrin almost snatched her from the circle right there. Uaine grabbed his friend's shoulder, it would do no good to make a scene in front of everyone; not against *him*.

Curious silver eyes stared down at Nia, a crown of silver leaves adorned his jet-black hair, he had been the one beating the drum that carried her feet forward. He looked vaguely familiar. Nia did not miss the triumphant look he threw Torrin. "Who are you?" She asked as she stilled, an air of danger surrounded him; yet there was something in him, that familiarity, it was something she could not place. Nia found herself drawn to him all the same. Torrin could bare it no longer, as she looked through her lashes at the silver Fae, he yanked Uaine's hand from his shoulder to rip Nia from the circle.

Nia did not notice Torrin advancing on them, perhaps it was the wine which caused her mind to cloud; perhaps it was the magnificent stranger standing so close she could feel his warmth. With a mischievous glint in his eye the Fae leaned down to answer, his breath blew hot against her ear. Nia shivered, not from the coldness of the night, no; Nia suddenly felt hot all over. Before he could answer, as shivers ran down her spine; a silence hushed over the crowd. The air became electric. A stench filled her nostrils. Nia recoiled from the stranger. His silver eyes widened with alarm as he looked behind her, Torrin had stilled in his stride. Nia's skin crawled as she felt sharp daggers prod at her chest.

Then came a scream.

It clattered through her eardrums and sent Nia tumbling to her knees in agony. Chaos followed as the dawn broke. Fae scrambled, ran in all directions, all manner of creatures running for their lives. Nia had barely a moment to steady herself, yet another beast came into view; tall and slender with layers of razor-sharp teeth. It was ghastly and ghoulish, neither dead nor alive. Nia could not have created such a terror in her most horrific nightmares. It released the woman's neck from its mouth and turned to stare at the Elf on her knees.

A sinister smile spread across its sickly pale face. A bony finger rose in her direction, beckoning her towards it. Nia blinked, rooted to the spot as it glared; those soulless eyes bore into her. Darkness swirled around her. Wild eyed and terrified, Nia could only watch as it turned to bare its ungodly fangs at another girl. This lit a flame in Nias bones. The fear ebbed as she took a breath, glaring as the monster stalked the fleeing girl; it grinned back at her. Laughed at her. Nia jumped to her feet. Before Torrin, Uaine or her mysterious dance partner had a moment to react, Nia had hurtled herself towards the monster. As it lunged at the young girl in its tracks, Nia mustered every ounce of strength she could as she barrelled her body into its cold form. She would not let it kill that girl, if no one else would intervene; she would. It was pure instinct which drove her now.

Bile rose in her throat as the stench of it hit her nose, drunk on wine and music, and that damned man's eyes; the world around them had been drowned out, she had not felt its terrible presence approaching. Nia vowed never to make that mistake again. She owed it to these people to protect them, it was her family which had plunged this entire land into misery. Red sparks from Nia's body sent Torrin scrambling to push Uaine out of the way. If Nia had near knocked them out with panic, there was no telling what she would do filled with so much anger. None would wish to be in her path to find out.

Nia ignored the pit in her stomach as her hands wrapped around the creature's neck, she could see its darkness creeping up her skin as she gripped it tighter. Flames sparked within her, as if someone held a flint inside her core; slowly stoking a fire into a flaming pyre. The creature stared up at her and laughed through the blood gurgling from its teeth; even as it struggled in her grasp its darkness did not waver. It only met her gaze. Nia willed herself not to let go as shock filled her, she could see the emptiness of the creature's soul, in its eyes. There was no light, no love, no mercy; only evil, only darkness. "I will feast on every single one of them, you will watch the blood drain from everyone you have ever loved. You Elven bitch... I will start with the childr-" The word was stopped cold, the threat dead in the chill of the rising sun.

An explosion of blood red light had burst from Nia and in turn, the creature splintered into a thousand pieces.

Drenched in its blood and stench, Nia rose with fear.

They will kill me for it, my power, what it means.

Torrin saw the pure terror in the girls face and rose to pull her back to the Manor, only a silver crowned Lord had reached her first. Torrin cursed him as he watched. Nia felt the silk jacket drape across her shoulders and flinched. *This is the calm before the storm*, she thought as he grasped her shoulders. To her shock, they eased of their own accord. Nia searched for any indication he had used his magic, so many had already tried to use their powers against her, but none showed; instead, she felt a longing, something scratching at the back of her mind telling her that she should go with him. She realised, after a moment too long, that the girl who had almost been the creature's next meal was on her knees before her. Nia blinked, looking away from the mysterious stranger.

Barely hearing the cries of thanks that spewed from the girl's mouth, Nia found herself clutching the girls' arms and pulling her to her feet. "Nobody bows to me, not now, not ever." Nia said shakily, she had meant it to sound strong and decisive but considering the twisting in her gut it had been a fool's errand. To her surprise, the girls' eyes lit with respect. "Yet still, I thank you. Should you ever find yourself in need, the House of Avera will be at your disposal." And with a respectful nod she left, leaving Nia to think about what she had just done.

"Are you okay?" A quiet, concerned voice asked from her side. Nia had almost forgotten about the silver Fae. He smelled strongly of spearmint and honey. Her two favourite things. Nia drank in that scent, let it wash away the stench of that foul creature. "I suppose, I am only sorry that I could not save them both." her eyes darted to the older woman, withered on the ground. A sickening realisation hit her, as she looked at the limp and saggy body in the dirt. *"It drank her blood."* She gasped. Nia had seen animals rip each other to shreds but nothing could have prepared her for *this*. "A fitting end to the bastard then." He shrugged nonchalantly, as if she had not blasted the beast to pieces. As if she had not reached out to the blood within its veins and boiled it from within.

His calmness was a stark difference to Torrin's unease. "I hardly think it necessary, but I would much prefer to escort you back to your home, if your majesty would allow." There was a teasing tone in his voice, but Nia knew better now than to take the hand of a stranger; no matter how much her heart told her to. Her eyes searched for their faces and found Torrin and Uaine staring cautiously at the man before her. "Who are you?" She asked once again, as his mouth turned upwards to a smirk. His silver eyes flickered across Torrin and Uaine, Nia watched his smirk grow. "For another time, *milady.*" That time he *did* sneer as he said the word, it should have infuriated her. In all her exhaustion, Nia could only laugh as the stranger disappeared into thin air.

If she woke on that table, in her humble cottage, half mad with the wounds she had suffered from the Faelcu, it would have made more sense.

Torrin rushed to her now abandoned side, blood dripped from the tendrils of her hair; dishevelled and unruly. The colours barely separated from each other, two scarlet shades battling for intensity. *"What was that?"* Nia seethed at the remnants of the creature, what little there were, her arms outstretched in frustration. Wisps of white light flew from her fingertips, and she found herself suddenly clean again. On the surface anyhow, the stench still clung to her nose. Nia cursed the unpredictability of her magic as she glared at her fingertips. "That was the Abhartach; it is terror incarnate. How...?" Torrin was not sure what to ask, as she stood spotless and unsteady.

"I could not allow it to hurt another person." Nia's voice trembled as she remembered the sight of the woman falling limply to the ground, the shrill screech that almost burst Nias eardrums and the pain... *oh the pain*. Nia had felt the essence ripped away from the woman as her throat had been torn apart.

Torrin looked at Nia with a mixture of admiration and fear, if someone had stumbled upon the scene, they would never have imagined the young girl in the elegant gown was responsible for the blood painted across the glamoured grass. "What was it doing here?" Nia asked with worry as Uaine and Torrin led her towards the Manor. They shared an uneasy look. "I can handle the truth, if I can handle the bastard myself." Nia was surprised at herself, her language mirroring the silver crowned stranger whose jacket she realised she still wore. Her fingers caressed the soft fabric as Uaine sighed and answered. "Your return, your mother's kidnapping, it has set forth pieces placed hundreds of years ago. Old alliances, old feuds are resurfacing, creatures who are looking for Ciars favour will be on the hunt to bring you to him." Nia gulped at that. Only a fool would feel no worry at those words. She had faced not even a handful of monsters this world had to offer, what else could there be?

The silk beneath her hands lent a small comfort, its artisanry distracting her from her fear for a moment. "And who-" She hesitated before raising her chin, "who was he?" Nia finally asked, it was a question she had wanted answered more than she willed to admit. Torrin rolled his eyes. "That was Lorcan, one of five princes of the Silver Court." Uaine reluctantly informed her. Torrin outright scoffed at Uaine's words. "Prince of lies he is, silver-tongued bastard." Uaine gave his friend a warning look. "The silver and gold High Lords of the time, - Lorcans father and Duane- swore allegiance to Ciars forces during the war. That is why their lands have remained unscathed and their powers still prevail. Lorcan is the youngest of six vicious brothers, and while he is more trickster than anything I would still beg you to be cautious should he cross your path again. The savagery of his elder siblings is known in every Fae home." Uaine explained, there had been a coldness behind Lorcans eyes, yet she did not feel anything *sinister* from him.

Nia turned to Torrin then, with accusation burning in her gaze. "Why is it personal to you?" She queried; the Fae Lord had been baring his teeth since Lorcan had stepped into her song. Uaine cast a wary warning look in Nias direction, which she duly ignored as Torrins brows knit together. "My sister is married to one of his bastard brothers. *A gift from Ciar.*" He spat once again.

Surprise hit her, and she realised she had not seen a single family portrait in the Manor. "Is there nought to be done?" She found herself asking, Uaine shook his head sadly as Torrin stormed from the room rather than answer. "She has been cursed, her mind poisoned by dark magic, Tara is no longer the girl who Torrin grew up with." This sent sadness rippling through Nias core. "I will find a way." She decided, Uaines brows rose. "You will not, we have seen as many sorcerers as were willing and not one would aid us to pull the curse from her mind, its roots had grown too deep." His defiance only made her decision final. She would find a way to help Torrins sister. A start would be to return the jacket draped across her shoulders; to find a way into the Silver Court.

As she wrapped herself in the soft silks of her bed, Nia reached for the book of Fae on her nightstand. It held tales of Torrin, so she presumed it would give her some answers to who the Silver 'Prince' was. With the flickering lantern illuminating the room, Nia flicked through the worn pages of the book until she found the Silver Court. She found his parents first. Oisín was the last surviving of the Ó Cearbhaill line. He was not dissimilar to Lorcan, but his hair was lighter, no kindness shone in his eyes. Nia snorted at the meaning of the surname, 'valorous in battle', something told her they were anything but. He may have been a warrior, but he held no valour. The High Lord used whatever tactics he could to gain more lands, more power; no matter the cost. Nia's heart pained as she read of his atrocities, slavery, torture, witch-hunts; he was barbaric. Nia could not help the sliver of relief as she read the word DECEASED at the bottom of the page. She found Lorcan's mother then; Moire. Lorcan was a carbon copy of his mother, that raven hair, those light eyes. There was a bitterness behind her glow, Nia wondered if Lorcan's mother loved her husband or resented him.

As she flipped through the pages of his brothers and their crimes, bile rose from Nia's throat. They were savages, especially the eldest three. Aidan, the High Lord, led his Court just as his father had; like a barbarian. They stole women from other Courts for fun, sent pieces of children in parcels back to mothers who could not pay their debts, whipped their servants through the streets; whatever they wished, they did. Nia barely reached the washroom in time, as her stomach emptied into the ceramic bowl; her hands shook as she wiped the sweat from her brow. *What have I gotten myself into?*

Afraid, but still curious, Nia flicked past his brothers and found him, finally. Her hands trembled; the book gave her little hope as it followed the trend of the previous page, they called him cruel, said he joined his brothers with glee. Nia's stomach churned. She pushed past his crimes, as her eyes watered to find the section about him personally. It was the same section which had given her ammunition to tease Torrin. It seemed Fae men possessed the same traits, as Lorcan was also quite favourable with the ladies. Nia could not help but roll her eyes, they were all the same. With a frustrated sigh she shut the book and lay her head upon the soft pillow. A wicked thought filled her mind as she laid restless, *I could seduce him, convince him to bring me to his court and from there I can free Tara*. Nia decided to rest first before she made any decisions.

Chapter Five:

Dusk and Dawn passed without so much as a stir from Nia. Still unused to her magic, she had wiped out all her energy against the Abhartach. It was Rian who finally decided she had rested enough, as he jumped on her bed. Nia grumbled awake; no grace of the Fae could make one a morning person. "*Why*?" She asked as she sat up, hair askew. Laughter from the doorway had her scrambling to pull the soft duvet over her face. "Does privacy not exist in this damned land?" She groaned as she hurtled the book from her nightstand at Torrin, who carried a bejewelled tray of food that she had not noticed.

He sidestepped the book, barely, as it slapped against the wall where his head had just been. "By the Fates girl, stop trying to maim me." Torrin grumbled as he set the tray down on her bedside table. "Well, aren't you going to give it to her?" Rian questioned, to the disdain of his brother. "I was going to." Torrin murmured as Uaine entered the room. "He was in fact, not." Uaine confirmed as he sat in the lounge chair. "Well, what is it?" Nia asked with frustration, she truly did not enjoy surprises; no matter how much the world liked to throw them at her.

Torrin begrudgingly took an envelope from his pocket, crumpled but unopened. As if he had instantly thrown it away before deciding against it. He dropped the letter on

Nias lap with distaste. She could have guessed who it was from without the glistening silver '*Lorcan*' illustrated across the envelope. His handwriting was magnificent. "Stop examining the lettering and see what he wants." Uaine huffed, which caused Nia to send him a glowering stare. "For having a lifespan of thousands of years, you Fae have no patience." She *tsked* as she opened the letter. A delicate bracelet of silver leaves fell as she opened the pages.

It was so dainty, so delicate as she held it up to the sun to admire, she voiced her thoughts as it shone. Torrin scoffed once again. "Probably made by the children of slaves." A reverberating slap sounded within the room as the bracelet had been volleyed against the wall. "Excuse me?" She balked; letter abandoned. She had forgotten, in the haze of her tiredness. Nia's blood boiled. Her mind flashed to the white shackles which adorned the Fae men's feet as they had carried a trove of gifts into the ballroom. The human world had that disgusting practice, she still could not believe the Fae held the same ideals. By some miracle, the jewellery had not shattered into a thousand pieces.

"Most in allegiance to Ciar still carry out the practice, they see them as low-born Fae determined only worthy to serve the High Fae." Disgust ran through her. "That is the most horrid thing I have ever heard." Nia told them with honesty. She held true to her belief that no one man had been made better than any other. The bracelet forgotten; Nia returned her attention to the letter with curiosity. She knew even if she did not reply, her curious mind would not rest until she had read what he wrote.

Dearest Elvinia,

Though I did not have the pleasure of enjoying your company for long, I cannot contest the ache that you have planted in my heart; I must see you again. I know my brothers have sent gifts already, but I do hope you will accept a gift of my own, I am painfully aware it pales in comparison to your beauty, and I do not blame Torrin for hiding you away. You would do me a great honour if we could meet again, on neutral grounds of course; perhaps Avenere? I shall wait for you there.

x Prince Lorcan

"He wants to meet, on neutral ground, he calls it Avenere." Nia relayed as she finished reading, she decided it better to be honest than listen to his words and lie. This would work finely if she were to attempt to seduce him. "Absolutely not." Uaine answered first, Nia saw the gleam in Rian's eye as if to say, *'we will go no matter what'*. With that in her arsenal she let her shoulders fall with false defeat. "Fine, but if you must control who I see then I must demand privacy if this is to be my room." The trio left her at that and in the silence, she let loose a breath of relief. The triumphant look on Torrin's face made her chuckle. Since he had gotten over the shock of what she was, he had looked at her like no other man had; it gave her butterflies and sent a blush across her face whenever she thought of his caring eyes.

Nia decided she had no choice but to save his sister, for all they had done for her so far; she owed it to him. There was only one slight problem. She would have to gain favour with this Prince and use it to make her way into their Court; she would free their slaves and bring Torrin's sister home. From the letter, Nia knew Lorcan was already interested in her; she would use this to her advantage.

As she slowly became more conscious, the sounds across the land had come buzzing at her mind once again. It was a struggle to block it out, it felt wrong to ignore the pain and suffering, but Nia knew if she reached out to touch that dark abyss once more then she would be consumed by it. Instead, she ate as much of her breakfast as her stomach allowed and searched through the mountain of dresses in her wardrobe. Her eyes fell upon a beautiful set of silk trousers with a lace bodice. It was practical, beautiful, and *silver*. Nia grinned as she slipped the soft material over her body before she readied her belt with weapons. She would not trust a stranger so easily, not again.

As her dagger slid into its hilt a soft knock on the door told her it was time. Nia had found a soft brown hooded cloak and wrapped it around herself as Rian entered the room. "Are you ready? If they catch me, they will skin me." Rian half joked, her eyes darkened for a moment. "They would lose their hands before they lay a finger on you." Rian gulped at her ominous tone, he had no doubt that they would lose all limbs before they removed a hair from his head. She reminded him of Nessa for a moment. He shook that thought quickly from his mind.

Rian had scarce memories of his older sister, he supposed this was what it felt like to have one. "Stop being so serious lady, we're about to escape." The cheeky child flitted down the corridor before Nia followed him with swiftness. She had no idea where Rian was leading her, but she knew in her bones that to follow him was the right choice. It was not the same tugging, forced pull she had felt towards Duane. It felt like she was on a path to clarity. As they wound their way through the courtyard, past the barren field - Nia still could not believe how real the glamour the Fae cast had been, she could have sworn she felt the grass beneath her feet- except she noticed something in the distance that had not been before.

"Rian stop." She called out, he joined her to look in the direction she pointed. "What are we looking at?" He asked, squinting as the sun bore bright in their eyes. "Come on." She grabbed the boys' hand and led him towards it. There, he finally saw it, a small gleam of colour against the parched ground. "I can't believe it, the curse said once you stepped foot on Fae soil Ciars curses would begin to undo themselves, but you have been here for weeks with no change, Uaine and Torrin thought it had been remembered wrong." Rians eyes brimmed with tears as he stared at the solitary flower. A sudden realisation hit Nia.

"I took off my shoes." She said feverishly. "At the dance, I took off my shoes, my feet hadn't touched Fae soil until I danced." Her heart filled with joy; her presence would do at least this kindness to their land. "Should we return and tell the others?" Nia questioned, Rian thought for a moment before he shook his head. "No, if we return, they will not allow you to venture this far out again. I love my brother, but he can be a stubborn fool, he will want to protect you." Nia smiled at that. Save for her mother, none had ever deemed her worth protecting. Although, she supposed, they did have a personal stake in her safety, if it meant saving their world. They set forth, their hearts alight with the hope this revelation brought. "What is Avenere?" Nia found herself asking as they continued onward.

She felt the sadness ripple from him, it clogged her nose as she gasped for air. Rian looked up, wide eyed at her panic and cursed. It was a sound so foreign in his childish lilt that it snapped Nia back to focus. "Rian!" She exclaimed as the young fae broke into a sheepish smile. "I am a lot older than you may think." Rian laughed, he had said it so many times it began to turn his heart bitter; he shook it from his mind and nudged Nia to continue walking. "Avenere was the old city, once a bustling hub of art and music, abandoned, a ghost town now." Rian explained as he helped her climb the rocky ledge before them. "How old are you?" Nia asked. "Three hundred and five, you would think Torrin was four hundred with how he acts; he is only twelve years older." Nia stumbled at his words, Rian reached to steady her.

Nia stopped with a hand on her hip. "Wait." She told him as she did the maths in her head. "So you are seven years older than me and twelve years younger than Torrin, yet you look ten years of age?" It baffled Nia, she did not know much about the Fae, but she knew something was not right. Rian shrugged, it was an unspoken question in their household. "I think it is due to Ciar's curse on this land, I do not know how but I have not aged since my parents were killed." There was not much clarity when Rian thought back to those times; when he had been an actual child. Her heart sank for him, how awful it must be to live, trapped in a body that did not match his mind. Rian nudged her forward, up the hill, not wanting to dwell on the subject. Nia could see how much it pained him.

As she rose, dusting off her cloak, Nia gasped at the sight that came to be. Huge buildings, some stone, some wood, some glistening Sapphire, all covered in overgrown greenery. A vastness of ivy choked the town, its paths covered in mud and shrubbery. It was still beautiful, in an eerie sense. "A cruel joke, that the nature forbidden to thrive anywhere else should smother the remnants of our lives before." Rian scowled, a rearing animal cut Nia reply from her lips. A gleaming white horse, with elegantly braided hair and diamonds adorning its saddle. Nia could have cried at its beauty. The horse stared at the pair for a second, as if studying them, and with a huff it bowed its head and stepped out of their path. It took all her strength to pass the animal without jumping on that saddle and heading for the hills. Nia had always adored horses and the freedom they brought. She could have sworn it winked as they passed.

From one of the shorter buildings, Lorcan emerged. In another tailored suit and silk shirt, a shiver ran through her, Nia reminded herself she had a mission to free Torrin's sister. With a shake of her head to clear her thoughts, Nia took a step forward. She ignored the cautious look Rian threw her, he had brought her here but still he worried. Nia made a mental note to ensure Torrin laid no blame at Rians feet for whatever would happen. Lorcan smirked, like a cat who got the cream. He had seen her turn that creature into liquid, yet still he smirked? His arrogance irritated her for a moment, but she shook it from her mind and focused on why she had come here. Nia supposed she should have expected it.

Fine, she thought, *let him think I am a mouse in his trap*. Nia laid a comforting hand on Rian's tense shoulder and continued towards the Silver Prince with a soft smile and batting lashes. She used a memory of a girl from her village, who had every male wrapped around her finger, to aid her as she approached Lorcan. It felt unnatural, as she swayed her hips and smiled so sweetly at him. "I am surprised Torrin has allowed you to come." He said first, Nia almost growled as she swallowed her sarcastic reply. "He has been very gracious." She said softly instead. Lorcan smirked once again. "I see his grace did not extend to accompanying you." Anger welled in her stomach. It took every ounce of strength not to slap the smugness from his face. "He does not know I am here." It was a risk, she knew, to tell him they had come in secret; but Nia also knew he would relish in her choice to sneak away to meet him. As if to prove her point, delight filled Lorcans face. While this world and its power were still unfamiliar to her, Nia found men remained the same on either side of the border.

Slaves to their ego.

He was dangerous, this much she knew; but Nia found, in that moment, as his brows drew near, and those silver orbs burned into her own; she did not care at all. "So, you've snuck away, have you? Don't you know it is dangerous, meeting strange men in the woods?" His voice was husky, it sent shivers down her spine. Nia chuckled as she looked up at him, through thick lashes, Lorcans eyes flashed with hunger as she smiled. She relished in the irony, of how easily she had diverted his attention. "I have survived it once; I think I can handle you." His lips quirked at that. "Is that so?" He murmured as his lips dipped to her ear, she felt herself falling into *his* trap. "I would quite like to see you try." Every fibre of Nia's being lit aflame. If it had not been for the gagging noises of Rian in the background, she might have forgotten her objective. There was something sinfully alluring about him. The young Sapphire Lord glared at the pair. Lorcan flashed an annoyed look at the child.

"I have something of yours." Nia told him, breathless. She screamed at herself in her mind; *get a grip, you are better than this*. A dark voice questioned why she had to be. Lorcan smirked once more as his eyes travelled to her shaking hands, disappearing inside the fabric of her cloak. This was her chance, she noted, to weave her own web in which to catch the dazzling prince before her. Carefully, with feigned nerves, Nia retrieved his jacket from within her cloak and extended the bundle towards him. Nia made sure, as his hands wrapped around the fabric that her fingers brushed against his. Pulling back quickly with a sheepish smile Nia hid her hands back beneath her cloak. Rian watched the scene unfold with surprise. If he did not know better, he would have feared Nia was falling for the false Prince. *Torrin is going to kill me*, Rian thought. Lorcan, however, felt absolute victory at her shy advance.

"You could have kept it you know, given me an excuse to see you again." Lorcan winked, Nia chuckled with a shake of her head. Annoyance rippled in her core; she had not intended to enjoy his company so much. "And have me accused of theft? I think not." She continued their banter, despite the sinking feeling that she was no longer in control. Lorcan laughed at her, a twinkle in his eye; Nia did not wish to know what obscenity had crossed his mind, yet he shared it all the same.

"I think you would enjoy being my prisoner." Nia froze, Lorcan did not miss the shift in her eyes. She remembered the atrocities his brothers had enacted, how they treated their prisoners. Nia would rip him limb from limb before she allowed him to take her prisoner. The violence of her thoughts shocked her. Nia shook her head and turned her attention back to Lorcan, with a forced laugh she replied; "Three Faelcu tried and failed, I would like to see *you* try."

"Did you like my gift?" He questioned, noticing her tensing shoulders. She almost scowled, frustrated at her weakness. *Now I must try keep my focus.* Nia could have rolled her eyes at his cavalier demeanour; *does he really think me such a fool?* Nia took a seat beside him and beamed brightly as she raised her arm. The jingling trinket shone brightly in the sun as her cloak fell away from her body.

Lorcan's eyes darted to her nape, as she very much intended. "It is very beautiful." She paused for a moment and cast her eyes to the ground, pretending not to have noticed his gaze; pretending even more that she did not enjoy it. *What has become of me?* Nia questioned herself. "I would very much like to see where such beautiful jewellery is crafted, and I would like to thank the maker of your gift." This, she meant. Nia did not include how she would prefer to rip the shackles from every Fae in his Court; and possibly his heart from his chest for what he had done to them. He was gorgeous yes, but a pretty face would not absolve him of his crimes.

If I can free Tara and their slaves, at least some good will come of my presence, Nia thought to herself. "You are welcome in my court, whenever you please, I could take you there now." Lorcan shrugged and extended a hand. Nia gripped his palm as Rian took a step towards them. "Not now, please." Rians brows raised with shock at the sheer adoration on Lorcans face. She was far more skilled at manipulation than he would have thought. Nia could not bring herself to admit she was not entirely acting. "I must bring Rian home, for I would never wish to offend Torrin, he has been so kind in offering me shelter." Nia offered as explanation; she knew that revealing her thoughts of another man in his presence would throw him off.

The sparks of jealousy in his eyes confirmed her plan had worked. Lorcan swallowed a scoff and nodded thoughtfully. "This is fair. For I know I would chase you across the world to ensure your safety." Lorcan clasped the hand in his palm and brought his lips against her knuckles. At this, her heart fluttered. Nia blushed scarlet as he pulled away, those silver eyes twinkled as he smiled and stood. Nia stood alongside him. "When will I see you again?" She asked him, breathlessly. Lorcan winked at the beauty before him. "We shall meet again soon, under circumstances less likely to cause you trouble, I am very sorry for any I have caused already." Lorcan disappeared once again into thin air, her heart sounded like a thousand drums beating in her ears.

Rian cast a confused look to Nia, he thought that she had come to confront him. Nia shook her head and hurried Rian from the abandoned city. The white horse still stood, watching them curiously; Nia wondered if it somehow spoke to Lorcan. It would not shock her in this strange world; so, neither said a word until they reached the courtyard of Torrins Manor. Nia felt a queasiness in her stomach as he flashed in her mind once more, that smirk; those glittering eyes. Goosebumps raised across her flesh, something tugged in her heart; there was more to him than Etherea knew, she was sure of it.

"We walked for hours, risked my head, for mere *moments* of conversation?" Rian finally exclaimed as Nia closed the gates behind them. She noticed how he glanced in fear at the fountain, as if he were waiting for something. "Did you think I would walk up to him; bat my lashes and he would free every bound soul in the Silver Court?" Nia challenged, ignoring Rian's strange expression. "You *did what?!*" A voice boomed across the courtyard. Nia and Rian flinched at Torrins heavy steps. She rushed to shield Rian from his brothers' temper and pushed him behind her. Neither noticed the fear on the young Fae's face. "I can explain." Nia called out as she heard Uaine rushing towards them too. She had to resist rolling her eyes at them, Nia knew they were trying to protect her, but she was not just some fragile thing to be protected; she needed to help, to do *anything* besides sit in this Court while her mother rotted. Both Lords skidded to a halt at the frustrated look on Nia's face.

Her hands rested on her hips; her foot tapped with impatience. Torrin gulped as he took in her appearance, she had dressed to impress Lorcan; it sickened him. "I forced Rian to take me to Avenere, I met with Lorcan, and I have sowed the seeds to retrieving your sister and freeing their slaves." Torrin could not believe her words, Uaine looked between Nia and Rian for any indication of a lie. Rian knew neither would believe unless he showed them.

So, he did.

Nia watched wisps of blue dance between them before Torrin turned to glare at her. "You *flirted* with him? After all you know about him, you sat and let him look at you like a prized pig." His voice raised with each word, as did Nias temper. In a flash, she had stepped towards him and jabbed her finger in his chest to cease his verbal attack. "I sat there and let that smug little brat look at me like that so that he would think me nothing more and when his *prized pig* decided it preferred the company of another, I made him desperate for what he could not have. This ensures that he cannot suspect I have any intentions at his court, for he will ask me to join him." Nia jabbed Torrin once more for good measure, "and he will think me too much of a girlish fool to be a threat against him." Silence fell as Nia took a step back.

The trio shared a surprised and impressed look on each of their faces. Nia crossed her arms with a frown. "Don't look so shocked that I am *not*, in fact, a mindless fool." "You played the part very well." Rian shrugged with a laugh, attempting to ease the tension. It worked, as Nias shoulders relaxed, and a smile slipped onto her face. "You were my inspiration dear boy." She countered and ruffled the hair on his head. Nia knew out of the three it was Rian was closest to her age, but she adored teasing him about his appearing ten years old. "You will be the death of me." Torrin groaned as he rubbed his temples. "You might consider, sharing your *brilliant* strategies with us *before* you enact them next time." Nia grinned at Torrin. "I would not wish to insult your ego by kicking your ass should you try keeping me in this Manor." With that she sauntered to the dining room.

Torrin watched with disbelief as she walked, hips swaying confidently with each step. She infuriated yet enamoured him. Uaine laughed at the pained expression on his friends' face. "Women, the ficklest creatures of all." Uaine offered with sympathy as he lay a hand on Torrins shoulder. "And this one even more so." Torrin sighed while his brother and friend laughed at him. They joined Nia in the dining room as she piled her plate with food. "You had another visitor while you went wandering today." Uaine informed her as she spooned potatoes into her mouth. With all the grace of a rock, Nia replied a gurgled: *"who was it?"* Torrin frowned in disgust at her actions, Nia resisted the urge to stick out her tongue.

"Her name was Erin, she left these for you." Uaine gestured to a pile of fabrics Nia had not noticed by the door. "How sweet of her, could you send word that I would like to see her again? She was lovely." Nia smiled wholeheartedly, of the whole night filled with so many faces she remembered only three. Erin, Lorcan and that young woman from Avera.

Nia pushed the flashing images of the girls terrified face from her mind. "I would also like to send condolences to the family of the girl who was killed last night and to check on the welfare of the woman who was attacked." Nia voiced her thoughts and did not miss the look of admiration on Torrin face. She blushed and looked away. *Oh Gods, what has become of me?* She almost groaned aloud. "Consider it done." Torrin replied and with that settled, Nia dug into her food. Her heart thumped in her chest as her mind whirled, from her Golden Prince to her mysterious admirer, to Torrin; her saviour. They were all so handsome, it was exhausting; so, Nia excused herself and retreated to the library. *It was time to form a plan to save her mother*.

The moon illuminated the dark room as Nia stepped inside, with a lantern to light the way, she peered through the collection of ancient books. Frustration filled her as Nia found nothing of use, as she ventured further into room Nia collected a small stack of books filled with strategies used before. It was not enough. A whisper sent Nia twisting to look around, the room remained empty. It was just the wind, she reasoned with herself and set the stack down by her armchair. That whisper sounded once more; Nia narrowed her eyes as she stared at the shelves. They widened as she realised, one of these books was *speaking* to her. Filled with curiosity, Nia ran her hands across the spines of each until her fingertips burned hot and the whispers became screams.

She shook as the silver lettering shined in the light, *Etherea's History: Riona's Tale*. Feverishly, Nia grabbed the book and settled in her armchair. She could not believe it when she opened the first page, it truly was an account of her mother's entire life in Etherea. From her first adventure to her last, tears dripped from Nia's eyes as she absorbed each word. It began innocently enough, of Riona's journey to return health to a dying Oak Tree; it was called the Crann Bethadh, The Tree of Life. She felt bolts unlocking in her mind as she read of her mother's powers. Something bubbled in her blood. Nia gasped, momentarily distracted, as she found Duane had fought alongside her mother; they had been allies. She immersed herself into the book, unwilling to look away; hopeful that she might find inspiration from the one who knew Etherea best.

Chapter Six:

Torrin found Nia in the library the next morning, curled up on an armchair, with a book of battle strategies abandoned on the floor before her. *Riona's Tale,* nowhere to be seen. As he took a moment to take in her beauty, Torrin noticed the pain twisted on her sleeping face. As he put a hand on her shoulder to wake her from whatever plagued her, Nia voiced a name she should not know. "Bradach." She called out, desperation in her voice. "Don't go in Bradach. She is not me; I am not her; she will only fill your head with lies." Nia continued, fear mangling her expression. Only once her screams started did Torrin shake her to consciousness. *Her memories must be linked to her mothers,* he thought. All Fae knew the story well. Riona had travelled with his uncle Bradach to an oracle and that oracle burned Bradach's mind away. His uncle still lived, barely, an empty shell of the man that once was. The oracle, if that is what it truly was, had turned his brain to *soup*.

Nia woke, wide eyed, to a face so alike to the one in her dreams she screamed once again; gripping his arm as if releasing him would be to send him to his death. "Do not go in Bradach, do not go." She begged desperately. Torrin gently took her hands in his own. "Breathe Nia, it's Torrin, Bradach is safe." Not a lie, but not a whole truth. He decided it best to wait until she had calmed to explain what plagued her dreams. Her chest rose and fell rapidly until her breath finally steadied. Nia blinked twice as she realised it was Torrins blue eyes boring into her own. Nia released the death-grip on his arm. "I'm sorry, it was just a bad dream." She reasoned. Nia did not want to tell him of the book, she was unsure why; but she felt she must keep it secret. Torrin wrestled with a thought, should he bring her to that strange woman? Torrin made a mental note to find out more about the man in the tree. It sounded ridiculous. *A man in a tree, what use is that information?* Galeria was not a place one would wish to search blindly; many souls had entered; many had not returned.

"It was not." He began with a sigh as he pulled a chair before her and sat. "I think you are seeing your mothers' memories. I must tell you the truth, we found someone with answers to what you are. It seems that your magic is linked somehow, it is possible that you are also linked with Riona and that she is also a Fate-Swayer. We are still trying to find out exactly what it means." Torrin knew it was not an adequate explanation, but it was all he had to offer. "Who is this someone?" Nia asked, sensing that Torrin had not been exactly successful in getting information from them. Torrin shook his head and ran a hand through his copper hair. "She is not to be trusted." he simply replied. Nia groaned at this. "Torrin, please, if someone has knowledge of what I am then I must speak with them. Who is your source of information?" She pushed as she rose, her bones aching from sleeping in such an uncomfortable position. Nia made a mental note not to fall asleep there again.

Her waiting lilac eyes drew another groan from the High Lord. "If I say no, you will only figure a way to find her yourself, won't you?" He asked and received a pleasant surprise when she laughed. Tension eased from her shoulders and Torrin found himself smiling in return. "You are correct." Nia agreed, finding delight in his smile. "You have been a pain in my ass since you arrived, you know this right?" Torrin asked as he rose, Nia followed suit with a wide grin. "Ah, but how boring your life must have been without me." she quipped back, her nightmare forgotten. "We can only go to her at night, so don't pester me about it yet. It is time to have some food and if you would like to, we can continue to train while we wait for the moon to rise." Torrin extended a hand to help her stand. Nia took it gratefully and stretched her limbs, her bones cracked and creaked from sleeping in such an awkward position.

Nia yawned as she stepped towards the door. "For someone who sleeps so often, you're awfully tired all the time." Torrin commented, Nia scratched her neck sheepishly. "In truth it feels as though I haven't slept at all." Torrin frowned at her. "There was a tea my mother would make when we were children, when we feared the non-existent monsters beneath our beds." Torrin smiled sadly at the fond memory and Nia found herself linking her arm with his. He gulped at the contact. How quick she was to trust him, to care for him. Torrin could not believe he had thought her to be anything but good. "I do wish I could have met her." Nia said softly, sensing his sorrow. "As do I, she was a close friend of your mothers and I believe she would have doted on you as if you were here own." Torrin knew this to be true, it was her nature to take care of others.

He saw the hesitation on Nias face as they approached the dining room. "What is it?" He pressed, worry in his eyes as he scanned her; waiting for that red mist to appear once more. Nia shook her head. "I cannot phrase it without sounding harsh." She admitted, Torrin squeezed the hand still holding his arm, it sent warmth through her. "Considering your circumstances, I would expect some harsh statements." It was true, he had expected much more anger that nobody had stepped up against Ciar in the hundreds of years since Rionas disappearance. Torrin was still surprised she had not grabbed her weapons and stormed from his manor the moment her powers appeared; it seemed fitting to her character. "Why would no-one shelter us?" Nia asked the question that had been swirling in her mind since that first day in his court.

Torrin sighed as his eyes drifted around the corridor. "Trust me, it was not that they wouldn't. Riona knew that half, if not all, the Fae world would sacrifice themselves for you both. It was her last act of protecting those who had protected her, to leave them a chance. They had just won an epic battle and were approaching Ciars gates with force. My mother revealed to me a secret I swore never to reveal, but I suppose it would be fair to tell you. Riona begun to have visions, my mother guessed they were triggered by your life growing within her. That night, while her army filled themselves with whiskey and wine, Riona had a terrible vision of what would happen should they storm Ciars castle. They would fail, our world would burn. It had shown her a way, though, to save us all. So, she ventured into the darkness of night, as the merriment in camp grew, and slipped through the wood into Ciars Castle. She knew of a secret chamber that led to the throne room, and that is where she lay her curse on Ciar and fled these lands."

Nia drew in a shallow breath. She had seen their bloody faces in her dreams, watched dozens of Fae cut down in their stride. To know that these were not just dreams, but what her mother had witnessed, it brought tears to her eyes. Torrin saw the pools forming, threatening to spill over her lashes, and he could not stop himself from pulling the young woman into his embrace. Nias breath became shallow and quick. "I have seen them." She sobbed into his chest. "Stood beside them on the battlefield, heard their screams, watched their blood salt the earth, knowing that it is real... That the man responsible is my father... I am so sorry." Nia choked on her breath, panic rising in her chest.

Torrin gently placed a hand on Nias chin and tilted her head until her watery eyes met his. "You have *nothing* to apologise for, neither does your mother. Ciar came to this land on a boat filled with exotic spices and jewels with tales of his royal family from an undiscovered land, he spent years courting your mother. He learned everything about her, she saw him as nothing but another suitor. For a princess has many, and so she assumed his eagerness just the same as every other Lord vying for her attention. It was Rionas father, King Ainmuire, who pushed the pair together. Ciar knew he would not win over the Princess alone, so he used her father, made him see an alliance between Ciars false kingdom and Etherea; and so, he aided Ciars pursuit of Riona. She really did not stand a chance." Nia felt slight relief, that her mother had not willingly given her land to that barbarian, yet she was filled with sorrow for Riona. He had tricked her, Riona had not just blindly fell for a handsome Prince. Nia felt shame as she realised, *she had*.

"Do you suppose Duane had similar intentions?" She asked, guilt filling her core. Nia had fallen for pretty gardens and glittering jewels- yet here she had been, judging her mother. Torrin sighed and nodded. "I still feel it, a pull, like a rubber band stretched wide, waiting to snap back into place. There is something scratching at my mind. I must see him again." Nia forgot that she had not mentioned this before. Torrin pulled back with surprise. "He could have put an enchantment on you. I shall ask Uaine what can be done." Nia was grateful for that. She did not like how her soul lunged for Duane each time she thought of him, how her clearing mind became murky as she tried to remember her moments with him. Nia had not noticed it before, she supposed that when her mother dampened her power, she had inadvertently made Nia more susceptible to manipulation.

"Am I interrupting?" Uaine asked with a raised brow at the sight before him, Torrin held the girl still as if she would disappear should he let go. "Ah, just the man I was looking for." Torrin turned with a grin, Uaine groaned, and Nia ignored her disappointment as Torrins warmth left her. She wished for nothing more than comfort in this unfamiliar world. "What do you want from me?" Nia laughed at the surly nature of his tone. "Come, let us eat before our hunger causes quarrels." The trio entered the dining room to finally break their fast. As Nia raised her spoon to her lips, a booming crash sounded from the other side of the Manor. She surprised them all by clattering her cutlery against the table and storming out of the dining room. She had quickly grown tired of the dramatics of this world and presumed it to be yet another creature out for her blood. That book had done something to her, opened a channel within her; it felt like a damn preparing to burst.

"So, help me God's, whatever you are you better run." She roared through the hallway, Uaine and Torrin shared an amused look. They knew that sound well, Rian had taken up potions. Well, he had tried to. Nia stopped dead in her tracks as a smouldering Rian turned the corner into her path. His face smeared with charcoal, his mousy hair singed and stuck up in all directions. Nias anger disappeared instantly at the frustrated look on Rians face. "What have you done?" She asked with exasperation as she wiped the ash from his cheeks. Rian grumbled his response, swatting her hands away. "I was trying to make a healing potion; it did not do what I intended." At that, Nia could not help the laughter that bubbled through her chest. None noticed the sheer rage behind Rian's eyes; along with his body, his magic had not grown as it should.

She swung an arm around his shoulders with a smile. "This is the way of the world Rian." She chuckled and returned to her meal with the sulking boy trailing by her side. Torrin eyed his brother with amusement. "Should we ever need to tear the Manor down, at least I shall save coin on the labour." He teased, Uaine held his cup in toast. "To Rian the demolisher." He winked, Rians eyes lit at that. Nia laughed at the young Fae and finally began to eat her food. She reflected as she watched her companions, how so much had changed in such a fleeting time. Her thoughts drifted to her village. She had been much like Rian in her childhood.

"If you cannot control that child Riona so help me, this is the third time this month." The old woman scolded; Nia glared up at her. She had hundreds of fabrics, why should she care if Nia took her scraps? "She is but a child Breda, perhaps she would do best as your apprentice, it would save you chasing her down every week." Her mother was good at that, getting her curious child out of trouble. Nias fingers gripped the soft ribbon she had stuffed in her pocket, determined to flee should Breda demand it returned. The woman huffed and grumbled to herself as she eyed the red-headed pair. "Fine, but only because you helped my grandson." Breda finally relented. The frost had almost killed the boy, sent fever through his blood, but Riona had been there to aid him. Her medicines were probably the only thing keeping the villagers

from throwing the troublesome child in the river. Riona had managed to spell the entire village through their food, no matter how many generations came and went none would be the wiser to it. Not even her own child.

The memory brought a small smile to her face, Nia had a knack for getting into things she was not supposed to, a new sense of admiration hit her for her mother's strength. How Riona had managed to keep Nias curiosity curbed, was a question for the ages. "So, pray tell, what is the agenda for today?" Uaine asked as he leaned back in his chair, his stomach fully sated. "You will search for a reversal of the spell Duane has cast on Nia and I will be bringing Nia to the fountain." Uaine rose his brows in shock at his friend. The spell did not surprise him, he had seen it wrapped around her mind when they first found her; Torrin's decision, however, chilled him to the bone. "Have you lost all sense?" He asked with so much fury it surprised Nia. He had grown fond of her and did not enjoy the thought of her in that woman's presence.

Nia waved her spoon at Uaine as she spoke. "You are welcome to join us if it worries you so." He shuddered at the memory of that smothering magic. "I will not go near that woman again, and you should leave her to rot where she stands." This surprised Nia, in her time at the Manor, he was the more level-headed of the bunch. It almost made her reconsider, but Nia knew she would not rest until she found answers. "I appreciate your worry Uaine, but I promise you, at the first sign of danger we will turn and leave." Nia knew herself well enough to know she might break that promise, she had made it to herself enough times. Gods knew she tried, but Nia could not help but jump headfirst into danger. Uaines shoulders relaxed an inch as he let loose a breath. "I hope you stand by that." Uaine gave her a warning look before excusing himself from the room.

"We should go to the training grounds, if we wish to make any progress before the days end." Torrin stood, his chair scraping against the wood floor. "Can I join you?" Rian asked, still covered in soot and embers. "Go clean yourself up first." Nia told him before joining Torrin in the doorway. Once again, the courtyard had been laden with practice dummies. "Do you use your magic to set this up?" Nia asked, since they had been together all morning and there were no staff at the Manor, it made the most sense. Torrin shook his head, "I came out this morning. Before, we could use our powers to do almost everything, but now we are limited." Nia could have cursed; her father had truly ruined this world. "We will begin training your magic soon, but first you should be able to hold your own travelling through Etherea."

He let her begin easy, her bow in hand, to build her confidence. Rian joined them soon, clean and smoke free. He had jested for her to go easy on him, yet Nia soon found he proved a lot stronger than he looked. As sweat dripped down her brow, Nia narrowly dodged Rians blade lunging towards her. "I think that's enough for today." Torrin announced, painfully aware of the descending sun. "I can keep going." Nia protested, her breath a gasp, Rian threw his sword on the table. "If you want to meet *her*, then we should take leave." Torrin sighed, Nia had almost forgotten. With renewed determination she abandoned her own sword, yet she could not leave her dagger behind. Something within her core told her she may need it that night. With trepidation and silence, Rian trailed behind the older two as they walked towards the fountain. *Why did I show them this rotten place?* He silently cursed himself. Rian did not understand why he also returned, why his dreams became filled with flashes of this chamber; it began weeks ago, before the Faelcu attacked. When he found his father's journal.

Nia felt it then, as they drew closer to the stone monument. A ghastly stench of decaying flesh permeated her nose. A gushing wave of power rolled over her body, licked at her bones, tempted her mind. Its sinister nature whispered to her, of all the darkness that could be hers. Nia swallowed the temptation that chased her and filled her mind with light and happiness as her mother advised, it gave Nia the strength to step forward, as the monument opened its jaws, and the full force of that stench assaulted her soul. Something screamed inside of her, *run*, it told her, *run or be ready to kill her*. Nia shook the voice from her head and continued down those dark steps, unaware that she had left Torrin and Rian behind.

The pair stared after Nia and found her eagerness to be a shock. A sickly feeling filled Torrin, *this has been a mistake*, he thought. Each step brought more dread to Rian as his brother chased Nia down the steps, he glanced wearily at the open door behind him. He followed the pair downwards. It was only as they reached the bottom did Rian realise, he no longer had the amulet which could control her.

Nia took the last step into the darkened room and ice filled her heart. As her eyes struggled to adjust, her thoughts flashed to her mother's tale; how she lit the passages beneath the Ruby Court. Nia took a chance and willed a light to illuminate the room. Regret filled her once it did. Staring back at Nia was a mirror image of herself, hunched and pale, a sinister grin on its sallow face. The rotting carcasses of small animals were scattered around the stone floor. *"You stupid child."* She bellowed with glee, a laughter so hollow and cruel it pained Nias ears.

Behind them, an even worse sound echoed through the chamber.

The stone door had *closed*.

Chapter Seven:

The woman laughed, low and sinister at the fear on their faces. A haze fell over Rian's eyes as he prayed that he had not led his friends to slaughter by showing them this dreadful place. "Your mother will be rolling in her grave at your stupidity." She spat with delight at Torrin. "Who are you?" Nia demanded as she stepped towards the woman. "And why should I answer you?" Nias temper rose to a boiling point. Their similarities were eerie. The Fae watched the pair before them. "I should think the fact that you are wearing my face is reason enough." Nia sneered. The hatred in the room had begun to seep into her skin. It made her skittish and aggressive. "My name, foolish girl, is Nessa and this face; sorry to disappoint, *is my own.*" Nessa bit back at the dim-witted princess standing before her.

"How?" Nia asked as she took another step, Nessas eyes gleamed. Torrin reached to pull Nia back, she shrugged his hand from her arm. "Our souls entered this world at the same time. Two born of the same power to balance the other; unless one shall become the other." Nia had quickly grown tired of her vagueness. "Do not speak to me in tongues, what have you done to earn this imprisonment?" She had to know, for if they merely locked the girl up for being powerful, Nia would feel required to free her; she did not think this would be the case. Nessa smirked, she could easily lie, yet knew she need not. "I grew tired of pretty girls with sharp tongues, so I boiled their blood until their beauty ceased to be." Nia felt sick. Nessa's cheerful tone as she recounted the memory only worsened her queasiness. "You foul creature, how could you do such a thing?" Nessa's eyes burned bright red with anger at Nia's disgust, the wards had been placed hundreds of years ago and their casters mostly dead- Nessa had tested their resolve daily.

Torrin jumped towards Nia, only to find himself barrelling backwards against the stone wall. Rian followed shortly, both found themselves bound and unable to move. They could only watch as both women glared at each other. Nessa had made a mistake, while Nia could not summon her magic at will, the sight of her friends bound swelled the rage in her core. Her own lilac orbs turned scarlet. The air became electric. "*They* are the foul creatures." Nessa snarled at the two High Fae. "A plague on this land with their high-society and glaring hypocrisy, their knees should bleed as they bow to their betters." Torrin and Rian found it harder to breathe as Nessa spoke. "They are weak, pathetic little creatures that cannot handle power greater than their own. They will throw you in with me the moment you show them what you can do."

Nia knew this to be false, it had been her first fear once she discovered the things she could do. They had committed the same heinous act when she boiled the blood of the

Abhartach- but Nia had not done so out of petty revenge. She had done it to save another's life. With this thought to steady her, Nia stepped forward once more. Nessa watched her counterpart curiously. "We are not the same." Nia growled as she reached within her cloak, her back straightened.

"You are a wicked, selfish thing. They have seen what I can do. I did not do it to sate some murderous lust, I acted to save the life of another. *We are not the same*."

The sureness of her words gave Torrin and Rian some hope that they could be saved. Nia had stepped closer with each word. "You only lie to yourself, I see the truth, you will burn this world to ashes by my side, and you will *relish* every moment of it." Her laughter broke what little resolve Nia had left and before Nessa could react, Nia had pulled her elven blade from her waistband and held it firmly against the decaying woman's chest.

The blood red jewel adorning the hilt grew so hot that Nia winced; but she did not miss the sheer terror that filled Nessa's eyes, as the silver steel almost pierced her skin. Torrin and Rian fell to the ground with a thud, their lungs greedily sucking in air. Neither one realised how grateful they were for breath until that moment. "Get that thing away from me!" Nessa screeched, Torrin and Rian covered their ears. Nia merely winced, Nessas fear was paltry compared to the tsunami that assaulted her mind, it blended with the screams she had been battling each day she spent in this realm. The blade burned hot at Nia's fingertips; she almost dropped it. Nia would rather scald her skin than release her grip on Nessa.

"*Open the door.*"

As Nessa cast a glare at her, Nia pressed the blade harder against that greying skin. They heard the scraping of stone as the entrance flew open. Nia came to a terrifying realisation.

If Nessa had the ability to open it, she had stayed for a reason.

Torrin yanked Nia from the wretched woman and dragged her out into the rising sun. The door behind them snapped shut once more as they fell to the ground, hot tears stung Nias eyes as she pulled herself to her feet. "I am not like her." She repeated to herself as she paced towards the manor, Torrin threw a worried look towards his brother and ran to follow the distraught girl. That stench of evil, that wicked voice in her mind that had told her not to go into that chamber. She had been willing to kill Nessa, within moments of speaking to her. It unnerved Nia, that willingness to kill - even if it meant protecting another. At what point would those lines blur? Would she eventually take the life of another for simply offending her? "Do not believe a word that woman says, I was a fool for bringing you to her." Torrin started as he caught up to Nia. She was awfully fast for someone so small, he noted.

"You were right to bring me, I would have gone by myself, and I would have drove my dagger into her chest without a second thought." Her words surprised him as he followed her to her chambers. Torrin felt it was not the right time to leave her to wrestle with her mind. Nia sighed and sat on her bed as she examined her scorched hand. Torrin rushed to her side, his own hand gripped hers with such gentleness that Nia almost smiled. Her skin was seared. "How did this happen?" Torrin questioned, worry shook his voice. "The dagger, it burned when it touched her skin. I did not want to let go; I could sacrifice a hand if it meant saving you and your brother." Torrin frowned at that as he began muttering the same healing spell that he had used on her that first night.

"Stop that." He said firmly, Nias teary eyes shot to his blue orbs with confusion and Torrin breathed a sigh of frustration. "Stop thinking that your life comes second to those around you, you do not have to kill yourself for the sake of another, the war will wage, and the world will turn without me or Uaine." Torrin couldn't bring himself to say his brother's name, "but without you, Nia, my world would end without you." Neither noticed the innuendo of what Torrin had said, *his* world, not *the* world. They were both too filled with worry for one another, to notice the care swirling in the other's eyes. "You are worth much more than you think, so please stop throwing yourself into danger as if you are not important." Torrin begged.

Nias tired heart swelled with gratitude, and she found her arms flying around Torrins neck. As he wrapped those strong arms around her waist, Nia sighed and squeezed him tightly. "I cannot promise I will not fall on my sword for any of you, but I will try not to put myself in another situation such as this." It was the best Nia could offer. She was too curious for her own good. Torrin had been given a glimpse of this curiosity and it had already frustrated him to no end. Nia stretched her tired limbs as she rose. "I am still no closer to finding my mother, or the full extent of what I am." She huffed as she ran a comb through her unruly hair. True, the book that had appeared in the library gave her much insight; but Nia had a feeling it also omitted many details. Torrin, with a heart filled with guilt, drew his hand across his face. "I used the dance to reconvene with some old allies of mine, they should send word soon of where Duane is keeping your mother and what is going on in his court. I am sorry I could not do more." Nia shook her head and took Torrins face in her hands, his stormy blue eyes met hers as she spoke. "You have done more than enough for me, thank you for everything." With that she lay a soft kiss against his forehead.

Torrin felt the world disappear for a moment in her soft embrace, his eyes fluttered closed with peace. When they opened once more, Nia was retreating towards the washroom. He could not see the scarlet shade her cheeks had burned. It was only once Nia sank into a steaming bath; did she notice her hand had healed. As the warmth of the water soothed her skin and the scents of raspberries and rose washed away the stench stuck to her nose, Nia found her eyes heavy with sleep.

She dragged herself from the water before she could drown herself and wrapped her body in the softest peach nightwear. Her feet dragged along the ground until she reached her bed, Nia had nothing left within her. As she prayed that Torrins allies would report to them soon, so she may finally set out to find her mother; all energy she once had disappeared like a puff of smoke in a storm. The moment her body hit the smooth silk, exhaustion sent her tumbling into a fitful sleep. Her dreams ready to plague her once more.

Ash choked the air, embers flying across the ground, flames licked at her skin. It was stifling, Nia could only stare as always. Her feet rooted to the scorched ground as beasts flew, plumes of smoke and fire billowed before her. Tears stung her eyes as vast stretches of forest suddenly turned to dust, at either side Fae collided. The gnashing of teeth and the snarling of beasts churned her stomach as she watched. Men, women, it did not matter, Ciars forces cut them each down in their stride. As blood soaked the ground, Nia felt the hope seep away from the earth. Her limbs moved of their own accord, feet burning as she tore through the army before her. Rage unlike no other had cast a red mist through her vision. When her eyes cleared and the smoke thinned, Nia saw not herself, but her mother stood amidst a sea of bodies. Drenched in blood and soot her chest heaved before an agonising scream left her lips.

Nia shot from her bed with sweat cascading down her back. Relief filled her that it had been another memory and not a vision, Nia could not stomach the thought of her own companions cut down on a battlefield. She drew a cold and clammy hand across her brow as she rose from the bed, she had to save her mother. Nia could not bear thought of her suffering, not after all she had been through. As she bathed and thought, Nia contemplated her options. She knew she had spent too long in Torrins Manor, yet she had promised to free his sister and she could not just disappear in the night. Her stomach lurched and Nia found the contents of her supper splattered across the marble floor. With a groan she pulled herself from the molten bath, shivering violently, and began to clean as her mind wandered.

Too many things needed to be addressed, the curse Duane had set on her mind, the raging power bubbling beneath her skin, the mysterious man who could give them answers. Nia did not necessarily trust that he *would* have answers, for it had been Nessa who provided the information and Nia knew she did not trust the woman as far as she could spit. Most important, she still needed to find and free her mother, but how? *My mother knew storming those gates would end the Fae, but it is not as if I can just knock on the front door.*

"Take me with you to Galeria." Uaine stared across the short table as if Nia had grown three heads. He had been unable to find a cure for the curse Duane had set upon her, much to

Nia's disappointment. She refused to sit around any longer. It was futile to spend her time in the Sapphire Court, if she wanted her mother back; she needed allies and information. "Absolutely not." Torrin snapped, Rian begrudgingly sat quietly to his side. The younger Fae threw Nia a sympathetic look as she opened her mouth to argue. There was no stopping either once they had decided something. "Have we not determined that I can protect myself?" Torrin glared in response, his jaw taught at the idea of her trudging through the swamps of Galeria. "You cannot control it, who is to say blindly throwing yourself at an enemy will work every time?"

Torrin knew it was harsh, and unfair. As a mere mortal Nia had torn through a pack of Faelcu and lived to tell the tale. Even before they had been turned into the mindless, cruel servants Duane had made them, the Faoladh had been some of this land's fiercest warriors. With access to her powers, she had already won against a creature so terrifying even the eldest Fae did not wish to cross its path, she was far stronger than he gave her credit for. The flames that danced in her eyes gave Torrin the feeling she had been thinking the same thing.

Cannot control it? Blindly throwing myself at an enemy? I'll show him.

Her temper soared; Nia hardly knew where the anger had come from. Perhaps it had all finally caught up with her. Nia stood, it had been so easy to summon light into the chamber beneath the grounds it gave her pause and she thought for a moment. Torrin felt unease as a smirk grew on Nias face, white rope wrapped around his middle in a flash. A blanket of magic wrapped around him. "Nia what are you doing?" Uaine asked as he stood, torn between the decision to speak to her or lunge for her.

Nia's eyes widened as she heard Uaines internal struggle like a whisper at her ear. "You lunge for me, and you will find yourself in a similar predicament." Uaine could only pause in his advance, shocked that she had heard the words he had not spoken. They were gurgled and unclear, but there all the same. "You have proved your point." Rian said curtly. Three sets of bewildered eyes turned to the young Fae. "Torrin, lest you have forgotten you threw the same spell at her when Duane visited, she cast a light beneath ground protected by sacred wards, she is advancing quickly. Bring her to Galeria and train her on your way." Nia released Torrin with a shaky breath, not quite sure where that act had sprung from. Duane's gold eyes, his breath-taking smile; they filled her mind. Nia clawed her way back to reality, shook his charming face from her thoughts and let out a heavy sigh as she turned to her companions.

"I'm sorry, I am just so very tired of people treating me as if I might break. I was injured when you brought me here, but even before all of this," Nia gestured to herself with frustration, "I was strong, my mother raised me to hunt, to barter, to fend for myself. I am not some mortal village floozy, my days were spent setting traps and skinning my dinner before I ate, marriage and grand celebrations were never in my cards. So please, if I am to do what I must, then you must understand that. If you cannot... Well, I am afraid we must part ways."

A lump had formed in Torrins throat at that, while Uaine still looked at the girl with trepidation. Something had changed in her, he could not place it. "You need never prove anything to us, I... I am sorry for any offense I have caused." Torrin meant it, she had been through a great ordeal and proven the better for it and he had treated her like a child. Uaine and Rians faces filled with shock, neither believing their ears. They cast a look to each other as if to say, '*is this real?*' Torrin seldom apologised, even when he was wrong. Nia shook her head with guilt and regret swirling in her chest. "No, I am sorry, I do not know what came over me." She raised a clammy hand to her forehead once again before stumbling towards her chair. Black spots danced before her eyes and suddenly, the world went dark. Uaine barely caught Nia as she fell like a dead weight to the floor. She convulsed violently; her eyes sprung open. Torrin, Rian and Uaine watched in shock as white orbs glared at them.

Nia watched as wind whipped through a silver ballroom, the doors swung from their hinges, the crystals of a chandelier shattered across the room. She saw Torrin in a set of glorious Sapphire armour, claws of silver piercing through his knuckles as he slashed against the wall, his screams turned her blood cold as a woman with straw coloured hair attempted to comfort him. "Where are they?" He roared to an injured Uaine; the blonde's green eyes lit with pain. "I don't know!"

Uaine screamed back, sobs bubbling up his throat. A woman stood at his side, with auburn hair and golden irises.

Nia and Rian were gone.

She woke with a start, sapphire and emerald eyes stared intently down at her. A frost bit at her bones, Nia lurched and ran on shaking legs until she reached the courtyard. Her stomach emptied once again, ruining a line of wilted shrubbery, *what was that?* It shook her to the core, the pain on their faces, the crumbling room around them, *the claws.* Nia wretched again.

Uaine found her first, his magic allowed him to see the burning aura around the girl, such sorrow and fear surrounded her that it made his heart constrict. Torrin had not shared with him the secret of Rionas visions, but Uaine had seen that aura thrice before. The first as a young boy, when the inklings of war began to appear, his father had desperately implored a local seer for strategy against Ciar's lieutenants. The second as a man, when he himself sought a seer out for guidance after his lands had been stripped from him and finally, around that gods-forsaken woman beneath their feet. That final thought unnerved him, but Uaine forced himself to focus on the girl before him as she heaved once more.

Uaine took a tentative step towards her, afraid she might startle, as if he were approaching a wild animal. It was a fair comparison. He lay a comforting hand on her back as she lay her head against the stone pillar to their left. "What happened?" He asked, although he already knew. "I think," her voice shook, "I think it was a vision." She did not want to say it aloud, to make it real, but Nia knew she could not hide it; not as Uaines green eyes watched her. Slowly, with wavering breaths, Nia recounted what she had seen. Torrins heart clenched as he stood in the shadows.

She knew his secret, and it terrified him.

Uaine embraced her once Nia ceased her heaving. The warm act soothed her quivering limbs. Uaine's heart stung as his mind flashed, to someone he had not thought of in a very long time; the sister he had lost so long ago. With a sigh Uaine combed his fingers through her hair, comforting her as a sibling would. "Torrin comes from a hidden line of Faoladh, his father was an advisor to king Ainmuire, and his father before him. They have been bound by secrecy, so that they may be the final line of defence should their king be attacked. Advisors were thought to be scholars and the Royal family kept it that way. When Ciar brought Duane to his side, keeping Torrins family secret became paramount. Even Tara..." Uaine paused for a moment, Nia pulled back as she felt the sorrow and longing seep from his essence. It stung her soul. She would never get used to this, the emotions of others pouring into her veins; twisting her heart. "Before she was sent away, Torrins father bound her abilities so that she may never reveal what they were." Nia felt even more sympathy for the girl, gifted like an animal to another, unable to be her true self. It strengthened her resolve to save Tara, although they had never met; Nia felt a familiarity for her situation. Torrin felt his gut twist as Uaine spoke, the memory of his sisters' pleas to their father. Her screams as Torrin pounded against the doors, it was *horrific.* Nia gasped as she came to a sudden realisation.

"Do you mean, the Faelcu, they were as Torrin is?"

Her words were feverish, her hands shook. She gripped Uaines shoulders. He felt her fingers dig into his skin and winced; Nia loosened her grip with a flinch. "Yes." Uaine replied, as he rubbed the flesh her hands had almost bruised; it was easy to forget how strong she had become. Nia held her face in her hands as tears poured from her eyes, she thought of those beasts she had killed, as Torrins face flashed in her mind. Their eyes became his, Nia saw the beast who had fallen with her dagger between its brow and saw it twist and transform until Torrin lay dead at her feet. Nia blinked furiously, Torrin had stepped from his hiding place. His face awash with panic and pity "Nia?" He started cautiously as he walked towards them, not entirely sure what had caused her to fret. "I killed them, I may as well have killed you, they were people." She spluttered

"I didn't know they were people."

Torrin was surprised. He had expected her to be terrified of him, furious even at his deceit; not riddled with guilt at defending herself. He rushed to comfort her. "No, Nia, it has been centuries, the Faelcu are no longer the men they once were. If anything, you freed them when you killed them, loosed them from their beastly prisons and released them from Duanes sinister grip. They cannot be brought back; he has poisoned the very essence of their souls." It was true. Whatever morality they held once, had been long snuffed out by Duane. It gave Nia little comfort, for she had fallen for that monster; she felt her body give out once more. Torrin caught the exhausted girl and locked eyes with his worried friend. "We must help her." Uaine sighed, and so it was decided.

They would venture to the swamps of Galeria.

Chapter Eight:

Perhaps this has been a terrible idea, Nia thought; as they trudged through slop and sludge, covered in dirt; bruised and battered. It had not begun that way, no, their journey began in the scorched lands of the Sapphire Court. Nia longed for the burning heat of the sun once more, all she had known for days now was a murky mist. One would not think a place such as this existed in a land so mystical, yet the stench of despair stung their senses.

Torrin eyed his companions wearily, he did not wish to set forth on this journey, but they had been left with no choice. With scarcely anyone left above the earth he would trust enough to ask for help; their best chance was to find the seer in Galeria and gather information on Nia so that they might stand a chance against Ciar. He took some comfort in the unwillingness of Nessa to share the location of Abbán, Torrin hoped this meant he would help them.

Nia climbed over a dusty hill, keenly aware of Torrins blue eyes watching her like a hawk. She wiped her brow of sweat and glanced towards the horizon, burnt trees, and glaring sun stretched as far as her eyes could see. It pained her to know this was once lush forests and bustling towns, homes once stood where they walked, turned to ash, and blown away with a strong wind. It was devastating. She pushed the thought from her mind, felt her magic reach out once more towards the light. She embraced the warmth of the sun on her face, let it fill her bones with heat.

Uaine walked ahead cautiously, his eyes ever watching their surroundings. Rian trailed by his side, Torrin trusted none to keep his brother safe but himself and so, he was forced to be brought along. Uaine had argued with Torrin, of course. The arguments of the two Fae Lords had woken Nia from her slumber, she had chosen to ignore them as they would bicker with or without her. Torrin had won, clearly, much to Uaine's disappointment.

Rian was not disappointed at this, however. Always ready to get into trouble, he had danced inside as Torrin told him to pack his things. His eyes, like Uaines, scanned the horizon; but Rian, unlike Uaine, had a different objective. He jumped with delight as his eyes found their target. Nia had forgotten, they had taken this same path to Avenere and there -where that lone flower had broken through the earth- a bushel of flowers had sprouted from the dust.

Torrin and Uaine stopped dead in their tracks.

Too shocked, too delighted to speak they simply looked from the unexpected life growing from the earth to Nia and finally, to each other. The sheer joy which rippled from their auras almost knocked Nia over, it filled her with such lightness she felt almost drunk. *Is it possible to get drunk on the happiness of others?* Nia wondered. She supposed it would make sense, if she could feel their emotions as if they were her own. Uaines eyes were firmly locked on the cluster of flowers, while Torrins darted to the glowing girl at their side. The light that framed her contained a hundred colours, yet it was translucent all the same. Her eyes, like the lavender that once grew in their gardens, were hazed as she grinned at the horizon. "Are you alright?" He asked, his joy only outweighed by the care that had grown in his heart with every moment she spent in his company.

Nia beamed brightly at him, quite literally. White light surrounded her, one did not need the gift of half-sight to see it seeping from her body. Joy bounced between the pair as Nia's power unwittingly flowed outward, piercing Torrin's heart with a weightlessness he had never felt. "You need to calm down." Torrin guffawed, nothing was particularly funny-yet he laughed all the same.

Uaine looked at the pair, too enthralled in their own joy to notice those they had travelled with. His eyes widened with surprise as wisps of sapphire and scarlet danced between them, it was like their magic reached out to one another. Uaine did not wish to see what would happen should they collide, not as the light grew brighter with each second; he pulled the two apart. Torrin took a deep breath to steady himself, Nia supposed it would take something stronger than calming breaths to settle the glowing aura around her. So, she did what she could and pulled the hood of her cloak over her head. It worked a small amount; if nothing else it curbed the magic seeping from her.

Nia realised just how dangerous her power could be, she could bring joy to illuminate this world, or she could smother it in darkness. The thought unnerved her, she understood she had a choice, yet she feared the journey might cloud her morals. Even so, they pressed on, a renewed sense of determination alight in their hearts. Uaine understood more than the others, his ability to sense magic around him allowed Uaine to see the sheer power still rolling from Nia, it was like a wave of iridescent light. Uaine hoped that Abbán would have the answers they had set forth to find.

Before long, they reached Avenere. "We should stop here for the night." Uaine told the group as they entered the abandoned town, he knew it would pain Torrin to stay there but they would be fools to venture further as darkness fell. It would do them no good to be attacked while weary from their travels. Nia stretched her limbs and agreed. Rian and Torrin looked around the town with sadness in their eyes. Torrin felt the weight of Ciars destruction heavily, for although he could not have done much to aid their cause he still felt that he should have done more; but what good could a child have done against a King?

Nia lay a comforting hand on his shoulder, the light finally dimmed around her. "We will rebuild Torrin, I swear it, this town will be alive once again." Her words rang with such honesty that Torrin found himself hoping that somehow, she was right. "Why don't we begin practicing her magic now?" Rian suggested, it was about time they helped her use her power rather than continue to be blindsided by it.

Uaine nodded in agreement. "Come, Nia, Torrin may be more adept at physical activities," Nia did not miss the innuendo or the playful glare Uaine cast to his friend, "but I am far more skilled with magic." Torrin opened his mouth to protest, until Uaine had lifted him five feet off the ground and turned him upside down. Nia could not help but laugh at Torrins surprise. "Put me down you fool." Torrin groaned. Then, as if realising his mistake, he rushed to add, "*don't drop me on my-*" it was too late, Uaine *had* dropped his friend on his ass. Rian and Nia howled with laughter as Torrin grumbled, dusting himself off as he rose. He shot a glare at the trio; it only caused their laughter to grow.

"Focus Elvinia." Uaine said for the fourth time as she stared at the ivy covering the sapphire building before them. They had left Torrin to set up camp. Nia glared back at the blonde Fae. "Stop calling me Elvinia." She snapped back, it was difficult to focus. Her mind raced at every moment. "Why do you hate your name so much?" Uaine questioned, allowing her a reprieve for a moment. Nia groaned and kicked a rock by her foot. "Mortal children are cruel beings." She did not wish to explain, he did not wish to pry. The look in her eyes as she cast them downwards told him enough. Bredas grandson had proved less than grateful for her mother's help. She still bore the scar of the day he had thrown her into the creek.

Nia returned to the task at hand, she had little interest of speaking of her past and glared at the ivy ascending the building before them. She thought of how she had summoned the light within the chamber beneath the manor and used that thought to comfort her. *I can do this,* Nia reached out to the ivy and closed her eyes, watched it retreat in her mind, until the walls became clear of debris. She repeated this, several times until a soft gasp escaped Uaine's lips.

Nia finally opened her eyes and took in the sight before her, she had not just cleared the building, she had cleared the entire quarter in which they stood. "I can tell you I am very glad you did not meet Ciar first." Uaine admitted as he looked around in admiration. Nia nodded in agreement. "We should head back to the others." She said as she felt her fingers shake. "Are you alright?" Uaine asked, noticing the change in her demeanour. "Yes, thank you, sometimes it takes a lot more energy from me than I realise." Nia admitted.

Torrin stepped through the trees, his eyes alight with worry as he looked at the staggering girl; without hesitation, he scooped her into his arms. Nia sighed gratefully, as she lay her head against his chest. Too tired to protest as he carried her back to their camp. Uaine and Rian said nothing as he lay her beside the campfire; only shared a knowing look. Nia wished the memories of her mother's teachings were not so fragmented; if only so she could use her magic without exhausting herself.

They returned to their makeshift camp within a building still overgrown, they did not want to be found in the darkness by any of the creatures that roamed these lands. That first night was filled with laughter and joy before they retired to their makeshift beds. Uaine took the first watch, as his friends lay their heads to rest. Neither knew, as they slept, what would come in the days ahead. Each prayed silently, for the strength to withstand whatever may come.

Chapter Nine:

Nia awoke in the darkness, her eyes struggled to adjust, for a moment she forgot where she was. Panic trickled through her, until her eyes fell upon a sleeping Rian by her side. A breath of relief fell from her lips as she scanned the crumbling room, Uaine lay across the floor; Torrin was not there. The beating of birdwings and the scratching of insects in the dirt plagued her senses; she knew sleeping was a fool's errand. Nia rose softly, careful not to wake the sleeping Fae and ventured out into the night. She wrapped her cloak around her tightly as she stepped out of the building.

The cold nipped at her skin; the fabric offered little reprieve. She could see Torrin, he had not ventured far, seated on a stone bench. Nia took a moment to look at him, there was something hidden; deep within his soul, she could not reach far enough to uncover it. Nia felt a familiarity in his internal struggle, there were two parts of him battling each other for control.

He glanced up as she approached and smiled, Nia cursed the blush that crept up her cheeks. Oh, how he looked at her, like she held the stars within her eyes. "Can't sleep?" He asked and gestured to the empty spot beside him. Nia sat at his side and nodded her head. "I can hear... *Everything.*" She sighed. "The world is like an old house, cracking and creaking at every moment." It was the best comparison her tired mind could manage. "It must be exhausting." Torrin could only understand from the fraction he had experienced when that darkness had shot from her. He would not wish it on his worst enemy, yet she coped with it exceptionally well. The screams he heard had been harrowing, he could not imagine hearing them daily. "The longer I spend here, the more my mother's spell wears away, I have remembered pieces of her teachings and they have helped me to keep the darkness at bay," Nia paused, pursing her lips before deciding to continue, "but I fear if I remain ignorant to either one, then whichever I push away will be unmanageable." She remembered a line from her mother's tale which sent shivers down her spine.

'Drunk with power, Riona abandoned her friends.'

Torrin looked at Nia in the moonlight, admiration filled his eyes, it knocked the wind from her lungs. "Your mother would be proud." A sob rose from Nia's chest. It was a thought she could not bear, what *would* her mother think of her? For all Riona had done, with her armies and her power against Ciar, Nia felt as if she had achieved nothing in comparison. Torrin embraced her, his warmth offering comfort in the darkness. "I am not so sure." Nia admitted as another sob bubbled up her throat "I have done nothing to help her."

Torrin shook his head and held her tighter "Nia, I have known you a short time and you have proved to be nothing if not selfless. You wrapped yourself around a stranger's child and let a beast tear you to shreds to protect him. With no knowledge of your power, of your heritage, you would rather die to protect a stranger. I have no doubt that your mother will be brimming with pride at the young woman she has raised, and we *will* find her." Nia pulled back as her breath steadied, his blue eyes bore into hers. The urge to close the distance overwhelmed him, yet he resisted. Torrin almost groaned as her eyes flickered to his lips, her beauty radiating in the moonlight, it would be so easy to just press his lips to hers. Torrin loosed a breath and pulled away. They sat in comfortable silence; Nia rested her head upon his shoulder. Guilt wiggled its way into her heart as Duane flashed in her mind, her lids fell heavy at the thought of what should have been between them. An elegant castle by the sea, fields of flowers at her feet. Nia knew she should not, but she longed for it still.

Uaine found the pair, Nia bundled under Torrins arm, when he woke some hours later to take over the watch. Torrin rolled his eyes at his friends unsurprised expression. "Do not start Uaine." He whispered, for fear of waking Nia from her peaceful slumber. Uaine raised his hands in surrender. "I said nothing." "Your face said enough." Uaine laughed at that. Torrin looked once more at the sleeping girl curled beneath his arm. "She *is* breathtaking." Torrin admitted. "In all the years I have known you Torrin, I have never seen you look at a woman as you look at her." Uaine admitted as he leaned against a towering tree. "I have never met a woman such as her." Torrin breathed, it unnerved him- the care he felt for her.

Nia found her dreams interrupted by a scream, warning of what was to come. The sleeping Elf woke with a start, a stench in her nose, her eyes filled with confusion. That scream rang in her ears once more and her mind cleared. "We must leave, *now.*" She jumped from the bench, ignoring Uaine and Torrin's shocked faces. Nia pulled Rian from the building, they fell to the earth as a snarling bear barrelled through the adjacent wall. Its claws slammed against the ground where Rian's head had rested seconds before.

Uaine flung a bolt of lightning towards the animal, striking it down in its path. Rian looked around with laboured breath, his eyes still filled with sleep. "What-" "There is no time Rian, get up, we must go." Nia scrambled to gather her weapons. Uaine and Torrin followed suit. When Rian did not rise Nia scooped him into her arms and took off north, in the opposite direction of the horrible stench permeating her senses.

Uaine and Torrin did not dare question her as they followed. Soon they had their answer, an agonising shriek pierced the silence of the woodlands they had entered, followed by a horrendous growl and the rumbling of paws pounding the earth. Their pace quickened.

Nia did not fully understand *who or what* had warned her that they were coming, but she had heard it in her slumber as clear as though her eyes were open. A wrongness had been creeping towards them and that voice had rung shrill like an alarm. As the Faelcu chased them, Nia begged her power to guide her. By some grace, *it answered*.

A path of light opened before her as she darted left, praying the others would follow; they did, but Torrin and Uaine cast a look between them as they ran. Uaine watched the light cascade before them, like a guide from the Fates. She had turned towards Rulaine, a sector of the Silver Court, and neither wanted to set foot in *that* High Lord's territory.

Nia sensed their hesitation and ignored it, as she ignored the burning of her lungs and limbs. Rian clung to her as she ran, no longer confused, now deathly afraid of falling as Nia ran at a pace he could not describe. Nia saw their salvation ahead and allowed instinct to take over. She crashed through the invisible barrier before the riverbank, her eyes allowed her to see the silver wall of light that separated the Courts.

With Rian safely- albeit a bit aggressively- thrown across the water, Nia skidded to a halt and turned to the treeline. It marked a barrier between lands, Nia could see where the curse began to seep through the decaying trees leading towards the Sapphire Court. The sight fuelled her anger.

Torrin and Uaine slid to a stop at her side as she faced the border. The sounds of the Faelcu grew closer. Torrin grabbed

Nias arm, her neck almost snapped as she turned her head to glare at him. Her eyes glowed blood red once more, Torrin released her arm, and she glared back to the forest. Uaine choked on the power rolling from her. Nia raised her palms. She stepped past the barrier. Uaine opened his mouth to protest, for his eyes also allowed him to see the divide between lands. She allowed instinct to guide her.

As the snarling shapeshifters stepped from the forest- ten in total- Nia clasped her hands together with a clatter. A gust of wind barrelled towards the beasts; it knocked each back with such a force their whimpers carried through the wind. Nia drew from the raging river at her back and a furious wave rolled over their injured forms, it washed them back towards Avenere. Only once the howls stopped, did Nia let herself relax.

She turned with a start then, to look at the child she had thrown. "Oh, Rian, I'm so sorry!" She shouted sheepishly to the young Fae covered in mud across the river, as he brushed himself off; mumbling a sarcastic, "it's fine." "We should not stay here." Uaine told them, for he knew that as soon as they had stepped foot over the barrier, warning bells had rung in the minds of the Silver Princes. Nia hoped that if any were to find them, that it be Lorcan. Him she could handle. They trudged across the river- Nia was grateful it only reached their waists- to join Rian and set off again; slightly off course now. Neither Torrin nor Uaine wished to venture any further into the Silver Court, yet both knew they were safer within its borders.

Nia shot another apologetic glance at Rian as they walked, she had essentially manhandled him. Rian supposed he could not be *too* mad at her. After all, he would have been minced by the bear that burst through the wall of their camp; if she had not acted so quickly. He glowered at his inability to help, he had only embers of the magic he should possess, and he knew in his heart he should have grown by now.

They had not discussed it, but Rian's stunted growth had become suspicious in recent years, most Fae his age already looked like men. Torrin reasoned as Rian did; that Ciars curse which limited their powers had trapped Rian into a painfully slow growth cycle.

Too soon, the sun began to dim while they walked. Nia cursed as its light receded. They had lost most of their supplies as they fled the Faelcu. The older Fae shared the same thought. As they continued through the wet grass, the sound of the rushing river breaking through their silence, Uaine stopped as a light came into view. The sound of hooves in the distance sent the four of them scrambling to hide. "Nia?" A soft voice called out in the darkness and Nia could have dropped with relief as she scrambled from Torrins grip. He had pulled her along with him, to a nook beneath the riverbank. Droplets of water fell from her cloak, and she resisted the temptation to glare at Torrin as she grinned up at the blonde woman in the carriage. "Erin!" Nia replied, the others cautiously joined her side. "What are you doing out here? Are you mad?" Erin questioned as her eyes scanned the forest behind them. "Quickly, get in."They did not need to be told twice, and as the four climbed gratefully into Erin's carriage, the blonde said a silent prayer that none had seen her aid their enemies.

Chapter Ten:

Silence filled the carriage as they journeyed forward. Torrin did not miss Erins brown eyes darting from her companions to the translucent glass at her side. "We do not wish to cause you trouble, your kindness thus far has been more than enough." Torrin told her truthfully. The journey was theirs to bear and he would not want to burden another with their troubles. Erin shook her head as they drew nearer to her home. It was not grand, like Torrin or Duanes Manors, yet Nia felt at ease when the carriage pulled to a stop outside Erin's homestead.

It was made of wood and stone and grew from within the earth around it. "You have a lovely home." Erin cast a grateful- albeit uneasy- smile at Uaine. "It is not much, but it is mine." Nia could relate to that as she remembered the thatched roof and stone walls of her own home. It felt so far away now, she longed for supper at that table with her mother. "It is wonderful." Nia told her, truth rang in each word. At this, Erins shoulders eased; her smile was grateful as she led them to the door. They stepped into the doorway and a refreshing warmth filled Nias bones. The coldness of the night had caused a chill to creep within her.

Erin guided them into her home, it opened out into a vast space and Nia noticed lights illuminating entrances to various tunnels. Uaine and Torrin shared a knowing look at the awe and wonder that glistened within Nia's eyes. Most Fae homes outside of the cities were built within their surroundings. Before their powers had been drained, many Fae had fashioned grand homes within giant Toadstools and Broad cap mushrooms. Winged Fae would carve their homes in the side of the tallest mountains, some preferred the trees. He vowed to show her one day, those grandeurs that had been forgotten, Torrin imagined the delight on her face, and it filled him with warmth. Rian tiredly followed the group, the cold still nipped at his bones, and he felt himself less inclined to care about his surroundings as he stepped in line with the others. He had been almost killed, handled roughly, and thrown into a river. Rian was most definitely in a foul humour as his feet squelched alongside him, none had thought to dry the scowling Fae. Rian did not dare attempt it, for his magic was so unpredictable he feared he might accidentally set himself alight.

Nia noticed, as they walked, portraits adorning each side of their path. She scarcely had a moment to look at each, as her companions kept a quick pace towards a hot meal. A striking painting of Erin and a broad man with chestnut hair caught her eye. By the loving looks they shared within the canvas, Nia assumed it was Erins husband. The sight of a table laden with a feast made their stomachs growl. Erins shoulders released their tension, and she laughed while gesturing to the table laden with an assortment of breads, meats, cheeses, and fruits before them. "Help yourselves." Rian needed no further prompt.

The young Fae lunged towards the bounty in his sight. Torrin gripped the collar of the hasty child's' shirt and gave him a stern look. "Where are your manners?" He asked, his jaw taught. Nia felt her hands slide across his shoulders of their own accord. "Let the boy eat." She said gently, and Torrin felt his grip loosen on Rians collar; yet Rian knew his brother was right. So, he turned to Erin and bowed with as much grace as he could; still covered in mud. "Thank you." Erin shook her head with a laugh. "Eat, before you fall over, and I shall have hot baths drawn for each of you." Erin left them as they sat at the table. Rian almost cried at the thought of being clean again.

They were famished, neither had realised how much so; not until that first bite of food crossed their lips. It did not take long for each to fill their bellies. Sated and safe, they rested in their chairs as Erin returned to the room. She laughed at the sight of them, but Torrin noticed that her smile did not reach her eyes. Erin guided each to their own personal washroom. Nia marvelled at the size of the building, it seemed to go on for days. "What has brought you across the border?" Erin asked as they walked. Nia had expected to be questioned eventually. Her shoulders slumped as she wrestled with her answer. Nia decided Erin had done nothing to prove she could not be trusted but knew better than to reveal too much. "We are traveling to meet a man who might know more about my history." A half-truth, it was the best she could muster.

Erin's face filled with sympathy. "It is awful what has happened to your family." The blonde said as she rested a hand on Nia's shoulder. Nia had not thought of Ciar as her *family*. For it had always just been Nia and her mother. Sure, she had been curious as a child, but Nia had never felt like she was missing anything. It was still strange to think her father was out there at all, never mind what he was. "I shall leave you to get some rest. Goodnight Elvinia." With that, Erin took her leave. Nia entered the grand washroom, a steaming tub stood proud in the middle of the room. Nia almost wept at the sight.

She sunk, gratefully, into the hot water once Erin had left. Nia let it soak her aching limbs as her mind raced in the silence. The Faelcu had been so close to catching them, she had scarcely had a moment to think. Nia scrubbed at her flesh as she willed Rians frightened eyes out of her mind. When a strong knock sounded against the door, Nia realised she had almost scrubbed her legs raw. "Just a minute!" She called out, fresh nightwear and a silver silk robe lay folded neatly atop the sink. Nia had not noticed anyone bring them in. *Perhaps*, she thought, *the Fae here have more power because of the loyalty their Lords have shown Ciar*. The thought sickened her. Nia could not hold it against Erin, as she donned the fresh clothes.

Nia found Torrin, leaned against the doorframe, in all his magnificence. His intense blue eyes raked over her; the silk nightgown peeked from the slit of her robe. Torrin sucked in a breath as he forgot his words. "Yes?" Nia questioned, her eyes sparkling up at the Fae Lord. Torrin shook the wicked thoughts from his mind as her tongue traced across her lips. "If you don't mind, I have asked Erin that we share quarters. Uaine and Rian shall room together, as shall we." Nias pulse quickened at that. Goosebumps raked across her flesh. "If, that is, it's alright with you?" Torrin asked, suddenly nervous. Nias voice betrayed her as she whispered, "that's alright with me." She had meant it to sound nonchalant. Instead, her heady tone sent Torrins mind into a whirlwind. She cursed herself as she followed Torrin through the hallway to their room for the night. Her mind flickered back to the dance, to his lips at her ear and his hands at her waist. Nia willed her mind to calm itself as they stepped into the room. While Nia glanced around and absorbed her cosy surroundings, Torrins eyes lay squarely on the singular bed in the middle of the room. It took Nia a moment more to come to the same realisation.

"I can ask Erin if there is another bed, or I can sleep on the floor." Torrin offered, ever the gentleman. Nia shook her head. "Erin has done enough for us, we should let her rest. This bed is big enough for us both, I will not have you sleeping on the floor." Torrin decided not to argue with her, giving in to that selfish part of him which wanted to lay in the same bed as her once again. Nia was highly aware this time would be much different than before; she had been terrified of the Púca and what may come for her within the night. This time, despite her worry about the Faelcu, Nia knew she could defend them should anything attack while they slept, and it gave her comfort to know Torrin would be at her side.

The crackling fire in the corner of the room flickered soft light across Nias skin as she slipped the robe from her shoulders. She did not miss the subtle glances Torrin chanced as she stepped towards the four-poster bed. Torrin could barely hide his disappointment as she slid beneath the covers, until he realised, she too was sneaking glances. Nia could not be blamed, for although she had never been bothered with the boys from her village; she did not claim to be blind. Her mind scrambled as Lorcan's face flashed before her, followed by Duanes. *What has become of me?*

Nia felt her heartbeat race as he shrugged off his coat and kicked off his shoes, each landing with a soft thud. His fingers gripped the edges of his shirt and Nias breath hitched as he pulled the fabric away; his muscles flexed as he moved. Her mind clouded. Torrin had heard her gasp, had clung to every ounce of self-control he had as he removed his belt. Nias thoughts turned wicked, it surprised her. She almost checked herself for a fever. *Surely, I am ill to be thinking like this*, she thought with a frown. Torrin's lips tugged upwards at the disappointment on her 'sleeping' face when he climbed into the bed next to her. Nia could not lie to herself; she would have enjoyed seeing the rest of his clothing fall to the floor. Guilt wracked her as the chains of Duane's enchantments tightened around her heart for her betrayal of the Golden

Prince. Too tired to curb her thoughts, she drifted into a frustrated slumber.

At some point throughout the night, the sleeping pair became entangled. This proved to be a problem as Erin attempted to shake them awake. Torrin woke before Nia, saw the girl wrapped in his arms first; then he noticed the fretful look that blanketed Erins face. "You must leave, I have prepared supplies and horses for you. It is the best I can do." Her eyes darted to the door. "My husband... he would not be so sympathetic to your... *situation*." She cast a worried look at the waking girl. Erin rushed them to the road; where Uaine and Rian awaited. Nia turned and thanked Erin for all she had done for them. Erins eyes welled with tears as she gripped Nias hands. "Be safe, I will do what I can if you should need aid in the future. You need only ask." Nia felt her heart constrict as Erin released her hand before running back to her home. It had been a brief respite, but a welcome one all the same; and so, they set out once again.

Chapter Eleven:

The air had turned cold, the further they ventured North. Nia found herself grateful for the horses Erin had gifted them as day turned to night and then back again. Their green surroundings were a welcome change to the barren Sapphire Court. It only strengthened her hatred for her father, he had done this. Fractured the lands and their people. *For what? Control?* Nia found herself scoffing outwardly.

Uaine looked to her curiously as he conversed with Rian. He said nothing as her brow creased. Fury licked at her bones as her thoughts turned bitter. Ciar was her blood, her *legacy* was pain and suffering. *My father,* it made her sick to think, *brought this land to its knees.* A wicked thought crossed her mind, she would see *him* on his knees before her. She would force him to beg as she ripped every ounce of power from him, as she stripped the earth of every darkness that he had poured into Etherea.

Vengeance will be mine, she thought as she looked at her friends, *and justice shall be theirs*.

A violent wind rushed through the group, Torrin and Rian thought nothing of it. Uaine *saw it*. Her rage, a billowing gust rippling across their path. Leaves were torn from their branches; the trees groaned as they bent. She would rip Ciars heart from his chest; he would watch before he fell, as she burst the blackened thing in her hands. She did not want his end to be swift, he deserved no peace.

For all that he has done, he deserves no mercy. He gave none, why should he receive it?

The horses reared as the wind grew, Uaine turned to the girl as crimson light shined around her. "Nia, whatever plagues your mind, you must let it rest." Uaine called above the wind. Rian and Torrin turned then, had not noticed the burning rage that grew in Nias heart. "My father will rue the day he took my mothers' hand." She told them softly, yet the winds carried it like a roar. Uaine scanned the forest around them as her power shook the earth.

Nia felt it coming. Did not know *what* was coming, but she was ready for it.

The horses bucked.

Nia jumped to the ground and pulled her supplies from the animal. "What are you doing?" Torrin asked incredulously, as he barely managed to steady his steed. Rian found himself struggling to cling to the reins of the fretful horse. Uaine followed the girls lead, for as powerful as his sight was; Nia could see things that were to be, and he would not question her again after the Faelcu attack. Torrin groaned as he jumped from his own horse, he grabbed the bucking pony beneath Rian and settled it so his brother would not be thrown into the forest. That would be the last thing he needed.

A glistening silver light glowed, seconds before Lorcan stepped from it. Nothing could have prepared him for the sight that met his eyes. There she was; the girl that had plagued his mind since he left her in Avenere. Her eyes grew wide, Torrin drew his sword. Uaine stepped in front of Nia as Rian grabbed his bow. Nias heart swelled at the protective circle they had created around her. Lorcans stomach dropped at the fear which flashed in her lilac eyes.

"This... This is unexpected." Lorcan laughed, trying to ease the tension of the situation. It did not work. Torrin stepped towards the Silver Prince and raised his sword towards the man's neck. Lorcan had a choice. He could call his brothers, watch them rip the Fae men apart and take Nia to his Manor while the carnage raged; but it would solve nothing, it would not aid his plans.

So, Lorcan merely glanced at the sharp steel aimed at his throat and raised a brow. "Pray tell, Torrin, what brings you and your merry band-" Lorcan looked once more to the scarlet haired girl within their shield of bodies, "to my lands?" Nia steadied her breath and shut her eyes, letting her power fill her. It rolled over Lorcan, examining him. The fear that flowed from within him had her eyes widening once more. He was just as uneasy at their appearance in his Court as they were for trespassing. Confusion filled her as she found light in Lorcan's soul, far more than there should be; for all the cruelty he had wrought, it did not make sense.

Nia decided to trust her instincts, for they had not yet led her astray. "Forgive us please, your grace." It took every ounce of strength Torrin had to keep his eyes squarely on Lorcan; to not whip his head around and ask the girl what in the Fates she was doing. He cared about his sister, yes, but he would sacrifice all hope of saving Tara to keep Nia from the Silver Courts grasp. Nia laid a hand on Uaines shoulder and gently pushed the Fae aside. Torrin heard her footsteps and moved himself into her path. Nia struggled not to smile at his protectiveness.

She would never grow accustomed to it, to others stepping up for her. It had always been the reverse.

With her eyes locked on Lorcan, Nia side-stepped Torrin and willed herself to ignore the accusing look he cast at her. Lorcans silver eyes watched the scene curiously, how she said nothing yet everything all the same; as she stepped around the Fae. Torrin was poised to cut him down where he stood. "They have travelled with me, for me. We did not mean to cause offense; in truth we did not mean to trespass." Nia summoned her most desperate, devastated expression as she looked through her lashes at him. "We were attacked by the Faelcu, we had no choice." The false sob that bubbled up her chest surprised even Nia. It unnerved her; how easy it was to switch her demeanour, to suit the target. *There it was again, that word*. Nia shook the thought from her head and brought her focus back to Lorcan.

She had him.

They could all see it; his focus evaporated at the doe-eyed look she gave him. He groaned, low and guttural; frustrated at the position they had put him in. His brothers would have his head for this. "When I set out on my morning patrol, I did not expect this." Lorcan scowled towards the Fae men before him. "I can't just let you go." He shook his head, as her desperate eyes pierced his soul. He sighed as he came to his decision.

I can make this work.

"I shall make you a deal." It was Rian who scoffed this time, raising his bow once more. "Deals with the devil are for fools." The young Fae spat at the High Lord; it surprised them all. Despite Rian never knowing his sister, he knew too well the pain her loss had caused his brother. Torrin may be strong in physical strength, but his mind had been a wreck for far too long after Ciar stole her away.

"I think you will find you have little choice, child." Lorcan bit back, his features softened as he looked back to Nia. Rian's eyes darkened. "I will let you go, but we must make it believable that your companions fought me and won; and you will return to my court on your journey back. You would be surprised at the rumours which have already circulated in my Court, the dark and vengeful Elvinia; captured by High Lord Torrin. I have but one condition, *you come alone.*" Lorcan did not miss the scowl on Torrin's face.

Nia contemplated it, he was correct, they had no choice. Unease filled her at the perception the people here had of her. It served another purpose; this would give her access to his court and Tara. Nia thought it might help her find Duane and her mother, perhaps she could convince the two 'Princes' to battle each other for her and she could run with her mother in the chaos.

"How should we make them believe you lost?" Nia asked, although she suspected it to be something Torrin would enjoy. "I suppose I shall have to let your *protectors* land a few shots, a rare opportunity for them, I am sure." Lorcan confirmed her suspicions. Nia tried to ignore the smirk on Torrin's face as he sheathed his sword and raised his fists. Torrin wanted to *feel* the Silver Lords bones break. For they had ripped his sister from his arms and poisoned her mind so terribly that he had not heard from her in years. Gleefully, Torrin swung his fists at Lorcans face, Nia looked away. She did not wish to see the satisfaction awash Torrins features as he beat the Silver Prince. *It is necessary*, she reasoned; *so that we might find a way to defeat Ciar*.

As the men mounted their horses once more, Nia turned back to Lorcan; his face battered and already bruising. "I am sorry we have put you in this position." She told him truthfully as she used the fabric of her cloak to wipe the blood from his brow. Lorcan forced a smile through his wince and winked at the girl, ever the charmer. "I will find a way for you to repay me."

Before Nia had a chance to reply, Lorcan had snapped his fingers and they found themselves miles away; in a completely different environment. "Bastard." Uaine cursed as his stomach churned. Nia stumbled as her feet hit the ground with a skid. Blankets of blinding white snow covered their path. Towering mountains stood above them. Nia looked around for her horse, only to find it had been left behind. She was grateful that she had grabbed her supplies at least.

Torrin noticed her predicament and extended a hand, she gripped it gratefully and allowed him to hoist her on to the saddle, glad it could fit them both. "Where are we?" She asked as she wrapped her arms around Torrins warm waist, he shivered at her touch. "The edge of the Silver Court. We must travel through the mountain pass, into the Emerald Court, and there we will find Galeria." Unease filled them as they ventured towards the mountain path. The darkness of the stone above threatened to swallow all who dared enter. It would not have been Uaine or Torrins first choice, but it would take days to change their route to a safer path. With cautious steps and bated breath, they began the treacherous journey between the sharp stone walls of the mountain.

Mountains that encased their people deep within.

#

"They what?" Aidan growled at his brother, fierce and towering above the youngest prince; Lorcan winced. "Torrin *has* kidnapped the girl, I suspect he will be using her as leverage for his lands back." Lorcan rubbed his aching jaw and watched his elder carefully. As he suspected, Aidan raised a fist and brought it barrelling down into his brother's face. "And you let them go?" Aidan seethed, his eyes aflame with fury. Lorcan spat the blood from his lip and returned his brother's glare. "By the Fate's Lorcan, you better get her back, or I will feed you to the Faelcu myself. She is the key to Etherea, to returning Ciar. We must be the ones to bring her to him. Duane already has her mother." Aidan spat as he spoke. Lorcan cringed but bowed his head all the same. "As you wish brother. She will be ours."

Chapter Twelve:

They shivered in the darkness; night had fallen far too quickly. Hooves scratched against stone as they walked in eerie silence. Uaine took the lead once more, they kept Rian in the middle of their pack. This left Nia furthest behind as she gripped Torrin tighter, her head whipped at every creak that came from the snow-capped mountains. Its jagged stone jutted out towards them as the path narrowed, Nia realised they should not have brought the horses along. They had long left behind the yellow aspen trees that lined the entrance to the stone valley. Deep purple coral bells sprouted from the base of the stone, a small reminder of life within the hollow crevice of the mountain. Traders had once filled this route. Nia heard, for the third time, a rustling beneath the mountain. "What is that sound?" She asked, her voice barely a whisper in the catacomb silence that wrapped around their group.

A heavy sigh from Torrin made Nia wish she had kept her mouth shut; his shoulders tensed as he spoke. "This... this is where it happened. Ciar had tricked us all, the Fae of the Sapphire Court and the last Elves of the Ruby Court, any who dared still support Riona. They met here... And Ciar trapped them beneath the earth." Nias stomach churned as her eyes darted around the jagged rocks. She could not imagine it, people trapped beneath their feet. "You said before, that you had found ways to communicate. Are they alright?" Nia knew it was a silly question, she would *not* be all right should she be encased in stone.

It was a cruel fate, to never see the light of day again. To live with the memory of a beautiful land; to know you will never touch the earth again. "They are surviving, I do not think Ciar expected them to. They govern themselves, but they have not found a way to escape." Torrin need not say more, Nia heard the words unspoken. *Surviving, but not living*. Her arms wrapped tighter around his waist, offering what little comfort she could. It only brought anger bubbling back within her, she took a breath to calm the swell in her stomach. That scratching noise sounded once more; this time, Uaine drew to a halt. It was in fact, *not* the rumbling of the people beneath them; *but a creature stalking them*.

In a flash, Uaine turned to warn his friends.

It was too late.

Nia felt herself ripped from the saddle; jagged stones jabbed her skin as the creature dragged her down a winding path; through a crack in the rocks that they had not noticed before. Nia screamed as its talons pierced her shoulders. White hot liquid gushed from her flesh. Agony shot through her. Torrin tried to follow, but the magic that entombed the Fae prevented him from entering. Her wails echoed through the chambers of the mountain, Rian threw himself at the crevice; it was useless.

Uaine said a silent prayer and placed his palm on the bedrock and sent magic, carrying whispers, through the earth.

He hoped his friends would hear him; *hoped that they remained*.

Although they received word from time to time, Uaine and Torrin still feared that Ciar would find a way to eradicate the people he had left beneath the earth. To finish what he started.

Nia struggled to peer up at the creature, white spots filled her vision at the burning hot pain in her shoulder. She blinked twice at what she saw, almost did not believe it. The thing which gripped her, had *three* heads. After what felt like forever and a day, its' claws screeched to a halt as it threw Nia into an open cavern. A pool of water rippled as she rolled across the earth, liverworts and lichen littered the walls. Long winding crystalised stones dropped from the ceiling like icicles, some rose from the cave floor. Her breath rasped in her chest; crimson blood poured down her arms. Nias knees knocked as she scrambled to her feet. Her hands fumbled for the dagger at her waist.

Glowing moss gave her little aid as her eyes attempted to adjust to the darkness. Fear and pain clouded her mind, she relied on her ears as she listened for its razor-like claws scratching the bedrock. She stumbled backwards as that harrowing scraping noise drew closer; and found herself falling backwards. Stones fell beneath her body as she dropped to the ground, the whoosh of air above her head told her to be grateful for her clumsiness.

Nia willed herself to focus, to draw from within and pull that light outward once more. She wished she had not, wish she had learned her lesson the first time she had illuminated a room hiding a horrid creature. Three jaws of serrated teeth came gnashing towards her, Nia scrambled backwards. Her stomach lurched as she glanced down, the stones she had pushed aside were not stones.

The room was filled with *bones*.

It terrified her, sent a sickening wave of unease through her body.

A surge of adrenaline gave Nia the strength to roll to the left and pull herself to her feet once more. A pool of black water at her left, the winding path she had been dragged down at her right. Nia did not know how far they had come, nor did she know the path; but she also could not swim. Her body ached already; she was not sure she would survive this event. The beast took her pause to its advantage, it whipped one of the three tails Nia had not noticed. It knocked her off her feet, sent the breath wheezing from her lungs. Nia choked on a sob and willed herself to do something. Anything.

Protect yourself, you fool, that voice snarled in her mind once more.

Nia growled as she rose, her vision blurred as the blood still poured from her shoulders. It dripped from her fingertips at her sides, running would be no use. She would leave a trail. So, it was decided, she would fight.

Nia summoned what little strength she had left; her eyes found the glowing hilt of her dagger behind the beast. If she could reach it, her luck might change. The head closest to her snapped its jaw once more, she narrowly avoided it, and she put herself squarely in the path of its left head. Snake eyes stared back at her, furious, as if it were angered by the protests of its meal.

Nia dived and tumbled beneath its lengthy form, it was almost like a lizard; if a lizard stood eight feet tall, three tailed and three headed. Her fingers scraped the earth, she resisted a shudder as her nails cracked. Nia had grabbed the dagger; a tiny sense of triumph filled her as she lunged. No time for celebration; she could not hesitate.

Nia plunged her dagger into the scaled flesh of the creature.

The shriek that resonated through the mountain sent sweat trickling down Torrins brow. He did not know that it was the creature that released that harrowing sound. Terror filled him as he thought of her, trapped and alone within the mountain. Uaine heard the whispers beneath the earth as he held firm to the stone and turned to his friend. The mountain groaned, as if Ciar's spell knew they had intruded.

"We must go, we will be met by the pools of Linn." Torrin had no choice but to trust Uaine's words as he mounted his horse once more. The trio took off with haste, none willing to think she might not meet them on the other side.

The beast snarled at the girl; its blood mixed with her own on the cavern floor. Nia found some solace in the thought that if she were to die here, it would die alongside her. She knew the thought to be cruel, but in that moment, she did not care. Another whip of its tail came towards her, Nia jumped backwards, the sharp edge of its arrow-like tip sliced her forehead. Nia cursed as sticky warm liquid rolled down her face and stung her eyes; but still, she resisted. She pulled what focus she could to her mind and begged the earth for strength as she clasped her hands around the dagger. Once more, it glowed furiously. The white-hot hilt burned her flesh yet again, a crackling static filled the air. Wisps of crimson riveted around her, and a blindingly bright scarlet beam shot towards the creature. It fell like a dead weight, the sound boomed around the mountain. Loose stones and piles of bones shook as it clattered to the ground.

Her breath came in gasps, her chest cracked as she weakened. Relief turned her adrenaline to dust as her limbs shook. So, when the creature rose and lunged for her; Nia was blindsided. She flew backwards, her hands scrambled to grab the centre head coming towards her. As the ice-cold water slapped her back, Nia shoved her dagger upwards, through the gaping mouth of the monster. She had no choice but to breathe in the stench pouring from its gnarled teeth as she slipped beneath the water. As if to add insult to injury, it fell with her.

The water warmed as she descended. Nia was faced with two problems; the weight of the beast was dragging her quickly to her death and, if she somehow managed to free herself; she still could not swim.

Chapter Thirteen:

The water was shockingly warm as Nia sank to the bottom. It was a small mercy, at least, to not die in freezing depths. She watched the duckweed disappear above her, its roots slid against her arms. The light she cast faded further as she drifted towards the bottom. Nias eyes shot open wide as a body swam around her, half fish, half woman. *A mermaid*. She could hardly believe it. Nia did not fight as the beautiful woman wrapped her hands around her. *This is it*, she thought as she recalled Torrins words of how deceitful merfolk were, *I am surely dead*. Nias head spun as they glided through the water. It took only seconds, yet as Nias breath quickly ran out; it felt like eons.

The surface did not arrive quick enough, her eyes shut of their own accord. Torrins fretful pacing stopped as the water rippled. The woman pushed Nia to the earth. Without a second thought, he rushed to her side, his knees skidded across the mud as he shook her lifeless body. "*Nia wake up.*" Torrin pleaded as he checked her breathing. Panic coursed through his veins; no healing spell could reverse the damage that had been done. When no breath came from her lips, Torrin rushed to push on her chest. "This is not the end for you." Torrin desperately prayed for her eyes to open, to no avail. He had no choice, he brought his lips to hers; if she would not breathe alone, he would give his breath to her. Nia spluttered as the water gurgled up her throat.

Greedily she drank the air around her as her consciousness returned. Rian looked on with shaking hands. She had been lifeless as she was dragged to the surface. Her skin, a deathly shade of pale. Uaine loosed the breath he had been holding and turned to thank the woman who had saved her. "Thank you Airna, I owe you once more." The glistening creature smiled at the Fae, her skin shimmering green. Algae clung to her shoulders. "What was that?" Nia gasped as she bolted straight up, still desperate for oxygen to refill her lungs. Airna cast a sorrowful look at the girl, Torrin worked quickly to heal the gaping wounds that pierced Nias shoulders as much as he could. This far from his Court, his powers waned even more. "That was the Ellén Trechend of the Mallaithe mountains." Airna told them.

The Fae stared once more at Nia with disbelief. They had not seen what took her in the darkness, only heard her cries as it stole her away. Nia looked at them with narrowed eyes. "You said mermaids were not to be trusted." She said to Torrin, an accusation in her tone. She had believed the woman had arrived to drag her to her death.

Nia was not so impressed with Lorcan either, she understood the strange Elven words that they used; he had sent her to 'cursed' mountains. No sane person would expect safe passage through a place with such a name. Airna scoffed. "I am not a mermaid." She laughed, but Nia saw true offence in her eyes. "Airna." Uaine gave her a stern look before turning to Nia; the light had begun to return to her face. "She is a Merrow, a much gentler people than their cousins; who enjoy trapping mortal sailors with their song." The blood had stopped gushing from her wounds, Nia noticed the exhaustion on Torrins face and rested a bloody hand on his before she turned to Airna. "Thank you, for saving me." The Merrows eyes gleamed as she looked curiously at the Elf.

"Our folk will always be here for you and your kin, miss Elvinia, for what your mother did for us many years ago." Airna gave a respectful nod, Nias brows furrowed. "What did Ciar do to your people?" She asked, her curiosity always getting the better of her. "That fool?" Airna laughed once more. "He could not hurt my people if he tried, we were here before the first Fae and we will be here long after. No, your mother saved someone particularly important to us, it is a tale I will let her tell you; for the years have no doubt done it little justice." Nia wondered if there was any part of Etherea her mother was not revered.

"What news of faoi thalamh?" Uaine asked as he sat by the lakes edge. *Underground*, Nia recognised, he was asking about the Fae. Nia looked at the merrow with curiosity, could she travel through the mountain? Were there pools so far below? Airna rested her arms on the bank and sighed heavily. "Not good Uaine, the darkness is ebbing away at their spirits. I fear the Dorchadas will consume them." Merrows were honest creatures, unlike their deceitful kin; it gave Uaine pause. *Darkness*, that is what threatened the trapped. Nia rang the water from her cloak as she looked back at those towering, pointed peaks above the mountain, capped with snow; one would never presume by looking at them that an entire people was within. Sorrow filled her, the Merrows glistening green eyes examined Nia before she reached into the water beneath her.

Nia watched as Airna pulled a small shell up to the surface, it was beautiful. Gleaming white, with a high, curled, spiked spine and a siphonal canal. "A conch shell." Airna explained as she handed it to the girl. Nia felt the coolness of Airna's skin, it was sticky. She resisted the urge to recoil. Airna gave her a thankful look for her politeness. "Should you ever find yourself in need once more, as long as there is water near, my people will rush to your aid." Nia took the shell with still shaking hands. Airna frowned at her. "You could dry yourself, you know." She looked between the Fae men curiously, Nias thoughts flashed back to the night of the dance; how she had cleaned the blood from her body in the blink of an eye.

"Your mother used the earth." Airna continued, sensing her confusion. Nia had been too exhausted to remember much more of her training; sometimes trying to remember felt like chipping away at an enormous wall and sometimes it was like she could smash right through. Nia dug her fingers into the earth and shut her eyes. With a steadying breath, she willed herself to listen, carefully. She did not wish to go too far and suspected they were closer now to the darkness of Etherea than they had been in the Sapphire Court. Nia could hear everything, the wings of birds beating above, worms wriggling within the earth, the heartbeat of the horses at their side. She could hear the fish beneath the water. Then, she felt it, the life force of the ground beneath her. It crept up her fingertips, wrapped around her arms, and filled her with warmth. Nia focused on her dripping garments and willed that warmth to fill her, to rid her of the cold wetness that covered her.

Torrin, Uaine, and Rian watched in awe as glowing red tendrils wrapped around her; and covered her in iridescent light. Heat filled her as her garments dried, it was a welcome feeling. Nia gasped as flowers sprouted beneath her palms, wriggling through her fingers. Airna cast a sympathetic smile to Uaine. "Safe travels, my friend, I shall look out for you should I venture near Galeria." Her eyes twinkled as she looked once more at the odd group; before disappearing beneath the depths of the lake. Famished, and filled with exhaustion, they took rest in a nearby grove in the woods. The snow had thinned. As Torrin and Uaine set up camp, Nia took Rian to forage nearby. She did not wish to go too far but knew she would find more near the lakes. She was grateful to be proved correct, as her eyes scanned the earth; and for the bounty that grew at their feet. "What are we looking for?" Rian asked as he looked at the plants around them. He had never paid much attention to what grew around him, a fact he came to regret. He did not know what would quell their hunger, or which would poison them.

Nia shook her head; she had relied on the forests around her home for years. She knew each plant like the back of her hand. As she peered around, she saw plenty she could use and began teaching Rian how to identify each plant, from white rounded petals of arrowheads to the tangled mass of thorns that adorned the hawthorn bush. Nia set Rian the task of collecting red Clover, for it was easy to recognise, and got to work on the rest of the earth around them.

The pair returned to their camp with glee on their faces, both carried a basket filled with greens and berries. Nia had found more than enough to feed them for the night, she would prepare some of what she had gathered for the journey ahead. Torrin eyed the bounty of plants in their basket and grimaced, he had hoped for a fish at least. "I thought you were a hunter." Uaine voiced his thoughts. *'You are braver than I'* Torrin shot at his friend, Uaine continued to glower at the basket. Nia grabbed a stick of rhubarb she had cut and whacked the Fae with it, much to Torrin's shock and amusement. "Don't be so ungrateful." She scolded the blonde as Torrin laughed at him.

Nia got to work, determined to change Uaines opinion of her bounty. She was ever grateful that Erin had packed cooking supplies along with her weapons as she emptied her bag. Torrin watched as she prepared the food. She washed it thoroughly, in a nearby spring. Nia sliced the arrowheads thinly, chopped the roots of dandelions, took the leaves from the clovers, took the seeds from the hawthorn berries, broke through beech fruit to reveal nuts within. She cursed her stinging fingers as she chopped the young leaves of the nettle plant. Finally, once it had all been prepared and her stone pan had heated, Nia threw all but the berries into the pan.

The smells that rose drew Rian, Torrin, and even Uaine closer to the cooking flora. Citrus sweet and nutty earthiness filled the air and their stomachs growled in response. Nia laughed at their sudden change of heart as she dished up their meals, sprinkling lightly roasted hawthorn berries atop their salads. A bowl of washed and pitted berries sat before them, blackberries, bilberries, cranberries; Nia could not have dreamed to eat so many all at once, oh how she despised waiting for the change of the seasons to bring about her favourites. Silence fell over the group as they ate gladly. Uaine had forgotten all about the lack of meat in the meal as he wolfed every bite. "You must," he swallowed, "you must teach us how you do this." Uaine finished. Nia looked around them with disbelief, Torrin sheepishly avoided her gaze.

"Do you mean to say, that none of you know how to live off the earth?" Nia questioned, she should not have been surprised, they were *Lords* after all. She presumed mortal lords would be just as clueless. Torrin scratched his nape as he shook his head. "We have never really had the need." He admitted. Since the theft of his people and the desolation of his lands; Torrin had his ingredients delivered and used what little magic remained in his veins to prepare his meals. Nia supposed she could not fault him for what he did not know; she forgot sometimes that they had not lived as she had. After a moment of silence, Nia looked at the crackling fire between them. Darkness had begun to fall.

"Sometimes, when the weather grew harsh and the animals ran north, it was the only choice we had." Nia held her shaking hands closer to the fire as she remembered. "One winter, it grew so cold that even the sturdiest plants began to freeze and die. With nowhere to turn, we turned to the trees; and found them ready to save our lives. We found acorns in the oak trees, and an abundance in the pine trees. We used their needles for tea, their bark for flour and the pinecones for their nuts." Nia shivered once more as she thought back to that desolate winter.

"People were desperate, they ate the bark of the tree first, gorged on raw nuts until each crawled back up their throats as they emptied their stomachs, retching and writhing; they had poisoned themselves in their haste to eat, for we were miserable and starving. It did not happen overnight, but with my mother's guidance we learned to survive with whatever the earth gave to us." Torrin looked at her with admiration, there was such strength within her. "It grew easier then, we learned what would keep until the winter, which plants grew when and where. It is different here, spring herbs grow next to autumn berries." Rian yawned. Yes, the meal had been delicious, but he found himself exhausted from their day of adventure. With a full belly, he took leave of the group and laid his weary head down. Uaine followed suit, leaving Torrin and Nia to bask in the firelight alone.

Chapter Fourteen:

The cool night air carried only the crackling of their campfire and the chirping of crickets. The light of its flames flickered across their faces. Nia wove together a crown of chicory, astor and shamrock she had collected earlier. Torrin marvelled at her in the quiet, as her nimble fingers created an arrangement of purple and green. "One day you will have a real crown." He whispered absentmindedly; he meant it. She chuckled and shook her head. "I could not care any less for crowns or titles Torrin, I care only about the safety of my mother and your people." She replied honestly. Her ears still felt the onslaught of pain in the west. "You deserve everything Etherea has to give." Torrins words rang with certainty.

Nia quietened once more, as she remembered similar words Duane whispered in her ear.

Her heart still ached for him; but in the scheme of things, it was the dullest ache she felt.

It disgusted her, that her soul still felt that pull towards him. He was cruel, she could never love someone who took pleasure in enslaving people. "Those words tricked me into Etherea, set every foul thing that has happened since in motion." She scowled; her fingers ripped the flower crown apart. Torrin felt a pang in his chest at her bitterness and laid a hand over hers.

"It also set in motion every wonderful thing that has happened, without your intervention; Rian would have surely died, life grows once more in the Sapphire Court, you saved the Lady of Avera from the Abhartach and you have slain the Ellén Trechend of the mountain. You cannot blame yourself for the cruelty of others, for you have shown at every turn that you defy their wishes to trap you in the darkness."

An uneasiness ran through her, still unsure of the path the fates had laid for her.

"Tell me more about your mother, I don't think you told me her name." Nia wished nothing more than to change the topic from herself. Torrin looked to the fire with a soft, sad smile upon his lips. "Her name was Aoife, my grandfather's youngest daughter. She was wild and defiant, so he sent her into service at the castle. Our families have a long and winding history, but at that point we held favour with the crown. So, Aoife was shipped off to be your mother's maid. It's said Riona was so angry at the decision she did not speak to King Ainmuire for two months and tormented his training soldiers at every wake in revenge." Torrin chuckled as he looked at Nia, he could see the resemblance now; questioned how he had not realised it the moment he laid eyes on her. "She set out with Riona on every adventure, I have been told you could not find one without the other. It is no surprise that they stood shoulder to shoulder on the battlefield."

There was pride in his eyes at that.

"My mother was determined to die at your mother's side, but Riona knew this and used her magic to send Aoife home. I will never forget; the defeat in her eyes, as she bundled me and Rian in her arms, tears streaming down her face. We had mere weeks together after Ciar stormed the Courts, and somehow, she ensured our safety. The blast that decimated my court killed everyone who had not gone to the mountain." Nia gasped at that, she had presumed that Ciar had rotted the earth, not burned it with fire.

Torrin decided to move away from that depressing subject. "In the weeks we had together, she told me wonderful tales of her adventures in the Ruby Court. She had spent years in their service, though she said your mother refused to treat her as a servant; so, she did not mind it. It is through our mother's perseverance that women were allowed to fight in the royal army. The law did nothing to stop them, Ainmuire had two choices; let his decree be undermined by his daughter and her *maid* or repeal the law."

Nia laughed at that. Her heart swelled with pride. "I suppose he had no choice at all." She beamed, Nia knew her mother; a woman who believed women were just as strong as any man, would never let a man tell her what she could not do. "No, I'm guessing he did not." Torrin chuckled alongside her, "and what of your father?" She regretted asking the question the moment those words left her lips. Sadness had filled his features, no light in his eyes as he had for his mother. Nia placed her hand over his. "Forgive me Torrin, I am curious to a fault, you need never answer questions should the answer cause you pain." He sighed and kicked the dirt beneath his foot.

"His name was Uilliam, they called him Liam. He did not start as a bastard, but he sure became one in the end. I do not know exactly what happened but in the early years, before Ciar revealed his true nature, they were all friends. Riona had managed to grant my mother a pardon for her service, allowing her to return to the Sapphire Court. Liam returned with her, a babe on the way and a wedding to plan, but jealousy drove him insane. My mother had loved another on their travels, a lowling Silver Fae, and my father cut him down. She did not know this, until they had sent Tara to the Silver Court."

Nia cursed at that, how cruel; to kill another for fear the woman you want would choose him. "He loved her, I suppose in his way, but she could not love him after that. He ran away, she ran to Riona. Myself and Rian were left with a trusted friend until she returned. Battered, bruised, screaming that Riona had gone, I was blessed she held strong for the last few weeks. For I did not understand, not until it was too late." Sorrow filled her, as the fire dwindled in the frosty night air.

"We will avenge her, I swear it Torrin. I will be the first to admit I have broken many promises, but this; I swear he will suffer, for your mother, and mine." Torrin shook his head. "Something tells me the journey ahead of us will be long Nia, do not trouble yourself with my woes." "I wish I could have seen her, seen them all; before it all went to shit." Torrin nodded in agreement. Nia did not know it yet; but she should have been far more careful what she wished for. They took their leave of each other as the fire ebbed; Nia crawled into their makeshift shelter with a snoring Rian at her side.

They awoke to no dramatic event; it was a welcome reprieve. Nia had struggled to sleep, every crack in the woods had her clutching her dagger. She did not know if it was better or worse that sleep escaped her, for her dreams were plagued with darkness and death. They ate their breakfast in silence, their thoughts occupying them as they sat. Uaine thought of stepping foot in his court once again, it had been years. He wondered who Ciar had dredged up to oversee his lands, the thought made him sick. He would have been the High Lord if his father had not done what he did. Torrin felt sympathy for his friend, he remembered Uaines mother crashing through the manor; the last High Lord of the Emerald Court dragged behind her. It sent a shiver down his spine. Nia thought of what she might ask Abbán when they reached him... *If* they reached him. Rian thought simply of his bed at home, he had been filled with adventurous spirit when they first began; it had quickly faded. He had grown cold and bitter on their journey.

They set off again, through the forest path. Neither wished to be caught on the main roads of the Emerald Court. Nia thought to question why, but the grave silence around them made Nia hold her tongue. The Emerald Court was truly as green as its name. The lush forest around her filled Nia with energy, she heard the buzz of bees in the distance and her heart sang. "What are you at girl?" Uaine questioned as she rushed ahead, he cursed her as he followed. Nia found her target quickly, a huge hive rested nine feet above them. Its weight pulled at the branch it clung to. Uaine watched with pursed lips as she stuck her hand into the hive. Torrin nearly had a heart attack at the sight. Rian became filled with curiosity. "Can I do that?" He asked, his brother glared in response. "Nia so help me take your hand out of that beehive before you get stung." Nia struggled not to laugh at that, to keep her hand steady, "you sound just like my mother." She said as calmly as she could, as her fingertips felt the stickiness they searched for. Carefully she extracted the honeycomb, the buzzing of the bees matched the pulse in her ears.

Uaine watched with disbelief as she removed her hand, a bee sat squarely on her knuckles. Nia looked at the fuzzy creature in awe; she could not help herself as she raised her other hand and gently ran a finger across its back. "It is softer than a thousand feathers." She whispered; her eyes wide like a child. She had been stung many times in the forest by her home, honey was her weakness; but here, they merely hummed around her. Torrin watched with shock as the bee fluttered its wings and buzzed back to its hive, Nias face alight with wonder. *This girl will be the death of me*, Torrins pained voice in his mind caused Uaine to chuckle. Nias eyes shot between the two Fae men, wisps travelling between them.

"Stop that."

Blue and green eyes stared at her. "Stop what?" Uaine asked her curiously, her own eyes darted to the wisps between them. He marvelled at her; she was filled with so many surprises. "Stop speaking to each other in your minds, I do not know what you are saying but I can see it and I do not appreciate being spoken about in secret." She had guessed the topic was about her, Torrin felt relief that she did not know *what* they said; for he did not wish to impose on her his feelings. Uaine's eyes glittered with amusement, he would have enjoyed watching his friend be caught out. At her frustrated frown, Uaine coughed to cover the laugh that threatened to escape and turned to her.

"Apologies, Nia, it is an ability many Fae share. We forget that you have not been here long." Uaine sighed; in truth, he would not enjoy others whispering about him either. Rian snorted. "*I* say cut it out, *for years*; yet you persist, a pretty girl asks you once and you fold like a deck of cards." he mocked his older brother and their friend. Nia chuckled at that as Torrin punched the little lords' shoulder; gently of course.

They continued as they ate the honeycomb, they had to admit; they were glad she had stuck her hand in that dangerous hive. It was a surprise, that none of the bees had attacked. Perhaps they recognised her magic, knew what she was; what she would do.

A rustling ahead gave them pause, Nias ears pricked as a low grumble sounded. Not Faelcu, she thought, but what? Weapons drawn; the quartet watched the shifting grass as it came towards her. Her heartbeat furiously as it drew near, until the hedge split, and a great big hound flew towards them. It hit her like a tonne of bricks, she fell to the ground with the animal on her lap.

Tufts of black, silver, and white fur covered her body. Nia felt panic, until a wet, slobbery tongue lapped across her face. She blinked. It was like a wolf, yet twice the size, and a face so majestic, one amber eye, one milky white. It stared back at her with laboured breath, its tongue hung from its mouth, it cocked its head to the left, pointed ears flapping lightly in the wind. It sniffed at the flower chain she had wrapped around her neck and sneezed, giving a surprised wide-eyed look to the girl. She laughed. Yes, the animal was huge, its paws could crush her face should it choose, but the sheer dumb look on the hounds' face filled her heart with awe.

Nia noticed Torrin and Uaines advance and scrambled to her feet. The hound sat tall at her waist as it watched them. "Nia, come here." Torrin warned as he drew closer, his sword in hand. Nia outstretched her arms in a protective shield.

"Leave it be, he is no threat." She pleaded; they looked once more to the animal. As if on cue, to prove her point, the hound stuck its head into a stinging nettle. It retreated, scratching its nose as it sneezed. Uaine burst into laughter at this. "Oh, he is a cute beast." He cooed as he scratched the dog's ear. "What shall we call him?" Rian asked, dutifully ignoring his brothers frustrated stare at the group. *They cannot possibly be serious*, he thought. Much to his chagrin, they began to discuss names for the wolfdog.

Almost an hour later, as they came to the barrier of the Emerald Court, they decided. "How about Madigan?" Torrin grumbled, he had grown tired of their bickering as the dumb dog stomped through the forest. They had little chance of stealth now that it had joined their ensemble. Rian's brows drew close as he stared up at his brother. "Little dog? I hardly think that applies." Nia grinned at that. "I do not see you coming up with anything better. Her heart warmed as Torrin begrudgingly scratched the dogs' ear, she saw the twitch of his mouth as it lapped at his hand. So, it was decided; his name would be Madigan, and they could keep him.

Not that Nia intended to listen if Torrin said otherwise.

They came to another riverbank and Nia gasped as she looked across. There, a hundred feet ahead, was a town. *A town filled with people.* Nia could not help herself, nor could she be blamed as she ran towards the bustling city; for they had not told her of the harrowing history they shared with this Court, and for this they would pay.

Chapter Fifteen:

Nia could scarcely believe as she looked around; Fae of all sorts bustled about; oblivious to the wide eyed, slack jawed Elf girl in their midst. Torrin acted quickly as he yanked the hood of her cloak over her head, the soft brown wool covered her face. Nia almost turned to yell at him, until she noticed what she had not before. In her wide-eyed wonder, she had failed to realise the calibre of Fae that walked amongst them. Cutthroats, mercenaries, folk with horns and wings.

Then, she noticed, *there are no women*.

Nia felt suddenly uneasy.

"Take my hand." Torrin told her through gritted teeth. She began to protest, until a shrill voice stopped her cold. "Who is responsible for this woman?" Nia could hardly believe it was a man who spoke. He wore a navy button-down uniform with gold bezels and a flat black hat. He glared at them with his beady green eyes, his thin lips pursed in a scowl. Nia could not help but grimace at his scarred jaw. "I said." The man screeched. "Who is responsible for this woman?" Nia felt unrest growing in her middle. *How dare he speak of me like this*, she glared back in return.

Torrin pulled his hood from his head, the uniformed man stepped back. "I am, will this be a problem?" The authority rolled off him in waves. Nia admired him as he stepped before her. "Lord Torrin, forgive me, we were not aware that you would be visiting." The man stuttered; all bravado lost. "You know how they are, always finding trouble." It took every morsel of self-control that Nia could muster, to stop herself from smacking the smug look from the man's face. "I'd say leash her, but you seem to have a pattern with the animals you keep." he snickered with a glance to the giant dog lapping at a nearby puddle.

Nia could not do it, could not keep her mouth closed as they spoke of her in this way. It pained Torrin to do so; he would have warned her, had she given him a moment, but there was no time. Nia saw wisps of Sapphire weaving towards her before an invisible hand covered her mouth. Torrin had felt the unrest from the girl, and knew it was only a matter of time before she lit herself and this town aflame. Her eyes scoured the crowds of Fae around them, until they rested on a scene which turned her blood molten.

There, in the centre of town; five women, *in stocks*.

Uaine felt the panic, the fury, unrelenting and unyielding crashing from the girl.

His eyes followed Nias and he struggled to keep his resolve. *What have I left my people to be subjected to?* Nia could not look away as she scanned the women bound to the stocks, the bruises that covered their skin, their gaunt hopeless eyes; their dresses askew. It all made her sick. A single woman raised her head, defiant; and glared at the crowd which hurled insults at her. Her glowing gold eyes met Nias, '*they fear what they cannot control. We cannot be used, we cannot be broken, Ciar will burn for what he has done, the world will be brought to its knees by a woman someday.*' Her silk voice slipped into Nias' mind.

"Trouble?" Uaine asked. It was a vague question, yes; but he did not trust his voice to ask more. Torrin could have cursed his friend for asking anything at all, he had been ready to announce their leave. The man scoffed and spat towards the women, Nia felt her lips curl in a snarl and dug her nails into her palms to resist thumping the arrogance from him. "Bloody witches." Nia could hardly believe the term that had passed his mouth.

A witch-hunt? In a magical land? Have they lost their minds?

"Wicked creatures." Torrin agreed, Nia felt blood pooling in her palms. *I cannot take this; I cannot listen to this one more moment.* Uaine gave his friend a warning look. They were teetering on a thin line with her, something dark had grown within Nia in the weeks since they had left the Sapphire Court. "I am afraid we must take leave; we have urgent business to attend to." Torrin didn't dare give the smirking man a second look as he tugged Nia by the elbow.

"Should you grow tired of that one, visit the Brookes, there are plenty far more beautiful than *her*." At that, Nia felt the anger rippling from Torrin. It would do no good for them both to be furious. If his anger persisted it would do nothing to quell her own; she would turn and burn that wretched man where he stood. *'Run, fellow sister, for those of us who are shackled; you must free yourself from this court.'* A mirage of flashing images coursed through Nias mind, the golden eyed girl lead her into the mountain which she had been dragged, and down to a bustling city beneath the earth. *'Be safe, sister, may we meet again in the summerlands.'*

Uaine rushed the furious pair back to the path then further into the cover of the forest; as soon as he had been sure there were no eyes watching them. Madigan had taken Rian on his back as the Fae walked at an impossible speed. Finally, they stopped; Rian soon wished they had not. Nia turned and burst into a blinding light of burning red.

Her Ruby eyes shone in the low light of the sun, those wings; which had appeared only once before, sprouted at her back. Talon's sharper than the dagger she held bit through her already blood-soaked palms. Panicked, Torrin shouted at the wolfhound to get his brother to safety. Nia snarled at him as Uaine jumped between them. The sight of her almost burned their eyes. "Nia please, there are things in this world you do not understand." He began, she remained enraged. "Why have you not stopped this?" she growled at them. They had not discussed it, but Nia knew he was a Lord of this Court by his eyes; why he had not challenged this barbaric practice, she could not understand. It was true, the knowledge of what had become of his home almost drowned Uaine with guilt.

She felt it too, the sorrow, the regret; he reeked of it.

Nia felt no remorse.

The image of those women, humiliated, battered; tears for them scalded her eyes. Fire danced in her gut until it swirled at her fingertips. "It has not been my court since I was a child, I do not know which bastard is in control. I had no idea..." Uaines sobs cut through her, Nia glared back at the town. "If I find out that you knew of this and let it be, I will tear you down myself. *And you.*" She seethed at Torrin. "Don't you dare speak of me; or any woman, in the manner which you spoke today or by the Fates you will never spend the night with one again." Nia stormed away as they called after her. There was no chance she would continue their journey with what she had witnessed.

When night had fallen and her glow had faded, Nia watched from the edge of town. Flickering torches offered scarce and scattered light across the path. *Perfect.* Nia drew her cloak closer and stalked through the night. It was a large city; she had not realised how far she had run earlier; in all her excitement. Nia had thought, as she ran towards its bustling streets and emerald buildings that she would find merriment and friendship; instead, she found an entrance to a woman's hell. *It is a shame,* she thought, *that this city is so wicked.* For it had stores, taverns, and homes; the means of becoming a wonderful eutopia for all Fae.

As she drew nearer to the centre, to where those poor women still stood, the golden eyed Fae's head snapped upwards. Astonished, she stared at Nia as the girl approached without a word and ripped the stock apart with her bare hands. Nia worked quickly with her help. When every woman was released, she turned to the gold eyed woman. "Where is 'the Brookes' and that man?" Nia snapped. She was not satisfied, she wished to watch the smile melt from that bastard's face. "You must go, Elvinia, go beneath the mountain and tell them Cliodhna sent you." The woman pleaded. *How does she know my name?*

Nia did not need to ask again as a party of drunk Fae men fell from the doorway of a decrepit building. Enraged once more, with the wind stirring behind each step; she did not stop until she reached the entrance. Nia did not have to move, the door exploded as she willed; women screamed as men jumped to their feet.

She roared at the women to go, to leave this rotten place and its corrupt occupants; as they ran by, she noticed more and more injuries adorning their frail bodies. Fire burst from her fingertips as the last Fae ran from the whorehouse. Nia watched with satisfaction; the flames danced in her eyes. The women ran, scrambling in all directions for freedom. Nia remained, as the men dragged themselves from the fire; spluttering for air.

Finally, *he* stumbled from the building. His gold bezels melted against his uniform shirt. Nia glared bitterly as he slid to a halt before her. Those beady eyes widened as much as they could in his shock. "Who are you?" He spluttered as the heat warped the air around them. Nia laughed, yet there was no joy in her. "My name is Elvinia Ó Mordha. Daughter of the rightful Queen of Etherea and *you*, have made a grave error this day." She had not said it aloud before, not so decisively; Nia relished in the power she felt as she raised her hand. Fear filled those green eyes as he begged for mercy, Nia feigned thought. Why should she give him mercy when he had given none before?

#

Torrin paced for the fourth time as Uaine attempted to track Nias aura. You would assume it could be seen for miles, for her rage burned brighter than a thousand suns; yet the girl had managed to hide her tracks. Uaine worried whether she had intended to or not. "Where has she gone?" Torrin then asked for the seventh time, Uaine glared at his friend. If only they knew what Nia was doing, neither could have imagined it. He was trying his best to find her, Torrins constant commentary did not aid him. "As far away from us as she can get, I would think, and who could blame her?" Torrin groaned at Uaines answer, he felt sick with worry, they had not been able to find his brother either. "Rian could not have gone far though, right?" "I would like to say so Torrin, but that hound is twice the size of any; I fear it could bring him a fair distance." It was not what Torrin wished to hear, but it was needed to bring some sense to his mind. They must return, retrace their steps, and pray to the Fates that they were both in one piece once found.

Torrin reached the town first, as Nia raised a fiery fist in the air, the officer of the court on his knees before her. Uaine stopped in shock. They could scarcely believe it, sorrow rippled through Torrin at the pure hatred in her eyes. He could not blame her, if it had been the reverse, he would have burned this town down too. Uaine pulled his friend to run towards her, *we must try to stop her; try to save her from the guilt that would come from killing another Fae*.

Before anyone could react, before they could reach her, Nias onslaught was cut short as two hooded figures snatched her from where she stood.

Chapter Sixteen:

You would think, in a world of wonder, that the Fae could live peacefully. One would suppose, however, that darkness lives within us all; it is our duty to resist, to pursue the light at every chance. Nia reminded herself of this, as best she could, as she struggled against two pairs of strong arms; the men wrestled the wriggling woman. Nias nails dragged across the stone walls they passed; to no avail. She could barely see through the hood over her head. Despite this, she would not give up. Nia cursed as her magic failed her and swung her leg once more. They dropped her. Nia felt a fleeting whisper of hope; until a boot came crashing into her face. It knocked the wind from her lungs.

Fists smashed against her body, a hundred whacks against her skin. The all-too-familiar sound of scraping steel filled the darkness. Barely, she rolled away as that whistling noise coursed through the air. It crashed against the ground with a clatter. Nia counted her blessings as it sparked against the stone beside her head. Nia cursed as she felt cold steel slice through the skin of her calf. She would not give them the satisfaction of knowing the agony she was in. With grit teeth as they assaulted her, Nia silently scolded herself for running towards this barbaric town.

She bit back her screams as another foot connected with her spine. A memory flashed, of the Faelcu ripping apart her flesh. Nia winced once more. 'P*lease, get up.*' That mysterious voice rang in her head again. It became clearer each time, Nia realised it was a woman's voice. It was softer this time too, not harsh and disgusted like the times before. Another kick connected with her ribcage, Nia spluttered, and a sob escaped her lips. Their laughter brought her shame as she curled herself inwards, the hood fell from her face. In the darkness, it hardly mattered. *'They are going to bind you with foxglove, you need to get up. Now.'* Nia decided to listen, for this voice had not steered her wrong yet.

Uaine ran frantically through the city, following faint trails of her, scarlet light lined the cobblestoned path as he pressed through. Panic had already begun as Fae ran towards the burning parts of their town. Torrin searched through the forest for his brother, praying his friend would return with Nia. Uaine cursed as he took in the smell of the city, it reeked of foxglove. *That is how they have kept the women under their control for so long*, Uaine realized. It turned his stomach, *why would they poison them? To what end?* Torrin tore through the wood like a madman, he would not rest until he found Rian. *I was a fool to bring him*, Torrin thought; but he knew in his heart there was none he would have trusted with his brother, and he would not have been capable of focusing on their mission.

Nia did not know of foxglove, for Riona had burned every sprout within a thousand miles of their home, but she knew by the rotten stench that crept up her nose; she must heed the voice in her mind. With that decided, Nia took a steadying breath and rallied the strength from within. As she closed her eyes, she thought of every foul thing she had encountered in this world. From the women in this court, bound and beat; to the beasts that chased them towards this treacherous path. Nia let thoughts of Torrin, Uaine and Rian fuel her. She would have preferred to draw from a happier place; but her anger greatly outweighed her joy. The two men could not have anticipated the sight they would witness as the young girl leaped into the air. Her magic still subdued; Nia relied on every carnal instinct she had. Their shock did not last long as both men lunged for her.

Torrin found his brother, tucked beneath the legs of the wolfhound; sleeping peacefully. The animal cocked its head at him, as if to say, *'what did you expect?'* Torrin almost wept with relief as he shook Rian awake, the young Fae looked at him with sleep filled eyes. "What's wrong?" He asked as the terror on his older brothers face registered in his hazy mind. "We have to go; I will explain on the way." Rian had little choice but to run after Torrin. The night air pinched his cheeks with frost as they sprinted back towards the city. Rian had a horrible feeling about this as his tired limbs ached. He reminded himself to stretch before bed next time, it had become a regular occurrence that he would be woken from his slumber to a threat to his life.

Uaine said a prayer to himself as he stepped through the eerily silent streets of the city, he hoped he would find her in time. *It is all my fault, I should have done more*, Uaine thought bitterly to himself. He could not fail her; not like he had failed his people. She would be their saviour; he would not let her die at the hands of some city thugs; he would not let her die at the hands of *anything*. While Uaine did not share the rapture Torrin felt when he looked at the long-lost princess, he found himself compelled to always ensure her safety and wellbeing. He had a sister once, who had died when Ciar seized the court; but if he could choose one now it would be the blazing spirit that had crashed into their lives.

A meaty arm clubbed towards her head once more, Nia ducked and dived. Sweat ran down her face as she fought the thugs, her body ached, her bones screamed at her to surrender and end her own misery. Still, Nia resisted the temptation as she grasped something cold and metal. *Thank the Fates*, she thought as her hands found a cutlass in the belt of one of her attackers. Nia almost beamed with happiness, almost; for she was not out of the woods yet. She could not give it a second thought as she swung the blade at her foes. Her eyes could still barely see. Nia relied on her ears as she had done within the mountain.

Uaine heard the scraping of steel ahead and gulped as he recognised the forgotten entrance to the High Lords personal prison, where one would be thrown for the greatest offenses towards the High Fae of the court. It looked derelict now, the wooden door had been split and torn away. This did nothing to calm his nerves, if the prison was empty; where had its occupants gone? "Bloody witches." A man shouted from within. His pulse spiked as he pulled the remnants of the door aside and ran to rip the men to shreds. Uaine had a sneaking suspicion Torrin would be displeased with anything less for the bastards.

Nia smirked in the darkness as she felt a tingle of her magic return, *they must have drugged me*, she realised. This realisation brought a whole new wave of anger; it seemed to evaporate what poison they had inflicted upon her. Nia thought of the women in this court, what they must have endured. *No more*. Her palms burned with fire; it lit the room around her; *they had dragged her to a cell.* Some cells around her had been blasted open, some held the skeletons of those unable to escape. She did not wish to think of their intent when they brought her here, it sent a shiver down her spine, but Nia had no time to dwell on this as the larger of her attackers lunged for her once more.

He was a balding man, with a wide and harsh face and a smugness in his dirt brown eyes that sent fire billowing from Nias fingertips. The cell burst with iridescent scarlet light, it licked at the stone walls. The air began to twist and bend in the sweltering heat. The Fae brutes scrambled backwards at the sight before them, only to find the iron gate of the cell had snapped shut behind them. It was a wonder the bars had not bent. Uaine descended the steps to the underground prison and cursed as stacks upon stacks of Foxglove came into view before finally, he found Nia.

He really should have realised at this point, that Nia did not need knights in shining armour to run to her aid.

She needed a reason not to burn this city to the ground.

Nia felt those cold wings at her back and wondered if she could keep them long enough to fly. The shorter man cowered as he fell in his hurry, his slim face bounced against the cold metal of the gate; his hazel eyes wide with panic. Nia felt no remorse, no sympathy for them as they rattled the metal bars; desperate for escape, clinging to the scalding metal as it scorched their palms. "Nia?" Uaine called out to the girl as flames danced around her body, licking at the boots of the two brutes. Her head snapped up, her eyes like ice in comparison to the blaze around her as she glared back at Uaine. "They must pay." She told him, her voice dark and distorted.

Fear rippled in Uaines gut, he pushed it away, determined to calm the swell of fury in the Elf. "This is not the way Nia, you will start a war within the courts, and they will not band together to defeat Ciar."

"I will not need aid to rip that bastard apart."

The surety in which she said it stopped Uaine, even the two scrambling from the flames took pause. "Be that as it may, you will need aid to stop his army tearing through the streets of other courts; ones who have done no wrong." Nia suppressed a groan as she shut her eyes, *he was right.*

Thoughts of Erin filled her mind, the woman from the Golden Court, the young Fae that had run through the ballroom. Torrin, sweet Torrin; *he will be furious with me*. Her heart softened as she resisted the urge to explode like a bomb and burn them all to hell; instead, Nia swung the metal gate open. The men lunged for escape.

There was one thing she could burn, if not these foul excuses for men. The Foxglove around them burst into flames. If Uaine thought the city reeked before, it was positively horrendous now. He held his sleeve to his face and grabbed Nia. Her skin was boiling, still he held firm and ran. *Foolish girl,* he thought, *yet it is our fault for not teaching her of this world, for allowing her to skate through on instinct and raw power.*

Torrin skidded to a halt as they reached the town centre, The town was aflame; brothels, taverns, the stocks, it all burned bright in the night air. Bushels of Foxglove transformed to white hot fire; by some miracle, their flames did not travel to anything else, only the Foxglove. It seared his nose; they had no choice but to return to the forest. By chance, Rian spotted their friends scrambling through the streets as chaos filled the air.

Fae ran in all directions from the explosions around them. Nia had not intended to release the poison. She prayed the mist would not last long. The world around her shook as she breathed it in. Torrin reached the pair as they stumbled to their knees, Uaine shoved the girl towards his friend. "Go!" Uaine screeched. His emerald eyes grew luminous.

Nia struggled to free herself from Torrin's grip, as the poison dug into her mind. As he pulled her away from their friend, away from the burning city. She could not believe it, they had left Uaine behind. His pained eyes and dust covered face haunted her thoughts. Her hands thrashed against Torrin as he dragged her further away; back through the forest where he had left Rian.

"What are you doing?" She roared as he eventually released her, no longer able to hold the thrashing girl; it sent her tumbling to the ground. "We have to go back." Nia struggled to stand; her legs shook as she pulled herself up. Her lungs burned. "We cannot go back Nia, not until that damned Foxglove clears the air. *What were you thinking*?" Torrin snapped as he paced, running his fingers through his copper hair for the hundredth time that night. "I was thinking if I could not burn that hovel to the ground, I would destroy their means of torturing my sisters." Nia snarled back. *How dare he question my intentions?* Her mind raged. Torrins brows raised at the venom dripping from her tone. *What is she talking about?* He asked himself as she paced.

"*Your sisters?* I understand you might find some solidarity in their situation, and Nia I am sorry for the cruelty of this court, it is something I would change in a heartbeat if it were so simple, but you have no idea what you have done. That city will be filled with carnage for days, that much Foxglove can send the strongest Fae to the brink." Regret battled with her fury. She had not meant to cause more suffering.

Nia had wished only to end the torture of the women. Instead, she had caused them much more pain. "Will it clear?" Her voice shook, Torrin sighed; the night had truly exhausted him. As her eyes still burned, he knew it was not yet over. "It will, but I do not know how long it will take." Torrin told her honestly, Nia glared in return. "We must press on, Ciar will know you have moved on from the Silver Court and the Faelcu have much less restrictions here." Torrin groaned at her protests, as she crossed her arms and sneered at him; as she argued that they would go nowhere, except back into the fog to rescue their friend.

He had to drag her once more, kicking and screaming through the forest; hoping that eventually she would tire, and that foul poison would leave her blood. Nia cursed him, screeched at him; calling him everything from coward to bastard. He could not find the strength to cover her mouth, to hush her screams; even as Rian covered his ears. Too exhausted to do much else but pull her away from the city, he let her roars blend with those of the hundreds of Fae still trapped beneath that deadly violet mist.

Chapter Seventeen:

Uaine choked as he looked around, everything a haze of violet, from the buildings aflame to the purple dust floating in the air; It was as if a woollen blanket had wrapped around the city, suffocating it. His lungs burned with that bitter stench as Fae scrambled around, the women were much better off; although that was not saying much, they had built a resistance to the toxin. The men did not share this same fate. Uaine cursed them, they were fools to use such a vile method of torture and more foolish still for never creating a defence for it. He looked around as Fae scrambled past him, some covered their faces with cloth, others scratched at their skin; as if trying to purge the poison from their blood.

It was no use. The toxic mist would take days, if not weeks, to clear. They had no choice but to attempt to endure what may come. Uaine did what he could for the women fleeing, until he felt his limbs grow skittish and his mind grew bitter. As he crawled to the town centre, to find a building he might hide in; Uaines vision began to fade. He barely felt the hands that clutched his shoulders and dragged his lifeless body into the air. He fell with a thud onto a pile of limbs atop a cart; his destination? He did not know.

Nia and Torrin had not spoken since the night before. Violet fog still rippled from the South, Nia could not stop the guilt that washed through her as plumes of it flowed and ebbed nearby. Rian sat awkwardly between them, his furry companion at his side. The young Fae did not know what to say, there was nothing he could muster that would ease the tension. Even the hounds' ears dipped, as if it sensed the unspoken anger coursing between the two Fae. Torrin thought of his friend, trapped in that toxic city, and dug his boot into the earth once more. He did not look up as Nia left the camp they had made in the night; when she had stopped screeching to return to the burning city.

Rian looked pleadingly at his brother. Torrin turned his head. Nia scoffed and grabbed her bow before storming in the opposite direction of the billowing smoke. She let the peace of the woods fill her as she traversed through the tall grass. She did not know where she was going, only that she needed to escape Torrins accusing eyes and the eerie silence that had fallen over their group. Nia tucked her bow at her back, no animals wandered this forest.

It is strange, she mused, *I have seen neither squirrel nor deer; save for Madigan and the bees, animals do not dwell here.*

This thought unnerved her, if even the animals would not roam this court; she had been an utter fool to run into the jaws of it. Nia took rest upon a fallen tree; glossy red capped mushrooms lined its base; white spots scattered across its top. Mushrooms grew all around, stranger than she had ever seen before. On the ground some had bright orange stalks and a deep red cap, others climbed up the tree like a sheet of blue velvet. One caught her eye; it was a bright red ball. She brought her face closer, and her nose wrinkled as the stink of rotting meat invaded her senses. Nia reached to prod at the odd surface, she had never seen a mushroom like it; for it was not just smooth and round, it had smaller holes indented on it and a design within the smaller circles that almost looked like flowers. It was beautiful, even if it stank of rotting meat.

Her finger had almost reached the squishy cap, when a flash of silver blinded her, and a cold hand wrapped around her wrist. "I would not do that if I were you." Lorcan chuckled. Nia nearly fell with fright. His silver eyes turned serious and dark, still bruised from Torrins onslaught, as he looked at Nias deathly pale face. Her eyes, which neither Torrin nor Rian had met, flashed between burning red and soothing lilac.

"Who did this?" He snarled as he took in her appearance. Nias scarlet hair was frazzled, singed at the ends where the flames had almost swallowed her, pale skin dotted with purple welts and yellowing bruises. Lorcan could barely look at her face, at the healing gash on her forehead or the fresh bruises sprouting across her cheeks and neck.

It angered him far more than he thought it should.

Nia felt true tears well in her eyes, she was no longer acting to gain his favour; she still cared for her plan, still wanted to free the slaves of the silver Court. Yet, she had never felt *so alone* and for a moment, Nia decided to wallow in her own guilt. "I have made a horrible mistake." Nia sobbed and threw herself into the arms of the Fae prince. Lorcan stumbled backwards at the unexpected strength of the girl. Still, he wrapped his arms around her as her shoulders shook. "It could not have been that bad." He reasoned, yet he scarcely believed his own words; news had travelled like fayfire of the burning city of Bréaga. Lorcan had smelled it the second his feet touched the ground, rotten bitter fruits. The sky above the city had turned a shade of plum. "I killed Uaine." At that, Lorcan stilled. *Surely not,* he thought.

"I do not believe you would do such a thing willingly." Lorcan said cautiously, some flowers were known to drive Fae insane and turn even the purest Elven heart to darkness. Foxglove had been banned in most courts for this exact reason eons ago. *What has the Emerald Court been up to?* He wondered. Nia hiccupped as she pulled away and wiped her hand across her face. She winced as she received a painful reminder of her state. Fresh bruises littered her skin. "We left him, he rescued me, and we left him to die... Torrin left him to die." She knew this was not fair, Uaine had begged them to run, he had screamed at them to leave him behind.

"No, that is wrong of me." She scolded herself before Lorcan had a chance to insult Torrin. "I was foolish, I acted on impulse. They had women in stocks for using their magic." At the memory of this she shuddered. Lorcan held his tongue, for he knew his own Court was no better. "I could not leave them, could not let them rot in their wooden prisons for all to torment... So, I freed the women and set fire to the stocks and their brothels." She would do it again too, regardless of how it had ended.

"They... They were not too happy with me for this, two men took me to the cells. I have a fair idea what they intended to do to me there." Nia shuddered once again as his eyes burned with more fury than she had ever seen. Lorcan cursed the cruelty of Fae. "I'll skin them alive." He seethed. It surprised her, the sheer honesty in his voice. Nia had no doubt as she looked at him; that he would have torn them to pieces.

"I almost flayed them where they stood, they thought they could contain me. They were mistaken." Lorcan smirked down at her, a stark contrast to Torrin's judgement. He was impressed, this much he could not deny; she had grown far more vicious on her travels. "I would warrant they were quite surprised when this pretty little thing turned against them." Nia was in no mood for his condescending compliments. In truth, he spoke sincerely, he admired her strength; he would have enjoyed watching the shock on their faces as she turned against them.

Lorcan wondered how much damage she could do with a suit of armour and a sword in her hand.

"Uaine tried to warn me, that burning the city to ash would bring no good. I should have listened, like a fool I thought I could do them one favour if we were to abandon them. I set alight the purple flowers they had tried to poison me with. I turned it into a gas and now it is burning my friends' lungs because I thought of myself as their saviour, like a zealous idiot." Nias chest heaved as she finished speaking, gasping for air.

Lorcan helped her to a nearby rock to rest her shaking limbs. "They deserved it." Lorcan shrugged, only to backtrack as Nias eyes glared up at him. He raised his hands in surrender. "Okay, *Uaine* did not deserve it, but he would have willingly thrown himself onto a pyre of that poison if it meant saving you." At this her brows furrowed. "You say this as if you know it." "I do know it, because as he would; so would I." He relished in the bright scarlet shade her face flushed before continuing. "You forget Nia, we have a long and painful history. We were once friends, before our fathers ruined our families. Uaine has always wished to return home, to retake his court."

"What do you mean *retake his court*?"

Although Nia knew Uaine was an Emerald Lord, they had not divulged his history and she had just assumed he was an estranged Noble of the court exiled for siding with Torrin. Nia reminded herself not to assume anything about this place again. His brows rose. "Do you mean they did not tell you?"

Lorcan was surprised, for how could they not tell her when they passed this city on their journey?

"They are the fools then Nia, for they should have known how you would feel once you saw this place. Uaine is the last true High Lord of the Emerald Court, his father sold his Court to Ciar in return for his mother's whereabouts. She made it to the Sapphire Court just in time to hide Uaine before he struck the deal. I assume she told him that she killed the child for none have ever searched for Uaine. None have met the High Lord whom Ciar appointed, for an emissary attends any meetings that may take place, but even Torrin knew what happens here."

Several realisations hit Nia at once: Torrin knew of this wretched place and did not warn her, Uaine had lied to her about who he was. If Lorcan knew of him and still none had come looking, then Lorcan had kept their secret. *Why would he do such a thing if they were enemies? She* wondered. Everything felt backwards. "You should return to Torrin, if he awakes and you are gone, he will level the forest to find you. I know I would." Nia scoffed at that, Lorcan cocked a brow with curiosity. "He would rather I be gone; I am no more than a risk to their lives. They are better without my interference." Lorcan shook his head. Nia watched as his demeanour changed, his shoulders became stiff; his eyes filled with worry. He could sense his brothers travelling towards him, goosebumps rose across his skin. If Aidan caught him there, speaking to the girl, he would drag them both to the Silver Court. Torrin would be dead.

"I do not have the time to explain but you are wrong, utterly and totally wrong. Now, you must listen to me; run back to your camp and get out of this damned court. Tell Torrin my brothers are coming." Lorcan warned, for a parting gift he laid his palm against her cheek. Nia felt a warmness like no other fill her, from the tips of her toes to the roots of her hair, she felt refreshed.

Without questioning him, Nia turned and ran as she felt the air crackle. The same static which had hummed in her bones just before Lorcan arrived. Nia did not dare turn her head as she heard them arrive, not wanting to see the monsters she had read about; if only so that she could convince herself, Lorcan was not like them. *I must warn Torrin*, Nia gasped for air as she ran, whether he would heed her words or not; she would still protect him. Even if she was furious at his lies.

If only I had known, this could have been avoided.

Chapter Eighteen:

Duane glared venomously as billows of violet smoke erupted from the Emerald Court, he had been in the tavern sleeping peacefully when the whole city was engulfed in chaos. Barely, he escaped as barrels and carts burst into flames. *It must be her,* he thought. He knew his enchantments had not entirely failed him, for she had accepted his gifts and sent his emissary along with words of forgiveness. *Now to find her*, he spat on the earth at his feet as he wiped ash from his coat.

"Duane!" A voice called merrily in the distance; he stifled a groan as he turned to greet the six Silver Princes. It was an insult to him that Ciar had forced him to share his title. The eldest of them, Aidan, approached him first. They were all the same to him, with their silver eyes and jet-black hair, only by the sigils on their cloaks could he tell them apart. They greeted him in chronological order, Duane resisted the urge to laugh at their ridiculous formality. He hated it, the politics of the Fae world. He could rip them to pieces if only it would not displease Ciar.

Bradan, Caden, Eoghan, Keegan and Lorcan followed Aidan. To most, it was an intimidating sight. Duane had lived too long, seen too much to fear them, they were children to him. "Some event, eh?" Aidan nudged the Gold Prince. Duane was good at keeping them oblivious to the threat he posed, and his own grin grew on his face. "What a shame, I should have visited a brothel first." Duane laughed as they looked back towards the city. Eoghan snorted at this. "You would have met the Scarlet Death should you have done so." Duane howled with laughter at that. Thinking of the soft, pathetic girl he had toyed with brought tears to his eyes as his laughter grew louder. "The Scarlet Death? Who in Etherea named that stupid little girl such?" He asked as he guffawed. Keegan looked curiously at the golden eyed Fae. "You know her?" Keegan asked when Duane had regained his composure.

Duane rubbed his eyes of the tears which flowed; he had laughed harder than he had in an exceptionally long time. "Know her? I had her wrapped around my finger until that bastard Torrin got in the way." Lorcan eyed him curiously, Nia had not spoken of Duane once to him, although he had only spent a fleeting time with her. "Forgive us, Duane, but our scouts have reported many things that contradict your words. Not forgetting how she killed not one, but two of your Faelcu as a mortal, she has since boiled an Abhartach from within, survived and killed an Ellén Trechend beneath the mountain; now she has burned those brothels to the ground and poisoned half of the Emerald Court." Lorcans brothers laughed as he came to the girls' defence. "Our brother has become a lover of hers it seems." Caden nudged his younger brother in jest.

Duane scoffed at that. "I *will* admit her ass isn't half bad to look at." he chortled. Lorcan felt his fists curl in his pockets. Aidan sensed the shift in his little brother's demeanour and threw his arm around Duanes shoulders. "We have come to aid the evacuation of the city on Ciars command, as I am sure you have too." Duane had not heard from Ciar since he revealed his failure to capture Elvinia. Duane grumbled a response as Aidan handed him an antidote before they trudged through the thick purple fog. Bradan coughed as it took a moment for the antidote to take effect. "Lorcan, Keegan, take the carts and gather any survivors. Eoghan, Bradan, set up camps outside the city. Duane, Caden and I will find the women." Aidan's smirk made Lorcans gut twist. He pitied any who found themselves in the path of his brothers, especially Caden.

The group disbanded, Lorcan kept the grimace from his face as he looked at the carnage Nia had wrought. He knew he was different from his brothers, but he did not know why. They had no care, no sympathy for anything. Maybe it was because they had known their father much longer, had served under Ciar and tore through Etherea with little consequence. He had spent only a fraction of their time at war and found he enjoyed it even less. Keegan kicked the Fae at his feet as Lorcan rolled them over. He scoffed at his brother's softness. "We do not have time to be gentle Lorcan, Aidan will have our heads should we fail this task, come on." Lorcan rolled his eyes, Keegan would do anything out of fear, but he listened all the same.

As they dragged the lifeless, yet living, Fae from the ground Lorcans shoulders ached. They pulled the carts, brimmed with bodies, out of the city. On their third run, as Lorcan grabbed the cart handles to leave once more; a glint of green caught his eye, Uaine lay in the dust. His eyes still wide open, terror on his face. Lorcan dropped the cart and hoisted him onto his shoulder. He could not leave him but knew taking him to their camps could still prove fatal. *It is better*, Lorcan decided, *to give him a chance.* With that thought he threw Uaine atop the pile and grunted at the weight of the cart as he dragged it away.

"Of course, *we* get stuck with lifting these stinking assholes through the mud while *they* have all the fun." Keegan groaned as a woman's scream rang through the air. Lorcan prayed Nia was far, far away. He did not want her to attack his brothers, not yet anyway; not if he was to gain her favour and ask for her aid. They would never trust her in their Court should she attack this day. He wished that she could, as more screams began.

Uaine awoke as his face slapped against cold mud. The air was clean at least, but it would do no good until he received an antidote. The fog still clung to his lungs, scratched at his mind as he looked around in fear. Silver sigils lined the camp on flags and cloaks. Uaine choked on a cough, he would rather suffocate than draw attention to himself. He proved unbelievably unlucky as boots walked towards him, squelching in the wet mud, he barely had the strength to change the colour of his eyes. "I recognise this one, that's the little bastard Torrin took in." Duane laughed at the wide-eyed Fae, *so she is close*, he realised. "Leave this one to rot for a while." He told Lorcan, who scoffed in return. "I do not take orders from you." "Oh come on dear brother, Duane has suffered enough in his failure to capture the princess, let him have his fun with the low-born." Aidan chuckled, he knew enraging Duane was not worth it and he could handle his little brother; although he could not resist his own jab towards his rival.

Lorcan begrudgingly walked away but did Uaine the mercy of setting his eyes to a permanent hazel. Uaine wondered why Lorcan did not tell them who he was. *He must want to take me to Ciar himself,* he reasoned; although reason was the last thing Uaine could muster. Duane kicked the low-born Fae. Uaine felt the last of his strength leave him as he glared up at Duane, surely, he would see the Emerald eyes staring up at him. When Duane did nothing but kick him again, Uaines fading vision cast to Lorcans retreating figure.

#

Nia ran through the woods as fast as she could, her feet sloshing against the wet grass. Torrin jumped, sword in hand as she crashed through the treeline; breathless, Nia grasped the bark of a towering oak as she gasped for air. Torrin studied her appearance, there was not a single mark on her; only fear in her eyes. "Lorcan... Brothers... Here." Was all she could manage. It was all that was needed. Torrin whipped up their supplies as Nia helped Rian on her back. The young Fae was not happy about this but knew he could not keep up with them. "Are they really so terrible?" Nia asked as they took off North, opposite of the city, opposite of Uaine. Her heart clenched at leaving him behind once more. Screams erupting in the forest answered her question. Torrin gripped her hand as pain ripped across her face.

His anger disappeared as he finally looked in Nias eyes, still violently flashing between scarlet and lilac. *Tormented*. He faltered at the guilt that wracked his gut. "That could not be him." Nia cried, flinching at the jealousy that rippled from Torrin. "I am sure it is not, he would be gathering survivors." It pained Torrin to admit it, but he knew deep down Lorcan was not *terrible*. He had been painted with the same brush as his brothers and as the centuries passed without sign of salvation; Lorcan had no choice but to allow them to consistently torment Etherea or risk their barbarity on himself. It had been the theft of his sister which had turned Torrin cold toward the youngest prince.

Nia hoped that Lorcan would protect Uaine should he find him- *if he found him alive*. "We must keep going." Rian said hurriedly as he clung to her neck. "They will be rounding up the women who escaped." Nia tried desperately to ignore their screams, to push away their pain as it crashed into her. Torrin gripped her hand tighter as they ran once more. They did not stop until another sun had fallen and risen again. Their limbs ached, their bodies caked in mud, they were exhausted. Rian had pointed to an opening in the hill before them, to a cave which might offer them rest. The screams were a whisper, the stench of the city barely tickled her nose. Nia sobbed with relief as they veered towards the cave. Torrin was sure they would not go this far to retrieve the runaways. Rian clambered from Nias back with a grunt and scratched the ear of the hound as it rested on the cave floor.

Their stomachs screamed at them. "I will find us food." Nia decided as her hands shook. Her mind was scrambled; she had been ready to kill them all. Without waiting for a response Nia left the cave, she did not wish to sit in the silence; to see their eyes judging her, watching her. Rian glared at his brother once more. "If you do not follow her and apologise, I will find her and we will leave your ass behind." Rian hissed at his elder, Torrin rolled his eyes at his little brothers' stubbornness; it mirrored his own. Torrin found Nia nearby, clutching a handful of dandelions and wild garlic. "How can I help?" He spoke softly, unsure of how to begin. Nia jumped and cocked a brow as she turned to glare at him. "You can tell me why you did not inform me who exactly Uaine is." Torrin's eyes widened at the accusation in her tone, she watched frustration wash across his face. "It was not my business to tell you." Nia scoffed, unwilling to accept his excuse.

"In the scheme of things, I think at least a *warning* of the vile practices of this court was deserved; you saw it fit to tell me quickly of the Silver Court slaves but not the tortured women of the Emerald Court, or how a usurper sits in Uaines stead." Torrin let loose a breath to calm himself; if he argued he may lose her once again. Her eyes still wavered, two halves battling for control. "I am sorry Nia; I did not mean to cause this." He said truthfully. Nias shoulders eased as she picked comfrey, sweet woodruff, and sorrel; stuffing them into her pockets. "I am sorry too, I should not have been so stupid." She chastised herself once more.

Blue eyes filled with guilt as they looked at her. "You are not stupid Nia, you went with the purest of intentions." Torrin reasoned as he reached for her, Nia shook her head as his hands took hers. "Look at me." He told her firmly, Nias tormented eyes met his reluctantly. "We were fools to think we could keep anything from you, especially if we are to journey across Etherea to Galeria. Uaine will be okay, he will join us on our way or meet us at Galeria. It was noble of you to try; I am ashamed to say I cowered from interfering for far too long." Nia frowned at him and raised a hand to cup his face. Her breath had steadied, for a second her mind cleared.

"You lost *everything* Torrin, no one could blame you for wanting to keep your peace." Tears welled in his eyes at her conviction. Nia threw her arms around him; she could barely fit around his wide frame but hugged him tightly all the same; she drank in that sweet smell of apples and cinnamon once more. "Thank you." Torrin choked. He would rarely show it, but the loss of his people had devastated him much more than the loss of growth in his lands.

"Still, I must admit, before you arrived, I was preparing for a journey to Ciars castle. I was ready for whatever may come if it would return my people, I would have bent the knee... I would have done anything." It sickened him to admit it. Nia rubbed his back and let out a sigh. "You were willing to brave my father's cruelty for the sake of your people, I would not call that cowardice Torrin, I would call that courage. If my mother could not defeat him with an army at her back, you had no chance with half of Etherea trapped beneath the earth." Her reasoning was sound, Torrin could not argue and pulled back to give her a grateful smile.

Nia released him when his tears had dried. "I shall make soup and we shall rest, and then we will find Galeria and hopefully Abbán will have answers." Nia spoke decisively, Torrin could only follow her as she gathered more herbs. He had come to comfort her, and yet it was she who helped soothe the ache in him. Feeling useless, Torrin praised the Fates as he spotted a nearby birds' nest. Nia watched him curiously as he climbed the tree to their left. "What are yo-" Her words were cut short as he dropped from the air in front of her. He held in his hand four eggs.

Nia felt pity for the bird even as her stomach grumbled and took two from him. "Return those to the nest." Torrin cocked his head at the girl, he heard her stomach growling. "Nia, we must eat." "And we will, this will be enough." She snapped at him. Torrin sighed with defeat and climbed the tree once more. He could have eaten the bird itself at that moment. They returned to the cave with a plethora of herbs, berries, and the eggs. Rians eyes lit with excitement as Nia began to cook, the smell of their oncoming meal wafted within the stone walls of the cave. Their stomachs roared by the time

Nia had finished. They swallowed the food quickly, even as it burned their tongues. Finally fed, the exhaustion of their journey finally overcame them. Rian and Madigan curled at the back of the cave, Nia found herself under Torrins arm and let his warmth soothe her restless bones until finally, her heavy lids closed.

Chapter Nineteen:

Uaine woke once more, still in that miserable camp. He had been left out in the mud as rain cascaded from the heavens. It stung his face, not enough to burn through his skin, but it hurt all the same as it slapped against him. Lorcan sat in his tent while his brothers bickered. He found his mind filled with thoughts of Nia, he hoped she had reached safety. Uaine grit his teeth as he realised his hands and feet had been bound. An emissary trudged through the camp, filled with groaning men, and captured women. His lips curled with disgust as he stepped over the dirt covered Fae on the ground- including Uaine.

Lorcan and his brothers glanced to the entrance as the emissary entered their tent. Duane sneered at the brunette's faltering confidence as he looked upon the seven Princes of Etherea, he had not expected to find them all sitting together as chaos reigned outside. "Good evening your Grace's, I have been sent by our Lord to retrieve witnesses to what attacked the city." The emissary explained, hoping it would be a brief visit. Aidan, ever the politician, smiled warmly at the man. Lorcan rolled his eyes behind their backs as Aidan swung his arm around the emissary and squeezed him just a tad too tight. "Of course, for what kind of Princes would we be if we did not aid our people? Choose who you will and send our regards to your Lord." A ghost could run the Emerald Court for all they knew.

They watched as the emissary nodded and scurried out of the tent. Lorcan could not blame him, they were the seven most powerful Fae men in Etherea; it was just a pity they were all barbarians. The emissary scoured through the camp. He took three women and four men. Lorcan clenched his jaw as Uaine was dragged along with the others. He had managed to slip him the antidote in the night, but it would take time to truly reverse the Foxglove effects. Duane grumbled that he had lost his plaything, Lorcan contemplated warning Nia and Torrin.

Lorcan had no doubt that Nia would tear the High Lords Manor down, brick by brick, if it meant saving Uaine. If he could convince his brothers to leave this place, he could help. Lorcan sat silently as he pondered how he might enact his plan. As long as he remained blameless, he could cripple the Emerald Court from within; return Uaine to his birthright, and he would have an ally in what was to come.

As if the Fates had answered, a young boy ran into the tent. Wearing the traditional green scout uniform, his eyes darted between the towering Fae before him. "They are north of here, in a cave by the Nimae river." The scout told them, breathless. His brothers whooped and cheered, Lorcan joined them. "Lorcan, you man the camp, do not worry; I will let you have your way with that pretty thing before we hand her over to Ciar." Aidan winked with a grin before they set out on the chase. Lorcan thanked the Fates for his brothers sadistic need to chase their prey as he disappeared in a flash.

Cold steel pressed against his throat as his feet landed inside the cave.

Nia blinked twice and jumped as a strange man appeared before her "Torrin!" Nia yelled as she dug her dagger against the stranger's neck. "Nia." The man sighed; her brows knit close as she stared at him. Spearmint and honey wafted in her nose. "Lorcan?" She gasped. Relief coursed through her. Nia almost threw her arms around him. "I do not have time, they know where you are, Uaine is in far more trouble than I thought. I can take you to your destination or I can take you to Uaine, but you must choose." Lorcan knew it was no choice at all, she would not abandon Uaine again. Torrin and Rian ran into the cave, weapons drawn. Nia panicked, as Torrin raised his sword and swung. The shining steel came whistling towards Lorcan, a spark within Nia flickered; pure instinct overwhelmed her.

"Wait!" Nia jumped to knock Torrin's sword from its swing without a second thought, cursing as the steel sliced her flesh, *"It's Lorcan."* They stilled as she hissed, holding her gushing arm. Lorcan audibly gasped, he could not believe she would do such a thing. Without hesitation, she had taken the blow meant for him.

Torrin blinked, before he could move Lorcan had gripped her arm; her blood coated his hands. Nia watched as silver ribbons wrapped around the gash, in an instant it was gone. Lorcan sighed with relief as she smiled up at him in thanks. "Never do that again." He pleaded as he pulled her into his embrace. Torrin's jaw fell slack at the love-struck haze in Nia's eyes as she pulled away.

She has never looked at me that way.

He looked between the pair in disbelief as Nia relayed their situation to them. Torrin grit his teeth. "I have to save him, but you need to reach Galeria." He sighed; Nia glowered at him. She had grown tired of his constant need to push her to safety. *It has done me no good so far,* she thought bitterly. "Galeria is not going anywhere, Uaine might die. We go to Uaine." Nia did not give Torrin a moment to argue as she grabbed him and Rian before shoving herself into Lorcans arms. "Go, now." She snapped. Lorcan laughed, her stubbornness gave him joy. Torrin should have known better than to suggest she leave her friend behind. They whistled through the air. Nia felt nausea rip through her as her body morphed into the air around them.

Uaine dipped in and out of consciousness as they dragged his body through the mud, until they threw him on an icy marble floor. *The High Lords' home*, he realised. There was uniformity to their homes, always adorned with the highest quality marble infused with the mineral from their court. Uaine could barely raise his head as he was dragged across the floor; they threw him to the ground before an empty Lords chair. The room cleared, Uaine pulled himself to his feet. The clicking of heels behind him had Uaine spinning around. A *woman* stepped across the floor, her blonde hair tied in a sinister bun, Emerald eyes glittering in the light.

Uaine blinked twice, she looked just like his mother. She did not spare him a glance as she took her seat upon the Lord's chair.

The woman looked at him then, her eyes cold narrowed as they assessed him. "Who are you?" She demanded, Uaine faltered. "My name is Brady." Her lips curled into a snarl, sensing his deceit, with a wave of her hand she sent whisps of jade coloured light clattering against his cheek. Uaine stumbled backwards as his face stung, her eyes burned with fury. "Do not lie to me." She seethed. "I have not lied my lady." Another blow struck his face as she stood from her throne. "Test me once more and you shall not walk out of this room." She threatened, slighted by his insolence, infuriated by his lies. "Uaine, my name is Uaine." He relented as he felt his throat close. Her eyes narrowed even further; she took a moment to consider his answer before releasing his neck.

Uaine gulped a breath of air as she peered at him through those narrow slits. Her teeth bared as she waved her hand once again. Lorcans spell dissipated and Uaine's eyes glowed green once more. "*You.*" She snarled and lunged for the confused Fae. Uaine barely side-stepped her and raised his fists to defend himself. He did not enjoy fighting women, but he would not die in his own home at the hands of this one. "Who are you?" Uaine gasped before her fist connected with his jaw. She laughed, shrill and manic.

"Do you mean to tell me you do not know?" She hissed as he returned her blow. "I should have known, *you* were always her favourite." She used her magic to shove a blast of air against Uaines chest, he flew towards the marble wall. His back clattered against the rigid surface; it knocked the air from his lungs. "Have you never wondered why *you* survived? We were born in a war, twins, entering this cursed land seconds apart. When they demanded her first-born, she handed *me* over like it was *nothing.*" she spat at Uaine, detested the shock on his face "Maeve?" Uaine gasped. He had not thought of her in centuries. Technically younger by a fraction of a second, they had entered the world in the same breath.

He had searched for years after the last war, when their parents failed, but assumed his mother did not have time to save them both. He thought her to be dead, not ruling a court of torture. A sinister grin spread across his long-lost twins' face. "So, you did not forget me entirely." Maeve snickered as she shoved her brother once more with her power. Uaine gripped a nearby table to help him stand, he could not stop the glare he gave her. "I looked for you, for *years*, how was I to find you when none knew of your existence?" He snapped back at her, they were children, he would not be blamed for what happened. A snort escaped Maeve. "I have given up *everything* for you and here you are, beaten, broken and captured. Our father may have been a rotten bastard, but for *you* I grit my teeth and took Ciars abuse; until he grew tired of me and tossed me out like I was trash. By the time I slit the throat of the cunt ruling our

Court, it was too late, one woman against a hundred thousand men? I think not, so I allowed it to continue in hopes that you would grow a pair and storm the gates with Torrin and whatever allies you may have. Yet, it seems to have been in vain." There was no remorse in her tone.

Maeve had no regrets; she had done what was needed to survive. Uaine stared at her, slack jawed as she paced the room, fury rippled from her. "Where are your companions?" She demanded. Uaine cast his eyes to the floor, a vase crashed against the wall behind him. "Uaine Ó Loinsigh, so help me if you do not answer me, I will send soldiers to find them, and I will have Torrins pretty blue eyes ripped out and boiled." Maeve seethed, Uaine glared at his sister. "You will do no such thing." He snapped back at her. "You are a coward!" She flung another vase at him, Uaine ducked the ceramic whistling through the air.

The air crackled behind him; the vase did not shatter.

Maeve's eyes widened with shock. Uaine spun on his heels. Torrin, Nia, Rian, even the damned dog, and a stranger appeared in the room. Lorcan held the vase in his hand as he took in the scene before him, the furious emerald eyed woman glaring back at them. Nia choked on the suffering in the camp below, felt the poison tickle her nostrils once more. As if by instinct, Lorcan entwined his fingers with Nia's, sensing her discomfort. His jaw dropped as he absorbed Maeve's appearance, the crown atop her head. "*You* are the High Lord?" He asked in disbelief; Maeve bared her teeth as a whip of air swung towards him. Lorcan's disguise disappeared. Nia glared at the forest green rope and raised her hand without a second thought. She gripped it in her hand, hissed as it burned, twisted it around her knuckles and *yanked*.

Maeve stumbled in shock before fire flew from Nias fingertips. Fuelled by the agony flowing from the women of the court to her veins, Nia felt her teeth bare. Lorcan tried to pull her back, Nia yanked herself from his grip. "She will burn for what she has done." Uaine ran to his sister, shoving her out of the way as the flames flickered against his back. Nia jumped back with surprise, extinguishing the fire in an instant. Torrin looked between the two, carbon copies of each other. "Is this her?" Torrin asked Uaine softly, Nia blinked and watched with disbelief as Torrin stepped towards the blonde woman. Lorcan gripped her hand once more to comfort her, *how have they left her so blind to their histories?* He wondered, they were fools to do so; for it left her unprepared and vulnerable in a world where so much was intertwined.

Maeve wrestled herself from Uaine's grip, glaring at him as she dusted off her elegant green gown. "So, this is the Scarlet Death?" Maeve grinned at Nia, there was no coldness behind it this time. Even she had heard of the Elven girl, tearing across the Realm. Nia frowned at the name, Lorcan almost laughed at the grimace on her face; it seemed she was not a fan of her new nickname. "My name is Nia, not... *that.*" Nia said cautiously, still utterly confused. Uaine sighed and ran a

hand through his hair. "Nia, this is my sister, Maeve."
Annoyance filled Nia once again. She no longer held control
of her emotions, she had succumbed to her instincts;
whether they be good or not.

"Do you mean to tell me that not only did you withhold
information that you are in fact *the* High Lord, but that you
have a sister who runs a court of torture?" Nia seethed, her
eyes snapped to Maeve, her thoughts as fractured as the
colours swirling in her orbs, "*and you*, you have the audacity
to torture the women of your city as if the men here would
not turn on you in an instant?" Nia snarled at her, ice in her
veins. It disgusted her. A man at the helm would have been
no surprise, but a woman inflicting such misery? Nia could
not stand it.

The ice that shot from her palm shocked them all.

Nia felt it appropriate, it was a cold fury that raged within her
after all. Maeve bit back a scream as the ice pierced her
shoulder, pinning her against the wall. Torrin stepped
towards Nia, the pain on Maeve's face sent a shiver through
him, only he found himself rooted to the floor. Rian had no
choice but to bitterly watch it all unfold. As always. "*Oh,
excuse me*, we are not all gifted with the power of a
thousand suns, *your majesty*. I survived, and I would do it
again." Maeve seethed as pain coursed through her. Nia took
pause at her words and ripped the ice from the girl's limb.
What am I doing? Nia questioned herself as she shook her
head. Maeve whimpered as the wound healed. Uaine stared

at Nia with worry, her eyes had not settled; her actions were not usual.

Nia stepped towards the blonde on the floor and reached to aid her to her feet. Maeve sighed as she peered at Nia's hand, there was only one way to explain. Lightening shot through Nias body; her limbs shook as a thousand images flashed within her mind. "Do not touch her." Uaine yelled as Lorcan ran to pull Nia away. It felt like eons for Nia, as she lived through every awful thing Maeve had experienced at the hands of her father.

 As she fell away, tears cascaded down Nia's face. Maeve glared at her. "Now you know, do you disagree?" Nia wretched and shook her head. "She had no choice... *No choice at all.*" Nia sobbed, she had felt the abuse Ciar inflicted on Maeve, she wanted to scorch her own skin. It was too much; it was all far too much. Like a crack in a dam, each ounce of pain around her threatened to release the floodgates of darkness in her mind.

Lorcan looked at the troubled girl, Nia felt his pain. "I will stay, if you need me to stay, just say the word." To hell with his plan, to hell with his Court. Lorcan could not deny he cared for nothing else, only her. Nia shook her head, tears still brimming against her lids. "You must return to your brothers, before they realise you are gone." Nia blushed at the adoration in his eyes. "You are truly unbelievable, until we meet again."

Maeve rose as Lorcan turned. "Wait, take this letter. It will send them away and give us time to escape." Maeve quickly wrote and sealed a letter thanking the princes for their aid and a false sighting of Nia towards the South to keep them occupied. Lorcan took it gratefully, Nia gripped his hand before he left. "Thank you." She told him before placing a kiss on his cheek. Filled with a genuine sorrow at leaving of her, and a sliver of triumph as Torrin glared at him, Lorcan evaporated. The room filled with eerie silence, tempers still flared, unanswered questions filled their minds. Nia rubbed her tired eyes and looked between the Fae around her.

"We need to talk."

Chapter Twenty:

Lorcan took his seat, just as hit brothers re-entered the tent. "Where are they?" Lorcan asked, Caden spat on the ground. "The scouts were wrong, we found nothing there." They were displeased. His brothers only enjoyed one thing more than the hunt; the fear on their victims faces once they were caught. "Perhaps they heard you, hooting through the forest, and took their chances with the river." Lorcan scolded, Aidan laughed once more at his youngest brother. "Perhaps we should send you, *oh wise one*, since you were so sure you had gained her favour after Torrins little dance." Aidan teased, Lorcan wanted to agree; but he knew appearing too eager would raise suspicion. Duane raised a brow at this, so Lorcan had met the little Elf; and she had not ripped his head off. *Curious*, he thought, *curious indeed*.

"I would not wish to embarrass you, by succeeding where six of you have failed." Lorcan teased in return, Bradan howled with laughter. "The ways of wicked women still escape you little brother, I would not go chasing this one alone." He grinned as he slapped Lorcans back. "A letter came while you were gone." Lorcan told them, wishing to change the subject before they began describing how they could tame wicked women. Aidan took the roll of parchment from his hand and frowned as he read the words. "We have been tricked." He started, Lorcans pulse quickened. *I should have read that damned letter*, he thought. "They have gone back south; we are to follow this lead. The High Lord will send troops to aid the camp and thanks us for our aid." Lorcan knew if Duane were not here, Aidan would have scoffed at the thanks and cursed the unknown lord.

"I will take my leave then, as I have other business to attend to; for our King." Duane did not believe for a second that Nia had returned south. They would not have come this far unless they were looking for something, nor would they turn and abandon their pursuit. So, they parted ways. As Lorcan suspected, the moment Duane had left earshot, Aidan ripped the letter in his hands. "Who does this obscure bastard think he is? Thanks for the help, now off you go. If he did not have favour with Ciar I would rip him to shreds." He seethed, Lorcan struggled not to roll his eyes; the High Fae had such tempers. Despite their contempt, the brothers packed up and left the camp of recovering Fae. Lorcan said one last silent prayer for Nias safety as they vanished.

Duane did not believe the letter one bit, the cave reeked of her; she smelled just like her mother, citrus sweet. *She must have infiltrated the High Lords home*, he realised, *clever bitch*. Duane turned his attention to the towering Emerald Manor atop the hill before the camp. If Nia were anything like Riona, Duane knew she would be swaying the High Lord in her favour. He could not return to Ciar without Nia, and he certainly could not return with news of a lost ally. So, he set upon the hill with determination that he would succeed.

#

"You must be joking." Maeve balked at Nia. Even Uaine doubted Nias sanity as she relayed her plan. "I most definitely am not." Nia returned. "It will be simple, if you can live with the loss of your foyer." She shrugged. Torrin could not help the chuckle that escaped his lips at her cavalier attitude, only Nia would suggest it would be easy to feign an assassination on the 'High Lord' to return Uaine to his birthright. The act itself would be simple, but convincing the court to fall in line would be an entirely different feat. "And how do you suggest we defend against the mutiny of the court?" Maeve asked, voicing Torrins thoughts.

Nia rolled her eyes once more, Uaine watched her carefully. He caught Torrins eye and frowned. *Something is wrong with her*, his mind whispered to his friend. Torrin looked at Nia once more, she looked normal; save for her eyes. "Have you not been listening to me?" Nia snapped. "The court will not mutiny when I am finished with it. I am the daughter of powerful magic, lest you have forgotten." Her voice warped as she said it, as the men had witnessed once before. Maeve hesitated in her response as the room darkened, an unnatural wind whipped around them. Nia, in her exhaustion, had been struggling increasingly each day, with each tragedy, to stop the screams, the agony, and the darkness from piercing her heart. The torment of the women in the camp below ripped at her soul. The hands that tore at their skin, she felt them on her own. Maeve ignored the protests of her ego and stepped closer to Uaine.

Disbelief filled her as Rian stepped towards the Elf; a shadow cloaked Nia now, Torrin reached for his brother. *How little they understand me still*, she growled in her mind, *I would never hurt them*. What Nia did not realise was that although they knew she would not *wish to*, her powers were going haywire; no matter how in control she felt.

Rian shrugged Torrins hand from his shoulder and took another step, he had realised quicker than the men; they had not once asked Nia how she was coping with the raging storm in her mind. "We have done you a great disservice, your majesty." Nia could not look at him, at the childish face staring up at her. "We have taken you throughout a land you do not know, without telling you anything of it, we have not helped you train, nor have we asked you if you are okay." Torrin raised his brows at that, had he been so selfish? He thought of their journey and realised with regret, *he had*. Nia glared at the Sapphire Lord as realisation washed across his face.

"We have allowed you to protect us and scolded you for defending the women of this court. We have failed to understand you, to listen to you, forgive us; your majesty." Conflicting emotions whirled within her; sorrow, guilt, fury. It dissipated into shock as Rian lowered to his knees, his hands clasped as he looked up at her. As she opened her mouth to respond, that mysterious woman's voice roared in her head. Nia could hear clashing swords in the background as she spoke *'Duane is coming, you must act fast'*. Nia swallowed her panic and threw her thoughts to Rian; it had worked before, she prayed it would work again. *'Tell the others that whatever is about to happen, you must trust me'.* Rian nodded, although he did not fully understand. Darkness still cloaked her. He received his answer as the doors swung open.

Duane stared in shock at the scene before him. Nia had Rian in her arms, her dagger at his throat. A cloud of smoke surrounded her. *Just like her father*, he realised. Uaine held Torrin back. "Take one more step and I will flay you like that pathetic *High Lord*." Nia sneered; her eyes turned to Duane. He stood slack-jaw in the doorway. "My love," she cooed. Although Nia still felt the trickle of a pull towards him, it was nothing compared to what he thought; and she would use that to his advantage. "Why did you not come for me?" She asked, her lips in a pout. "They said you did not want me." Torrin glared at her. "You are a monster." He growled, he did not mean it of course. Duane could hardly believe it. He had thought his spells had failed, he did not entirely trust her. "I am here, as they kept you from me, I too was kept away." Duane purred as he stepped into the room.

Nia prayed as he came closer, *'when I reach for him, you will escape. Torrin will drag me from the room and then the room will explode, you must be ready'* Rian gulped at her plan, fear filled him at the wild look in her eyes, yet he relayed the message all the same. "Please take me away from here." She sobbed and outstretched her hand. In an instant Riad had jumped from her arms, gripped her hands and thrown her into the clutches of his brother. Duane hurled himself towards them, leaving the doorway vacant. Nia screamed for Duane as they approached the exit before fire burst from her fists and the room shattered into a million pieces; along with her plan to retake Uaine's Court.

Chapter Twenty-One:

Singed, bruised, exhausted; they staggered from the crumbling manor. Maeve did not look back as Uaine did. He *had hoped* that one day he might retake his home; as he watched it crumble and fall, that hope was lost. Nia gripped his hand. "We will take it back one day Uaine, I swear it." She told him, pulling his attention from the chaos behind them. "We must go, before the guards regain enough sense to chase us!" Maeve's words rushed together as she ran ahead of the group.

She had scarcely known them and was unwilling to be caught alongside them; however, Maeve was smart enough to stay close should she need them. The light of the burning manor quickly faded as they sprinted through the forest, ignoring the ache in their limbs and the burning of their lungs. Nia begged for guidance once more, as she had while they ran from the Faelcu in Avenere. White light lit the path before her, its suddenness almost blinded Uaine and Maeve. "By the Fates what is that?" Maeve asked, Torrin and Rian shared a curious look; for they did not share the gift of half-sight which the Emerald twins had. "A path to safety." Uaine answered before Nia could. "You can see it too?" Nia questioned, she realised Uaine had left a great deal out about himself.

"We are descendants of seers, while we do not share the gift of foresight; we do have a *different* sight. We can see what is hidden, what others cannot; but we cannot see the future. Watered down seers, if you will." Maeve explained, she found herself pitying the princess for enduring her brother's stupidity. "That explains so much." Nia shook her head, exasperated by their continuous omissions. With no time to dwell on her thoughts, they took off running yet again. Nia led the way, Torrin at her side; sword in hand as footsteps began to sound from all directions. They trusted in the scarlet haired girl as she ducked and weaved through the woods, past the clearing in which they had argued and beyond the cave where they camped.

Torrin gulped as the river Nimae came into view. Legends of creatures travelling through its waters were known across Etherea. Nia still faced the issue that she could not swim. She reminded herself to learn, soon. To her surprise, drowning seemed to be her most likely demise in this world. He looked at the panicked girl as his friends dove into the river, even the dog jumped without hesitation. Nia stared at the rushing water. "I can't." Her voice quivered. It reminded her so much of the river in her village. She remembered their cold and coarse hands on her as they carried her to the riverbank, as they bound her hands and feet. She could hear the rock they had tied to her waist crash into the water before it dragged her deep below, felt the ice water as it flooded her lungs.

Torrin had not seen such fear on Nia's face before, not for herself at least. It unnerved him, how her eyes seemed far away, remembering a painful point in her past; her hands clutched at her throat as her breathing quickened. "What happened?" Torrin asked, half afraid of the answer. Nia glowered at the raging river. "I was ten, and a terrible child." Torrin could believe that as he thought, *if she is this wild and impulsive fully grown then she would have been unbearable as a child*. "I got into just as much trouble as I could without losing my head. I did not know it then, but I had been a child for far too long; my soul was bored." Nia had come to understand it, that she had re-lived her childhood fifty times over; only the faces and names around her changed each time without her noticing. "I stole from a local seamstress, Breda wanted to lash me through the streets." Nia had loved that woman, despite her initial temper and her bastard grandson.

Torrin watched the emotions battle on her face, love, pain, regret. "My mother convinced her to take me as her apprentice, knowing I would probably be caught again and lose a hand for it; Breda was a fierce woman, I missed a stitch once and she told me she would cut the hair from my head and I could use it as thread instead of wasting her fine silk," Nia had not fumbled with a needle ever again "but she was a wonderful woman, she taught me everything she knew." For Breda, Nia could never hold ill will. "She had a grandson, a trite fellow; bitter that the world had not handed him a lordship like his uncle- he was a bastard you see, in all sense of the word." Torrin glowered at the darkness of her words, he knew it would only get worse as she spoke.

"It was one of the worst winters, not the very worst but close enough; Tristan caught the frost, a plague that riddled the village. The fever that followed almost killed him, we nursed him back to health for weeks; he was worst affected, and he could not stand it. When his strength had recovered, he beat me senseless for being a witch. Tristan corralled his group of hooligans and bound my hands and feet, they tied a boulder to my waist and flung me in the river. My mother found me, and thus began my training with the dagger. Tristan always knew something was wrong with me."

Nia laughed bitterly at the irony. "There is nothing wrong with you." Torrin told her through clenched teeth. "I will teach you to swim, but not in this river." And so, he guided the trembling Elven Princess on to his back and trudged through the raging waters. The others shared glances of sympathy as Torrin reached the riverbank at their feet, Nia scrambled to return to dry land. Her breath quickened as she stumbled away from the group, her hands shook violently. Beneath the mountain, she had no time to dwell on her own trauma; it was do or die against the Ellén Trechend. Here, as fire and smoke raged far behind them, as they ran for their lives, as her mind scrambled; Nia found it was all she could think of. It had not been the last time the children of her village turned against her at the command of Tristan, they had teased and tormented her; he had tortured her. Nia jumped as a cold hand slid across her shoulder. "Men are bastards." Maeve said softly behind her. "It is our duty to survive their stupidity and bring what sense we can to this twisted world." Nia turned to face the blonde woman; Maeve held no animosity in her eyes.

"We did not meet under the best circumstances, nor have I decided if I have lost my mind joining your band of misfits, but you have done what I could not; you returned my brother to me, you freed the women of my court-" Nia scoffed, Maeve gave her a stern look, "you *tried*, you saved many more in one afternoon than I have done in a lifetime. You have given me a glimmer of hope that something can be done to end this awful era of death and suffering and for that, I thank you." Nia threw her arms around the blonde; Maeve almost lost her footing; her hands hovered in the air for a moment before embracing the girl. Both women could have cried, it was like finding a sister; a small light in the darkness. "Come now, if we wish to live another day we must go. No doubt Duane survived; that stubborn bastard has been alive for centuries." Maeve was correct, for as they ran Duane dragged his battered body from beneath the rubble. *Seething*. His suit in tatters, dirt and dust covered his face, his gold eyes burned furiously as the manor fell to pieces above him. The roar he let loose rippled the earth beneath Nias feet as she ran. It sent a chill through her spine.

It took far longer than they had hoped to feel safe enough to stop, but exhaustion had hit each of them like a tsunami. Nia left the others to set up camp, she could not keep herself from sliding to the grass and closing her eyes. She had

nothing left in her. Maeve glared at her brother once more as Nias chest rose and fell peacefully. "You fools, you absolute fools." Uaine groaned as she began, the sapphire lords remained quiet. "That," she threw her index finger in Nias direction, "is our future Queen, and you absolute-"
"Fools, we know, what is your point?" Uaine snapped. Usually a patient man, he had been through a great ordeal; his mind needed rest to recover from the Foxglove. Maeve rolled her eyes. "How is it that you have dragged her across Etherea rather than rally the loyalists, band the courts and burn that damned castle to the ground? How is it that she is clueless?" Torrin looked away at that, it was his fault. He had been distracted by his own fear and then he had been too raptured by her beauty to think of her as the warrior she would become.

Uaine shook his head. "She was mortal Maeve, she did not know-" Annoyed, Maeve gripped her brother's arm. Rian watched in surprise as Maeve's eyes turned milk white. She watched it all, from the moment they found Nia's broken body on the cottage floor; Maeve gasped as she watched everything that had transpired. You should have told her more, trained her more; she is a lamb to the slaughter with her magic so fractured." Maeve shook her head, frustrated at the inability of the men around her to understand the true power of any woman, never mind the royalty sleeping at their feet. Nia stirred then, pain washed across her face, whimpers escaped her lips.

Nia found herself somewhere terrifyingly cold and dark, her eyes refused to adjust to the pitch blackness; her hands reached before her for something, anything, solid to hold on to. It felt as if she was falling, blindly into the nothingness. *"Finally, my child, I have been waiting for you to call out to me."* The voice froze the blood in her veins, it was hoarse and cold. "Who are you?" Nia asked, although she knew the answer. A cackle echoed around her. *"You know."* He spoke, mirroring her thoughts. "No." Nia gasped, the blanket of darkness wrapped around her and grew tighter every second. "Yes." He laughed. *"Why do you detest me so, my daughter?"* Ice ran down her spine at the confirmation, it was him.

"You are an evil, rotten bastard." She spat, Ciar chuckled in return. *"So they say, but did they tell you why?"* He asked, Nia could hear the taunt in his tone; but she could not quell her curiosity. "What do you mean, *why?* You have plunged Etherea into darkness, they should have killed you." Ciar laughed once more. *"I offered them salvation, they refused to bend... What does not bend must break."* Nia scoffed at her father's reasoning. *"I will be waiting for you Elvinia, for when your friends abandon you; as all Fae will."* With that, flashes of a burning Etherea ran through her mind. Nia awoke, eyes like saucers, gasping for breath once more. Torrin sat by her side, patiently waiting for her to awake from whatever nightmare plagued her. "It was him," she gasped, "he spoke to me." Torrins brows knit together in confusion. "Who?" He asked, he soon wished he had not as her wide eyes met his. *"My father."*

Chapter Twenty-Two:

The air within the castle dungeon was icy and damp, water trickled through cracks in the stone. *Drip, drip, drip*. Riona had not seen the sunlight in… she did not know for sure how long it had been. She awoke first as the Faelcu dragged her through the woods, cursed the sun and moon and all below as she felt that long forgotten buzz in her veins; they had entered Etherea. It was nothing like it had once been. Even during the war, the land remained strong; fighting against his decay. Riona knew they would pass through the Sapphire Court first but could not believe her eyes at the sight of lifeless earth before her. She could see the High Lord Manor in the distance, a paltry speck of sickly green; where were the forests? The babbling brooks? Where the Faelcu ran, was once a crystal-clear river filled with fish. Riona remembered it so clearly, she began to question her decision to flee.

Riona slipped in and out of consciousness until, at last, they reached a towering gold castle. She had been relieved, on their journey, to notice that not all courts had suffered the same fate. What had they done to deserve such cruelty? Riona knew from experience, that it did not take much to set off Ciars terrible temper. Relief abandoned her as they came upon the towering golden gates of Duanes Castle. Not content with a High Lords Manor, he insisted upon having something bigger and better than the rest. Riona could not believe she once called him friend; even *enjoyed* his company. She cursed herself for not seeing his ambition for what it was; a danger to Etherea. The Elves had been here long before the Fae, yet some Fae still held the belief that Etherea belonged to them. Riona had been mistaken in allowing that belief to fester. She could never have imagined the strength of bitterness in a Faes heart.

She had been a foolish girl, once. Too sure of her power, headstrong in her belief that she and her Fateful were untouchable. That her good intent could rid this land of eons of animosity. She had been wrong, so wrong. *My daughter,* she thought, *my poor daughter.* Riona felt riddled with guilt as she thought of Elvinia, alone in the world. She prayed the girl had run deep into the mortal world, crossed the great sea, and never looked back. Riona knew it was a foolish hope, she had watched it unfold all those years ago.

It would be days before Duane decided to visit the lost Queen in his dungeon, he had stormed through the castle furiously.

Riona did not know it then, but this had been the day Duane visited Torrins Manor. The iron gates of the dungeons screeched open, waking her from her restless slumber. The floor was like ice beneath her, Riona struggled to lift her bruised body from the ground. Duane stomped through the hallway until he reached the silver gates holding Riona, adorned with glittering jewels enchanted by Ciar himself; it was no ordinary cell. The Golden Lord laughed at the pathetic woman before him. Once tall and defiant, he remembered the shining gold armour she had worn; encrusted with rubies, glowing as she tore through their enemies. He stepped inside the cell, Riona flinched as the gates slammed shut behind him.

"You could have been something you know." Duane sneered at her. Riona supposed she should not be surprised that in the two hundred odd years she had been gone, he remained consumed by his selfish whims. "Only with you by my side if I recall correctly." Riona spat back, it astounded her still; men could not envision a woman in power, without a man at her side. She had relented to her father's wishes and allowed herself to perpetuate this fallacy and look what good it had done. Duane scoffed. "I was a fool, you are a blight on Etherea, Ciar could have saved us all. You crippled him." Riona gawped at Duane. "You cannot be serious, Duane, this is all he has ever wanted; the world clawing at his feet, since he stepped on the shores of Ranere. What lies has he told you?" She should not have been shocked, Ciar had always been an excellent liar, Duane had listened to his lies for centuries.

Duane could not help himself, his hand moved of its own accord as it raised and crashed against her pale face. Riona hissed as his golden rings sliced through her flesh. "Your daughter is just as much of a stupid bitch." Duane snapped as he wiped the blood from his jewellery. At this, Rionas head whipped up. Her violet eyes pierced him, Duane felt a ripple of unease as he glanced once more at the gems lining the cell, questioning their strength. "My daughter will rip you limb from limb." "Oh I think not." Duane cackled as he reached into his pocket, a plethora of letters fell at Rionas feet. Her mouth fell open as she recognised Elvinia's handwriting. They were love letters. Riona glared at Duane. "You are just like him, plying on a young girl to get to her power; she will see right through you, as I do now." He was still the same arrogant, selfish boy she had known all those years ago. Only, in the clarity of age, it no longer enticed her; it infuriated her. "We shall see, we shall see. For now, rest *your majesty*. Your husband has been looking for you." Before Riona could retort, Duanes fist came crashing into her face once again.

Her mind raced as she slept, she felt suffocated. Riona reached out for her daughter but found nothing in return. The cell blocked her magic almost completely. *Almost*. As Elvinia's screams rang throughout the Sapphire Court, as a thousand tendrils of her magic stretched across Etherea; a bolt of lightning crashed through Riona. Riona jolted from her sleep, sweat pouring down her back. *It has happened*, she realised, *Elvinia has begun to transform*. Guilt filled her once more as she cursed Duane for finding them.

The weeks continued like this; Duane grew more restless with each day Elvinia did not run to him. Riona grew to find relief in his attacks, for it meant her daughter had escaped him once more. One day, as she leaned against the scalding silver bars of her cell, Duane had left the doors above open. Riona could hear him, roaring at his Faelcu for losing Elvinia to the Silver Court. Her heart stopped at that, *not Oisín's Court, please*. Riona prayed to whatever Gods were left to keep her daughter safe in that treacherous court. She shared Torrins opinion of the Silver Lords, only she did not know this yet. What she remembered of Oisín was not good, he took what he wanted and struck down all in his way. Mistakenly, she had not made him a priority; despite his barbarity he had been a damned good politician. Now, she wished she had cut him down when she had the chance.

Three days later a servant girl appeared at her cell. Riona eyed her cautiously, golden shackles disguised as bracelets rested on her wrists, her chestnut hair cut jaggedly to her ears, frightened hazel eyes looked back at her. The girl said nothing as she stepped into the cell, holding a shaking tray of food and medical supplies. "I will not hurt you." Riona told her softly, those hazel eyes darted around the dungeon as she placed the tray in front of Riona; before she ran from the cell. Riona watched her run, startled at her suddenness. Cell doors snapped shut once more and she stifled a groan. Tentatively, Riona poked at the food. She had not eaten much since she arrived, nausea had wracked her stomach as a stale bread loaf had been thrown through the bars each day.

Her stomach grumbled as the smell wafted upwards, *oh to hell with it*, Riona thought and tucked into the meal gratefully. As she ate, she noticed a slip of paper beneath her glass, glittering silver letters caught her eye. *The servant girl could not have written this*, she realised, as she scanned the magnificent handwriting. '*She is safe, she is searching for you, she is fighting.*' Rionas heart swelled, so all was not lost as it had seemed. A new purpose filled her as the slip of paper evaporated into smoke. *If Elvinia is fighting, I will not leave her to fight alone.*

Chapter Twenty-Three:

This has been a terrible idea, Nia thought; as they trudged through slop and sludge, covered in dirt; bruised and battered. It had not begun that way, no, their journey began in the scorched lands of the Sapphire Court and oh how Nia longed for the burning heat of the sun once more, all she had known for days now was a murky mist. They had crossed that dreadful river, rested for the night, and found in the morning light that Galeria lay just ahead. One would not think a place such as this existed in a land so mystical, yet the stench of despair stung their senses. Unease still rattled her as she thought of Ciar invading her mind. How had he done so? Had he done so before, without her noticing? Her thoughts raced. They had not spoken of it.

The air that choked them was different from the purple fog that still swallowed Breága, a green vapor that hissed from the swamp itself. Nia wrinkled her nose in disgust as she heard something squelch beneath her boot. Maeve glared at the lot of them as she hiked her dress above her waist, it would do little good; the gown was destroyed.

The Emerald Lady questioned her sanity for following them, although she knew to turn down a journey such as this would be a regret she could not live with. Torrin held Rian above his shoulders, Madigan rested in Uaines arms. The poor dog whined as the swampy water rose to their waistline. Nia found her feet walking of their own accord as her mind wandered. Nia felt scattered, lost. There was too much suffering, far too much. It pierced her heart like a million daggers, grief, pain, anger, sorrow, she felt it all. It was suffocating, she struggled to keep her head up as she walked; *I am their last hope*, she winced, *I must ignore the darkness*.

None acknowledged the internal war raging within their future Queen. She squashed the storm threatening to burst from her bones and quietly attempted to quell her anger. Nia could not control her emotions much longer.

"Tell me once more, why are we doing this?" Maeve grimaced as dirt and algae sloshed around her. "Nia is a Fate-Swayer, Ciar has cast a spell so that we do not have any idea what that means, we... found a woman who told us of a man in Galeria who could help us." Uaine explained to his sister, Maeve narrowed her eyes at his hesitation; she recalled his memories to her mind and flicked through them until she found the hidden chamber beneath the Sapphire Court.

"That woman must be destroyed." Maeve said instantly. Nia's eyes flickered with annoyance. "Of course *you* would think so." Torrin glanced sideways at Nia. "Lest you have forgotten, you almost drove your dagger into Nessas heart." She glowered at him for defending Maeve, Torrin felt himself stepping back. Nia said nothing, just stomped ahead. *That was different*, she had wanted to say; but found herself choking on the words. Instead, she followed her feet once more. She had known for a while now, exactly where Abbán hid; she did not know how, just that she felt where each step should be without thought.

Torrin shared a look with Uaine, something had drastically changed in her. Rian cursed that he could do nothing but watch, they had not spoken of it; but Rian had been aging so unnaturally slow, even for a Fae. In truth, he felt useless. Even Maeve could see, from looking through Uaines memories the girl had grown darker. They had made a terrible mistake, what if she chose her father? They followed Nia nonetheless, until the mist thinned, and the water turned clear.

The twins looked around in wonder as wisps of light magic danced around them. An island sat in the middle of the crystal lake, and atop it grew a towering hawthorn tree. Torrin gripped his brother tighter as the bells of pixie laughter rang in his ears. "So, you have come at last." A wheezing, scratching voice echoed across the water. Nia looked at the tree as it began to rustle, its bark split and unravelled to reveal a frail man; he stumbled from the bark with a crackled breath.

Nia reached to steady him and walked him to a bench beside the tree. "Abbán?" Nia asked, the old man laughed; she could have sworn dust spilled from his breath. "What is left of him, and you... you look just like your mother." Nia sighed at that, *my mother, now we are one step closer to finding you.*

Abbán eyed her companions curiously as he struggled to sit. Torrin and Maeve looked at him with disdain for his frailty, Rians eyes filled with curiosity, Uaine looked on with sympathy. Nia ignored his studious glance at her friends and sat at his side. "Is there anything I can do to help you?" Nia asked with sincerity, Abbán smiled; his milk-white eyes glistened with relief. "So, you are not entirely lost." He said to the Elf at his side, Nias eyes widened at that. "What do you mean, lost?" Torrin asked, before Nia could.

Abbán scoffed. "Torrin Ó Cinnéide, surely you are not blind?" Maeve snorted at that, she had known them all of three days and she could see Torrin *was* completely blind to the power within Nia. No matter how many times he witnessed it, he could not see it consuming the redhead. His attraction had cast a blanket across his vision. Uaine had realised as Lorcan had, the moment he had looked into her flashing eyes.

Rian had been unwilling to admit the similarities growing between Nia and Nessa, for he had spent the most time with the rabid woman beneath the Sapphire Court. *Nia does not share her cruelty for cruelty's sake at least*, Rian thought. Abbán looked at the young Lord. "You may be right, Rian, but cruelty for any sake, is still cruel." Nia frowned as she looked between them. They were having a conversation of their own. "You have been cursed." Abbán muttered as he peered at Rian closely. This was news to them all, yet it made sense, for although Nia did not know much of the Fae ways; even she suspected Rian should look older.

"You must not search to undo this curse." The old man warned, Rian glowered at him. "Why not?" He asked, it was a fair question, for his youth had plagued his mind throughout their entire journey. "You will unleash havoc on this world." It was cryptic, but enough to send a chill through Rian. Abbán turned to Torrin then, his eyes narrowed.

"You have been too stubborn to understand your role in this journey." Abbán *tsked* at him. "The last Faoladh above ground and what have you done to protect your Queen? Blinded her to the truth of Etherea." Torrin opened his mouth to speak, Abbán cocked a brow, he found his mouth shut of its own accord. Abbán looked to Uaine and Maeve then. "You have both been silent for far too long, hidden figures on the chessboard. It is time to stop hiding." The twins looked to the ground; they knew he was right.

Abbán looked at Nia once more, his eyes filled with sympathy. "The life of a Fate Swayer is a turbulent one. It has always been so. Many have forgotten that the Elves were created alongside the Fates. Two races forbidden to interact; the Fates began to dwindle. A pair of defiant lovers abandoned their oaths to keep their races separate and escaped deep within Etherea. From their love, the first Fate Swayer was born. It is thought that the powers which create us had granted the Fates the gift of absolute sight and the Elves the gift of siphoning the earth, and in realising they had not created balance, they created a singular anomaly which would correct this imbalance. The lineage of these two lovers became the answer to this problem, they are challengers of the Fates designs; for better or worse."

Nia blinked as she absorbed the information.

"It started a war between the Fates and the Elves, both accused the other of creating this power for themselves. The first Fate Swayer united the races and became the first Queen of Etherea. So, it continued, each first born daughter in your family has been granted this gift, each mother suffered the curse of an early death as their power transferred from one vessel to another. Until Riona. I did not know why she survived then, I do now. The evil that faces Etherea is so great, so deeply rooted from the choices made over the eons; it will require the power of two to overcome." Abbán looked at Nia once more, at the dark shadows slipping around her. Abbán reached into the tree, a velvet bag emerged from the crevice.

Nia watched him curiously as he dug through the bag. "You must ground yourself first, the curse of a Fate Swayer is the ability to feel everything, everywhere all at once. The good, the bad, you must find a balance between both; or you will be consumed." Nia had suspected this; she had said so to Torrin once. She let out a frustrated sigh. "I understand this, but *how, how do I find balance?*" Nia asked. The old man paused for a moment before turning to the side. He raised a frail, shaking hand and pointed a finger to the forest lining the swamp. Nia watched in wonder as a white hare bounced across the grass. It was the first animal she had seen roaming freely through Etherea.

Shock evaporated her wonder as Abbán snapped his fingers, the hare dropped to the ground with a screech.

Nia's stomach churned as a cold darkness overwhelmed her. "Push it back, wait, watch." Abbán advised. Nia reluctantly listened, to her astonishment a fox appeared from the treeline. It sniffed at the dead hare and raised its head to look around, two pups emerged from behind it; the three began to gnaw on the animal which had lived and leaped just moments ago. "Should they have starved to save the hare pain?" Abbán asked, Nia chewed on her lip as she watched the tiny pups. "I suppose not." She sighed. "Some pain is necessary to endure; for without pain there cannot be life." She may not entirely agree, but Nia could see his point.

"As for the visions of your father, you must not listen to him. Ciar is a master manipulator, a skill he seems to have passed along; it will serve you well in your journey to come. I have some items which may help." Abbán reached once more into the velvet bag. "Take these, you may have noticed your mother has a similar one. It will help you hone your magic and protect you against any curses that come your way. As far as I am aware it will also eradicate Duanes grip on your mind." With these words he handed Nia a pocket-sized leather-bound book and a glistening ruby and silver ring. She had seen her mother wearing a similar one, as she slipped it onto her finger the overwhelming noise in her mind quietened to a hum.

Tears sprung to Nias eyes, their pain was still there; the darkness still whispered to her, but it no longer *screamed* and for that she would be eternally grateful.

Nia threw her arms around the old man as serenity filled her. "Thank you." She sobbed, Torrin stared in shock at her. He had done nothing to help her, *absolutely nothing*. For that, he was filled with shame. Abbán smiled as she released him. "You must not ignore either part of you, this book was your mothers; it should aid you on the journey yet to come." He told her, Nia wasted no time as she opened the leather clasp of the pocketbook. Her mother's handwriting made her heart swell. The missing pieces of Riona's Tale. Abbán turned to the others with a sigh. "You will not like the words I am about to speak, but I have seen what will happen should you follow a different path." Nia looked curiously at her comrades, who looked just as confused.

Abbán looked at the twins first, as he pulled an ancient scroll from the bag, along with two Emerald Sigils. "You will return to the Emerald Court, both of you and return what has been lost, take this as proof of your heritage should any question you." The pair took his gifts gratefully, albeit unsure. Abbán turned to Torrin again, his eyes judging the Sapphire Lord once more. "You must return to your court, life grows once again, you will find people you thought long gone have returned and are looking for their Lord." Torrins brows rose, there were no Sapphire Fae left above the ground. *Could it be?* Torrin shook his head in shock.

Finally, Abbán looked at Nia. "Your journey takes you backwards now Nia, you must go to the Silver Court as you promised; trust in Lorcan, you will find your intentions far more aligned than you realise, you will go beneath the mountain and you will find friend and foe alike; it is your choice who you follow." Nia looked to Torrin, saw the jealousy in his eyes. "We will do as you say." Maeve spoke first as she saw the hesitation on Nia's face. *Stop being a bastard*, Maeve shot at Torrin. Nias eyes narrowed as wisps of light travelled between the pair.

Torrin clenched his jaw as he nodded. "As will we." He bowed his head to Abbán as Maeve rolled her eyes. Abbán stood and looked to Nia. "I will."

"Do not feign innocence with Lorcans brothers, they are alike in looks alone. Remember, you are not Rionas child to the darker folk of Etherea; *you are Ciars.*" With that final piece of cryptic advice, Abbán clasped his hands. They stumbled backwards as light exploded from his palms, sending each spiralling towards their destinations.

Only Nia did not reach hers.

Chapter Twenty-Four:

Nias gut tightened and twisted as she dissipated through the air, shadows and sparks contended with each other before her; battling for control. She felt as if she was being torn apart and rearranged, until suddenly; she crashed against the earth.

She spluttered as she clattered against the ground, mouth filled with wet earth. Nia struggled to pull herself to her feet, limbs shaking as her hands found a nearby tree. Wiping the dirt from her eyes, Nia took in the scene before her; she had landed in a dark and murky forest. The land looked as though something huge had crashed through, for it was mud and water and not much else.

She groaned as she looked down at herself. *I cannot approach Lorcan like this,* Nia shut her eyes and focused for the first time in weeks on the light around her. Warmth filled her as her clothes transformed from her filthy britches and tunic to a simple ice blue silk gown. Her messy hair tamed itself into an elegant low chignon beneath her hood, two ringlets framed her face.

Nia peered around as she caught her breath, feeling better about her appearance at least, glints of silver poked from the earth beside her. Filled with curiosity, she dug her fingers into the dirt; clawing until she freed what had been buried underneath. Nia gasped and threw the helmet to the ground; for there was a skull within the armour, its wearer struck down in battle. Her stomach churned as she looked around once again, noticing more glints in the earth; more bodies buried. Nia doubled over and wretched at the sight.

She had landed in a graveyard of war.

As the thought settled in her mind, as she rose her shaking head and cringed at the vomit at her feet; a shriek split through the silence overhead. Nia's eyes were drawn to the sky, to find a sight so terrifying; she wished she'd never set foot in this land.

Three women, ghastly pale; almost ghost-like, flew overhead. Nia felt nothing but horror emanating from the women and as she prepared to run; they swooped towards her. Cackling and shrieking still; they circled the terrified girl. Nia watched in terror, rooted to the spot, as the skeletons buried within the earth clawed their way to the surface. Their armour, once fitted and strong, now worn and hanging on their skinless bodies. The spectres howled with laughter as the skeletons drew closer to the girl, Nia could hear their words of encouragement to their conjured army. They spoke the old tongue, no new-world language met Nia's ears.

For the first time, she thanked the Fates that she could understand them. Raising her hands to fight the advancing convoy of dead men, Nia glared at the almost transparent figures flitting around their heads "Wait!" She screamed at them, though Nia heard it come out as Fanacht. The skeletons paused; their weapons drawn. The women cocked their heads at her, before. floating down to glower at her.

Their white eyes drew shivers from within Nia's core. She felt cold all over, like she had never felt heat before; and as if she would not again. "Give us a reason." The middle woman snarled, her voice warped, like they were at opposite ends of a tunnel; not five feet apart. Nia's mind scrambled as fear took over. At her silence they sneered. A sword, held by a hand of bones, swung towards the girl as the women cackled. Without a choice, Nia drew her own sword.

Her bones ached as they advanced, with every blow they landed; she returned two. It was futile, for how could one kill dead men? Nia's arms grew weak as they swarmed her, with their clanking armour and rattling bones. Her feet sank in the mud as she scrambled, while those wretched wisps of women screeched above her. They relished in the violence; welcomed her death with jagged grins. Nia looked around for an escape, but there was none, for she was truly surrounded.

Nia cursed them as she lost her sword, stuck in the hollow sockets of a skull whose body stumbled backwards. Her efforts were futile. As her back met the callous surface of a tree, Nia knew she was done for if she did not act. The women watched her curiously as she shut her eyes; expecting the girl to surrender to her fate.

Nia drew a breath, willed the wind to aid her; let her magic whisper to the earth at her feet. Her eyes flew open, glowing bright in the murky clearing. Roots sprang from the earth, coiled around the bones of the decayed soldiers before her and ripped them from the surface; dragging them back to their graves. The winds blew furiously as she looked to the women flying above her. "*An leor do shaol ar chúis?* Is your life enough of a reason?" She spat at them. They screeched as the wind battered against their ghostly forms, they glared at her once more before they turned and fled; screaming that this would not be forgotten.

Only once they had left, and the bones below ceased creaking, did Nia fall to her knees. Sobs wracked through her; she could not stop the screams which left her lips. Approaching footsteps sent Nia tumbling backwards, her bow in hand; an arrow perched, ready to fire.

A man stepped from the treeline. Nia could have laughed. Oh, how familiar the scene was, for this was how Duane had found her first; albeit she had not been covered in her own blood back then. Nia recognised him as Lorcan's brother, Eoghan, if she recalled correctly. They looked the same, yet different; they shared that black as night hair and those silver eyes, yet Eoghan was broader, clearly older, with a spiralling tattoo across his neck.

Nia glared at him still, she knew the horrors his family inflicted on low-born Fae; heard their glee as they hunted the women of the Emerald Court. Eoghan raised his hands in surrender, eyes wide with shock. They knew Lorcan had met with the Princess; heard tales of her power. Witnessing it, however, had shook him to the core. The Bánánach were ancient creatures made guardians of the Silver Court; appointed by Ciar himself. For they relished in violence and destruction, they were the perfect protectors of his most loyal subjects. "I wish only to help you, your grace." Eoghan said softly. Nia's head spun as she lowered her weapon. Too tired to argue, she staggered to her feet. *This will all be worth it,* she tried to convince herself, *when I find my mother and free this land.* "Take me to Lorcan." She hissed; the adrenaline had left her.

The pain had begun.

Eoghan caught her as she stumbled towards him. Covered in blood, clothes torn to pieces; his brother was going to kill him once he saw her. "Let me carry you." Nia glared at him as he held her steady, Eoghan grumbled and continued to walk with her. He could see why his brother had become so enthralled, even covered in dirt and blood; she was radiant. He had watched her, as the Bánánach set the dead against her.

How she fought with every ounce of strength she had, how she returned their onslaught twice fold. If they had been living men, they would not have lived for long. Eoghan had never seen the spectres run from a battle, he almost wished they had stayed to face the Princess; if only to see how she would have handled them.

Nia watched her blood drip scarlet against the blinding white snow of the Silver Court. She fell over the steps leading to the Silver Princes Manor as Eoghan struggled to keep hold of her. It was an enormous structure, fashioned into the side of ice peaked mountains; fitting for the cold High Fae which roamed its halls.

In stark contrast, unaware of the staggering girl his brother carried towards him; Lorcan stalked past his servants in the warmth of his home. He detested the practice; his family had treated the Fae of their court like dogs for far too long. Most of his brothers had returned, with news of the destruction of the Emerald Manor; how only Duane had survived. *Of course, that cockroach survived*, he thought to himself as he cast a glare to Aidan and returned to his chambers. Aidan had watched wearily, Lorcan's retreat, and reminded himself to ask Eoghan to speak to the boy.

The youngest of their clan had always been troubled; their relationship even more so. Lorcan could not believe his eyes as he looked through the frosted window.

There she was; the girl who consumed his mind.

Dripping scarlet and dragged through the snow by his brother.

Nia could feel his gaze upon her, could not explain how; but she felt it all the same. Like a wind caressing her skin. "Lorcan." She rasped; throat thick with smoke. Eoghan cursed her, knowing his brother was on his way already. He did not want to face Lorcan's temper; not here, with Nia by his side; she would cut through him like a hot knife. Nia had no clue, no idea whatsoever of what had attacked her. One moment she could feel the desperation of battle, saw those bones half buried in the ground; the next, she was surrounded by those... those things.

Lorcan was by her side in an instant. His eyes first laid on her torn dress; the dress she had worn to impress him, it was covered in mud and blood. Destroyed. Lorcan swallowed, hard, as his gaze travelled upwards; to her snapped sleeves, to the gash across her chest, the blood oozing down her frame. Nia watched his eyes turn dangerously dark; their sparkle almost gone. Fury burned brightly within him. Nia could feel it seeping outwards, almost choking her.

"Who did this to you?"

She only sobbed in return. Lorcan clenched his teeth and lunged for his brother.

"I'm going to kill you."

At this Nia startled, she threw her arms around him. Shocked by his anger, Nia snapped from her haze, panic coursed through her veins. "No, Lorcan, it was not Eoghan. I don't know what happened. I was in a graveyard, and these women... They appeared from nowhere. Dark, and hungry. Eoghan found me." Lorcan blanched at her words and took a step back. Still furious, he could not help but scowl as he watched the blood gush from her veins. Warmth filled her as light poured from his hands.

"Are you insane?" He growled as he healed her wounds. Nia could see the panic in his silver eyes. It calmed whatever annoyance his words sparked. Her heart fluttered as she looked up at him. Eoghan watched the pair in silence. "I promised I would return; *you* did not warn me of crazed spectres that would attack me should I do so." Nia replied with a shrug, she winced as her shoulder burned. Eoghan stifled a laugh beside her, Lorcan cursed himself and shook his head. He had forgotten the bargain they had made. He glared at his brothers' smirk and returned to healing the girl. Neither missed how his hands shook as they hovered over her, how his eyes burned with such intensity Nia had never seen before. Her nonchalance only worried him more. When he was sure her wounds had healed and the blood had ebbed, Lorcan met her gaze.

"Your eyes." Lorcan breathed.

No longer flashing between violet and red, both were split in two halves of each colour. Nia sighed and ran a hand through her hair. "I am finding balance." She could not explain what Abbán had done, what she had felt. She was not cured, no, but it was much easier now to breathe; to think.

Lorcan sensed there was more to her story as she twisted the glittering ring now adorning her finger, but did not pry.

Instead, he extended a hand. Nia took it gratefully and turned to Lorcan's brother, still quietly watching them. "Thank you, Eoghan, for helping me." She told him honestly. Eoghan's eyes were filled with admiration for the girl, for her clothes were still torn; yet she stood proud and tall.

"I must say it is a great honour to meet you, your grace, for my brother has not stopped telling us tales of your beauty and power." Eoghan bowed low, Nia resisted the urge to tell him not to as she remembered Abbán's words. *The daughter of their King*, that's who she was in this court of treachery. "I only told the truth." Lorcan scoffed as his cheeks twinged pink. "We are quite infatuated with your reputation. My brothers have been dying to meet you." Eoghan laughed at Lorcan's embarrassment and grinned at Nia.

"Aidan will shit himself that you have arrived at his front door, I shall tell him." Eoghan disappeared into the air as they ascended the steps. Nia laughed at that; she seemed much lighter now. Lorcan could not smile alongside her as they stepped into the entrance chamber, no matter how much he adored the joy on her face. She had stepped into a wolf's den, without a care.

Nias eyes widened with delight as she looked around the Manor. It was sleek, elegant, and much warmer than she had expected. Glittering silver and cool blues adorned the entrance room. A grand white door separated them from the main hallway, Nia stopped as her breath caught. Lorcan looked at her worriedly, checking her once again for injury.

She remembered the doors of Torrin's home, how she adored them. Nia had not felt such adoration in an exceptionally long time. Lorcan watched in silence as she stepped up to the doors. Her fingers trailed against the carvings; it filled her with serenity. Tears pricked her eyes; she had forgotten what peace felt like. How she would have loved to step inside a beautiful painting and leave this world and her responsibilities to it behind.

A smile slipped on her face as she traced the outlines of the mountain landscape carved into the wood. Nia closed her eyes, hearing the trees rustle in the wind outside, snow crunching beneath the feet of Fae. It was almost enough to transport her there. Almost. Nia sighed as her eyes opened, staring at those beautiful doors once more.

A memory flashed, of Uaine's frustration at her love of detail and her back straightened with embarrassment. *I have much more important things to dwell on, I must let go of these foolish whims,* Nia scolded herself. "Apologies, I have a love for craftsmanship." Nia explained as a blush crept to her cheeks, awaiting his taunts for her idiocy. "Do not apologise, my great-great grandmother carved that door." Lorcan told her, Nia jumped; she had not realised how close he had gotten. She turned to look at him, the awe in her eyes threw Lorcan off; he had never seen such... happiness in *anyone's* eyes.

"It is magnificent, she was a very talented woman." Nia told him honestly; it filled him with pride as she looked back towards the carvings. She supposed it was derived from her own past, most of what Nia owned or wore; she had made herself. She had no choice, so she knew how difficult it was to create something with your own hands. "I made, well, I tried to make a harp for my mother once. Oh, it was awful, I had splinters for days, the skill this would take... it is unbelievable."

Lorcan could not help but smile at her as he reached to push the grand doors open. "Wait!" Nia exclaimed. Lorcan cocked a brow as she yanked the doors closed. "Look at me." She groaned; he stifled a laugh. "Only a woman would face death and care about her outfit." Nia's mouth fell agape, without thought; she swatted him. Not hard of course, but hard enough that Lorcan jumped backwards with wide eyes. "What was that for?" He asked, rubbing his cheek. "For being an ass." Nia told him sternly before waving a hand across herself, returning her appearance to before those damned things attacked her. The laugh that bubbled through Lorcan could be heard throughout the Manor. "You are something else." He chuckled with a shake of his head.

Her body still ached; her heart had not stopped pounding; his sparkling eyes were burning into her soul, but she did not have time to dwell on such things.

Sensing her discomfort, Lorcan offered a reprieve. "Perhaps I can ask our grandmaster to teach you a few things, should he refuse, I could show you a thing or two." Nia's eyes brightened as a smile tugged at her lips. Lorcan shrugged as she looked around the hallway before wisps of white light surrounded her. He thanked the Fates that the servants had scurried away; no doubt telling each other of the mysterious woman that had stepped into their home. Lorcan did not mind their gossiping now, he only feared her judgement once she learned they kept slaves in their home. Lorcan struggled to keep his breathing level as she appeared in a silk silver dress and glittering jewels across her nape. Her cloak floated from above, wrapping around her like a warm blanket.

Nia whipped her head to look at him, she could not decide if he were trying to save face; for she knew of their slaves, and how could a slave refuse their High Lord? Nia began to suspect her initial thoughts of Lorcan had been correct. There was nothing sinister about him, she had sensed it the moment she met him. He was tormented, yes, but she had not seen a single piece of evidence to show he relayed that torment against anyone else. With Abbán's words in her mind, Nia opened her mouth to reply.

Her words died in her throat as Eoghan appeared before them with four equally giant men at his side, Lorcan cursed his brothers as her eyes turned to saucers. She had seen them in her book of Etherea's Fae, but nothing could have prepared her for the menacing force of standing in their presence. They were almost identical, with their jet-black hair and silver eyes, strong jaws, and sharp cheekbones; Nia could tell them apart by their height and by the different scars and tattoos littering their arms and faces.

It was silent for a moment, as the Silver Princes' took in the sight before them. Nia spoke first. "Forgive me, your Royal Highnesses, for the intrusion. I have come to visit your dear brother, if he will have me," Nia took Lorcans hand in hers, "for we were very rudely interrupted at my dance, and I have been terribly busy since." Aidan could not believe it, the key to Etherea; to Ciar's return, had fought off their guards and waltzed into their home. He looked at Lorcan with a respect he had never before felt for the young Lord. Nia examined him, the coldness in his eyes, the claw marks adorning his jaw, the swirling black tattoo across his left eye.

Lorcan watched Nia's eyes shift, from light and adoring, to cold and calculating. She examined his brothers like a hunter glaring at their pray. For the first time, Lorcan questioned Nia's intentions with his Court. He had his own of course, at first; every moment he had spent with her since Torrin's dance had filled his cold heart with warmth. When he found them at the border, Lorcan had contemplated it; taking her, sending his brothers for her friends, letting her rage loose on Aidan and the others. It was strange, when she had looked at him with that fear in her eyes, Lorcan could not bring himself to do it.

He could not become what Etherea made him.

Not if it would destroy her.

Keegan laughed, breaking Lorcan from his thoughts, shaking his shaggy hair from his eyes. His tattoo wrapped around his right arm, barbed and twisting; Nia could hardly make out the designs. "Busy burning down the Emerald Court." He chortled; Aidan could have killed him with the look he cast. Eoghan nudged Keegan, who choked on his laughter. Abbán's words gave her the courage she needed as she raised her head with defiance. Lorcan watched her cautiously. "Their Lord was an ass." At this, Aidan howled with laughter. He doubled over as he struggled to regain his composure.

"I cannot believe it, for centuries we have wanted that shadow Lord gone; you spend a *day* in the Emerald Court and tear it down." Aidan extended his hand, Nia let herself laugh alongside him, for a different reason; Maeve would enjoy the name of shadow Lord, this she did not doubt. "I would like to apologise first, for our guard's overzealous behaviour; the Bánánach are fiercely protective. Although I heard the Scarlet Death made quick work of them. Not a scratch on you." Nia glowered as she shook his hand. Aidans eyes flickered down her body, she felt her skin crawl. Insults danced on her tongue, curses and spells ready to turn him to dust. The ring on her finger warmed and Nia took a steadying breath.

Lorcan prayed to the Fate's that she would keep calm. Her eyes flickered to Eoghan; she had most certainly not escaped without a scratch, why would he lie? "If you wish to keep your own court standing, I recommend you do not call me that again. It is your majesty to you." Aidan laughed once more and looked at his brother.

"I like her already."

Lorcans head throbbed as Bradan exclaimed, raising tattooed hands, "come! We must have dinner and you must tell us all how Torrin managed to keep you trapped for so long." Nia resisted a shudder, she had forgotten; distracted by the attack, Torrin was an enemy here. Her eyes glittered as they entered the dining room, a long table sat in the middle, it was much larger than the Sapphire Courts. She could not help the look of disdain she gave the table, despite its beauty and the bounty upon it. For Torrin no longer had a reason for so many chairs, *they* had taken his family from him. Nia slipped her cloak from her shoulders and looked up to find six sets of eyes staring hungrily at her.

Nia supposed they would have their charm, if they were not such foul people. Still, she blushed furiously as she took a seat next to Lorcan; for Nia was still a girl, one who had never held the attention of so many before. "Now who cares more about my outfit?" She mocked Lorcan as jealousy burned in his eyes.

"Where are your wives?" Aidan turned to Caden and Bradan, both shared a look with each other. "Where do you think?" Caden groaned, Aidan shook his head. "We will have no slaves left if they must all suffer Taras's wrath, control your woman Caden." Lorcan cleared his throat dramatically; his eyes darting to the girl at his side. Aidan opened his mouth to speak, but before he could; a younger brother asked a question that stiffened Nia's back. "So, Nia, is it true that Torrin trapped you in that Gods awful torture chamber beneath the Sapphire Court?" Keegan asked, Bradan kicked his brother beneath the table.

So, they know of the hidden room that holds Nessa, Nia realised, *I must send word to Torrin.*

"He tried." Nia shrugged as she noticed their eyes awaiting her explanation. "And what pray tell, did the brothels of Breága do to deserve your wrath?" Eoghan whined, at that Nia outright scoffed. Truthfully, she was grateful for the change of subject. Lorcan sent a silent thanks to his closest brother, Eoghan did not even meet his brother's eye. "If you receive a woman's touch only because you have paid for it, I am afraid I have some very dire news for you." The men laughed at that, even Lorcan snickered at her side. "I have been telling him this for centuries!" Keegan grinned as he raised his cup.

The meal continued like this, Lorcans brothers bombarded her with questions of her adventures; twisted versions of the truth, how she had battled the Ellén Trechend and escaped the mountain only to be caught by Torrin once more, how he had dragged her to the Emerald Court where she freed herself and poisoned the city, how she tortured the men in the cells; it was all distorted, Nia could scarcely believe how easily her deeds sounded evil.

"I think it is time to let our guest find rest, God's knows *I* need it listening to you baboons." Lorcan teased his brothers as he took Nias hand once more, Aidan's eyes fixed on their interlocking fingers and a smile slipped on to his face as she squeezed Lorcans hand.

Who would have thought it? He mused to himself, *the youngest of our clan has taken the interest of the most powerful woman in Etherea.*

Aidan grinned at his brother. Malicious plans forming in his mind already. "Go, we will not begrudge you for stealing away such a beauty." Lorcan groaned as his older brother winked at them. Nias cheeks flushed pink, fuelling his brothers whoops behind them as they walked away.

"As if Lorcan would know what to do with her."

Nia turned as they reached the doorway, Caden's words lit a familiar fire within her, Lorcan watched with trepidation as she cocked a brow at his brothers. "I can assure you, fine *Lords,*" she sneered, "Lorcan knows well what to do with me." She did not give them the chance to gather their thoughts, not even a second to close their mouths. Nia had turned and left. Even Lorcan paused, shocked in the doorway; he looked at his brothers and shrugged, gathering his composure. "You heard her." Aidan slapped the table with a grin at his brother's words. "It seems we have all underestimated you brother, I'd recommend you go after her before something explodes; seems you share a temper." His eyes glinted with humour, Lorcan did not bother forming a reply; he just turned and chased after Nia.

"I know what to do with you, do I?" Nia laughed as he caught up with her. "Oh you wouldn't know where to start, but I couldn't very well let them tease you could I?" Lorcan feigned offence at her reply, she rolled her eyes with a smile. "Where, pray tell, will I be resting?" Nia asked as she realised, she did not know where they walked. Lorcan's gulp told her all she needed to know before he spoke. "In my chambers." Nia cocked a brow at him, "do not look at me like that, Tara and Lana are devious bitches and no doubt they will try to harm you the moment they learn of your presence." Nia chewed on her cheek, Torrin had said they had poisoned Tara. Had they ever considered Tara did not *want* to go home? The thought shook Nia to the core.

They came upon a silver door, the only door in this section of the Manor. Lorcan hesitated as he turned the handle. "I just want to make it clear, Nia, I do not expect anything from you. Despite the reputation of my Court, I would nev-" "I know." Nia did not need him to explain, she *felt it*. With her powers settled, it had become much easier to use her senses. Lorcan blinked at her surety. She hardly knew him; he could not understand how she trusted him so easily.

Nia drew a breath as they stepped into his chambers. Soft blues and glittering silvers adorned the room, a huge window overlooked the mountains outside. She was glad they did not have a view of that gloomy forest. It took her breath away. Lorcan watched as she stepped around the room, taking in every detail, from the sky-blue couch in the corner, to the adjacent bathroom. Her eyes rested on the bookshelves beside the huge silver bed, a book lay open on his pillow. Nia smiled at that, "what are you reading?" Lorcan felt heat rise in his cheeks. "It's nothing." he shrugged and stepped towards the book; Nia was quicker.

He groaned as she read the page that he had left open, Nias grin grew as her brows raised at the steamy scene her eyes rested on. "My my, it seems your brothers are *very* wrong about you." Nia teased as he reached for the book, Lorcans face burned beet red as she evaded his grip. "Nia." He warned, it only made her laugh louder.

"It is nothing to be ashamed of, Torrin was always quick to boast about how ladies fell at his feet." Nia rolled her eyes as she laughed, Lorcan stilled. His silver eyes turned cold as they met hers, Nia gulped as she took a step back. The book fell to the bed, its place abandoned. Lorcan stepped towards her, until her back hit the wall with a thud.

Those silver eyes traced her face, from her scarlet hair to her pink lips which parted ever so slightly. Lorcan watched her chest rise and fall as a wicked smirk slipped on to his lips, his breath on her neck rose goosebumps across her flesh. "I prefer," Nia gasped as his lips pressed against her throat, "to let my women boast for me." And with that, he was gone.

Nia raised her hand to her neck, where his lips had been, her fingers shook as her heart pounded against her chest.

Chapter Twenty-Five:

Uaine and Maeve returned to a court in chaos, men and women alike were chained and paraded through the city as livestock. The twins shared a look of disdain as they stepped through the city, the hoods of their cloaks wrapped tightly around their faces. The situation had become much worse in the few days they had been gone. Fae, turned crazed by the poisonous fog, beat their heads against stone walls; as if to purge the Foxglove from their minds. Some did not stop, until their skulls split; Uaine could not stomach the sounds of their bones cracking against the stone. The roads ran red with the blood of their people.

Neither stopped, until they reached the glimmering Emerald gates. Maeve gulped as the Manor sat half in ruins atop the hill. Guards scattered around the rubble, roaring orders to each other. It was no use. The courtyard was in absolute chaos. Uaine took his sisters hand, and together, they walked towards the mayhem. They were thankful for the weapons they had kept, as the Court Guards raised their swords against them.

Maeve had not realised that the same note she used to divert the Silver Princes had also ceased their distribution of the antidote.

Purple veins grew beneath the skin on their faces, the whites of their eyes had turned a sickly yellow. Uaine threw himself in front of his sister as the guards stormed her. Maeve grunted as she swung her sword in all directions. Uaine fell in step with her as they defended themselves against the masses. Sweat laced their brow and their arms grew tired. Their swords felt as though they were made from lead. Maeve faltered as a break formed in the line of men coming towards them, she had one ally in this entire court; and there he was, fighting against the plethora of navy adorned guards. Uaine jumped to block the sword whistling towards Maeve's head and cursed her loss of focus.

"We must help him!" She shouted above the growls of the men clambering to maim them, Uaine looked at his sister in disbelief as he glanced towards the man clad in emerald armour. A sentry of the court. Their luck may change yet. "Rowan!" Maeve called to him, her voice drowned by the clattering of steel and silver before she took off through the swarm towards him.

Rowan's honey-coloured eyes widened as Maeve lashed whips of white magic against their attackers, clearing a path to him. They grew only wider as Uaine came crashing through behind her; cutting down any who reached for her. Rowan blinked twice at the pair. They were identical; save for the obvious difference. He thought her dead, cut down by the Fae who lost their minds. "Thank the Fates, I don't know what happened, we were on our way back from patrol when we saw the city in flames, I thought..." Maeve had just enough time to give his armour-clad shoulder a reassuring squeeze before another sword whistled through the air at them.

"What good is this damned scroll if no-one has a clear mind to understand it?" Uaine cursed as he struggled to keep hold of the parchment. "Abbán would not have sent us if it would not work, but if it does not; I am glad to have tried." Maeve was defiant, she had spent far too long hidden away; no longer would she disguise herself, no longer would she send orders from her chambers, skulking through her own Manor in fear. Rowan eyed the glittering scroll as he ducked and dived away from the weapons whizzing at him. "The councilmen have retreated to the high tower, perhaps they have not been effected." He reasoned, although he did not know what the scroll entailed; he would do all he could to assist Maeve. Rowan had kept her secret for decades and been a faithful friend; they could not change the ways of the Court, but they could keep its cruelty from leaking past the borders.

She had found him, wandering the outskirts of her court; on a day in which sense had left her, when she had all but given up on the hopes of Uaine returning to her. Maeve had thought he was a trapper, out hunting for wild women to sell; like so many others in her court. Instead, he had stared at her; wide-eyed and terrified. For Rowan *had* come to trap women, with his father and his brothers; yet he could not bring himself to do it. Instead, he helped her to flee. Rowan never understood why Maeve returned to the Manor, when she could have fled to another court; not until she told him of Ciar's intent to destroy her family, how she lived to protect the sibling her mother had hidden. It was three days after, when Maeve saw the bruises littering Rowans face, that she made him her sentry. His father had beat him, allowed his brothers to attack him, until he was a bloody mess and still; he did not tell them of Maeve.

Uaine did not miss the warm look his sister gave the burgundy haired sentry; but he did not see a broad man barrelling towards him. Rowan knocked Uaine to the side, both narrowly avoiding the blade the crazed man wielded. The scroll sprung from Uaine's hand in the turmoil, through the air it went before landing with a thud in the muck; as dozens of feet ran across it. The seal broke as the rocks scraped against it, Uaine cursed as the parchment unfurled. Blinding white light erupted from the scroll as it fully unravelled.

The trio watched in wonder as the purple haze disappeared from the sky, the air cleared in the lungs of their people. The men around them blinked, as if seeing clearly for the first time in eons and paused their advance. Ciar had cursed this court too, it seemed; for they looked disgusted with themselves as they threw down their swords. One man, with fair hair and a gaunt disposition reached for the scroll. His eyes lit with realisation as he read aloud the words Abbán had written.

"By order of her royal highness, rightful heir to the throne of Etherea, Elvinia Ó Mordha; The Emerald Court is hereby released of any and all curses set upon it." Murmurs filled the courtyard as the man cleared his throat. "Furthermore, for his wilful crimes against the women of Etherea; the High Lord of the Emerald Court has been sentenced to death. The last remaining heirs to the Ó Loinsigh line have returned to reclaim their rightful titles as High Lord and Lady of the Emerald Court, any who dare challenge this; will face the wrath of Etherea." The men bowed instantly. Maeve could hardly believe it; she had spent centuries hidden and afraid; so sure, that she would never be able to step back into the light of her court as its leader.

Uaines heart swelled, Nias presence had not just cracked Ciars hold on Etherea; she had blown it wide open. Nothing proved this more than the sun splitting through the clouds, illuminating the hill they stood upon. Maeve turned to the crumbling manor behind them and raised her shaking hands. Like the Sapphire Court, Ciar had dampened the power flowing to the Fae of the Emerald Court. Maeve felt a surge in her veins as his hold slipped away. The manor shook in its stead, Uaine raised his palms to aid her. Rowan and the crowd watched in awe as the siblings rebuilt the manor to its former glittering glory.

The council men emerged then, from the adjacent tower. Uaine could have scoffed at their formal attire and stern faces. Their vision too had cleared, yet they remained sceptical of the legitimacy of the twins claim. One could not understand their reasoning, for it was obvious the emerald eyed pair were the heirs to the Court; but the old ways ran deep within Court officials. Uaine had never understood it, how some still clung to the politics of Ethereas nobility. Maeve had never met them but knew of their stubbornness.

She held her head high as she approached them, the Fae who had read the scroll handed it to the eldest councillor. They huddled together in their matching emerald robes; golden brooches adorned their chests. Maeve's eyes narrowed at that. They should be wearing emerald gems on their collars, not gold on their chests. The man holding the scroll pursed his lips and looked at Maeve, she cursed his eyes as they scanned her before turning to her brother. "The council recognises your legitimacy. We welcome you, Lord Uaine." The smile on his face did nothing to calm her nerves. Uaine felt Maeve's trepidation and found himself stepping towards his sister. "You have forgotten your Lady, kind sir." Uaine had grit his teeth, his patience waned as their callous eyes scoured his sister; their sneers boiled his blood. The councillors tittered behind their leader. "Forgive us, Lord Uaine but no woman may sit at the Emerald Courts helm, it simply is not done." he spoke with a smugness that only a councillor could.

Rowan snatched the scroll from the stubborn fools' hands. "It is done, she is your High Lady. Now bow your fucking heads." Rowan snarled as he pointed to the writing which clearly stated they were to lead the court as a unit, the lead council member scoffed. Maeve smiled and shook her head. She knew the truth the moment she saw the gold on their chests. They had no authority here.

"Good sirs." Maeve said politely, ignoring Rowan's incredulous look, as she stepped beside her brother. "Would you be so kind as to tell your Lord why you wear the sigil of the Golden Court? A symbol of allegiance to Duane if I am not mistaken." They paused. Uaine *had* noticed the gold on their chests but did not realise it was out of place. The men's eyes widened. The bystanders watched anxiously, realising they too had been misled. "By royal decree, we have been returned to our birthright; yet you presume to tell me it cannot be done, because the parts between my legs do not suit your preference?" The crowd around them murmured. More of her people climbed the hill to their High Lords home, the fog cleared from their minds; men and women alike, ashamed and confused.

The council member looked around; Rowan raised his sword. "Lord Duane owns this court!" The shortest of them called out. A gasp rippled through the crowd. Maeve howled with laughter before pointing a finger at the huddled council members. Uaine watched as streams of Emerald light burst towards the men. "Run and run far; should you reach your precious Lord, tell him should he or his beasts set foot in my Court, I will rip him to shreds." As if to prove her point, Maeve clenched her fists and the fine robes they wore fell to tatters on the ground.

Naked, they ran through the crowd.

Uaine stifled a laugh at their bewildered faces; their shouts that they would pay for this one day. One could not take their threats seriously, not as their pale and wrinkled skin flapped in the wind. Maeve gripped his hand and turned to their people. *She is much better at this than I,* he realised as she raised their joined hands in the air. Maeve smiled warmly at the concerned crowd. "Good people of the Emerald Court, we have been reunited at last; we must work together now, to rebuild our Court as our own. No woman shall be harmed within our court, never again. General," Maeve turned to Rowan, his eyes widened at the title, "please ensure that all devices used to enslave or torture the people of this court are destroyed. We would like to welcome you all, to our home, but first, go forth and rest. For we have much work ahead of us."

Uaine could hardly believe it, they *cheered* for them. Women wept with relief as men begged for forgiveness. Maeve blinked furiously at their pleas for their wives, their daughters, to forgive them for what they had done. For it was not their nature to be so wicked towards their counterparts; Ciar had poisoned their minds, Duane had worked to keep it so. Maeve had been powerless to stop it. Up the steps they rose, to the chorus of cheers behind them. It was surreal, they were finally *home.*

Chapter Twenty-Six:

Lorcan had returned to his chambers late that night, weary from the day's events; he still found a smile slipped on to his face as he eyed the sleeping girl in his bed. He lay across the couch, facing the doorway; ever ready for whatever his brother's may do. Lorcan found his eyes travelling towards the Elven woman in his bed. In her slumber, she glowed effervescent. His heart yearned for her; she was light incarnate; everything Lorcan had ever dreamed of. He shook his head; he would not do her the disservice of distracting her from her mission. *Perhaps, when all is said and done, we may have a chance.*

Nia awoke the next morning filled with confusion. It had been weeks since she last slept in a bed, in this very Court; when Erin had kindly offered up her home as a haven for them at the beginning of their journey. It all seemed so far away now. Lorcan sat in the armchair by the window, drinking his morning coffee, and watched with amusement as Nia jumped from the bed. Wearing the same silk blue gown that she had arrived in, her scarlet hair askew, Lorcan could not believe how she managed to remain breathtaking. His brows rose as Nia withdrew the bejewelled dagger she had strapped to her leg. Nia blinked twice as she reviewed her surroundings. Embarrassment burned her cheeks as she realised where she was, and who sat watching her.

Lorcan laughed as she sheepishly lowered her weapon. "I think you may survive this madhouse yet." He teased as he poured her a cup of coffee, Nia closed her eyes at the smell that wafted towards her. "What is that?" She asked, taking a step towards the pot of steaming chocolate coloured liquid. "Do you mean to tell me you have *never* had coffee?" Lorcan asked, astounded. Nia groaned, she had barely survived Torrin and Uaines High Lord ignorance; once again she found herself in the presence of privilege. The genuine shock on his face gave her pause, perhaps she should cut them some slack; for they did not know of the hardships that faced humanity. Lorcan knew he had made a blunder as her lips pursed before she answered. "I have had coffee," Nia told him matter- of-factly, "but it was not this, my mother made it from dandelion root." Lorcan crinkled his nose at that, his nurse had loved dandelion coffee; he could not stand it.

Lorcan nudged the cup towards her. "Swill, compared to this." Nia rolled her eyes as he put his foot in his mouth once more. "A delicacy when you have nought else." She bit back, Lorcan sipped quietly as she lifted her cup to her nose. He resisted the urge to laugh as she sniffed it with trepidation. Nia almost sank into her chair at the aroma wafting to her nose, it was heavenly; with hints of citrus, spiced nuts and chocolate, Nia had never smelled anything like it. Lorcan almost spoke to warn her of its heat, until she blew the liquid of her own accord; he could have sworn she looked at him as if she knew his thoughts.

Nia did not need to read his mind to know he was about to warn her, as if she were a child. Her senses erupted as she slurped the boiling liquid, it *did* burn her tongue; she would never admit it. Lorcan chewed the inside of his cheek as she winced just the tiniest amount, if she wished to be stubborn, then he would leave her to it. Her eyes like saucers, Nia slammed the cup down. "This is wholly unfair." She whined; she could still taste the heavenly liquid on her tongue. At this, Lorcan did laugh; causing Nia to narrow her eyes. "Dandelion coffee is better though." She reverted; it almost hurt Nia to say it, to insult the absolute nectar in her cup, but she could not relent. She never could. His silver eyes sparkled as he grinned at her. "Whatever you say, your majesty." He winked as he said it, sending butterflies crashing around Nias stomach. She mentally scolded herself and remembered herself distinctly telling Torrin that she was *not* some village floozy. *Torrin*. Nia wondered how he was faring. She thought of Uaine and Maeve too, back in that dreadful Court.

"Lorcan?" He watched as she fiddled with the spoon aside her cup. "Yes?" He prodded as she fell silent, Nia pursed her lips once more before sighing. "Forgive me, but have you heard word of Uaine or Torrin?" "Why would you need forgiveness for asking of your friends? By the Fates what *have* you heard about me?" Lorcan despised his reputation more than anything else. Nia sighed before placing her hand over his. "Considering Etherea has called me the... scarlet death," Nia flinched every time she heard it, aside from being an utterly ridiculous name; she did not wish to be associated with death, "then your reputation means nothing to me." Lorcans heart swelled as he looked at her, she was not teasing him. She simply meant the words she said.

A rare occurrence for the Silver Court.

"Uaine and Maeve have reclaimed their Court, with a scroll carrying a royal decree from one Elvinia O'Mórdha." Nias widening eyes told him she had little to do with writing such a scroll. "Their curses have been undone; the Foxglove has cleared." Her shoulders eased, he debated whether to continue. "There were some... issues regarding Maeve," Nias brows creased as she sat up, "they are fine, it seems the councilmen had sworn allegiance to Duane; they had grown tired of being led by a secret Lord, Maeve and Uaine rectified it fairly quickly." Nia sighed with relief. Anyone in the Emerald Court who preferred the old ways had no place in Etherea. "I have not heard word of the Sapphire Court, although there have been sightings of folk scurrying towards its borders over the last few weeks." Lorcan wished he had more news to share, but Nia simply took another sip of her delightful drink and leaned back in her chair. "No news is good news." She repeated a mantra she had heard her mother say a million times to folk in her village. Lorcan wished he could share in her optimism; he knew the shifting of the Courts meant politics would rise its ugly head once more.

As if on cue, a knock sounded at the door. Nia had forgotten for a moment, where she sat; in the heart of the most vicious court in Etherea. With lightning speed, Nia removed her dagger from the table and hid it once more in her garter. She did not miss how Lorcans eyes lingered just a second too long on her exposed skin. Nia felt her heart flutter once more and cursed herself. Lorcan blinked as white tendrils wrapped around the fiery woman beside him, her silk blue gown replaced with a simple silver off the shoulder day dress, her hair loose but tidy. "Now, *that* is unfair." Lorcan teased as he rose to open the door. He glanced nervously at Nia as she raised her cup to her lips, a twinkle in her eye. Lorcan knew which of his brothers stood outside his door. He would have preferred Aidan. At least *he* would have been polite.

Caden grinned at the pair as he swung the door open, inviting himself into the room. "Sleepless night?" He asked with a smirk, eyeing the pot of coffee on the table. Nia glanced at him through her lashes. "A lady never tells." She told him, sickly sweet as she sipped from her cup. Caden clicked his tongue at her. "Then we are in luck that you are not a lady." Lorcan growled at his brother, a warning in his eyes as his jaw tightened.

"Say that again."

Nia gulped at the dangerous look in his eyes, for although she knew of his reputation; she had yet to see him live up to it. Fire flared in Caden at his brother's challenge. "She may have been born into royalty but, honestly brother, look at her-" Nia gasped as Lorcans fist connected with Caden's face before he could finish his sentence. "She is your future Queen, lest you forget again, I shall be glad to remind you." Lorcan roared at his brother. His voice was so furious, so sure, a coldness coursed down Nia's spine. She always forgot, one day she could be Queen. If she were to survive this ordeal at least. The older Fae stumbled backwards; she watched him spit the blood from his lip before raising his head to glare at his little brother. Nia thought he would speak, curse Lorcan for hitting him, but no; Caden lunged for him.

Nia raised her feet to escape their tumbling bodies as they crashed into the hallway. Her mind whirled as she jumped to her feet. Nia crossed the doorway, and all diplomacy left her at the sight of Caden hunched over Lorcan; his fists pounding into Lorcan's face. Fury ripped through her in an instant. Caden was vicious, out of control, blood poured from his younger brother's face. Nia wanted to rip him to shreds.

Aidan reached the commotion- he had heard it from across the manor- just in time to witness Nia wielding a glittering dagger at his brother's neck. Aidan paused, took in the sight before him; Lorcans battered face, Caden's smug smirk, Nias burning eyes. He blinked at that last image; the rage rippled from her.

Ciars daughter through and through, Aidan remarked to himself. Nia saw it clearly, for the first time; not just wisps of silver magic or gurgled whispers, but *words*. Nia almost choked on Aidan's thoughts before a wicked idea ran through her mind; she could use this to her advantage. "I wonder if my father would like to know how his princes are treating his daughter." Nia sneered as she pressed the cold steel harder against Caden's throat. The men stilled at her words, Lorcan eyed her from the ground; *please, tell me she is bluffing*, he thought. Nia could not believe he doubted her, she realised she would have to speak to him; to reveal her plan. Aidan studied her for a moment, the calmness in her eyes as she returned his gaze; it unnerved him.

Caden glared at both of his brothers, his eyes darting between them; for their hesitation. "Forgive my brother, Elvinia." Aidan started gently, ignoring Caden's burning hatred. "He has felt the fist of many against his head, and I am afraid it has cost him his sense." At this he glared at Caden, for his stupidity. Nia clicked her tongue at the Fae. "Do see that it does not cost him his life." She removed the dagger from Caden's neck and shoved him towards his elder, Lorcan could not believe it as Caden rose to his feet and turned to face Nia. Tension fizzled between the two. "Ah, it is like she is already family." he grinned, breaking the thickness in the air.

Nia fumbled for words; Lorcan pulled himself from the ground to save her from her confusion, for she did not yet know that this was a regular occurrence. While Lorcan could not go against his brothers in war, they tormented each other regularly within the privacy of their home. "Yes Nia, forgive my idiot brother; for it was I who knocked him upon the head and murdered his brain cells." Lorcan grinned as he slapped his brothers back. Blood still gushed from his nose, Nia glared once more at Caden and Aidan. "Perhaps we can knock some back into him one day." Lorcan laughed nervously, he knew she meant it.

"What in the Fates is going on here?" A shrill voice sounded from the end of the hall. Nia's head snapped to the woman storming towards them, it was not Tara; no, this woman looked nothing like Torrin. She had long ringlets of silver hair, olive eyes, a high nose, and a stink of entitlement. Lorcan groaned, cursing his luck; or lack thereof. "Lana." Aidan warned, the woman shrugged off his extending hand as she bee-lined towards Nia. "So, this is her?" She asked, Nia raised her chin to lock eyes with the taller Fae. There was much less fear in the woman than the men around her. "I don't care who your father is, keep your claws off my husband." Lana growled at her; Nia rolled her eyes. "He wishes." She scoffed. Lorcan sucked a breath through his teeth, Aidan reached for Lana too late.

A loud clatter echoed through the hallway, Lana lowered her stinging hand; Nia turned her head to stare back at the woman, Lorcan's heart almost stopped as she smirked. A red handprint adorned her cheek. She curled her hands at her side as she stepped closer to Lana. Nia snapped her fists open, a terrifying gust of wind sent Lana barrelling towards the wall.

"If you wish to keep those pretty hands long enough to calm your prick of a husband down, then I suggest you never raise them to me again." Lorcan could not believe the fear that flickered in Lana's eyes; Nia was full of surprises. She turned her attention to Caden.

"Get her out of my sight."

Caden looked between Aidan and Nia, Aidan nodded his head and without a second to spare; Caden dragged his protesting wife from the hallway. Lorcan beamed, she had spent hours in their presence and already his brothers feared her, he did not doubt that Caden would have taken Lana away whether Aidan gave him permission or not. In their own barbaric way, Caden and Lana loved each other wholly.

Nia turned to Aidan, her eyes no longer burning with rage; she took a calming breath. "I apologise, for the commotion I have wrought within your home, Aidan. My threat of my father, an empty one made in anger. I do hope you will allow me to stay." Lorcan felt he had whiplash, one moment she was murderous, in the next she became perfectly poised; a picture of the crown which she represented. For either side of Fae, light and dark; she fit both roles flawlessly.

He was in awe at the skill she had, to balance both sides of herself at a knife's edge. It had not been long since he found her, fractured, and devastated in the woods. Aidan's grin surprised them both. "Yes, definitely part of the family." He boomed. "Go, clean yourselves up; then we shall have dinner and discuss the welcome reception we will hold for our wonderful guest." Aidan left before either formed a reply; he would not admit he also feared her temper.

"I do not know why you look so smug." Nia *tsked* at Lorcan as she re-entered his room, her coffee ice cold; she sighed as she held the cup in vain. Lorcan sauntered in after her, shutting the door behind him. His once crisp suit now crinkled, he threw his jacket across his bed.

"I will not lie to you, as you already know my brothers are," he paused for a moment, "not my favourite people." Nia was not shocked, for every time he had spoken of his brothers he had done so with a glimmer of fear in his eyes. "Nor am I theirs, we have fought each other for centuries. After the questionable death of our father, Aidan followed in his path and bowed to Ciar; binding us here, together. These walls have seen plenty of brawls, you need not come to my aid." Nia stood, his emotions rolled towards her in waves, she took a shaky breath and clutched the ring on her finger. Shame, pain, guilt, anger, hopelessness. It burned her blood; tears pricked her eyes at the sheer strength of devastation that struck her.

Lorcan reached for her with worry, it sent Nia to her knees. She gripped the burning jewellery tighter, willed it to work; to do anything to dull the ache in her heart. Two days without the world's pain assaulting her mind and she had already forgotten its gut-wrenching feeling. She cursed herself for her weakness. Lorcan misunderstood and reached to remove the ring from her finger. Nia opened her mouth to scream but no sound escaped her lips; instead, she knocked Lorcan backwards, she felt just as she had that very first time. Nia remembered Torrins rage, Uaine's fear; the pain on their faces as she sent them to their knees, writhing in the agony which probed her mind every day since. She could not do that to him.

"Lorcan please, run, I am dangerous." Nia begged him as he struggled against the forces pushing him away. With each step, black ink trickled from Nias fingertips. Lorcan felt it then, his own emotions at a magnitude that sent his head spinning. Still, Lorcan advanced, care overwhelming any regard he had for his own safety.

Shock filled her as he reached her and wrapped his arms around her. "What is happening?" He asked, Nia squeezed her eyes tight. "I feel it all, every ounce of happiness, every wave of sorrow. Everything in the world is happening all at once, this ring has dulled it; but... your pain, it is *so strong*." Lorcans eyes widened, he released Nia as if she had burned him; in truth, guilt wracked him for causing her pain. Nias nostrils flared. "Please, Lorcan, please stop." He staggered away from her.

"You are not what they think you are, I cannot see any evil within you; you must find peace." She wheezed as his panic grew, he wanted to help her; but did not know how. Nia clenched her fists and crossed the distance between them. The pain coursed through her body like a thousand knives against her skin as she embraced him. "What can I do?" Lorcan asked, finally shaking the shock from his mind. "You need to calm yourself." She told him, her hands shook as he held her once more.

Lorcan struggled but forced himself to take a breath and gather his emotions. He focused on the girl in his arms, the strength she had shown, her beauty, her laugh, her smile. It filled his mind and warmed his heart. The wave ebbed; Nia took a gulp of air as she found herself finally able to think again. "What was that?" Lorcan asked as she relaxed, although she still shook. Nia sighed as she unwillingly pulled herself from his embrace. Lorcan saw the exhaustion in her eyes as she told him of her journey thus far. Lorcan had not heard it from her yet, only rumours and stories that had travelled through the Courts. Nia decided not to speak of Erin's aid, she did not wish to cause the woman trouble for her good deed, even though she knew Lorcan would cause her no harm; she could not trust his brothers to share the same courtesy should they learn of it.

Lorcan shook his head as she spoke of the Ellén Trechend beneath the mountain, how she *had* fought it single-handedly and won but only barely; how she had been saved by the Merrow from the water which swallowed her. "I am sorry I sent you away, I should have stolen you from that fool the minute I found you in my Court." Lorcan groaned, Nia narrowed her eyes at him, Lorcan sighed. "I understand he saved you from certain death, but you must admit Torrin *is* a stubborn fool; he has always been protective to a fault, he would rather keep you oblivious than tell you your land is a shit-show and hurt your feelings." Nia blinked twice, her mouth agape. Lorcan paused as he awaited her reply, Nia laughed; wholeheartedly.

She did not know if she was delirious from exhaustion and suspected he thought the same as she wiped a tear from her face. "You are the first person to say it aloud, my whole life is a shit-show." She grinned at him; Nia had thought it many times. Etherea was upside down, as was her entire life since she stepped foot in it.

Surprised, but light-hearted once again, Lorcan returned her smile. "If you ever need a dose of honesty, I'm your man." He chuckled, Nia turned to the mirror to fix her hair as a blush crept onto her cheeks. She enjoyed the sound of that, far too much. It confused her, Nia knew Torrin felt something for her, and at first, she had shared his affection; but here she was, enjoying the company of another so easily. Perhaps it had been circumstances that drew them to each other, Torrin had taken her in like a wounded puppy and nursed her back to health; perhaps it had been that which created a bond between them. Nia had not much experience with relationships with the opposite sex. Tristan had made sure of it. She decided not to dwell on it, she had no commitments to Torrin; he had not expressed his wish to be with her, they had shared only fleeting looks and a dance. Surely that was not enough to mean she could not explore her feelings for another.

Nia turned to Lorcan then and raised her hand. He watched her curiously as warmth filled him, the blood disappeared from his face, his cuts healed. Nia smiled at him as he glanced in the mirror. "I could not stand being responsible for the destruction of such a pretty face." Nia shrugged, Lorcan smirked. "So, you think I'm pretty?" He teased; Nia stuck her tongue out at him. "Sure, for a pampered Prince." she shot back with a grin. Lorcan raised a hand to his chest. "You wound me, your majesty; you must teach me your humble ways." Nia snorted. "You and all the High Lords of this land would not last five seconds in my realm, without your precious magic to aid you." Lorcan did not doubt her, he knew at least three of his brothers would starve or poison themselves.

He quirked a brow at the wicked thought that ran through his mind. "Perhaps we *should* let them try." Nia shook her head with a smile. "I must say I am enjoying the irony that we both wished to seduce each other when we had the same intentions for my Court. Pray tell, your majesty; how did you plan to woo me?" Nia blushed once more and rolled her eyes. "Come on, I am starving; we can discuss maiming your brothers later." Lorcans eyes twinkled as he muttered, "perhaps we can also discuss our strategies of seduction." Nia groaned as he laughed and followed her through the manor.

He let her lead for far longer than he should have, Nia had realised quite a while ago she had no idea where she was walking; too stubborn to admit it, she continued forward until they reached a dead end. "Have we made a mistake?" He teased; Nia crossed her arms as she glared up at him. His grin only widened. "I do not make mistakes." She scoffed, knowing this to be a total lie. Lorcan clicked his tongue at her. "Oh, no? I was unaware the dining room had moved." His smirk only frustrated her more.

Nia glared at the blank wall before them, her eyes narrowing. "Admit it, you have no idea where we are." Lorcan teased once more, Nia wanted nothing more than to prove him wrong as he smirked down at her. His eyes betrayed him, as they flickered down her body. Heat coursed through her at the unexpected haze that covered his silver orbs, he looked at her as if he would *devour* her. A wicked thought flashed through her, along with a burning need stronger than anything she had ever felt before; *Perhaps I should let him*.

The hallway shook around them, breaking the pair from their revere. Lorcan stumbled, his arms wrapped around her protectively. Nia shuddered as his hands caressed her middle. Fire licked at her bones once more, and suddenly, the dining room appeared before them. Lorcan looked down at her in shock, Nia shut her eyes with a grimace, waiting for his fury. "Please tell me you did not just move the dining room to prove me wrong." Lorcan coughed as the dust settled. Her heart pounded in her chest, panicked that he would scold her for what she had done. Uaine and Torrin's reactions to her magic had been mixed to say the least.

The laughter that erupted from him had Nia opening her eyes cautiously, Lorcan held her face in his hands as he grinned. "You are amazing." Her heart swelled; tears pricked her eyes. Lorcans brows creased with worry. "What is it?" He asked, Nia sniffled. "You are not angry?" At this he embraced her once more. "I for one, think this is hilarious; I cannot wait to see Aidan's face." Nia chuckled as the joy rolled from him, easing her panic. "Come, we will say nothing, I think my brothers will enjoy having you around much more after this." Lorcan chuckled once again as he pushed open the door now before them. They entered the dining hall, Nia noticed they were last to arrive. She found her hand clutching Lorcans as she laid eyes on Tara. Nia had almost forgotten her.

The woman looked like Torrin, in a way; she was far more sinister. She had pin straight copper hair, a shade darker than her brothers, but those same glowing Sapphire eyes. Taras lips curled into a harrowing smile as they entered. Lorcan watched his sister-in-law carefully as she rose from her seat, Torrin had been entirely wrong in his accusations. Sure, Tara had been taken to the Silver Court by Ciar; but she had made it her *home*. Tara had found, quickly, how entirely she enjoyed the freedom of this Court. Without the ever-foreboding morals of her brother controlling her.

Nia said nothing as Tara approached, cocking her head as she surveyed the princess. Nia did not miss Caden reaching for Lana's hand; the comforting squeeze he gave it as the silver haired woman glared at Tara's back. She wondered, with their evil nature, were they capable of love? "So, how is my bastard of a brother?" Tara asked, Nia knew she must choose her words carefully; the men seemed much more afraid of her father than their wives. Nia forced a laugh and squeezed Lorcans hand once more. "Still a bastard." Tara grinned and threw her arm around Nia's shoulders. "You are much more palatable than your father." Tara informed Nia as she led her to the vacant chair beside her own. Lorcan took the seat across from them, a look of worry clear on his face. "And you are much saner than your brother presumes." Nia returned as she raised her glass to her lips.

The men around them tucked into their food but said not a word; all of them too focused on the exchange between the two women. It was notoriously known that High Ladies were far more ruthless than their Lords; and the Elves of the Ruby Court were known for far worse tempers than any Fae in Etherea. Highborn or not. Lorcan prayed the Fates would see him live through this meal. Tara chuckled and shook her head. "Men, slaves to their ego." Tara echoed a thought Nia had herself many weeks ago; when she met Lorcan in Avenere. Her violet-red eyes flickered to him. "They can be." Lorcan raised a brow at her, she winked in return.

Tara laughed. "You have made the right decision, to leave that soft court. I have heard the High Lady you have appointed to the Emerald Court is a force to be reckoned with, it is high time Etherea had a woman in charge." Bradan cleared his throat at his wife's words, he glanced nervously at his eldest brother. "It would do well to remember who gave you this life." Aidan said sternly, he would not stand for disrespect of their King; not even if it meant appeasing his daughter. "Ciar is a mighty ruler, we are blessed to have been his loyal comrades for so long; and even more so to have his daughter in our presence." Aidan raised his cup in salute, the others followed his lead. Nia cursed herself for coming here as she lifted her own goblet, a smile plastered on her face. It was not even noon and already her head throbbed. *How am I going to get through this?*

Chapter Twenty-Seven:

Torrin, unlike the others, did not leave Galeria immediately. Rian looked around the empty dining hall for his brother, to no avail. Torrin found himself still in Abbán's presence. The old man eyed him curiously. "You cannot love her, you will, but you cannot." He frowned at the vague words, defiance flamed in his heart. "You are not destined for her, only to protect her. You *are* a Faoladh are you not?" Abbán asked, Torrin gulped and nodded. The old man had said it already but did not believe Torrin had truly heard his words.

"Then you are the last protector of the last of the Ó Mordha line, you cannot be distracted by your love of her. She is to be the Queen, to bring peace back to Etherea. If you stand in her way, she will fail, she is destined for another, and you must not fight it." Torrin opened his mouth to argue but could not find the words. Abbán pursed his lips before clasping his hands. "Heed my words Torrin Ó Cinnéide and your court will thrive, ignore them and you will find only death and destruction. I fear my words have not been heard clear enough by another of your group, there are troubling times ahead." With that last warning, Abbán sent Torrin whirling through the ether; back to his home. Torrin stared in disbelief at the trove of people at his gates, Fae from all courts clattering against the steel. He could see Rian at the entrance, an equally baffled look rested on the young Fae's face. The court was alive with greenery, he had not seen anything like it since he was a child. "There he is!" A young woman yelled from the crowd, which promptly turned in his direction.

Torrin stumbled backwards as they advanced towards him. "Is it true?" "Is she here?" "Will she truly save us?" Their questions overlapped, bombarding him with their curiosity. Torrin opened his mouth to speak but found he did not have the words, he thought for a moment. "She is not here." Their faces fell. "But she will return, all who wish to find shelter here are welcome to do so." They cheered; the Sapphire Court had not seen this many Fae in centuries. Torrin realised they would have to rebuild Avenere if he had any hope of sheltering these people long-term. He began directing people, some he knew vaguely, most were strangers; he sent them to build camps for the night, find food and set up a guard by the border. He would not forgive himself if they were attacked for fleeing to his Court.

Finally, Torrin reached his brother. "Where were you?" Rian asked as the crowd disbanded; murmuring as they did. Torrin shook his head. "It does not matter." Rian suspected his brother was lying but decided not to push the issue. They returned inside their home; it had grown cold in the weeks since they had left. Both got to work opening the Manor to the masses, still in shock that they had been returned so suddenly. Torrin thought of his friends and hoped that they were okay. He did not doubt Uaine's sister would slip right into her role as High Lady; Uaine would take some time to adjust. He wished he could be there for them, to aid them;

his thoughts ventured to Nia. In the heart of the Silver Court; surrounded by enemies. He wondered how she would fare and prayed that they would not harm her. From the looks he had seen on Lorcans face, Torrin knew *he* would not harm her; he did not know how this thought made him feel. On one hand, of course, he was glad for it; deep down however, he could not ignore the swell of jealousy in his gut.

It felt eerie, the emptiness; Torrin thought it strange, for his Court had always been empty. He realised it had been *her*, Nia had brought a light and warmth into his home he had not even recognised until she left. He cursed himself for being such a fool. Rian stood quietly at his brother's side, contemplating Abbán's revelation. It made complete sense and yet no sense at all; who had cursed him and why could no one remember? Why would they curse him to stay young? He could not think of a reason, nor would anyone benefit from his perpetual youth.

Torrin noticed the silence of his brother, yet he could not find the words to say. He had not realised his own brother was cursed; although, Uaine had not seen it either. If Uaine and his sight had been fooled, then it was powerful magic which cursed Rian. Torrin squeezed his brother's shoulder. "We must help our people now, for we do not know what is to come." It would serve them both well, he hoped, to be distracted by the labour of restoring their Court. Torrin could not have known what he led Rian towards. Rian threw himself into aiding their people, despite their incredulous looks at the child; they had been blinded more than they realised. To their credit, neither Rian nor Torrin had made it a habit to leave their court; even if Rian *did* venture from the borders, they had not spent much time with other Fae in recent years. Torrin had become a recluse after the loss of his people to the mountain. Save for the dance he threw for Nia, Torrin had spent his time avoiding the other Lords at every opportunity.

Torrin scanned the perimeter as night fell, not entirely trusting of the guard which had formed itself to protect his Court. The moon illuminated the land, he still could not believe how much had grown since they had first set off towards Galeria. He remembered the dust in his eyes and the sun scorching his back as they had left, Abbán's words rang in Torrin's mind. Bitterness filled him, he would not do anything to jeopardize the safety of these people; not after his own had been trapped so many years ago, but he could not stop his heart yearning for that fiery redhead who had thrown his stagnant life into chaos and excitement.

He thought of Lorcan once more, how they had looked at each other; despite Nias claims that she had been manipulating the Silver Lord, he had seen her grow fond of him. Torrin hoped she could still free his sister, even if she fell for Lorcan; it would be a great weight relieved from his shoulders if she could do so. He had not seen Tara in so long, yet his heart still ached for her, still heard her sobs as they dragged her from his arms. *She should be here*, he thought, *not in that torturous Court*. Rian wiped the sweat from his brow, night had fallen without his notice, he wondered where his brother had gone as he gathered his supplies. Most of the Fae had already taken rest for the night, weary from their travels.

The moon shone high at his back, illuminating the path before him. As Rian stepped into the courtyard, his eyes fell upon the fountain proudly standing in his path. His gaze flickered to the hidden mechanism at its mouth. Rian knew he should not venture further. He had lost the stone which gave him a glimmer of protection against her, he assumed it had fallen from his pocket when they brought Nia. They never should have let them meet.

Rian could not help himself as he glanced around the empty courtyard before raising his hands to the structure which towered over him. It creaked and cracked as it opened, Rian felt goosebumps raise across his flesh. He had not felt so afraid of the menacing steps which led to her since that first time. When he had been caught, his father had been so angry. It had been a blur. Still, Rian was curious to a fault; despite Abbán's warning, he knew Nessa would give him answers at least. He would not ask her to cure him, would not go looking for the cure, as Abbán had asked. Rian was a fool to think this distinction would matter.

He could hear her, scratching at the stone around her. Rian shivered as he descended the steps; using what little magic he could summon to illuminate his path. The bitter stench of despair stung his nose as he finally reached the last step. Nessa cackled wickedly. "Oh you cannot be serious." She shook her head as Rian frowned; he could not find the words. "So, little one, Abbán told you." Nessa sneered as she cocked her head to examine him. "I could help you; you know. All you need to do is ask." Rian's eyes widened, surely, she was lying. "I would not lie Rian, I have always felt pity for you; what kind of father curses his own child to remain ten?" At this he turned to leave.

My father would never do such a thing to me, Rian thought; before he paused. His father would, he realised as he thought of Tara. His father had given her to the Silver Court without objection. Nessa clicked her tongue. "Fathers, they do tend to be cruel in Etherea." Rian scoffed, "and who are you to comment on another's cruelty?" He barked. It was easy to forget, with her ragged appearance, that Nessa was born of dark and powerful magic. Rian expected rage, instead she laughed; it was unnerving how similar she looked to Nia when she smiled. They could have been twins, if not for Nessa's gaunt and sallow skin. "At least I do not pretend I am not cruel, for all their posturing; the High Fae of Etherea are no better than the lowest street rat." Nessa spat. "So, do you want my help or not?" Rian could not believe he was contemplating it; he had opened his mouth to say no but could not bring the word forth.

Torrin felt an uneasy swirl in his gut as he looked across the land, something was wrong; but he did not know what. "Lord Torrin?" A woman's voice sounded behind him. Torrin turned from his post and looked at the golden eyed woman with long curly brown hair, she looked ever so familiar. "Yes?" He replied curiously. "I do not know if you remember me, but I was there the day you brought Elvinia to Breága." Torrin did remember her; the woman before him was the very same whom sparked Nias vengeful nature in the Emerald City.

"My name is Cliodhna, if it were not for Nia then I would have died a bitter death; is she safe?" The pain that flickered in Torrins Sapphire eyes gave her a clear answer. "If she finds herself in trouble, I have shown her where she will find allies; I only pray Elvinia remembers." Torrin eyed the woman curiously. Cliodhna stood tall, her eyes calculating as they looked across the horizon. "He has sent me to aid you follow your path." She whispered. Torrin frowned. "I do not know whom you speak of." He told her honestly; he had spoken barely ten words to her and yet; she looked at him as if he had said a million. "You found Abbán did you not?" Cliodhna clarified, Torrins brows rose in return. "What do you know of him?" He asked, suspicion clear in his voice. "That is for another time, you must go; for your brother is about to unleash death from within your court. I have seen it and I have come to warn you. For Abbán has been taken and he can aid you no more." Torrins blood ran cold at her words. *Nessa.* In all that had happened, he had forgotten once more about that wicked woman beneath their feet. He had been oblivious to so much... Torrin was beginning to question his ability to lead at all.

Chapter Twenty-Eight:

Nia had survived breakfast with Lorcan's family, at least. She was surprised with how normal their conversations had been. They spoke of taxes and politics. It was a stark difference to the conversations of prophecies and war she had heard in the Sapphire Court. It almost bored her. Eoghan stood with a grin as he noticed the glassiness of the Princess's eyes, he too was bored.

"Would our lovely guest care to join me in a walk around the grounds?" Nia glanced at Lorcan, his expression was unreadable, and rose from her chair. Lorcan rose also and wrapped his jacket around her shoulders in silence. Nia smiled as he winked. "I would not want you to freeze." He smirked, Lana still looked at her with disdain, Tara seemed more curious than anything. "I would be delighted." Nia replied to Lorcans brother and followed Eoghan from the dining room.

Nia sucked in a breath as he stopped, staring at the hallway. The meal had gone on for so long that Nia forgot what she had done. "What..." Eoghan looked at the girl, guilt clear in her eyes. A grin broke out across his face, he said nothing of it as they walked. "I do hope my brothers have not bored you to death." Eoghan chuckled, the tattoo cascading down his neck rippled as he laughed.

Nia smiled once more and shook her head. "I have never cared for politics." Eoghan snorted. "Then you and Lorcan are well matched, I am sure he was about to steal you away until I took his chance, I am only sorry we did not see Aidan's reaction to your handiwork." He winked at her. "Then what luck you had to have gotten there before Lorcan... and the dining room is in a much better place now." Nia jested, she scolded herself for enjoying his company as she remembered that this was just the guise he wore. Eoghan saw the shift in her eyes, he said nothing of it; instead, he reached for the door before them and opened it.

Her mouth agape, eyes wide, Nia basked in the sight before her. A blanket of crystalline snow covered the land, with the deepest shades of greens and reds peeking through. It filled her with peace, the air was clear and crisp against her skin. It reminded her of home. *Home*. Nia had not thought of it in weeks, how she longed to return to that forest; to force herself to turn and run when she had found that monstrous footprint in the ground.

They walked through the snowy garden, their footsteps crunched beneath them. "Aidan wishes to throw a ball in your honour, we were all sorry to have missed Torrin's dance when Lorcan returned; telling tales of a beautiful woman, more powerful than he had ever seen. Oh, and when he returned from Avenere." Eoghan bellowed a laugh as Nia blushed bright red. "We thought you had cast a spell over him, you are all we have heard of in months." Nia turned scarlet at that. She *had* intended to make him fall for her, but although she had not had much chance; Lorcan had begun to do so regardless.

We both began with the same intentions, she mused. The irony made her smile. "It seems the Fates have pushed you together, I do ask one thing of you. If it comes to it, do not hold our crimes against our younger brother. He is, as we are, powerless against Aidan; despite the title we share, he has the power of the High Lord in his veins. We must follow him." Eoghan's eyes shifted around the garden as he spoke in hushed tones, Nia said nothing; things were not so simple here. If she could rid this Court of Aidan, Nia could save them without much destruction.

Eoghan, unnerved by her silence; afraid that his hope was mistaken, turned towards the gardens. Nia did not entirely trust that Aidan had not sent him to test her. "I do hope you will be here for summer; our gardens are magnificent when in colour." Nia could see the passion in his eyes when he looked around. "Do you enjoy tending to the gardens?" She asked, Eoghan smiled once more as he revealed, "it is my favourite thing to do, if I am honest." Nia waved a hand across the earth before them. Eoghan stared in awe as burning orange and blinding yellow coneflowers sprouted from the ground, followed by bushels of bee balm in the richest red, wild columbine dotted around the garden; Nia wished they rang like the bells they resembled. She was not finished until the earth was littered with colour, from coral bells and irises to coreopsis and baptisia.

Eoghan's mouth fell agape as the garden came alive, instantly hummingbirds settled in the bee balm. Nia lowered her hands with a smile. "I do hope you were not lying to me; this garden will need much tending." She teased, Eoghan bowed to her. "Don't do that." She said it without thinking, Eoghan eyed her curiously; perhaps there was hope yet. "I am not my father, there is no need." She hurriedly explained. She could not trust that Eoghan's earlier words meant he would turn against Aidan if she gave them the opportunity to do so.

"Is it true that you can fly?" Eoghan asked, sensing her uneasiness. Nia snorted; it almost choked her. "God's no." She chuckled, "but you have wings, yes?" He pressed; she rolled her eyes. "Yes, I suppose technically I *could* fly; but I have not." Eoghan shook his head at that. "I suppose, Torrin would not have taught you; to keep you trapped." Nia frowned. "I did not see him grow wings, so how *could he* help?" Nia scoffed. "His mother knew yours, no? Surely, she would have kept a journal about it, they were close." Eoghan explained, Nia's stomach dropped as she realised, he was right.

Torrin *could* have done more to dig up information on her mother's powers so she may understand her own; it was too late to dwell on such things, Nia reasoned with herself as she took a breath. "I suppose he would have kept them hidden, so that I may not escape." She agreed. It pained her to play along with their fallacy. Aidan's shouts of confusion rang through the manor, Nia looked sheepishly at Eoghan as he doubled over with laughter.

"By the Fates Eoghan, I knew you had a green thumb, but I did not realise you had become so talented." Lorcan teased as he joined them in the gardens, he had been anxious to follow them the moment they left the dining room; although he did quite enjoy watching Aidan's shock as he discovered his home had been remodelled. Eoghan laughed once more.

"I owe it all to our guest, she has already given me much hope for our future." He winked at Nia and took his leave, allowing the pair to walk alone in the garden. "He does not seem as bad as the others." Nia chuckled, Lorcans eyes flashed with annoyance. "Do not let their charm fool you, they would rip you shreds for half of what you have already said if it were not for your heritage." Nia knew she would not change his mind; she had spent mere moments with them in comparison to the years he had lived here. "Do you really wish to fly?" Lorcan asked, changing the subject, Nia's eyes glowed with curiosity.

"I happen to know someone, they might be able to help; if you are willing to join me in a walk through the city." Lorcan did not actually want to bring her to the city of Gile but knew he could not hide it for long. "I must warn you, there are some practices here you may not agree with." He continued before she could answer, Nia sighed as she looked through her lashes at him. "I must confess, I know." Nia explained to him, how the shackled Fae arrived with his brother's offerings, how Torrin had told her when she received his gift; how she had intended to free those slaves. She revealed that she still intended to do so. Lorcans heart warmed at her revelation. "I had come to ask you to do so, alongside destroying my brothers; it has been my greatest shame that our Court continues the heinous practice." He confessed, Nia smiled and shook her head. "If only we had just spoken to each other, rather than play each other." She noted. "Hindsight, tis a bitch." Lorcan nodded.

Nia laughed at his crass words and linked her arm through his. "Let us go now then, and you may introduce me to your GuildMaster while we are at it." Lorcan could not help but return her smile, his eyes scanned her outfit. "As much as I enjoy the slip of nothing you currently wear, I would suggest something a tad warmer for our journey." Nia blushed as his eyes raked over her body.

She took his jacket from her shoulders and shivered, she had not noticed how cold it had gotten, with a wave of her hand Nia changed her outfit once more. "You must teach Keegan how to do that, he spends eons getting ready." Lorcan was not entirely joking, he had wasted much of his life waiting for his brother to choose an outfit. Nia stood in warm winter clothing of white and grey furs. They reminded her of Madigan, she hoped Torrin was taking care of the hound. "I prefer to make my own clothing, but I assume you would not have the patience to wait for that." She teased him.

Lorcan looked at her in awe. "What can you not do?" He asked sincerely. Nia's face flushed once more. "I cannot fly, remember?" Lorcan chuckled at her reply and led her down the steps towards the city. Nia groaned as a memory came to mind. "What is it?" Lorcan asked, his eyes scanning her for injury. "A friend had sent me magnificent fabrics; I did not bring them along for obvious reasons, but I would have liked to use them." She sighed before running a hand through her loose hair as the wind whipped through it. Lorcan had a twinkle in his eye as they neared the city.

Nia stared in wonder at the giant sparkling buildings in front of her. Unlike the other Courts, this place screamed wealth, silver entwined with crystal lined the streets along with massive statues of white horses and their riders. Lorcan watched her awe with delight, despite the faults of his court he still found it beautiful; it was a relief that she did too. "The City of Gile." Lorcan grinned, outstretching his arms to display the shining city. "It means-" "Brightness, the city of brightness." Nia finished his sentence, Lorcans brows rose at her knowledge of the ancient tongue; he supposed he should not be surprised, she was an Elf after all. It was their tongue that named many places in Etherea. "There is much more to you than a pretty face and a dangerous temper; isn't there?" Nia cursed her flushing cheeks, one would think the girl had a fever, and nudged him playfully. "You catch on quick, fine sir. Play nice and you might find out how much more there is." Lorcan revelled in their banter, the women he found himself with in the past always cared for one thing alone; his title. Nia could not care less if she offended him, she had a title of her own; why should she care for his?

It refreshed him as they came upon their first stop. Scraping steel and sparking flames drew Nia's attention, her heart sparked along with the sounds of the Fae hard at work. They paused as their youngest Prince entered the doorway, followed by a sight they could not have prepared for; all Etherea had gazed upon the drawings of Riona at some point or another. It was clear to them who this woman was.

Nia gasped as the entire room bowed to her, her heart broke at the shackles adorning their feet. "Please, do not let me distract you from your work; it is beautiful, your skill is renowned across Etherea." Nia did not know what to say. She wanted to break the chains at their ankles, they looked to one another with unease. A tall man with shaggy brown hair, kind eyes and an aging face stepped towards them. "We thank you for your kind words, your majesty. Your generosity is known by all slaves across this Court. Please, if you have the time; allow us to craft something for you to show our gratitude." At that, the Fae began to work once more. Nia opened her mouth to protest but held her tongue.

"Prince Lorcan, we were not expecting you, please join me in my office." Nia felt Lorcans hand snake across her waist as they walked towards a doorway in the back of the workshop. Dozens of eyes darted between the lost Princess and their favourite Prince. Lorcan knew there would be rumours spreading throughout Gile before the door of Thomas' office closed. He was entirely correct. It was a Fae's greatest fault, to indulge in gossip wherever and whenever they could. Lorcan supposed he could not blame them, as he took a seat in the homely office Thomas had made for himself, the Fae slaved away for their entire lives; he could not begrudge them a sliver of entertainment to pass the time.

Nia marvelled at the office carved into the stone behind the workshop, it was marvellous. Thomas smiled warmly at the young woman, her eyes twinkling at the crystal ceiling. "What brings you here Lorcan?" Thomas asked with unease as Nia looked around the room. Her eyes fell upon an open book upon his desk, a drawing of her dagger lay on the exposed page.

Nia looked curiously at the man, what did he know of the strange weapon she carried? "Forgive the intrusion, Thomas; I should have sent word." Nia's eyes could have fallen from her skull, this man was shackled as the others; the way Lorcan spoke, you would think he was the owner of this establishment. Her heart warmed once more as she looked at him; he was truly nothing like his reputation, or his brothers. "As you may have noticed, this is Elvinia Ó Mordha; I gifted her the bracelet you made my mother, she wished to meet the man who made such a beautiful piece." His eyes filled with pride, Nias mouth fell agape.

Torrin had said it was made by children, she had believed him; *she had flung it against a wall*. Embarrassment filled her at the thought, and she thanked the Fates that it had not been broken. "It is truly marvellous." Nia agreed, Thomas smiled at her. "I thank you, once again; it is not every day one receives such high praise and to hear it from yourself, well, that is all an old man such as myself needs." Kindness rippled from him, in waves, it soothed Nias heart. She felt her shoulders relax and returned his smile "I must admit, I do have a weakness for all crafts, but especially here in Etherea; I have not seen anything of its like in all my years in the human world." She felt sorrow for those separated from this world, that they would never see the beautiful things here.

"Do you weld?" Thomas asked, Nia shook her head. "The most I have made is some bows, I have not been gifted like yourself; should you need a new outfit sewn, that I can do." Thomas chuckled. "I shall make you a deal then, I have three daughters; if you would be so kind as to make them a gown each, I will teach you *my* ways." Lorcan quirked a brow at that, the GuildMaster was notoriously selective of his personal apprentices and had only grown more stubborn throughout the years.

Lorcan had expected to be turned away, or to be handed off to another with less skill. Nia clasped her hands with glee, instantly she knew what she would make; a gift to repay Lorcan for all he had done for her. "They shall have more gowns than they can wear, but I do have one more request." Her eyes fell once more upon the illustration of her dagger on his desk. She decided to take a chance, Lorcan trusted the man enough to drop his bravado around him; Nia felt she could do the same.

Lorcan watched with curiosity as she pulled the dagger from her boot. Thomas' eyes grew wide as she held it in the light. His nostrils flared as he stepped towards it. "Where did you find this?" His tone had changed, it became worrisome and dark. "It was my mother's." Nia explained as she lowered the weapon, not liking how he looked at her now. "It most certainly was not." Thomas ran his hands through his hair. "*That* was made as a set. A wedding gift for your parents." Regret filled his eyes at her blanching face. "Forgive me, your majesty. You have given me a shock is all, for I have not seen this dagger in hundreds of years. May I?" Nias hands shook as she held out the weapon, she did not wish to part with it; for it had saved her skin many a time.

Thomas held the blade expectantly as he turned it over, inspecting it. He handed it back to her within seconds, Nia took it gratefully. "That blade was your fathers." He explained, Nia felt her grip loosen as though she had been burned. The dagger clattered against the floor. Lorcan raised a brow at her, she had let it go as if it were her father himself. "A sword and shield for your mother, a dagger and a bow for your father. With rubies enchanted by High Elves. I should have known by their requests. Riona chose noble weapons of protection, Ciar wished only for deception and death." Nia paled at the comparison, Lorcan cleared his throat and gestured to the blanched face of the girl at his side.

Thomas quickly shook his head. With wide eyes he rushed to ease her fears. "That is not to say that this is the only use for these weapons. You have had them your whole life I suppose?" Nia nodded, she did not trust her voice to speak, "and as far as I am aware, the human world still stands. Ciar would be sat on the throne of men if he had access. You have also not burned down Etherea. This, I would say, makes you much more like your mother."

Thomas picked the dagger up from the ground and placed it in Nia's hands once more. "I have always held regret for making these weapons, it would do me a great honour to know they are in the hands of someone much more deserving." Thomas told her sincerely, Nia took a shaky breath. "Could you tell me about the rubies? Why do they burn me?" Lorcan frowned, she had not told him of this. Thomas sighed once more. "Your mother came to me one night, in secret, and asked that I change the spell the Elves would cast. Her addition made it so the blade would scorch its wielder, its intensity would depend on the level of pain one was about to inflict. So that one could feel the pain they inflicted upon their victim. I was blind to what it meant; she knew something was wrong with him. She had tried to quell his cruelty before they were married, and I had been ignorant to her attempt."

Nia looked uneasily at what had been her most used weapon, it did not help that her favourite weapon had also been his. "I have the entire set, is there anything else I should know?" Thomas beamed at that; he was glad that his creations were not hidden away in Ciars castle as he had expected, but in use to save Etherea. "Trust in them, and they will never fail you, they were enchanted as such. Do not let it bother you which of your parents owned them, they are yours now. You will make of them what you wish." Nia supposed he was right; they were only objects.

Lorcan stood and extended his hand. "As always Thomas, it has been a pleasure, but I would like to show our guest around Gile." They shook hands like old friends, Thomas bowed his head to Nia; whether she protested or not, she had earned his respect. "Wait, Lorcan, go ahead I will join you in a moment; your daughters' measurements?" Nia turned back to Thomas, he smiled and slipped her a piece of paper with the information she needed. Once Lorcan had shut the door behind him Nia leaned in close. "Would you help me make a gift for him?" She asked, Thomas' heart warmed; *oh, to be young and newly in love once more,* he thought. "It would be my pleasure."

Before they could leave, a young woman stepped towards Nia. Her hands shook as she raised a velvet navy box in the air. Nia took it with thanks and opened the box. A glittering pendant shone in the light; she was speechless. It was as if they had managed to encase snow within glass, a thousand colours shone within the clear crystal. "I have never seen anything so beautiful." Nia threw her arms around the girl. "Thank you, I shall return with something more tangible than words one day; I promise." Lorcan tugged Nia's arm, she released the shaking Fae girl.

Pity filled her, it solidified her intent to free them. One way or another they would not be shackled by the time she left this Court. Lorcan led her back out into the street, she shivered at the freezing air. It had been far warmer within the workshop, with its blazing fires and bustling bodies. "Where shall we go next?" She asked as she examined her gift. She could not look away. "We should visit the seamstress first, you will like her; she shares your disdain for royalty." Lorcan chuckled, Noirín was never shy to tell him what she thought of him and her brothers. She would never say it to the rest of his clan, no, they would gut her in the streets for it; yet he rather enjoyed her criticism.

A bell atop the door rang as they stepped inside the wide windowed store. Nia drank in the scent of fabric all around her, it filled her heart with joy. A woman scurried to greet them, she had short blonde hair that jutted out in all directions and piercing hazel eyes. Nia admired the shimmering black gown the woman wore, like the stars themselves had been woven within each stitch. "Good afternoon Noirín, I presume you have already heard of my guest; notorious gossip this one is." Lorcan grinned as the woman pursed her lips. "Tis a shame she has taken up such unseemly company." Nia snorted, she could sense the playfulness in Noirín; she knew the woman meant no harm.

"So, she knows you well." Noirín's eyes twinkled with delight at Nia's laughter. "Perhaps there is hope for you yet, what brings royalty to my humble store?" At this, Lorcan snorted. "Humble, ha! You would not know the meaning." He grinned as Noirín crossed her arms. "And why should she be? Do you know the patience it takes to sew a thousand stitches? The pain of your bleeding fingers each time the needle slips? I would be proud to make such garments."

Noirín glowed with pride at Nia's praise, Lorcan raised his hands in defeat. "We have come to purchase some fabrics." Lorcan revealed, as he pulled his coin purse from his pocket; Nia realised she had no money. She shook her head. "I cannot ask this of you." Lorcan rolled his eyes. "You did not ask, I have offered; let me do this for you." Nia relented as a pleading look washed over his face. Noirín watched the exchange in silence, she would not have charged Nia; whether she believed Nia to be good or evil, one would be a fool to try to charge a royal. Lorcan, however, was an exception.

Noirín took the coin he outstretched and led them to the storeroom in the back. Nia looked in wonder at the rows upon rows of different fabrics before her. "Choose as many as you like." Lorcan told her, Nia felt like a child in a sweet shop. It was not long before she had piled so much into her arms she could not see, a million ideas ran through her head; not just for Thomas' daughters, but for Maeve, Erin, and herself if she found the time. Lorcan had not seen her this excited before, it warmed his heart to witness the joy that shone on her face as she stumbled towards them; her bounty haphazardly balanced in her arms. He laughed as he took most from her, unburdening the poor girl before she could fall.

She had chosen all sorts of colours, in all manner of textures; along with threads and needles. "Would you be so kind as to have these delivered to my home?" Lorcan asked Noirín, Nia loved how he asked; he did not demand that they do as he wished for the sake of his title. Noirín held out her hand once more, Lorcan laughed and dropped more coin into her outstretched palm. "Ever the businesswoman," he jested, "come Elvinia, we should reach Shona before nightfall." Nia thanked the seamstress once more before they took their leave. Noirín watched them with curiosity, the rumours had been true; the prince of the people had fallen for the lost princess. Even if he did not truly realise it yet.

Lorcan and Nia trudged through the snowy city, until they reached a giant toadstool teetering on the outskirts. She looked at it in disbelief, a chestnut brown door had been placed into the stalk of the giant mushroom, along with three windows. Lorcan noticed her surprise and smiled, he could not wait to see her face upon seeing Shona. He knocked three times against the wood and stepped back. Nia's mouth fell open as a short, slender woman with huge white wings opened the door. Her snow-white hair fell in ringlets around her ivory face, pointed ears peaked from behind, kind olive-coloured eyes peered at her visitors; a sparkling dust fell from her wings as she shook herself awake.

Shona smiled, wide and sincere, at the pair on her doorstep. "What brings you by Lorcan? With such a gorgeous treat for my eyes." Nia blushed at the compliment, Lorcan groaned as Shona eyed his companion. Hunger in her eyes. "Elvinia, this is Shona; forgive her flirting, Pixies are notorious for their lust." Nia looked once more at the shimmering woman; a Pixie. She had not seen one yet, although they danced around Abbán's domain; none had ventured forward when they arrived.

"I cannot be blamed, when you have brought the prettiest girl in Etherea to my doorstep; I am not blind." Shona *tsk'd* at him, Nia shook her head with a laugh. "Please, you flatter me too much. We have come to ask a favour, should you have the time." "If this is too much, you have not been treated right." Shona gave a pointed look at Lorcan, he avoided her gaze. "What, pray tell, is this favour you ask? For you, I shall make time." Nia blushed once more as the girl winked at her. "She wishes to fly." Lorcan revealed.

Shona scanned the girl once more and scoffed. *"Have* I gone blind? She cannot fly without wings." Nia did not blame her for her scepticism. "I do, sometimes." she sighed, Shona's eyes widened. She had been too focused on Nia's beauty to realise who she was.

"You are Ciar's daughter."

Nia merely nodded.

"Then I will help you; but first, you must help me. I must see what I am working with." Nia thought it to be reasonable, yet her hands shook all the same. The young Elf had realised in that moment, she had no clue how to summon her wings.

Shona sensed the panic in the girl and smiled softly at her. "For now, use whatever has worked before; be it anger or pain, and then we shall work on summoning them at will." With Shona's encouragement, Nia recalled each moment those great wings had sprouted at her back. A mix of fear and fury filled her as she imagined herself back within the abandoned cells of the Emerald Court, how those men had cornered her; how she had almost given up.

Nia heard gasps from the pair beside her and opened her eyes. They both stared at her in awe, her silhouette burned red, her nails sharp as daggers and furious blood red wings hit the snow at her feet. "By the Fates." Shona whispered, Nia smiled sheepishly; it was an odd combination, her shy smile compared to her menacing form. Shona shook the shock from her face and grinned. "I can work with this." Hope filled Nia as they began their training. She was miserable at it of course, but Nia had not expected to master the art of flying within an afternoon. She had spent months in Etherea and still could only control her magic for paltry things. Every ounce of power she had unleashed had been in a fit of fury, it had served her well until it did not; Nia shook the memory of Breága from her mind as she tried and failed once more to lift herself from the ground.

#

Lorcan assured her that it would be no time at all before she flew, as Nia grumbled her way back to the Manor. He decided it better not to laugh at her disgruntled expression. She had fallen so many times; he would not add insult to injury. She had tried at least. Nia said nothing, just dropped into bed like a dead weight. Lorcan chuckled as he shook his head, she grumbled a response; muffled by the blankets which invaded her mouth. "You need to eat." Lorcan told her tentatively as he crossed the room. Nia rose to glare at him. "I need to free my mother, not sit around playing politics; what use am I? She had armies hanging on her every word, I have four friends whom I cannot even speak to." She snapped. The day had truly exhausted her. Lorcan sighed and took a seat by her side. "Your mother is alive, and safe."

Lorcan did not meet her curious gaze. "How do you know?" When he did not answer, Nia crossed the gap between them on the bed. Her suspicious eyes bore into his own. Lorcan could not look away. Nia watched as he swallowed, saw his jaw tighten as her breath blew against his face. "Lorcan," she began, "if you do not tell me, I will leave you to deal with your brothers alone." It was an empty threat, they both knew it; Nia would not do that to him. Still, Lorcan did not trust that her stubbornness would not outweigh her honour; and so, he sighed.

"I used a favour, a friend of mine has a relative who is serving in Duane's Court. When you destroyed the Abhartach, when you threw yourself in its path without a second thought; I knew you had come to save us all. It was a risk, but I managed to send word to your mother that you were alive; that you were fighting. She too has stayed strong since." Nia's heart soared at his words. He had risked it all for her, and he hadn't even known her. Lorcan awaited her reply, half afraid that she might scold him for not telling her sooner.

Nia threw her arms around him in delight.

"You are a miracle Lorcan, I do hope you know that." She murmured as she held him tight. His heart warmed at her words, at her soft voice slipping through his mind, Lorcan revelled in her embrace. "I am no such thing." He chuckled; Nia pulled back until her face was mere inches from his. Her brows drew close, determination shone bright in her eyes. Nia cursed him as his eyes flickered to her lips, she brought her hands to his face and held his gaze. "I may wear many masks in this chaotic realm, but this I know is fact; you are going to save your court, and I am going to help you. Whatever it takes; I will be here for you." Tentatively, Nia placed a soft kiss against his cheek before slipping from his embrace; too filled with exhaustion to allow him to argue, her lids grew heavy as her head rested against the pillow.

It was when her snores filled the room, Lorcan released the breath he had been holding. The feeling gurgling in his stomach was one he had never felt before. He was positively giddy. The warmth of her lips on his cheek remained as Lorcan took his rest on the couch. The next few days would follow the same pattern, she would sew gowns for Thomas' daughter; he would aid her to create a gift for Lorcan and then she would attempt to fly with Shona. Nia returned each night exhausted, covered in a little less dust and snow each time, but always grateful for the soft bed she fell into.

It was on one such night, when Nia had settled comfortably into her routine; did the visions of her mother's past plague her mind once more. She had drifted into a peaceful sleep, Lorcan snoring on the couch, it did not last for long. Shadows clutched at her, screams surrounded her. Ciar stood across the battlefield, smirking, cutting down all in his path; arrows flew from his bow, landing in the hearts of the Fae charging towards him. Nia felt the heartache, the agony of her mother as her father murdered her allies, her friends. They had no choice but to retreat; Nia realised as the gates closed behind her father, as he smirked at their fleeing figures, this was the first battle of many. This was when he took the throne. The scene shifted; Nia saw him sitting on an onyx throne before shadows engulfed the castle. His smile boiled her blood.

Nia awoke, in complete darkness, drenched in sweat from the visions which plagued her. So many faces, disfigured and dismayed; her father on his throne of the blackest crystal, that which could only match the empty cavern of his soul. His scarlet eyes burned bright in her mind; Nia could almost see them before her. As her hands outstretched, Nias blood curdled; the mattress beneath her, *it was alive*.

Nia startled as she threw the covers from her body. "Lorcan?" She called out, it was no use; he was not there. Nia reached for the light at her side and screamed at the sight before her. The bed, once soft silks and vibrant colours was now crawling with thousands of maggots. Bile rose from her throat as Nia jumped from the bed only to find rats sprinting in their hundreds around her feet. At this, Nia scarpered from the room, barefoot and in her nightgown; Nia was not hopeful for what lay ahead.

True to her fears, the cackling of Tara and Lana rang throughout the Manor. Nia cursed them both. "Foul creatures." She found herself muttering. Torrin had been utterly wrong about his sister; she relished in her power within this court, there was nothing they could do about it. Nia did not stop running, not until their laughter faded to a light hum.

She found herself upon a set of grand wooden doors, in the darkness she could not make out much. Something within called to her, had her hands wrapped around the handle before she thought to do so. Her heart beat wildly in her chest as the doors creaked open, Nia paused for a moment; waited for any of Lorcans brothers to find her and demand an explanation for her wandering. *At least I have a valid excuse*, Nia thought bitterly.

The moonlight shone brightly within the room; giant windows allowed the light to roam freely about the study. A huge oak desk sat before a towering marble fireplace, one which you could fit the entire desk inside and have room for more. Stacks of books lined the rich red carpet; it was much darker and cosier than the entire Manor.

Movement caught Nias eye, in the left corner of the room. She could not believe what she saw, there above yet another set of haphazardly stacked books; a tiny, three headed, winged little beast. *An Ellen Trechend*. Nia gasped as it turned its head, its beady black eyes peered at her. It was almost cute, with its tiny horns and spiked back; Nia would not have believed the carnage this little creature could cause, if she hadn't experienced it herself. This one was different though, with shining blue scales and a calm demeanour; it was nothing like the one beneath the mountain. Nia pitied it, locked in a tiny cage; it was cruel and perhaps the reason for the Ellen Trechend's attacks on the Fae. *I too would hate this world if I were locked in a cage*, Nia thought, it brought her mother to mind. Riona was still trapped, locked away from her own lands.

"What are you doing in here?"

Nia startled and spun around, Eoghan peered back at her. His eyes fell on the creature at her back. "Tara and Lana, they..." "Say no more." Eoghan shook his head. Nia almost sighed with relief. "Not what you were expecting, I suppose?" Eoghan mused, Nia could not help herself as she looked back at the cage. "It is hard to imagine the innocence of anything when there are three sets of gnashing teeth approaching your heard." Eoghan chuckled at her reply and stepped towards the cage.

It looked at her then, beady eyes narrowed as they fell upon her; as if the creature was examining her. Nia felt a calling within her, like a fizz in her veins. Eoghan watched in silence as she outstretched a hand, curious to see how the beast would react. It had not bitten her yet, so Nia took that as a sign to get closer. As her fingers brushed those blue scales, it shuddered with delight. Nia grinned as it rolled over, exposing the soft flesh of its belly, Eoghan's jaw fell agape.

"Well, you are not so terrible after all." Nia coo'd at the animal. She could have sworn it winked. "You best be off Princess, before anyone else finds you wandering in that slip of nothing." Eoghan grinned and hurried her out of his study. Nia glanced behind her curiously before returning to Lorcan's room. Perhaps there was more to be found in the study, which Eoghan did not want her to see. This only enticed her further.

Nia found Lorcan pacing the room as she re-entered, with furrowed brows he crossed the space between them and gripped her face gently in his hands. Nia found a smile slipping on to her face as his eyes scanned her for any sign of injury. "I returned and you were gone." Lorcan sighed, half relieved, half accusatory. Nia gave him a stern look in return. "I awoke, and you were not there." She retorted. Her words brought fire to his eyes. Lorcan was tired, weary of his brothers, and desperately afraid for the girl's safety.

Nia watched as his lids closed, he lay his forehead against hers with a heavy sigh. "I am sorry, I was called away." She saw his jaw clench, resisted the urge to ask him where he had been called to, and wrapped her arms around him;

brushing a hand through his hair. Lorcans nostrils flared at the gesture, choking back a sob his arms squeezed her tightly. "Did they hurt you?" Lorcan asked, after a long silence. Nia shook her head as he released her. "It was childish tricks, I ended up in Eoghan's study." Lorcan narrowed his eyes as Nia retreated to the bed.

Her twinkling eyes filled him with a different worry as he cocked a brow. "I found something magnificent." Nia continued, her voice hushed. "He has a baby Ellén Trechend, it is the cutest thing I have ever seen." Lorcan blanched, for he knew of the little beast which Eoghan had taken in. The foul thing had bitten him countless times. "You cannot be serious, you have fought one yourself; fully grown no less. How can you call that thing *cute?*" Nia rolled her eyes at his incredulous tone. "While I admit, the one I faced was much more terrifying, I will not brandish an entire species with the same brush. I only hope Eoghan does not hurt it, for it would break my heart." Nia told him, Lorcan did not doubt it would. Her eyes shone with wonder once more as her thoughts drifted, she thought of flying alongside the winged creature; how freeing it would feel. "You must rest, Nia." Lorcan sighed as her lids grew heavy. Too tired to argue, Nia obliged and fell into the bed; no longer writhing with maggots, she drifted into a more peaceful sleep.

Chapter Twenty-Nine:

Sweat laced the brow of the young Sapphire Lord as Nessa's eyes watched him. She had waited in that dark and damp chamber for centuries, patiently, for her moment to pounce. Ciar knew the Sapphire Court bordered the human lands and if his daughter were to return it would be through here, as cunning as Rionas plan had been; he had his own.

The young Fae could not answer her. Nessa's sickly-sweet smile unnerved him, it turned his palms clammy as his heart pounded in his chest. "Have you not longed for the day the world would stop treating you as a child?" He had not noticed her move behind him until those words were whispered in his ear. It was true, Rian resented his youthful appearance, each time he had been restricted by his age haunted his mind; every instance where he had been thrown into someone's arms because his short legs could not keep up with their pace.

Nessa could see the wheels turning in his head and knew her words were working. She smirked at his back before continuing, "think of it Rian, all that you could achieve if only you were returned to your rightful age. *You* could be the true High Lord of the Sapphire Court." At this his ears pricked; Nessa hid her grin as quickly as it had formed; the young Lord had turned to look at her. "Torrin is the true High Lord." He was sure he meant it to sound defiant, instead his voice had become a raspy whisper; betraying his curiosity at her words. *They are just words he* tried to convince himself.

"Oh, but you forget, Rian, the power that runs through my veins. I could grant whatever you desire... what a shame your brother is not loyal to you." Nessa sighed as she caressed his face, as a mother would. Rian frowned at the words she had spoken. "Torrin is loyal to a fault." He argued, unwilling to allow Nessa to insult his brother any further. At this she *tsked.* "He is selfish and ignorant, only a fool would allow one of the most powerful beings to be whisked away into the arms of another, and I suppose he had no objections when Abbán said you must not find a cure to your curse?" *How did she...?* The glint in her eyes sent a whole new wave of nerves quaking through Rian.

"He does not wish to save you, because he knows your power will outmatch his; you are far more cunning and capable of leading your Court to do great things." Nessa continued, watching the turmoil in the young Fae's eyes with delight. She could sense Torrin's approach, knew her window was drawing to a close; they had forgotten to reinforce the wards once, she knew they would not do so again. Nessa pursed her lips as she thought, she had wished for more time to sow the seeds of doubt within the little Lord.

 She glanced towards the stairs and scowled before turning back to look down at Rian. Her cold, bony hands gripped his face once more, squeezing his cheeks into his eyes. "Oh how I shall miss our talks, little Lord, we will meet again soon; this I promise. I leave you with a gift, in return I ask that you think of what I have said; I will find you when you are ready." Rian cringed and squirmed in her grip as she kissed his forehead, his skin burned. As he slipped from consciousness, Rian barely heard his own scream before his body crashed against the floor.

Torrin had run, as fast as his legs could carry him, towards the gaping statue centring his courtyard; it was not fast enough. *I should have spoken to him*, Torrin realised, everything had spiralled out of his control. His lungs burned, his feet ached; yet still, he persisted. Torrin almost threw himself down the winding stone staircase. A child's scream echoed throughout the chamber, Torrin's heart skipped a beat. Terrified that he would find his brother's lifeless body at the bottom of the steps, he pushed himself forward. Nessa was gone, and in her wake; she had left Rian writhing in pain on the stone floor.

Without a second to spare, Torrin scooped his brother into his arms and sprinted towards his home. Cliodhna stood waiting in the doorway, with hot towels and blankets. Her lips pursed as Torrin hurried past her, into the dining room. Rian convulsed as he laid him down on the table, crockery clattered to the ground around them, his eyes rolled into his skull.

Torrin did not care for the glass that fell and shattered; he cared for one thing alone, his brother. Cliodhna's hands shook as she wiped the sweat from the child's face, he wore a crown of barbed Sapphire light. Ruby embers flickered within the spell constricting the poor boy's mind.

The wards which bound Rian burst into a thousand pieces as a memory shot through his consciousness; like a meteor crashing against the earth. Cliodhna gasped and stumbled backwards as red replaced blue, two spells had battled for control; Nessa's had won. The pair looked on in astonishment as Rian's limbs began to stretch, he morphed and contorted until finally, he settled; no longer a child, but a full-grown man.

#

Rian found himself back in the courtyard, following his father to the fountain. The moon shone bright above him in the frigid night air, his footsteps light as a feather, Rian slipped through the courtyard unseen. He watched as his heart pounded; the great fountain split in half as his father outstretched his arms. Rian could not help himself as his father entered the passageway, his feet followed by their own accord. The power which slapped against him almost knocked him over, bile rose in his throat.

Rian wretched but persisted. He could not see his father but knew he would be at the bottom of the steps. With that thought to comfort him Rian steadied his feet, he did not wish to go tumbling down against the stone.

Chanting began from below; it sent a shiver through his spine; who else is down there? He wondered. Rian saw, finally, the bottom of the stairs. Light shone from an open doorway. Rian watched in horror as three High Lords and Ladies; his father, Uaine's mother and a woman he had not met from the Golden Court, circled a young girl bound by iron chains. His father stood before the girl, a vibrant stone of Sapphire, Emerald, Ruby, Silver, and Gold shone bright in his hand. Rian noticed then, the four young High-born Fae behind their elders, shock filled him; Torrin, Lorcan, Uaine and Maeve, their eyes filled with mist. How? He questioned. Nessa screamed and begged, pleaded as tears rolled down her face.

"They deserved it, for all that they have done to me." She screeched. "You wicked creature, we never should have let you live." Uaine's mother snarled and sent a wave of emerald shards towards Nessa. "You will be a blight on Etherea, and this we cannot have." Nessa glared at the High-Fae. "And you will regret this, when your children come crawling to me; I will take their pretty light and blind you bastards with it." She spat at them. "You cannot stop us, Ciar will burn this pathetic Court to the ground. Your children will be orphans, tortured and desperate. You will lose." Rian's father could listen no more.

He called the children; it was like they were in a trance. Rian felt his throat constrict as they formed a circle of interlocking hands, he realised then what they were doing; their parents were siphoning their magic, using it to imbue the stone with the power strong enough to bind Nessa. The girl screeched once more. "Ciar will tear you apart for this." She seethed as her bones burned. White flashed in her eyes and her signature laugh bubbled from her throat. "When the boy becomes a man, he will be mine and he will tear your cities down by my side." Rian's father glanced at Torrin with worry, Nessa laughed once more; her head snapped to the doorway, her burning red eyes met Rians.

"They underestimate you now, as they forever will." The terror that filled him could not be described, as the adults followed her gaze.

His father cursed at the curious child. "Get out of here Rian, do not return." He snapped at his youngest, Rian did not need a second warning. He vomited twice more as he ran out into the frigid air. Sweat dripped from his skin, his clothes soaked. His father found him later that night, as he lay sleepless in his bed. To his credit, Liam had tried to give the child the benefit of the doubt. "Do not return to that chamber Rian, that woman is a liar, she will say whatever she can to be released." It was vastly different to how Rian had remembered it, he only saw the adults in the chamber; he had thought his father caught him almost instantly and roared at him to leave and never return. How could he have forgotten? How could they all have forgotten? He realised then, their parents had lied to them, had used them like spare parts to aid their cause; no matter the cost.

Rian did not heed his father's warning, Nessa's words had spun in his mind; so, for the next few weeks he slipped from his room in the cover of darkness and crept beneath the Court. He could not understand, for she still looked like a normal girl; the magic had not yet stripped away her beauty. Nessa filled the young boy's head with wondrous tales of his future power, she weaved a wicked web; before long, Rian hung on every word she said. How could she be so terrible? He wondered, for she had told him he would be a powerful warrior; destined to lead Etherea to greatness.

It could only last so long, if only he had been caught sooner; Rian had delivered a book to Nessa, from deep within his mother's library. It was a red leather journal, the edges frayed over time. The wicked girl had just hidden the book and in return was teaching Rian to wield fire from his fingertips; magic far more advanced than he should be practicing when Rian's father stepped within the room.

He stopped dead at the scene before him. His eyes locked on the fire dancing across Rian's fingers, the coy smile on Nessa's face as she waved a shackled hand at him. Liam ripped his son from the room, this felt much more familiar to Rian. The High Lord cursed and kicked the grass beneath his feet as he gripped his child. Rian saw the torment in his father's eyes, the worry, the fear. "Forgive me." His father whispered to the sky before he held the boy tighter. Rian fought his father's grip as Liam began to chant.

Whirls of Sapphire surrounded them, and so; Liam had bound the child to remain a boy forever, had severed his ties to the magic within him, cursed him to be weak and vulnerable for eternity. Rian would not find Nessa again, not for many years; not until a certain Elven Princess returned, reversing curses across the land.

#

Rian gasped as he woke, dripping with sweat and a churning in his gut. His brother and a woman, so familiar yet he could not place her, stood before him; terror in their eyes. Rian felt stronger than he ever had. He finally felt like himself. Torrin looked at Cliodhna, who did not take her golden eyes from his not so little brother. *"We tell nobody."* He warned, at this Cliodhna turned to gawp at him. Rian did not understand their fear until he stood and found himself shoulder to shoulder with his brother. *So, it had not been a dream*, Rian realised. "Do not fear me brother." Rian began as he wiped his brow. "I have much to tell you." Torrin's knees almost buckled as Rian revealed what their father had done. "That bastard." he seethed, Cliodhna looked between the pair. It was a dangerous path they had begun to thread; she could do nothing but watch it unfold.

Chapter Thirty:

Uaine and Maeve's return had been a welcome sight for many, but there were those who had enjoyed the old ways; the dark souls of Etherea, ones who wished for Ciars strength to return. It was a tangled mess, trying to determine who they should trust. There had been only silence from Torrin in the past weeks. Uaine supposed he had been busy, as they had also spent their time tirelessly rebuilding trust with their people. It was this which saw Uaine and Maeve sat in a stuffy meeting room, with the traders of the Emerald Court who worried that Ciars wrath would fall upon them. Uaine could not blame them, for all knew what became of the Sapphire Court after their failed rebellion.

A young woman, with auburn hair and scars across her face stepped forward. "I was in Avenere, when folk rallied for the orphaned babes that Aoife had left behind; it was not enough to rip Torrins parents from him, Ciar sent his demons to sack the city before the earth beneath our feet burst into flames. We were blindsided once; I say we do not allow him the same opportunity." Her eyes twinkled with determination; Maeve smiled at the girl as a ripple of guilt ran through her core; she would not fail the women here again. The other traders murmured in agreement, until a bearded man pounded his fist against the table. "Are you all mad?" He sneered. "Forgive me, Grainne; if I don't put my faith in the strength of a *tavern wench*." Maeve stood before the girl could raise her fist, emerald rope wrapped around his neck. "The strength of a woman scorned could cut down a thousand men like you; it would do you well to remember that next time you speak." Maeve released the gasping Fae and returned to her seat, her anger scarcely quelled.

Uaine glanced at his sister with exasperation, before he could apologise another man stepped forward; he was clean-shaven and slender, he did not look like he had seen battle in his life. "Please, accept my apologies for Fearghal; I am Finn, it is just that we have lived under Ciars spell for far too long, some cannot cope with what we have done. The people cannot relive that, our wives... our daughters." Uaine shuddered at the pain in the young man's voice as it cracked. Maeve glowered at the table before them. "I swear it, by the Fates; your women will be avenged." Uaine abandoned all hope of keeping violence at bay as the Fae laid out their terms. They would support the twins claim, aid their cause, and begin preparing their people for war; in return Uaine and Maeve must eradicate those who resisted, those who enjoyed what they had done and wished to continue. With a deal struck, the traders informed the High Fae of where they would find a band of Fae working to usurp the court from the twins.

When the room had emptied, Uaine loosed a breath and looked at his sister. "Must we do this? Violence will only breed more violence." Maeve glared at him as he ran a hand across his tired face. "And what do you suggest? Do we allow them to fester? Let them regain their strength to rip us from our home once more, to trap the women here again; allow them to ravage and rape as they please? As they did before?" Uaine fell silent, he could not argue. He realised as he saw the guilt in her eyes, Maeve needed this. She needed to do something to make up for the years which she had done nothing. "Alright," he relented, "but perhaps we should consult Rowan, we cannot blindly go after these people if they want our heads on stakes." Maeve sighed and nodded her head, grateful that her brother did not argue.

The doors opened then, as a servant brought an envelope to them. Maeve did not bat an eye at the man, Uaine felt uneasy at the thought of having servants; voluntarily or not. When the man had left the room, he turned to his sister. "Can we adjust one thing?" He asked, Maeve looked at the envelope curiously before glancing at Uaine with a raised brow. "The servants, could we not call them servants? We should give them fair wage and board for the work they do, if they are to tend to us; it is the least we can do." Maeve smiled at her brother, "consider it done." He sighed with relief. Maeve questioned what her brother thought of her as she opened the envelope. "It is from the Silver Court." She told him, Uaine stared wide-eyed at the letter. "An invitation." He gulped as he read it.

Dearest Lord and Lady,

Congratulations on your recent victory. Elvinia assures us that your loyalty to Ciar is unbreakable; and so, we wish to cordially invite you both to our humble abode for a ball the likes of which Etherea has not seen in centuries.

Prince Aidan

Maeve resisted the urge to curse Nia. "Our loyalty to Ciar is unbreakable?" She guffawed, Uaine groaned. "We must trust her, she is in a court of snakes; we must put on the farce she expects, if only to ensure she is safe and sane." He reasoned, Uaine did not entirely trust Abbán had fixed Nia; she stood on a knife's edge between good and evil. He had also suspected that Nia's heart had turned towards a certain Silver Prince, Uaine could not be sure she would not shatter herself to protect him. In his journey he had learned one thing, Nia was a fierce protector of the people she loved; the looks she had cast towards Lorcan told him she would level the entire Silver Court to keep him safe.

Maeve grumbled at the letter once more. "Then we cannot be seen thwarting the rebellion against Ciars supporters, we must meet again with the traders; they cannot speak of our deal. They must appear to be rebelling against us, it is an exceptionally fine line we tread upon now Uaine. I hope she knows what she is doing." Uaine agreed with his sister at that, the war was fast approaching; they could all feel it.

They decided Uaine would speak with the traders, while Maeve set out to find Rowan. She found him peering over a map of Etherea, glaring tensely at the illustrations. Maeve chuckled, breaking his focus. Rowan smiled at Maeve, a glittering emerald crown atop her golden hair; it suited her perfectly. His smile faltered at the worry in her eyes. "What is it?" He asked. "Things have become... complicated" Maeve began, before explaining their situation to her general. Rowan tensed as she spoke, he did not wish to return to the way things had been before, but he knew it must be done. Rowan sighed and bowed his head. "If it will save Etherea, then I will do as you ask. The rebels will be swiftly dealt with, and no blame shall befall you or your brother my Lady." Maeve thanked the Fates for Rowan; she did not know what she would do without him. "You have been a blessing to me Rowan, how could I ever repay you?" She asked sincerely, she was unable to give him lands or titles before; she could do so now. Rowan shook his head. "I ask for one thing alone, that you make this wretched plan worth it; that Ciar pays for everything he has done to us." Maeve nodded in agreement. No words were needed; Rowan knew her hatred burned deep for Ciar. She needed no encouragement to make the terrible King suffer.

Uaine had less luck with the traders, who panicked at their plan. He could not blame them; the Silver Court was renowned for its crimes against the Fae. They would rip through this town just for fun at the revelation of their deception. Carefully, Uaine soothed the fears and protests of each Fae as they started, until finally they reached an agreement. They would continue to appear cruel by day, to whip their employees through the streets, to rebuild the stocks; but by nightfall, they would work to build their forces against Ciar.

It was a risky plan, with far too many variables. Uaine did not like it one bit, but he decided he must trust his sister; for she had been witness to far more court politics than he. So, reluctantly, the pair began to prepare for the *grand ball* they had been invited to.

Chapter Thirty-One:

Nia had flown, haphazardly, back to Lorcan's home; just in time to meet Aidan on his way out. She skidded to a halt as he marvelled at her. Nia had played the part well so far, joined in their praise of her father; even if it sickened her to do so. Aidan had plied her with gifts and flattery; his mind on one thing alone, *a marriage between his brother and the Princess*. "Magnificent." He grinned. "I cannot wait to introduce you as an ally to our cause, Etherea will cower before your excellence; but for tonight, *we dance.*" Nia's blood ran cold as she forced a smile on to her face.

"You are too kind Aidan, I thank you once again for your hospitality, I would ask one more thing of you; the Emerald twins are also devoted supporters of Ciar, without their help I could not have escaped Torrins grasp. I would like to invite them tonight." Aidan watched her for any indication of dishonesty; satisfied that he had found none, he agreed with glee. He still plotted to push her into the arms of his brother, to secure their place in the world she would create at her father's side. Nia bowed her head respectfully before she stepped out of his way. She could not help the glare she cast at his back.

Nia's newfound ability to hear the words others left unspoken had served her quite well; for Torrin had been correct about one thing, this was a court of *liars*. She knew Aidan planned to convince Ciar that a marriage between their two families would ensure Nia could not be swayed. She resented him for using his own brother as a pawn and loathed him further for not realizing Lorcan was *nothing* like him. It was his arrogance that would be his downfall, Nia was sure of it. She could be a patient woman, if it meant watching his ego shatter behind those sparkling silver eyes. A sliver of guilt ran through her at how many had been dragged into her journey to save this land, she hoped Maeve and Uaine could forgive her for the part they must play in it.

At least I will have friends nearby, she thought with a sigh. Nia looked towards the flourishing gardens, where Eoghan sat covered in dirt. She smiled despite herself. In their home it was hard to remember the nightmares they became once they were let loose on Etherea. Nonetheless, Nia walked towards the Fae; she had spent the past weeks watching and listening.

Each time Aidan spoke, every order he gave; their family seemed equally divided. The three elders stuck with each other, Bradan and Cadan followed their oldest brother without question.

Nia had witnessed Aidans temper in full force as he ordered them to search for the escaped women of the Emerald Court, to present as a tribute to Maeve and Uaine when he visited them; Keegan had paled but said nothing, Eoghan had held his head in his hands, his eyes tired. Lorcan had scoffed, questioning why they should waste their resources on 'paltry' low-borns.

She knew he had not meant it as an insult to the Fae, but to deter Aidan from his plan. Nia was also sure that if Aidan turned up at the borders of the Emerald Court with imprisoned women Maeve would rip him to shreds; as much as Nia would have liked to allow her this pleasure, she knew it would spark a war between the courts.

They did not need a war between the Fae, not when a much darker force loomed over them. Ciar had not tried to breach her mind again, Nia owed it to the ring gracing her finger. It held a powerful, ancient enchantment to protect its wearer; it would protect her mind from outside influences and hone her powers into a manageable force. It was the latter which had saved Aidan that night, as he attacked Lorcan.

Not so long ago, she would have torn his court to pieces without a second thought; it unnerved her, how quickly she had swayed in her torment. The evil in the world had soaked into her skin and turned her dark, Nia could not allow herself to be tempted once more; although she would have preferred to knock Aidan from his chair, the moment she saw the dangerous glare in his eyes. That night had been chaos. Nia had watched Eoghan's mouth open and close before Aidan stood; his chair scraped against the floor with a horrible screech. To her horror, Aidan used his powers against their youngest brother. As Lorcan writhed in pain, Bradan and Cadan smirked, Keegan looked away; Eoghan glared at his elder.

It was then, as Nia resisted the urge to gut Aidan where he stood, she realised that she could sway the two younger Silver Princes to their cause. Nia had been reading her mother's journal too, she had absorbed every word; found it re-arranged the jigsaw of memories that had fizzled in her mind. It was all so much clearer than the murky, muddled reels she had seen at the beginning. Lorcan had helped her in secret, to practice and control her powers. He still radiated sorrow and guilt, but Nia found it had strangely aided her to navigate the rush of sounds and feelings that bombarded her mind.

It was as if the strength of his pain had helped her build a resistance to it. The thought brought tears to her eyes.

"Do you detest us so, that the thought of an evening socialising with our allies has brought you to tears?" Nia startled at Eoghan's voice, she blinked the salt water from her eyes and glared up at him, he sighed in return. He had saved her from certain death on her arrival, and yet she could not bring herself to trust him. "Would you do an old man a favour and walk with me?" Eoghan asked, Nia's eyes narrowed at his polite tone. "I would hardly call you an old man, but I will walk with you all the same." With a shake of his head and a laugh, Eoghan took her arm in his and guided her away from the Manor. "How old do you think I am?" Nia glanced at him; he did look older than Lorcan, but only barely. Nia still could not wrap her head around the mechanics of how the Fae aged. Eoghan's eyes twinkled at her frown. "If you were born two hundred and ninety-eight years ago, and Lorcan was born three hundred and sixteen years ago; take a guess." He prompted; Nia's head spun at the reminder of her age. Her brows creased as she thought.

"Three hundred and twenty?" She asked, Nia honestly had no idea how to distinguish how old they were. Eoghan laughed. "You flatter me, but you are off by around sixty years." her wide eyes only made his smile grow "how old are your brothers?" Her face had blanched. "Bradan is four hundred years old, Caden is forty years his senior, Aidan will be five hundred this summer." Her mind reeled. *Five hundred years?* She could scarcely believe it. They continued in silence as Eoghan allowed the young Elf to wrestle with her thoughts.

As the Manor faded from view behind them, Eoghan sighed; a tormented look shone in his eyes.

"I must confess, I have brought you away from my home for a reason. Unlike my older brothers, I have heard not of the cruel woman with terrible power that you claim to be but of a brave mortal girl who wrapped her arms around a Fae child without hesitation. You paid the slaves who carried our gift to your debut, showed them more kindness in an evening than Aidan has shown anyone in his lifetime. You fought against the Abhartach, a creature so ancient that most Fae would turn and run; you charged towards it, within only weeks of your powers returning. Your mere presence brought nature back to the Sapphire Court, you found the hidden Lord of the Emerald Court and cut him down for his crimes. I do not blame you, for confirming their twisted versions. They have all but handed you the opportunity to infiltrate our court."

Panic rose in Nia's chest as Eoghan spoke. He did not seem angry, in fact, his voice had remained soft and quiet. "Do not fear, I have no intention of standing in your way. I am tired, so very tired of the destruction Ciar has wrought on this land. Aidan has grown far too violent to allow him to continue. I would not insult you by asking your forgiveness for what I have done, but I would be forever grateful if you allowed me the opportunity to make the right choice now; to stand with you, whatever may come." Nia's heart swelled as he kneeled before her, his sword outstretched in his arms. "Rise, Eoghan. Give me your hand."

Nia had learned through reading her mother's journal that she could in fact sense the very essence of a person. It was a skill Riona had not unlocked until it was too late, Nia had the advantage of her mother's step by step instructions; it also did not hurt that she had already expressed control of this power when the magic first began to flow through her veins again.

Eoghan gave his hand without question, Nia took it into her own and shut her eyes. He watched her curiously as the wind began to whip around them. Nia took a steadying breath and focused on Eoghan, on his life essence. It was dark, yes, but within the darkness a ball of light shone bright. He had a good heart; it had been encased in shadows through centuries of following his brother's orders, she could see he only wished to let that light glow.

Her eyes glowed bright, both halves working in harmony as her magic flourished. Eoghan winced as his palm grew hot, Nia released him instantly. "I am sorry, but if I have learned but one thing alone in Etherea, it is that I cannot trust the words of Fae men." Her eyes fixed on the redness of his palm and reached for him once more. Eoghan hesitated this time, it stung Nia's heart.

"I have looked inside your soul, and I have seen the truth. You are not what Aidan has made you. You and your brothers are victims of a tyrant's rule, stand with me and you will never need know the torment of torturing another innocent. I cannot guarantee you will not shed blood, that you will not face your brothers in the end; but I can promise I will be standing at your side when the battle comes." As she spoke, white light wrapped around Eoghan's palm.

He marvelled at her as the pain disappeared not just from his hand, he bore a lightness in his heart he had not felt in centuries. Eoghan questioned how he had ever followed his brother's rule; cursed himself for never stepping up, he knew Lorcan would have stood with him, Keegan would too. They were followers of what had always been, too frightened of their elders to stand against what they knew was wrong.

"Lorcan thinks he is alone, he is mistaken. It is ironic that our youngest brother, for whom Aidan has never held any respect, has been the bravest of us all. He has always challenged Aidan, in one way or another, while we have bowed our heads and continued our act for centuries."

Nia felt the shame rippling from Eoghan and sighed. "I cannot speak for Lorcan, but I think he will understand. You did what was needed to survive, Aidan can live with the youngest of his clan challenging him; he uses it to his advantage, to show his force. If he would cut down the baby of your family, then he would not hesitate to tear through the rest; but if the rest were to challenge him together, Aidan simply could not allow it. I am sure though, that the three eldest of your family are thick as thieves and I am sorry to say they would stand with him as he murdered your brothers." Eoghan fell silent but could not argue.

"I wish to show you how deep our facade goes." They had walked the path to the city. Nia noticed the differences instantly, nobody smiled at them as they did when Lorcan brought her. They eyed the pair wearily and bowed their heads. She hated how they scurried away and could see he detested it just as much. The disgust in his eyes worked in his favour, the people presumed it was his disdain for them which burned his gaze. Nia shook her head at how much deception ran through Etherea, so many did not wish to live under Ciars rule; yet they did nothing to challenge it, too afraid that they were alone. It was her destiny to unite them, but this court had been cloaked in darkness; for Aidan did not wear such a facade, he was terrible to his core. Men, women, creatures of all sorts were chained and dragged throughout the streets. If the Emerald Court had sickened her, this place sprouted from her nightmares.

It saddened her too, that Eoghan could not experience the city as Lorcan did. It was clear he had worked hard to maintain his act, terrified of his older brother. Nia's hatred for Aidan burned in her gut, she steadied herself; as much as she would have liked to turn around and blast the Silver Manor from the ground, Nia knew it would do no good. She could kill the innocents within the building if she attacked, and that was something she would not do.

Nia could not look at the true nature of the city, as she heard the crack of a whip fury bubbled in her blood. "I wish to return to the Manor." Eoghan looked at her with pity, he had spent years listening to the wails of his people; had grown used to the bloodshed, he forgot that this was not the world she had lived in.

"Let us return then, if I remember correctly, we must get ready for your grand debut." Eoghan could not stop his eyes from rolling, Nia chuckled. "If there is wine then we might survive the night." She joked as they walked away from the city, she ignored the pain in her heart at her abandonment of those poor people. Eoghan laughed alongside her.

"Your optimism gives me hope, your majesty." Nia groaned and shook her head. "I do wish you all would stop calling me that." Eoghan looked at her curiously. "You are a princess though, no matter which side the Fae take; that is one fact none can argue. You were born to the lost Queen of light and the reigning King of darkness; you are the Princess of Etherea whatever may come. Do not allow my brothers allies to see you question that. If you wish to be treated as Ciar's daughter, you must treat them as your father does; like dogs pleading for scraps at your feet."

As they entered the Manor, Eoghan gave Nia a final bow before leaving her alone in the entrance. The young Elf shook the snow from her cloak and sighed, the last thing she wished to do was get ready for a ball. As she walked towards Lorcan's room Nia felt a shiver run down her spine. Her feet stopped dead. Nia steadied her breath and focused her senses once more.

 Her magic rolled throughout the room, until in her mind she could see Bradan behind her; as clearly as if she were looking right at him. In his hand he held a bushel of Foxglove. Nia supposed she could allow her fury loose for this.

Bradan found himself suddenly questioning his choices as Nia burst into flames. She turned to glare at him, at the purple flowers in his palm. Bradan opened his mouth to speak, Nia did not allow him the opportunity. "What is this?" She screeched as she flung him against the wall, the flames singed his suit.

Bradan's brothers came sprinting to his aid as he roared in pain. Sweat broke on Aidan's brow as he looked at her, Nia had not shown them the extent of her power and would not still. She kept the fire to a minimum, Nia wanted to see the shock on Aidan's face when she turned against him in the end; at full power and with half of his brothers at her side.

Lorcan looked between them all, panic clear in his eyes. "You seem to have forgotten your place." Nia sneered as she stepped closer to Bradan, she ripped the Foxglove from his hand. He yelped as the flames burned his palm. They all watched anxiously as she held the poison. It did not burn as they had expected; Nia had learned that lesson the hard way.

Aidan glared at Bradan. "Please, your majesty; our brother is not himself, if he has been in contact with this poison then he is surely not in his right mind." Eoghan stepped forward, his eyes pleading. Nia glowered at the six of them until her gaze fell on Bradan. "Eoghan speaks the truth your majesty, I would never allow harm to come to the daughter of our great king at our hand. Please, release Bradan and I will ensure he is dealt with accordingly." Aidan bowed his head to her.

Nia resisted the urge to smirk down at him, Caden watched her closely. Nia extinguished the flames dancing around her body with a calming breath; sighs of relief began around her. Nia could not help herself as she turned and swung, her fist connected with Bradan's nose as a *crack* sounded throughout the room. "Sane or not, try kill me again and I will break your neck." She spat at him before storming to Lorcans chambers.

"If you do not win her hand and take control of her, *then I will.*" Aidan laughed at his brother's panicked face. Lorcan shook his head and followed Nia. He did not wish to hear how Aidan would do such a thing, especially if he intended to tell them in detail. As Aidan's voice faded behind him, Lorcan took a shaky breath before setting out to find the Elven girl.

He thought Aidan would have attacked her, or Bradan; but he had just watched. Lorcan had an uneasy feeling that his brother was testing their guest.

Chapter Thirty-Two:

Torrin had not left his Manor in weeks and had not reached out to his friends once; Rian told the court he was too consumed by his father's deceit. Torrin had begun to question everything he once believed, their parents had used them as conduits to bind Nessa beneath the court and erased their memories. His father had cursed Rian to never age for fear of the prophecy she foretold. Torrin pulled the manor apart to find any information he could.

His brother, on the other hand, was flourishing. As they sat for dinner on a cold night, Rian watched Torrin's torment tearing him apart with delight. Nessa had been correct; he had done nothing to aid Rian. Torrin had been blind to so many things, Rian was not entirely convinced he was not wilfully so. "Brother." Rian began, knowing Torrin's guilt was eating him alive. "I wonder if you would do me a favour." He took a sip of his wine as Torrin looked up from his food. "Of course, Rian, anything you need." If only Cliodhna had joined them that night. She had made Rian's efforts to thwart Nia's plans difficult, like a fly buzzing at his ear; she would not leave them alone. Rian had ensured that she had no choice this night, for he had poisoned a girl in Avenere; he knew Cliodhna would not leave the girl to die. "There was a book

Nessa spoke of." Already a lie, Rian had retrieved the journal he gave to her; it had told him of another, one bound in silver which would give him the answers he needed. "She was afraid of it, she wanted me to retrieve it as a child so that she could destroy it. Would you help me find it? Please? I cannot rest knowing she is out there." Torrin did not need to be asked twice, his guilt clouded his reality. He should have seen the darkness swirling in his brother's eyes. He still saw the child that once was.

It would be another week before Torrin found the book. He stepped into Nia's room, for the first time since they returned. It pained him as that citrus sweet smell wafted past his nostrils, it was almost like she was there. Her laughter haunted him as he saw a ghost of her, grinning, wrapped in her duvet. It was then that Torrin saw the silver book on her nightstand, he had never noticed it there before. *I really was blinded by her beauty*, he realised. He basked in her memory for another moment, before turning to find Rian. He found Rian in his own room, staring at his reflection in the mirror. Rian smiled at his brother in the doorway. "I found it." Torrin held the book in the air, Rian could have jumped with joy. Instead, he gestured for his brother to join him; to look at themselves. Torrin frowned at his reflection, the turmoil in his mind had made him sallow. His brows creased further as the glass began to twist and ripple, before Torrin could say a word; Rian shoved his elder into the glass. Trapping him within.

Torrin stared at him in shock, his mouth agape. He had remained unwilling to believe his brother had been manipulated so easily by Nessa. "What are you doing?" He asked, his voice muffled and distorted; Rian rolled his eyes and glared at his brother. "What I should have done years ago, you are not good. None of you are good. You are all selfish and blind, you think you are better than the rest of us. It ends now." Rian did not allow Torrin to respond as he left the room; leaving Torrin to pound against the glass in vain. There he remained as Rian made a name for himself within the Sapphire Court.

Cliodhna had nervously kept at Rian's side as he presented himself to the people. He was a natural, this much she could not deny, but there was something hidden in his eyes. *Torrin does not realise that his brother is taking his Court from beneath him,* she thought. Cliodhna had not seen Torrin in far too long. Rian relished in his newfound power, used it to build relations with his people. He was grateful for what Nessa had done but he would not say it aloud, for he suspected the golden eyed woman would run to Nia the moment the words left his lips.

As powerful as Rian felt, he was not foolish enough to think he could go against her; not yet anyway. Carefully he spent his days turning the people against his brother, filled their heads with tales of how Torrin had done nothing to protect his own people against Ciar; how he would do nothing to protect them now. Cliodhna watched it unfold, until she could do so no more. In the dead of night, after Rian had struck a trader in the streets for rotten produce, she sent a letter to the Emerald Court. Cliodhna knew she could not send word to Nia, for the Silver Court was filled with spies, but she hoped that Uaine could come speak sense to his friend.

The next morning, she found Rian smirking, an Emerald letter in his hand. Cliodhna had blanched, expected him to turn and strike her down. Instead, he looked at her and laughed. "The Silver Court has invited Uaine and Maeve to a ball, I think our invitation may have gotten lost. Have the servants prepare my things, I shall pay them a visit. I am sure Nia would be grateful for a friendly face." Cliodhna pursed her lips and did as she was asked, weary of the glint in his eyes. She supposed this was a good thing, if he were not in the Manor, she could find Torrin and speak some sense into him.

Rian watched the suspicious woman as she retreated, waited until she was out of sight before he returned to his room. Rian took a lingering glance at himself in the mirror and grinned at his new appearance before opening the mirror to reveal a hidden compartment. Torrin struggled against the magic which bound him. "How many times must you be told of your ignorance before you learn?" Rian sneered, Torrin could not believe the man staring back at him was his little brother. He cursed himself for allowing Nessa to poison his mind. Rian laughed as Torrin tried once more to free himself. "I will be visiting your beloved today." He taunted. "We shall see how she fares when I tell the Silver Court of her deception." Sweat dripped from Torrin's brow. Nia would be slaughtered if Lorcan's brothers turned on her. Rian laughed once more and slammed the mirror closed before getting ready. With one final, approving, look at his reflection he ordered his servants to ready his carriage.

#

Cliodhna's letter arrived, just in time, as Uaine and Maeve stepped from their home. Uaine read it first, his eyes alight with worry. Maeve took the parchment from his hands and gasped. "How could he?" Uaine asked, for he had known the Sapphire Lords much longer; never would he have expected Rian to turn against them.

Abbán had warned them, so clearly, not to search for answers. It seemed neither brother had listened. "I must go." Maeve shook her head. "No, it must be I; Aidan has no respect for women, he will not accept my title without you at my side. I will go to Torrin, you must go to Nia. She will need your skill for diplomacy." Uaine could not argue, he knew Nia hated politics; he would not leave her alone, even if it pained him to leave his friend behind. He trusted his sister would be successful, so they called for another carriage and set out on separate paths.

Maeve looked around in wonder when she reached the Emerald Court. They had rebuilt most of Avenere, skeletons of homes being built littered the land. Lights shone in windows once more, green covered the earth. It was a marvellous sight; one the Fae had not seen in hundreds of years. Maeve only wished the Fae trapped beneath the mountain could return to their home. As she stepped out of her carriage, into the eerie silence of the Sapphire Court, Maeve felt instantly the wrongness in the air which Cliodhna had described.

The golden eyed woman waited in the doorway as Maeve climbed the steps. "What is happening?" She asked in a hushed voice, fearing Rian would hear her. Cliodhna shook her head. "He is gone for the night, I do not know where, and I cannot find Torrin." Panic laced her tone; Maeve ignored the uneasy feeling in her gut and entered the Manor. The Emerald Lady used her gift of half-sight to search the Manor for Torrin. Cliodhna followed in silence. The quiet unnerved Maeve as they walked towards Rian's room. "How did this come about?" Maeve questioned, Cliodhna sighed and explained what Nessa had done to the boy. Maeve cursed as she pushed open Rian's door. "He is here, I am sure of it." The room appeared empty, but she had felt his essence strongest in this room.

"Torrin?" Cliodhna called out, a muffled thump sounded from behind the mirror. The women shared an uneasy glance as Maeve reached for the glass. She found it opened easily and gasped at the sight of Torrin; bound by Sapphire and darkness. He looked exhausted; in truth he was, he had been fighting against the magic holding him for days to no avail. Maeve cursed the young Lord as she outstretched her palms. "How could he do this to you?" Torrin groaned as the binds loosened. "He is not himself; Nessa has seduced him by granting his one wish. He is overwhelmed with power." Maeve shook her head and caught Torrin as he slumped, finally free. The two women dragged him to Rian's bed as he gasped for air. Torrin wiped the sweat from his forehead as he caught his breath. "You need to follow him; he intends to betray Nia." Maeve looked to Cliodhna. "Go, find my brother and warn him. I will stay, if Rian returns with any of the Silver Lords then I will be here to defend your Court." Torrin smiled, weakly at Maeve; his whole body shook as he leaned back. Cliodhna wasted no time, with a curt nod she ran from the Manor, to warn Uaine and Nia of what was to come.

Maeve looked at the High Lord with pity as he fell unconscious, still shaking, he had turned a deathly shade of pale. She would not leave him, for as much as his ignorance angered her; Maeve could not deny the similarities between them. He had been alone in his court, with no people to rule; she had been surrounded by Fae and alone all the same. For this, she would help him. So, Maeve set about healing Torrin as best she could while building a shield around his Manor. She would not die at the hands of a child or the false Prince's of the Silver Court. Not if she had a choice. Maeve only hoped that Cliodhna would reach Uaine in time.

Chapter Thirty-Three:

Lorcan found Nia, glaring at the plethora of gowns he had laid out for her. He sighed as she paced. She hardly noticed him step behind her, until his hands slid across her shoulders. "I should have broken his neck." Nia murmured as a content sigh escaped her lips, the tension disappeared from her back. Lorcan chuckled. "Aye, you should have; but I would much rather see you in a crown than in chains." Nia smirked up at him, a playful glint in her eye. "Tis a shame I do not have one." She teased as she ran a hand across the fabrics, Noirín had outdone herself.

"Remember, whatever I say; however I act tonight, it is not me. If I can convince Etherea I am on Ciars side, it will be much easier to infiltrate his castle." Lorcan sighed at the worry in her voice. Nia was not entirely sure her plan would work. "You bear a burden no-one should, whatever you need of me, I am here for you." Nia's heart warmed at his words. Scarlet silk caught her eye, Nia grinned wickedly and excused herself to go into the bathroom and get ready.

She trusted him completely; knew she could stand naked before him, and he would not come near her; not unless she asked. Nia did not wish to ruin the surprise. She had found over the weeks, he had become her best friend, her confidant; she had begun to wish for more. With his silver eyes and crooked smile, his constant defiance of his brothers and unwavering defence of her; she could not help how her heart yearned for him. It was unlike any feeling she had experienced, not like the poisoned lust that blinded her to Duane, or the allure she felt for Torrin for saving her. This was different, he had done nothing but be handsome and kind; yet she could not keep her eyes from searching for him in every room she entered, could not stop the disappointment if he were not there, revelled in delight if he were. She felt like a lovesick child.

Nia shook the silver eyed Prince from her mind and looked at herself in the mirror. She felt much steadier now than she had in the Sapphire Court as she eyed her reflection. She had styled her hair into an elegant chignon, two curled tendrils framed her face, the dress was magnificent. Carmine red and clinging to every curve on her body, lace slid down her arms, Nia almost decided against it as she eyed the lace bodice and its cascading neckline dotted with diamonds, sparkling silver swirls dancing along its edge. The skirt of silk felt so smooth against her skin before flaring into a soft mermaid tail. It left nothing to the imagination, yet she was fully covered.

Nia stepped from the bathroom, just as Lorcan was fixing his tie. His hands stilled, their task forgotten, as he drank in the sight before him. Nia eyed him just the same, in his perfectly tailored black suit, her heart warmed at the ruby cufflinks he wore. His silver sigil pinned to his lapel, his hair a mess of curls covered by a crown of silver leaves atop his head.

Neither spoke for a moment. "Well?" Nia prompted with a hand on her hip, delighted by his gaping mouth and wide eyes. Lorcan shook his head and blinked, his eyes ran over her once again. "Forgive me, your majesty; for I do not wish to let you leave this room... not like that." He whistled with a grin; Nia's face burned as dark as her gown. "In all seriousness, you are *breathtaking.*" Lorcan stepped towards her. Nia thought her heart might burst from her chest with the way his eyes bore into her.

"Will the dark souls of Etherea be impressed?" She teased once more, too nervous to be serious. Lorcan groaned as his eyes turned dark. "I can guarantee when we make our entrance, the entire room will wish you were on their arm." Lorcan paused as he stepped closer. Nia felt the air leave her lungs as his breath hit her ear. "And I will be selfishly enjoying that I have you on mine." Nia yelped as his teeth grazed her neck before he was across the room, in a flash. Flushed and breathless, she glared at him. "Fuck you." She muttered. Lorcan threw his head back in laughter. "That can be arranged." He winked and grinned once more as she burned red. "Here, I have a gift for you." Lorcan told her, serious now.

Nia did not know whether to listen to him or throw something at him. She decided the former was the better choice. Lorcan chuckled softly as he watched her struggle to keep silent. Lorcan took a midnight blue box from beneath his bed and handed it to Nia. She noticed how he had suddenly grown nervous, his hands stuffed into his pockets.

"If you do not wish to wear it, do not feel as though you must." He shrugged as Nia ran her hands across the velvet box; she eyed his curiously before opening it. Her eyes widened at the glittering silver and ruby baroque leaf tiara shining back at her. "This... this is beautiful." Nia had no words, it was so elegant; not gaudy like the crowns she had seen in books in the mortal world. Nia had always maintained she did not care for tiaras or crowns, but for this one she could make an exception.

Lorcan released a breath of relief and gently took the tiara from its cushion. "May I?" He asked softly, Nia nodded and allowed him to place the glittering tiara atop her head. Lorcan whistled once more as she raised her head and looked at him, her violet-red eyes sparkling in the light of his room. "Come, Nia." Lorcan extended his arm with a smirk. "Before I cannot resist the urge to tell my brothers we have fallen ill." Nia grinned as she joined him. "How confident you are, that I would allow you to keep me here." "I can be *very* persuasive." He teased; Nia was about to reply when she heard the Fae bustling around the ballroom.

Her focus shifted to the approaching doors. Lorcan squeezed her hand as his brothers joined their side and the doors swung open. Unlike the Sapphire Court, this room was filled to the brim. Nia's head spun at the plethora of Fae staring back at her as they reached the High Table overlooking the ballroom. She searched for Uaine and Maeve, but only found one of the two. *'You are not safe'*- That voice sounded in her mind once more. Nia almost stumbled as she realised *why* it sounded so familiar. *It was her mother's voice.*

Lorcan squeezed her hand once more as he noticed the panic in her eyes. He did not understand, as her gaze flitted across the room, that she no longer cared about the spectators gawping at them. Aidan began his speech, Nia paid no attention to him; no doubt he was boasting that they had rescued the princess, he would never admit she walked up to their front door. Lorcan tried with all his might not to roll his eyes at his brother. A pair of golden eyes moving across the room drew Nia's attention, terror shone on Cliodhna's face. Nia watched the woman stand behind Uaine, wisps of gold flew towards him. Uaine's emerald eyes widened and raised to meet Nia's worried gaze.

Aidan turned to Nia then, allowing her no time to communicate with Uaine. Nia paused, panicked, she had not heard what Aidan said; *'he wants to allow you the honour of introducing yourself'* Lorcan came to her rescue. Nia squeezed his hand in return and steeled her expression as the dark Fae of Etherea watched her.

"Do I need an introduction, Lord Aidan?" Nia laughed, none missed the slight in her words, Lorcan gulped at her side; Uaine shot her his signature warning look. She almost rolled her eyes; he had given her that look so many times in Torrin's Manor; when would he learn that she would not heed his warnings?

Nia looked outward, her head high, the jewels atop her head glistening in the light of the shining crystal chandelier above them. The crowd hushed as her eyes scanned them, Nia stifled a cough as their darkness clouded her. There were slivers of light, she could not deny that, but most of these Fae were evil; through and through. She was grateful that Duane was not there, she had forgotten him. If anyone could ruin her plans, it was he. Nia thought perhaps the warning would be about Duane and kept looking for him within the crowd.

"I did not think I needed an introduction, but so be it." Nia waved her hand carelessly, a freezing wind whipped within the room; ice filled the lungs of each Fae, she ignored Lorcan's whimpers behind her. Nia did not want Ciar to think she cared for anyone, even if Aidan reported to him his ideas of a marriage; she hoped if he believed she did not care for their lives then he would not use them as leverage against her. A wicked smirk slipped onto her lips as she fixed her tiara, allowing the Fae to breathe again.

Nia noticed Aidan advance upon her, she allowed the rage burning deep within her to explode until she herself burst into flames. The gasping Fae watched in terror as she burned so bright, they shielded their eyes, great furious wings outstretched behind her, her feet hovered above the ground as they whipped against the air. Nia's eyes glowed like stars in the night sky.

She did not need to say her name, did not need to call herself their Princess. Her claws, sharp as daggers sprouted from her fingers and the Fae fell to their knees. It sickened her, that they followed power alone; no morals, no care for their fellow Fae. Nia found herself on solid ground once more, her laughter cut across the room as she took her seat.

"My father will be pleased that you have shown me such a wonderful reception, I only wish I had some wine to enjoy." Aidan could have cursed as Keegan scurried to fill the cup which Nia had raised, *so he can be swayed with fear*, she realised; it was not her first choice, but her time was running out. Lorcan's oldest brother could not believe how she had made his guests her own within seconds. Nia smirked and raised the goblet towards Aidan. "Drink and dance my friends, for Etherea will herald those that stood beside me and mine." Nia winked at the crowd, a cheer roared throughout the room as they rose.

The Silver Princes sat dutifully next to her, Aidan to her right, Lorcan at her left. The music began, as dark and foreboding as her situation. Nia did not look at either of them as she rose. "I wish to dance." The pair watched as she traversed the floor, she relied solely on instinct to guide her from the hands of one Fae to another. Each bowed their heads as she twirled away, until finally she collided with Uaine. "Where is your sister?" Nia asked, her voice as cold as ice. If any were listening, which she was sure they were, it would have sounded like a reprimand.

Lorcan had heard and knew the truth.

Something is wrong, he realised instantly. "Forgive us, your Majesty; Maeve is protecting our borders." Uaine told her. Nia stopped their dance and raised her hand against him. The clatter that sounded around the room silenced the Fae. "Did I not decree that the Emerald Court were our allies?" Nia seethed. None answered. Uaine held his stinging cheek. "If I catch any of you advancing on their Court your flayed body will adorn the gates to their Manor. Your lands will be theirs. Your people will be theirs." Fear rippled around the room.

In a flash, Nia smiled at them. "Now, continue." She waved her hand, and did not miss how they flinched before they obeyed. It churned her stomach, she did not enjoy acting this way. *'Torrin was captured, Nessa is free, Rian is-'* Uaine had no time to explain, as an orb of blinding blue light burst into the room.

 A young man skidded to a halt before them, copper hair whipped by the wind, sapphire eyes danced around the Fae until they rested on a stunned Nia. She peered at him before she gasped. *It cannot be.*

"Rian?"

Chapter Thirty-Four:

Maeve cursed at Torrin's unconscious form; he had not woken since he tumbled from his cage. She paced the room as he muttered incoherently, she could feel the terrors plaguing his mind. Maeve could take it no longer, her patience had worn thin; she grasped his clammy hand and shut her eyes, allowing her power to show her what tormented him. It was an intrusion, this she knew; but it was one he would have to live with.

Torrin's father gripped him tightly, dread in his eyes. "You must come with me Torrin, I fear tomorrow will be too late. Whatever may become of me, I wanted to protect you all. You know what we are?" Liam feverishly asked the bewildered child as he dragged him through the Manor. Torrin nodded as they entered his parents' room; a room he still could not bring himself to enter. He watched in amazement as his father opened a door within a wall, he never would have noticed it.

"Ciar has granted Duane the power to manipulate us, to enslave us. You must never reveal what you are. Never." Torrin had no time to reply as his father yanked him into the hidden room.

Torrin looked up in wonder at the suit of armour standing proudly in the middle of the room. A glistening sword with a hilt of Sapphire and a matching shield rested in a case at its side. "You must forsake all you want in this world. There is one thing we, as Faoladh, must do. Protect our Queen. You are her last true ally; you cannot fail her as I did. I pray that she returns within my lifetime, but I fear this is a foolish hope. You will be the last of us. To protect you I must do terrible things, please, forgive me." Torrin's father did not allow him time to question his words. Before Torrin could react a flurry of Sapphire encased him. "When the time comes, you will remember your training. You will remember what you must do."

Torrin gasped awake, Maeve stumbled backwards. His father had been crazed, his eyes wild; a sickening realisation filled Torrin, Liam did not abandon him. *Ciar turned him into a Faelcu.* Maeve looked at him with pity as he struggled to sit up. "Rest Torrin, you have been through a great ordeal." He glared at the Emerald eyed woman as he pulled himself to his feet. Maeve ignored his sour look and rushed to his side as he slumped again. She cursed his stubbornness but knew in her heart, she would do the same.

With Maeve to aid him, Torrin staggered to his parents' room. "You cannot be serious." She groaned and pulled him towards the dining room, despite his protests. She knew Nia cared for the High Lord and did not trust that Nia would not have her head if Torrin arrived half-conscious and shaking. "You will eat, bathe and rest before you go protecting Nia.

Lest you have forgotten she does quite well alone." Maeve *tsked* as she sat Torrin down and fetched him food.

Torrin grumbled a reply which she ignored. "Yes, yes, protector of the Queen, the last line of defence. The last living Faoladh, I understand the burden you have been tasked with. What good will you do to arrive in the Silver Court with shaking hands and knocking knees?" Torrin glared at her once more. Maeve shook her head and pulled a chair close to him.

He watched her wearily as she raised a spoonful of soup to his lips. "I can feed myself." He muttered; her eyes narrowed in return. Torrin said no more as he opened his mouth and allowed her to feed him. Maeve sighed with relief as the colour returned to his face. "What happened with Rian?" Shame filled his eyes instantly, Maeve knew pieces from invading their minds; she was much more powerful than her brother, had spent years infiltrating the thoughts of those in her Court to eradicate any memory of herself; she no longer saw it as an invasion, it was just another tool to aid her now. "I should have seen it coming. I was too focused on my own feelings to heed Abbán's warnings." Torrin scoffed before continuing bitterly, "it seems to run in the family, Nessa offered Rian a cure and he took it without question." Maeve shook her head; she had said it once and she would say it again; that woman must be destroyed.

"He is going to expose Nia to the Silver Court, he had me find one of my mother's journals; I do not know what he found in it." Maeve pursed her lips, if he did not look so desperate, she might have called him stupid. For years she had silently protected herself, watched and listened with intent. It astounded her how unprepared Torrin had been, Ciar had hit his Court hardest; he had shut himself out from Etherea in return. Maeve swallowed the insult dancing on her tongue and asked instead, "where did he keep the journal?" Torrin stretched his aching muscles and pointed back where they had come. "In his room." Maeve stood and gave him a stern look.

"Eat more, go bathe, I will find his journal." Torrin scoffed, his strength had begun to return. "Are you implying that I smell?" He asked, Maeve laughed as she left the room. "Like a wet dog." Torrin's brow creased before his eyes widened, the dog! Where *had* Madigan gone? In the chaos of returning to his Court, he had forgotten about the poor hound. He distinctly remembered it chasing wisps around Abbán, perhaps it had stayed in the swamp.

Torrin could have slapped himself for his selfishness, the hound had done nothing but protect Rian since they found it and he had shown it no kindness; of course, he was not cruel, he could never hurt the silly animal, but he *could* have been nicer. He sighed before finishing his meal and retreated to his room, to relieve Maeve's nostrils of his stink.

Maeve shivered in the silence as she returned to Rian's chambers, it was an easy search; as soon as she entered the room her eyes fell upon the thick leather book on his bedside table. Maeve ignored the uneasiness in her gut as she picked it up, unintelligible whispers flitted from the journal. Power radiated from the cool binding in her hands. At first, it was a simple storybook; with her power of half-sight, she could see the secrets within. Maeve flicked through the pages, her eyes widening with each line; prophecies, enchantments, battle-plans, it was all there. Torrin's mother had documented every vision Riona had, every spell she learned.

Maeve's stomach churned as her eyes fell upon a dog-eared page.

Her face blanched.

"How could he?" She whispered and without a second thought, Maeve bolted through the Manor. Torrin cursed as she pounded against his bedroom door, he had just left his bath. Still wrapped in his towel, he swung his door open. "What now?" He sighed. Maeve paused, fist still raised, as her eyes travelled down his exposed chest. Torrin felt his cheeks burn as her tongue ran across her lips. Maeve shook her head and met his gaze, there was no time to ogle him; much to her dismay. Torrin watched her curiously as she caught her breath, absolute terror in her Emerald eyes as she opened her mouth to speak.

"I *know what he is planning.*"

Chapter Thirty-Five:

The room had hushed at the sudden intrusion, the Fae exchanged uneasy glances. Lorcan cursed at the smirking man in their midst. Rian gave the Princess a mock bow. "How nice it is to see you again, your majesty." Her skin crawled at his dark tone, he was nothing like the child she had left in Galeria; tall and glowering, he had gotten his wish, he had become a man. "I presume my invitation was lost?" He challenged; Aidan looked between the pair. He did not recognise the man who stood before them.

It was Lorcan who stepped forward first, shielding Nia, Rian's eyes glinted with delight. "Lord Rian, my how you have grown!" Aidan's eyes darted from Lorcan to the copper haired Fae with confusion, in all his years; Aidan had never heard his brother sound so... *Polite*. "You must share with us what Torrin has been feeding you, if I had known you wished to attend; I would have certainly made arrangements." Aidan glowered at the young Fae as Lorcan spoke.

"I would not wish to insult our Princess by inviting her kidnapper's kin." Aidan scoffed, Rian's smirk did not waver, if anything it grew. "Kidnappers, eh?" Nia's throat dried; it took every ounce of strength she had not to look at her friends for aid, instead she stepped in front of Lorcan once more.

"You did not seem to mind when you were in my brother's arms." Rian spat at her. Nia did not need to look back to know how Rian's words stung the Silver Prince. Lorcan knew he had no right to be jealous, yet he felt it all the same; could not stop himself wishing she was in his arms in that very moment.

He could take her away, far from this cursed land, he could let it all burn; but Lorcan knew he could not, for Nia would never leave her mother or her friends behind. "Blasphemy!" Aidan boomed. Lorcan said a silent prayer of thanks for his brother's tunnel-vision; Aidan saw nothing more than an opportunity to have his family on the highest seat in the Kingdom, he would not allow this child to ruin his chances. Uaine raised a brow in surprise, Nia had played her part well.

Nia stepped beside Aidan, cautiously watching Rian as she walked. He eyed her in return, like a wild animal. Nia could see the darkness in his heart, the betrayal, the rage; it saddened her. It had consumed him. She pushed all sadness from her mind as she placed a hand on Aidan's shoulder.

"Oh, how simple the world must look through the eyes of a child. Your brother found a pretty thing he wanted for himself, he slayed the creatures my father's lieutenant had sent to protect me and stole me from my mortal life before I could be returned to my home. It was either his arms or that torture chamber you dutifully showed him. You are as blind as he, an agent of chaos has sent you here to destroy Ciar's child." Nia sneered at him; fire danced across her fingertips. She did not like how easy it was to twist the truth, to paint Torrin as a villain; he had not been the cleverest Fae she met on her journey, but he had done nothing but help her.

Nia had treated him awfully in the weeks her powers grew dark.

Aidan eyed the fire caressing his shoulder, surprised that it did not burn. This strengthened his idea of her, that she was the key to Ciar; that she was his ally. "How dare you interrupt our evening to accuse your Princess of treason?" He roared at Rian, the Fae around them cowered; Aidan was renowned for his temper. Nia watched silver daggers of light whizz towards Rian. The young Fae groaned as he was thrown backwards. Rian spat blood from his lips with a laugh.

"My father's lieutenant." He mocked.

Aidan thrust his fists towards him once more, Rian's face gushed with blood as cuts opened across his flesh. Nia's heart clenched. Panic began to set in. Her hands shook at her side. "Duane found you first, wrapped that pretty head in enchantments and sent his pets to take you to your father. You murdered all but one and fell into Torrin's arms. Duane tried to bring you home twice more, the second saw the Emerald Court destroyed. *You* attacked *him*." Aidan faltered at his words and looked at Nia, his eyes flickered to her shaking hands, to his brother's terrified eyes; Aidan came to a sickening realisation, he had been tricked, "is this true?"

Her stomach dropped as her senses went wild. She was trapped, she knew it; they all knew it. Balancing on a knife edge, Nia knew she must choose her next actions very carefully. Nia wished she could scoop her friends into her arms and fly far away from here, but alas, this was a fool's hope.

"If I had known we would have entertainment, I would have come early." Duane grinned as he looked around the room. *Speak of the devil,* Nia almost cursed aloud.

His eyes widened as he took in the scene before him. He vaguely recognised the man standing before Nia; saw Uaine hidden in the crowd. Duane's eyes flickered to Lorcan's hands, protectively wrapped around Nia now. Aidan wasted no time as he growled at the Golden Prince, all formalities forgotten. "Did you send your Faelcu to protect her, or to steal her from the mortal world?" Duane frowned at them, stepping into the room nonchalantly. He basked in the sight of Nia in her blood red gown and glistening tiara.

Goosebumps rose across her skin as his eyes scoured her body, she wanted to rip those golden orbs from his skull. "Why, this pretty little thing? To protect her of course." Duane stepped towards her, Nia almost took a step back; Lorcan embraced her eagerly before she shook him off and walked towards Duane. Lorcan could not believe it as his jaw hung slack. He cocked his head at her. "Did she join Torrin willingly, or did he take her?" Aidan pressed, Duane sighed and scratched his chin. "It is hard to say." He revelled in Nia's panicked expression; Duane enjoyed playing this game. The Fae had grown quite predictable over the centuries, he enjoyed watching her struggle to weave her web.

Curious to see how she would handle the situation, Duane said no more.

Nia cursed him in her mind as Aidan's suspicious eyes met her own. Nia saw the panic rippling from Lorcan as she slid into Duane's arms, Eoghan stood silently at his younger brother's side; his hand firmly on the younger Fae's shoulder, willing him to remain calm. The Fae around them watched with bated breath. She looked at Rian, hoping he would return to his senses; still, he did not waver.

"My love, why do you play these games?" She asked Duane as she nuzzled into his chest, it sickened her; made every ounce of her flesh crawl, but she knew if she wished to free her mother, Nia knew she could not let Duane know she was no longer under his spell. She stepped forward; her confidence shook. There was a wildness in Rian's gaze, something feral.

She paused to consider whether he shared Torrin's gift. If he did, she would not allow him to show it; not when Torrin had kept it secret for so long. Rian saw her eyes flicker to his hands, watching for any sign of claws. Nia sighed as she made a choice, gone was the soft child she had once known. With a heavy heart she raised her hands towards him, fire swirled in her palms as she forced herself to glare at him. *'Do not make me do this Rian, please.'* She begged him in her mind, he scoffed in return.

"How dare *you* question *me?*" Nia snarled; her decision made. The fate of Etherea rested on her shoulders. Those wings sprouted from her back once more, her eyes burned wholly red, claws sprang from her knuckles; darkness shrouded the young Elf. The room stilled once more, awaiting the dark Princess's move. Nia prayed silently, for guidance.

Lorcan watched as his heart pounded in his hears, her eyes closed as she took a breath.

A furious wind ripped through the room. Rian fell to his knees with a scream. Gasps reverberated across the crowd as Nia's eyes shot open and white-hot flames coursed towards Aidan. None expected her fury to land on the Silver Prince, not even Rian as he struggled against her power. She could not do it you see, would not turn her magic on him completely; for he was still just a child, confused and poisoned by dark magic. Aidan, on the other hand, she could justify; he was unwavering in his cruelty, he acted this way by choice alone.

Bradan jumped in front of his brother; the flames engulfed him. Shock filled the room as he turned to ash, his wife's screams could be heard across the land.

Nia could not turn back now, not as Tara raised a burning Sapphire hand towards her. Aidan had roared for his guards, he did not care whose daughter she was; he had not lost a single brother in five hundred years, yet within weeks of her arrival she had murdered his longest friend. Before either could move, the silver doors of the ballroom burst open. Nia could have cried at the sight. Maeve and Torrin stood, furious in the doorway. Maeve was wrapped in a menacing cloud of venom green and Torrin... Nia could not believe it was him, in glistening sapphire armour adorned with her the sigil of the royal protector. Fae scattered all around them, it was less clear now than it had ever been which side Nia rested on; none wished to be caught in the crossfire to find out. Rian laughed, madness in his mind as they ran like rats fleeing a flood. "Ah dear brother, you have come to watch the show! To think, I could not have done it without you!" He cackled as he stood, groaning as Nia's magic pushed against him. Nia's shocked look at his defiance gave him pure joy.

"Nia run!" Maeve screamed as she shot emerald shards towards Lorcan's brothers. Her feet would not move, Nia could not leave her friends. Instead, she scrambled to join the fight. Torrin groaned at her stubbornness and struggled to get through Aidan's guards. Tara tore through anyone in her way, friend or foe, it did not matter. Her focus was on one thing alone, the bitch that murdered her husband.

Uaine saw Tara's fury as Sapphire light swirled around her. Vomit rose in his throat as she transformed, a towering menace of claws and teeth. He barrelled into her, knocking her off course before she could slice the Princess in half. Nia stared solely at Rian as she deflected the blows thrown at her, did not waver when the beast of Tara lunged for her, Nia's magic began to swirl around her; burning those who came close.

She watched as he pulled an amulet from his pocket. You see, Rian had learned; the same artifact which controlled Nessa, Ciar had used to trap the Fae within the mountains. If his brother had not given him that book, if it had never appeared in their manor; he would have never unlocked its secrets. Nessa had left it behind for him, she knew of course; for she had seen it all unfold. It screamed in Nia's ears. Her hands instantly went to her head, Nia sobbed as she looked at Rian. The shadows dancing across his face wracked her with guilt. *I should have seen this coming*, she cursed herself. The Fae around her fell to the ground as if their minds might explode.

Even Duane, for all his years in this Realm, could not withstand the screeching noise escaping the ruby gem. Fear struck in his heart as he realised what Rian was holding. "Foolish child, what are you doing?" Duane asked through grit teeth. The boy grinned in return. "*What Ciar commands.*" The gem burst into blinding light. Nia shielded her eyes as the room began to shake, the only one still standing. The Silver Prince's evaporated from the room, along with their guards. Duane dragged himself to the doorway as the walls began to crack and crumble.

Rian glanced at the amulet in his hands unsurely and ran from the room, dropping it to the floor. Maeve ran towards the burning artifact, Uaine tackled her; the pair smashed through the window at her back. Cliodhna gasped and ran after them. Torrin chased his brother, to catch him and drag him to a healer. Nia stood rooted to the spot as she looked around, something was nagging at her; something in the back of her mind as if this had already happened.

Lorcan, however, ran towards Nia as the floor beneath her opened. She yelped as she fell. With one hand gripping a nearby statue, the other grasped hers as the blackness of the earth below threatened to swallow her whole. Nia came to a realisation that turned her core to ice; she *had* seen this before, or at least the aftermath. This was the vision which assaulted her mind many weeks ago. "Let me go, Lorcan, save yourself!" She screeched at him, her heart thudded in her ears; the last thing she wanted to do was fall, but she could not drag him to his death alongside her.

He had not been in the room in her vision.

Nia would not allow that to come true, not now that she knew. Lorcan's eyes widened as she began to scratch at his hands, she began to slip. Lorcan did not think twice as he released his grip on the marble statue and held her with both hands.

"I would let Etherea fall a thousand times before I let you go." He roared above the wind, pure panic in his silver eyes.

Nia cursed as a wind yanked at her ankles, she was going down; this much she knew, she would not take him with her. "I'm sorry, I'm so sorry." She sobbed. Lorcan groaned as the wind below gripped her tighter, yanking them both towards the darkness. It only strengthened her resolve. "Nia don-" fire scorched his palms. Lorcan cursed as he held her until he could no longer bear the heat. Her friends returned just in time to see her disappear into the blackness that had destroyed the once glittering ballroom floor.

Torrin roared and raised his sword at the silver bastard, Maeve grabbed his shoulder; for she knew it was not Lorcan's fault, she saw his heart breaking before them. "What have we done?" Cliodhna gasped, staring at the spot which Nia had just been standing; the hole began to close. Uaine felt tears well in his eyes, she had been a faithful friend to him; had done so much for them all, and they had failed her.

Nia felt the whoosh of wind as she plummeted to certain death. She had failed, she would not save Etherea, had not saved Lorcan from his brothers or freed their slaves, nor had she saved Torrin's sister; if anything, she had left Etherea much worse than she found it. Nia had wrought chaos wherever she laid her head. Guilt wracked her as she cast one final apologetic look at her Silver Prince. Nia had never even kissed him, and in her final moments; as she looked at him, Nia selfishly regretted this the most.

Her heart almost stopped.

Lorcan had jumped.

Epilogue:

Dirt and dust clogged Nia's throat, her lips dried like bone and cracked until they bled. She was grateful at least, even if it hurt, that she had granted some reprieve from the desert on her tongue. Lorcan could no longer see, darkness had engulfed them, his body had hit the ground so violently his ribs had cracked. Pain reverberated through his body as he clawed against the stone between them. He could hear her, the wheeze of her lungs, the shortness of her breaths. He would not stop, not if he broke his fingers in the process. This would not be the end, not for her, not for either of them.

Try as he might, his magic failed him, he could not get to her; could not blast the stones away nor evaporate to appear before her. Lorcan felt useless, totally and utterly useless. Nia felt his despair, the defeat that coursed through his veins, she could not stand it. Nia could have screamed at him for following her, although a selfish part of her was glad he had. For at least she would not be alone in her death. As the pair drifted out of consciousness, whispering to each other in the darkness; voices sounded from afar.

About The Author:

Shannon Leigh Moore

Born in Dublin in 1999, raised in a small council estate, Shannon spent her days quietly tucked away from the chaos of the outside world. She fell in love with writing along with reading when she wrote her first novel at eleven years old, it was the first, if not the best, of many. With a mind constantly churning with stories, it would be another thirteen years before she found the courage to publish her work.

Printed in Great Britain
by Amazon